# Enoch's Children

### Jack Lauber

Enoch's Children
Copyright © 2023 by Jack Lauber



ISBN
978-1-960197-83-2 (Paperback)
978-1-960197-84-9 (eBook)

# TABLE OF CONTENTS

# CHAPTER 1

Cory felt the sand sift down the back of his tee shirt, and sputtered through mud-caked lips. He was hot and sweaty. He didn't like being hot and sweaty. He was in a dark hole, and he liked that even less. The hole was supposed to be a tunnel. It still felt more like a hole. He lay on his stomach with his feet stuck out the open end behind him. All of his body, except his feet, lay enclosed in the heat and dark of the tunnel he'd excavated. His lower legs were the only part of him free. He sputtered again as he chopped at the red sand in front of him. The sand had been there, undisturbed, for hundreds of years. It had packed down, and filtered in, packed again, and hardened in place. Over time it had grown almost as hard as the sandstone cliffs and the rock he was trying to dig under. Now he was trying to dig a hole through that packed sand and gravel. Somewhere in the back of his mind he was sure he was doing something insane.

The small camp shovel he used was nearly useless for anything else, even for most camp chores. However, it proved to be just the thing for the hole he was digging. The sand broke up and crumbled a little at a time. He exerted a great deal of effort to chop it up and move it. The sand, more gravel than sand, often broke into chunks rather than crumbling completely. He shoved the product of his effort along his body, and back toward the opening where his feet were. He could feel a pair of phantom hands taking it from around his legs, moving it out of his way.

Cory realized, suddenly, that the sand was backing up. It was piled around his legs. The hands outside the tunnel were not keeping up. It was hard to move, and harder to breathe. The sand was in his shirt, in his pants and shoes. It was caked to his face, down his neck, and in his hair. It was dark and stifling in the tunnel. Even in the dark he could see the red color of the rock and sand in front of him. He shifted his legs to try to get more room to move.

It was called "slick rock country". The rock was not true rock, and it wasn't slick, he thought wryly.

He sputtered again, and pushed more sand along the tunnel beside him. He was hot and tired, and it was time for a break. And it was Thomas' turn to dig.

"I've had enough," he muttered, trying to breathe deeply, and not succeeding.

The tunnel pressed too closely around him. He started to inch backward and, for the first time that day, felt a spark of panic. The sand had packed in around his hips and thighs. Thomas had not kept up. The sand had become an effective cork. He realized that he couldn't move. He was having trouble breathing. He tried again to inch backward out of the tunnel, and again failed.

"Hey!" he shouted. "Hey! Help me out!"

He knew the mountain muffled his voice. He became very aware of the mountain of sandstone on his left, and the massive boulder above him. Only someone very close could hear him at all. He kicked his legs, and felt familiar hands grab his ankles and pull. At first, he didn't move. There was a moment when he thought he might be trapped, that he might suffocate inside the tunnel. His breath was quicker, shallower, and almost frantic. The feeling of panic grew more acute. He thought a quick prayer. His breathing was too rapid to allow him to speak. Almost as if answering his unvoiced prayer, the sand gave way, and he slid out of the sandy prison. Light burst around him as he was pulled back on his belly. The sand fell off him in waves. His tee shirt slid up and the sand scraped his belly and chest and instantly caked to his sweaty skin. He didn't care. He was glad to be free. He thrashed free with his arms and shoulders. The helping hands released his legs.

He rose up on his elbows, and brushed at his face. The sand had invaded his shirt and was packed against his skin. Again, he didn't care. The breeze, which had earlier felt like a furnace blast, seemed cool and welcome. He breathed deeply several times.

He sputtered, wiping at his face, and took another deep breath.

"Wow!" he sputtered. "It's...hot...in there."

He looked over his shoulder into the face of his partner, his best friend. For one instant their eyes met. He could see he wasn't the only one who'd felt the fear.

"Are you okay?" The other boy asked, concern edging his voice.

"I am now," he said softer, brushing at his hair. "We've gotta be nearly through by now. We've been digging, and we just gotta be. How much further do you figure?"

"Are you sure you're all right?" the other boy asked.

"Yeah, I'm sure," Cory replied. "I'm all right. Really. Don't worry. I just got a little stuck, maybe a little scared for a minute. I'm okay now. Thanks for pulling me out."

Thomas, the other boy, nodded and said, "That's okay. You scared me."

"*I* scared *me*," Cory said sardonically.

He brushed more dirt out of his hair.

"I figured ten feet," Thomas said absently, watching Cory carefully, "assuming the candle is hollow under the other side like it was on this side. You're right. We have to be almost through."

Thomas was referring to the massive sandstone pillar that stood in front of them. It loomed like a predator on the ledge, and had for hundreds of years. The Native American tribes in the area called it the crow. From up canyon, in the right light, and with some imagination, it did look like a carrion bird waiting for the scraps from another animal's meal, waiting to swoop down into the canyon and feed, its wings folded tight against its sides. There was an Indian word, but Thomas didn't know it.

The early settlers, seeing it from down canyon, thought it looked like a candle hanging on the wall. It needed only a flame at its wick to light the whole canyon below.

The canyon itself was an ancient watercourse. The sandstone had been cut out, sliced by a massive amount of water, a great flood, leaving vertical red cliffs on both sides, and a rolling, sand-filled space between. The cliffs were particularly high just where the canyon opened up in a natural amphitheater. They fractured and split at intervals, sometimes because of water. Other natural forces, far more violent, had shaken the land and left their mark as well. Here, in a cataclysmic event before recorded time, the cliff on the east side of the canyon split, and the top layer slipped back ten feet, leaving a shelf, a ledge, across its face. Thousands of years of erosion had narrowed the ledge, but most of the way it was still several feet wide. The split was not perfectly horizontal, but it was continuous. It began deep in the sand, sliced up the face at an angle, and then soared out the top of the cliff a hundred yards further down the canyon. It formed a natural ramp, and it was the ramp that had attracted the boys. Except for the candle it was a natural path to the top of the cliffs. The candle blocked the ledge a third of the way up. It had stood sentinel for centuries guarding the way to the top.

Ages earlier the shard broke from the cliff above and fell. A hole remained in the face a hundred feet above roughly the shape of the shard. Years of erosion had softened both the hole and the shard, but it was evident where the shard had once resided. The sandstone rock, a thousand tons of it, fell over a hundred feet in less than three seconds. It hit the ledge and, against all odds, and, seemingly, against the laws of physics, stuck fast, and remained cemented to the ledge ever after. It should have fallen all the way to the canyon floor and exploded in a heap of rubble, probably taking a section of the ledge with it. But it didn't.

Cory looked up at the formation, and breathed deeply. The rock was an impressive, and imposing, obstacle. Until just the moment before he had not felt the weight of the rock. Now he wondered if their venture was wise.

Teens are prone to move forward when their imagination is sparked. Wisdom is a momentary thing, coming in flashes and often ignored, and danger is seldom an issue to contend with. It creeps in on cat's paws after an action. Then they take a moment to think. Sometimes it works its way to the surface before they hurt themselves, at least often enough for the majority to survive adolescence. It has been said that a teenage boy without bandages and splints is not truly living. The boys on the ledge were no wiser than most teens their age. However, there was that brief glimmer of thought as Cory looked up at the monolith.

He crawled backward till his shoulders cleared the overhanging formation, and then rolled over. Turning over was a mistake. The sand sifted from his hair into his eyes.

"Good golly!" he spat, brushing the sand off his face, and feeling the grit under his eyelids. "Listen, Thomas. This better be worth it. My mom's gonna kill me when she sees these clothes."

"Doctor," Thomas said whimsically, "it hurts when I do this."

"Then don't do that," Cory finished wryly. "Okay. I do most of my own laundry, too. I'll just make sure she doesn't see these. I don't want her to see these. If she kills me, Thomas, I'll come by your house and kill you."

"I've got a mother, too," Thomas returned. "If she sees my clothes you may not have to make the trip."

Thomas smiled. He was as dirty as Cory was. They'd been digging between the boulder and the cliff face for almost two hours. Their canteens were empty, and Thomas knew Cory's patience was about exhausted for one day. He took a deep breath.

"Let's come back next Saturday," he suggested.

Cory brightened for only a moment. Then he saw the lost puppy dog look on Thomas' face. Thomas was famous for it. He used it whenever he needed to get his way. His eyes turned down, his face grew long, and, on occasion, tears welled up in the lower part of his eyelids. It was a game he played, and all their friends knew it. Even so, it was almost always effective. Knowing about it and having been a victim many times didn't make Cory immune.

"I saw the lake," Thomas attested, a catch in his voice. "We flew right over it! That water spilling out of the gap has to be coming from somewhere."

"That water spilling out of the gap is just a wet spot on the side of the cliff," Cory said without much conviction. "Especially this year. It could be an underground spring just back inside the cut. In fact, that's probably all it is."

"Yes," Thomas returned, brushing at his shoulder, and slipping up to get his knees underneath him. "But, it never dries up. Not even after four drought years in a row. Look at the grove. I mean, it's an oasis in the desert! You're right. It could be a spring. That's what everyone's assumed till now. But it isn't. I saw the lake."

They were talking about the damp face of the sandstone cliffs. The water dribbled down the sandstone and disappeared in a small catch basin at the bottom. The sand absorbed it all, and it was gone. A skimpy coating of moss and clinging plants grew where the water kept the face of the cliff damp. A few trees, mostly cottonwoods, grew at the base of the cliff around the catch basin. They were always green and well-watered late into the fall, right up to the time their leaves turned. It was called "The Grove" by the first pioneers who settled the town, though there were hardly enough trees to make it a true grove. The grove was a gathering place for church services back then, before they finished the church in town. Afterward it saw only sporadic use. It saw occasional picnics and an odd party once in a while. Beyond that, the grove attracted little attention.

Cory was glad. The canyon had been their private territory for as long as either of them could remember. They seldom met anyone when they were exploring. They'd hiked the canyon before they got bicycles. When they got bikes they had ridden up as far as the forks, where the canyon split. Later, when Thomas got the Jeep, they drove all the way up to the mines, as far as the road went. The road got so bad further up only a four-wheel drive vehicle could make it. The Jeep was four-wheel drive, if only just barely.

Cory looked over the edge and tried to swallow in a dry throat. He wasn't afraid of heights, but this was a little different. It was 60 feet straight down. The face of the cliff was flat. There was nothing to break a fall except the ground far below. He didn't have to lean out much to see the wet section of the cliff. It was only a dozen or so yards on the other side of the boulder. The cut in the cliff where the water came out was hidden from him, but he knew it was there. It was a significant blemish in the cliff face, easily visible from below.

The cleft was half way up the face of the cliff. Over thousands of years the water must have worked the deep cut in the stone, at last settling and slowing when it reached the level of the ledge. Cory knew it didn't take much to carve away the soft sandstone. He looked into the tunnel Thomas and he had carved and wished it took a little less effort.

No one in town ever thought of it as a mystery. A little water oozing out of a crack in a cliff face was not unusual in the southern half of the state. Consequently, nobody had ever expressed any more interest in the water source than in the cliff face itself. No one had ever wanted to find out where it came from. But, almost as if it were put there as a temptation for the boys, the ledge climbed from the floor of the canyon, crossed the cut where the water flowed, and eventually reached the top of the cliffs. It was a virtual freeway for them. Though they'd climbed the ledge many times, the candle had always stopped them. It simply blocked the path without apology. They never put their minds to finding a way to defeat it because until recently it was simply the end of the path. There had never been anything on the other side they wanted badly enough until now. There were too many other things to explore in their canyon. They had been content to let the ledge alone, for the most part. But the seed was planted, and the mystery of the water source was ever present in their minds, deep down, waiting any excuse to burst out.

Thomas went out in the Highway Patrol helicopter with his father from time to time. The chopper was used mostly for traffic observation on the freeway 50 miles to the west. The Highway Patrol was always willing to lend the machine, and its pilot, when there was an emergency in any of the surrounding towns. A lost Scout troop fit that category precisely. They were almost a full day overdue, and parents and church officials in Salt Lake worried about their safety. Sheriff Brady, Thomas' father, placed a call, and organized the search effort from his office in town. He called Thomas to help, as he had a number of times in the past. At sixteen Thomas was old enough to be a good spotter, and his father used him as backup, each taking a side of the chopper to watch the ground sweep past below.

Every boy in town was jealous of Thomas' opportunities. Cory smiled to himself, realizing he was, too, especially this specific time.

Thomas came back with the story of the lake in a hidden canyon above the cliffs. No one ever went up there. No one else had ever seen a lake up there. However, the ground was sandstone, with many folds and crevices. Deep holes pocked the rock where water had once run freely from the mountains to the north. The land was too rough for a road, had too many deep cuts even for four wheelers, and was too barren to be of use for anything else. It was largely ignored. Occasionally hikers got lost up on the plateau, further north toward the mountains, but that was rare. When it did happen, Thomas was called by his father to help. With Thomas in the helicopter, his father's deputies were free to coordinate any search efforts from the town.

Thomas was more excited about the lake than he was about finding the Scout troop. The Scouts simply miscalculated the time it would take them to go up one of the slick rock canyons and back down the next one. A thunderstorm during the night washed away part of their gear. They were tired, wet, cold and hungry, but for the most part they were in good shape when Thomas spotted them on the slick rock up on the plateau.

"Scout troop off your right wing, Lieutenant," he said into the microphone. "Looks like the four wheelers can get to them if they go up Escalation Waterfold."

"I'll let them know," the pilot said, circling to get a better view. "Yup. There they are. You're pretty good at this, young Brady. Thanks."

"He's been up a few times," the Sheriff said, smiling at his son.

Thomas was already thinking about the lake. He was the only one who saw it. It was in the bottom of a cleft canyon. He saw it for no more than the blink of an eye. That was enough. He knew the pilot wouldn't go back for another look. Every minute airborne ate taxpayer's dollars. The pilot would take his father and him straight line back to town, drop them in the school yard, the best place in town to land a helicopter, and then fly back to the airport near St. George. Thomas didn't need the pilot to back track. He knew he had seen the water. Its very presence sparked his imagination and curiosity. A natural lake in the desert was an oddity and a wonder, if not an outright miracle. He knew he would have to explore that wonder, and he knew Cory would help. He wanted the two of them to be the first to find it.

"It's there, Cory. I saw it," he said emphatically. "It's lots bigger than the swimming pool. It's more than just a pond. And it's dark and clear blue! That means it's deep. We gotta go see it. It'd be a great place to swim in the summer! It's in the fold above the grove. I know it's there. All we have to do is get past the candle. It's just inside the cut where the water dribbles out. You'll see."

Thomas liked the mystery of a lake in the middle of desert country, but he knew Cory would fall prey to a private swimming hole. Cory liked to swim, but in the summer the town pool was always crowded with kids from all the towns around.

School still ate up the weekdays, so they spent the intervening Saturdays trying to find their way to the lake. They studied the steep ledge in the face of the cliff the first time they'd driven up the old mining road in the canyon. They'd climbed the ledge many times through the years. It would be tailor-made for their excursion except for the stone shard. They walked up the ledge, as they had a hundred times before. They never thought of going beyond the boulder until now, now that there was something above it. The candle blocked access to the source of the spring, and, beyond, the top of the cliff. Now they explored the boulder, trying to figure out a way around it, and were disappointed. They couldn't get around it, and there was no way to climb over it. It rested stolidly on the ledge as if to say, "This is as far as you go." Both boys listened to the imperative, and accepted it as fact. They abandoned the ledge and, over a period of several Saturdays, explored the plateau above the cleft. They hoped to find a way down to the lake from above.

The edges of the hidden canyon overhung, and sloped off at an ever-increasing angle like the break of a huge fossilized ocean wave. That wasn't unusual in the area, either, but it frustrated their attempts to see the water in the bottom of the crevasse. They couldn't even confirm its existence through direct observation. They found where the stream entered the crevasse almost two miles north of the canyon. The drop was steep, and again, overhung by the higher cliffs. The cleft it entered was narrow, dark and convoluted. There was no evidence of a pond or lake anywhere below. And there was no way down through the tortured passage.

They tried to find their way to the top of the ledge from above, as well, but the path to that part of the cliff was cut by deep folds and pits with steep and undercut sides. They couldn't get closer than a quarter mile away from where the ledge topped the cliff face. They could almost see the path down from their vantage, but couldn't get to it.

Three weeks passed, then four, and their curiosity increased in intensity until it drifted from compulsion to passion to obsession. The many frustrations they found only piqued their desire to get there. Finally, they returned to their first avenue, the ledge across the face of the cliff.

This time the boulder wasn't nearly as imposing as they had originally thought. Thomas knelt down at the base and began to claw at the sand between the boulder and the cliff. The gravelly sand was packed and hard, but seemed to promise a path they'd not thought of before. In a few minutes he dug out enough to convince them both that they could cut a tunnel under the thing and get beyond it. They could dig out the space next to the cliff where a sixteen-year-old boy might just squeeze through. The sand filled the space completely, and was hardened by years of weather, but they knew, with the exuberance of sixteen-year-olds, they could clear it. They went home that night elated, and ready to return the following Saturday.

The week in school almost seemed interminable, but the boys bore it. Most of the week was spent with finals in all their classes, so thoughts of the boulder on the ledge were largely overlaid with other concerns.

They were excited as they climbed the ledge with their camp shovels only a few hours earlier, in the cool morning air. Now, all Cory could feel was the hot, muddy sweat running down his back. He stretched his arms and let his t-shirt absorb the trickling sweat.

"I'll dig a while," Thomas offered, crawling over Cory's legs.

Cory grabbed the back of his shirt, and helped him over, then glanced furtively over the edge. The sixty feet to the canyon floor seemed further now than it did earlier.

"You're going to fall if you're not careful," he warned, but Thomas was already squirming into the tunnel, and the statement was lost.

A few moments later sand began to form humps around the younger boy. Cory started to shove the sand away from the opening, letting it flow over the edge of the ledge. Dust rose from the side of the cliff. The soft, warm breeze blew the dust in a gentle arc toward the center of the canyon.

It hadn't been his idea, he thought, to spend his Saturdays trying to find some lake in the hills. He had better things to do. He could be swimming at the pool in town, or going to the matinee at the show house. The show house was air conditioned! He could be fishing! He thought a moment, and smiled. He realized he was, in fact, exactly where he wanted to be. He was with Thomas, the person he most wanted to be with. What they were doing together had never really mattered much, as long as they were together.

He couldn't remember what it had been like before they met. He perceived a time when there was a kind of emptiness. Not altogether. There were other kids in the town his age, but he never felt really close to any of them.

Then, one day, in second grade, he looked up. The school principal, Mrs. Schuster, was standing in front of the class and introducing a boy.

"He's just moved here from Los Angeles. I know you'll all make him feel welcome. By the way, his father is the new sheriff, so don't drive too fast through town."

She laughed at her little joke, but Cory stared at the new boy. When their eyes met a realization washed over him. He knew this new boy. Somehow, somewhere, they'd met before.

"...Sheriff Thomas Brady," Mrs. Schuster said softly. "And this is Thomas Brady, too. That's 'also', not 'two'. Thomas Brady, Junior."

She held up two fingers, and smiled at her own joke again. The kids in the class laughed politely with her.

"Where shall we place him, Mrs. Nichols?" Mrs. Schuster asked.

Mrs. Nichols looked around the class, but Cory, familiar with the seating chart, jumped up, and said, "Here's an empty desk. Right here."

"I guess right there will do fine," Mrs. Nichols said, smiling kindly at Cory.

She ushered Thomas Brady back to the seat, then returned to the front of the room to talk with Mrs. Schuster. Cory leaned across the aisle.

"I'm Cory," he said, holding out a hand. "You're Tom?"

"Thomas," the new boy had corrected.

"Not 'Tom' or 'Tommy'?" Cory asked, smiling.

"Only if you're 'Core'," Thomas replied, a smug smile on his face.

And it had been that way ever since. He was always Thomas, never Tom.

"I don't suppose this school has a computer," Thomas asked, looking around the room at the old walls.

"Of course," Cory said. "The secretary uses it to keep track of things. Her name's Mrs. Bracken. She has kids here, too."

Thomas looked up at the skylights overhead, and sighed. Cory found out what had frustrated him so much that first day years later. But they'd been closer than brothers from that moment on.

"I'm through!"

Cory turned quickly on his knees, and scooted back as Thomas wriggled out of the hole.

Thomas rolled over, his blond hair matted with the red sand, his face dirty, streaked with sweat and mud, his clothes raising clouds of dust with each motion.

"I'm through," he spat again, and laughed.

Cory stared at his friend, and laughed with him. He laughed as much at the sight of Thomas covered with red sand as with relief that the job was finished. In a few moments the biggest hurdle they faced would be behind them.

Thomas became silent, seemed to study Cory, and then laughed again.

"I hope I don't look as bad as you," he said.

"You do," Cory confirmed.

"Shoot!" Thomas snapped. "Our moms *will* kill us."

"They won't have to," Cory returned sardonically. "We're gonna drown in this stuff!"

"I'm through!" Thomas repeated. "All we gotta do is dig the opening a little wider! Come on. You did most of the work. You ought to be the first through."

Cory stopped laughing, and grew serious. For the first time he thought about something neither of them had dared think during the morning.

"What if there's nothing there?" he asked quietly. "I mean, what if we did all this for nothing? What if the cut where the water comes out only goes in a few feet? What if there's no place else to go once we get past this rock?"

Thomas sat still a moment; the smile washed from his face by Cory's comment.

"If there's nothing there," he said slowly, his face brightening, "then we'll have had a great adventure! How many kids in town could say they've done what we've done?"

"As I recall, you and I have occasionally done what no other kids in town have done," Cory responded wryly. "Usually we ended up at your father's office facing both our fathers. Trying to explain things to both our fathers is something we're used to."

"Of course," Thomas chuckled a little, staring down at his knees. "You remember that time…"

"Not now," Cory said softly. "Let's finish this."

He took the shovel from Thomas, and edged toward the hole.

"Brighten up, Cory," Thomas laughed. "At the very least, we've opened a path to the top of the cliff. Maybe we could sell tickets! Cory, we've done it! We're through. We can get a drink of water out of the spring! What more could you possibly want?"

"A shower," Cory said practically. "We did this for the lake. That's what I want."

"The lake is there," Thomas assured him, working around and changing places with him.

Cory smiled and wriggled into the hole. He was reassured by Thomas' quiet confidence. He believed the lake would be there. He wanted to believe it.

This time the tunnel was different. There was a light at the end! It wasn't much, but it only took a few jabs with the shovel, and he was able to push the dirt ahead of him. A few more jabs and he crawled through. He pushed the shovel ahead of him, along with some more of the sand. He cleared the boulder and struggled carefully to his feet.

There was a moment of exhilaration and a touch of pride as he stood on the upside of the boulder. They were through! They were, perhaps, the only people in history who had been on this ledge, at this precise spot! He stared around at the canyon below, and felt his chest swell.

Thomas crawled out a moment later, and they stood together, looking down at the road, not much more than a two-tread track in the bottom of the canyon. The view was almost the same, but incredibly different. They didn't talk for a few minutes. There was a sense of adventure, of wonder now. They felt a reverence for the moment, a sense of accomplishment. Suddenly, and for the briefest of moments, neither Cory nor Thomas cared whether the lake was really there or not. Just being on the ledge above the boulder was enough.

It was Thomas who broke the silence.

"Yes!" he said, raising his voice slightly. "Yes!"

"Oh, yah!" Cory returned, raising both hands above his head.

"It's not even noon," Thomas said softly.

"It seems later," Cory returned.

They were both hot and tired.

"Well, I'm thirsty," Thomas said. "Somewhere over there is some water!"

Cory looked along the edge to where the cleft cut the face of the cliff, and nodded. There was a very shallow pool just where the water reached the edge of the cliff. Thomas couldn't pass him on the narrow ledge. Cory had to go to the water first. His moment of triumph was over, and he walked to the cleft.

The ledge was almost level here, above the rock, even dropping down a little before resuming its flight to the top of the cliffs. The pool was just a puddle. The wet sandstone made it appear deeper and wider than it was. Cory stopped as he passed the open mouth of the cleft. A cool breeze blew gently out of the deep cut in the cliff. He could hear water. Running water. Lots of water.

"Listen," he whispered, turning toward Thomas.

The other boy stopped, a broad smile breaking over his muddy face. In the midst of the mud was a bright, clean set of white teeth.

"I told you," Thomas accused, his enthusiasm almost bubbling over.

Cory smiled back, and said, "It's in there, somewhere."

Here, where the ledge opened into the hollow of the cleft, they could stand side by side and stare into the deep shadows of the crack. It was more cave than cleft, typical of many other streams in the southern part of the state. The walls were straight up, in a sense, but twisted and turned as if stirred by an ethereal cook, then allowed to set. They were four to five feet apart, narrowing at intervals where the batter was thicker. The stream was just a flat ribbon of water on the floor of the cleft for ten feet back into the gloom, and then it disappeared around a caramel turn in the stone. The unmistakable sound of running water, louder than the dribbling trickle they stared at, wafted from the cleft. The stream that crept out of the cleft was wall-to-wall, but barely deep enough to wet the soles of their shoes. There was something better inside. They looked at each other, smiled, and entered the cool shadows of the streambed.

"It can't be far," Thomas said. "The lake seemed to be just behind the cliff face."

He stopped, almost running into Cory.

Cory stood, staring at the waterfall falling from twenty feet above. It sprayed down and landed in a four-foot catch basin then all but disappeared. The dribble at the mouth of the crevasse was only a sniveling spill from what was a grander, real stream.

Cory reached out, and caught a handful of water. He rubbed it gently on his face. Then he took both hands full, splashed them on his face. He drank from his cupped hands, and let the cool, sweet water spill down his neck. He looked over at Thomas.

Thomas was on his knees, drinking hungrily from the catch basin. He looked up at Cory, and laughed. He splashed water up at him.

Cory responded, and in less than a second both boys were in the basin, splashing and dunking, and laughing and screaming. Almost as soon as it started, it was over. They sat on the edge of the pool, their feet still in the water, soaked, cleaned by the running water, and watched the mud from their clothes clear quickly, washed away by the stream that disappeared somewhere into the mountain.

"There's an echo," Cory said softly, wondering at the secret place they'd found. "Listen. You can hear yourself think."

Thomas nodded, and said, "This is great."

"It's ours, and only ours," Cory returned. "We don't have to share this with anyone else. We can come here whenever we want! All summer! This was worth all that work!"

He lay back against the rocks around the pool, totally relaxed. Thomas said something, and Cory almost decided to ignore the remark and just enjoy the cool water. He was close to sleep. Then he shook his head.

"What?" he asked.

"There's more," Thomas said again, this time with more force.

"What do you mean?"

"I saw a lake from the air," Thomas said. "I didn't even see this waterfall. This was a surprise to me, too. Hey, where does all this water go?"

"Underground, I guess," Cory said absently. "You sure it was a lake?"

"This water has to come from someplace," Thomas said.

"It goes no place," Cory said. "Maybe it comes from no place. Besides, we saw the upper end of the stream a couple of weeks ago."

He stood and looked up the waterfall. True to form, it was straight up, and overhung at the top. He looked for a way up. There didn't seem to be one. Then he saw the holes in the wall.

Next to the falling water, almost hidden by it, a series of holes pocked the wall in two neat rows running all the way to the top. They alternated left and right.

"Someone's been here before," Thomas said, pointing to the holes.

"I know," Cory answered, reaching into the ones in front of him. "But not for a while. These were made a long time ago."

Thomas looked up, and breathed deeply.

"The lake is up there," he said, motioning with his eyes.

"I sure hope so," Cory said, slipping his toe into the lowest hole, and gripping two more with his hands. "But, if it's not, this alone was worth all the work. Anything else we find is pure gravy!"

Thomas's hand rested on his shoulder, holding him back.

"The lake's there," he said firmly. "I saw it. Besides, someone thought there was something important enough up there to build a ladder to get to it."

"Well, we thought the lake was important enough to dig a tunnel," Cory said. "Let's go find it."

"What if we're not supposed to be here?" Thomas asked suddenly.

"No one's been here for a thousand years," Cory returned. "Not since long before the candle fell on the ledge. Besides, this was your idea. Come on."

Cory shook Thomas's hand off, and began to climb. The hand and toeholds were spaced carefully, with the holes angling slightly into the sandstone. Climbing was the easiest thing he'd done all day.

He felt the mist from the falling water running down his back. He stopped part way up and held on for a few moments, enjoying the cool water. A few steps later he reached the top of the ladder, and the top of the fall was within grasp. He reached over the edge, pulled himself up and into the slick bed of the stream above the fall. There were more handholds carved in the slick sandstone to help him over the edge. These, however, were worn almost smooth and only provided minimal help.

The water was swift and deep, rushing headlong over the edge into the dark below. He stood between the rocks to stare down into the chamber. Thomas was already halfway up.

"It gets better," he called out to the other boy.

Thomas looked up, and smiled. Cory reached down and pulled him over the edge. They stood and turned at the same time.

The walls were close for about ten more feet, then they opened, and beyond was a larger canyon, with sunlight pouring down into thick cattails! There was water there!

The bed of the stream was still smooth sandstone rock, but the sides became sandy near the cattails. As they stepped out into the sun they found the lake Thomas had seen.

The walls of this canyon were overhung, undercut by the force of a million times more water than flowed down the cut now, streaked with centuries of erosion and stained by the minerals that flowed with the desert seepage. A half mile away the canyon closed off again, but in between it was several hundred feet wide where it was undercut, maybe half that at the top of the cleft where the walls closed over. The lake was long, deep and clear blue, just as Thomas had described it. Cattails filled the overflow, but sandy beaches and sandstone ledges surrounded the rest of the lake. Here and there small trees overhung the water, or grew in small clumps near the cliff edges. High above, in the blue sky, a lone eagle cut the air currents looking for a meal.

Cory breathed deeply, and laughed out loud. There was a moment of silence before his echo returned.

"My echo!" He shouted.

"My echo!" His own voice returned.

He laughed again. Thomas laughed with him, and their echoes laughed back at them. The silence returned. Cory started to slosh through the water toward the lake. Thomas followed.

"I don't know about you," he said as they splashed along, "but I could really use a swim."

The echo splashed back at them as they dove into the water of the lake at nearly the same time.

# CHAPTER 2

The sun was hot. The warm rock drained the energy from Cory. He grew sleepy, and closed his eyes, letting himself sink comfortably against the stone. He rolled his head enough to see Thomas, stretched out on a nearby rock, and already sleeping.

The lake water rinsed most of the sand and mud out of their clothes, so they laid them out over the rocks to dry. Then they went back into the water again, wearing only their boxers. The cool water refreshed them, but it couldn't completely overcome the fatigue they both felt. They climbed back up onto the rocks and lay out like lizards basking in the sun.

Cory could not tell how long they lay there. It might have been just a few minutes, or an hour. He knew he slept some. He was suddenly awake and alert. The hair on the back of his neck stood up, and a chill ran through him. He knew there shouldn't have been anyone else there, in the canyon, but he had the distinct feeling he was being watched.

He brushed the hair away from his forehead, and sat up on one elbow. Thomas was face down on the rock a few yards away, and still asleep. His face was turned half toward him, his lips moving gently as he breathed.

They trailed water from the lake to the rocks when they climbed out. The rocks were dry now. Their clothes, still laid out a few feet away, looked dry as well. It had been at least that long. His watch was next to his pants.

He couldn't see the face. Both their wallets lay open, the contents scattered on the sandstone drying. It all seemed to be as it should have been.

Cory lay down, and closed his eyes again. There was a shock, almost like lightening, that gripped his belly, and he sat upright. He looked around.

A boy climbed into view twenty feet away, from behind the rocks at the water's edge.

Cory coughed, and reached for his clothes, and was surprised to find them out of easy reach. He sat still, and just watched.

The boy suddenly looked up from the water, saw him, and smiled. He was, maybe, eight years old. He wore a pair of shorts held in place by a simple tie string that hung down in front. The shorts were pure white, and appeared to be damp. From the waist up he wore nothing, and his legs and feet were bare. His hair was black, and plastered to his forehead. The boy must have been swimming, just as he and Thomas had, Cory realized. The boy smiled, and his teeth, in his deeply tanned face, were brilliant white.

"Hi," he said brightly.

Cory nodded, and said, "Hi."

He looked at his clothes again, and decided to get them. There would certainly be others around, and he didn't particularly want to be caught in just his underwear. He stood, and walked over to his clothes. His shorts were dry.

The boy climbed over the rock and toward him.

"Who are you?" he asked simply, watching with interest as Cory picked up his jeans.

Cory was surprised to find the rest of his clothes thoroughly dry, too.

"I'm Cory," he said quietly. "That's Thomas. Who are you?"

"Amium," the boy said, smiling. "Do you swim here a lot?"

"No," Cory returned. "We just found this lake. How did you get here?"

"I came here with my father," Amium said, waving vaguely up canyon with his arm. "He's over there."

Cory felt a surge of consternation, and asked, "How did you get here?"

"Our vehicle," Amium said simply. "What are those?"

"My shoes," Cory said, shaking the shoes out.

Even his shoes had dried. Loose sand shook out of them and drifted to the rocks.

"Those are pretty strange shoes," the boy said candidly. "We wear sandals, mostly." He raised each of his bare feet and put them down. It didn't seem to bother him that he didn't have sandals on at that particular moment. "Oh, and my brother and sister are here, too."

"What?"

"My brother and sister," the boy said. "Shoes? What kind of animal did you get that from?"

"That's vinyl," Cory said, brushing the soles off. "Your brothers and sisters?"

"Just one brother," Amium returned, slightly amused. "Just one sister. I have other brothers and sisters, but they're back home. My older sisters are married. So are my older brothers. My youngest sister stayed home with Mother. What's vinyl? An animal? Does it live around here?"

"Thomas, wake up," Cory said, shoving Thomas' shoulder.

"Huh?" Thomas said, pushing up to his knees. "What's the matter?"

"Better get dressed, pal. We're going to have company."

Thomas looked up, suddenly alert. He looked at the younger boy, then up to Cory, and understood. He got up and grabbed his clothes.

"Who's that?" he asked, and pulled on his pants.

"This is Amos—"

"Amium."

"Yes. What he says. He has a brother and a sister running around here somewhere."

"Oh, golly," Thomas said, his face coloring. "Do you think…?"

"I don't know," Cory said. "Where are your brother and sister?"

"Oh," Amium replied brightly, "you probably can't meet them. We didn't expect to find anyone here, and we're not supposed to interact. That means talk with anyone. Father will be upset to find out about you."

The boys stared at him, incredulous. The little one turned and stared into the deep waters of the lake. He breathed deeply, and sighed.

"What are you talking about?" Cory asked.

"Oh, I don't know," Amium said quickly, brightening. "Just some rules Father said we had to obey if we came here. I won't tell him about you. I want him to bring me back again, and he might not if he knows you're here. Anyway, where does the animal you call 'vinyl' live? Can we go find one?"

"He's off his rocker," Thomas said, pulling on his shirt.

"He's missing a marble or two," Cory agreed. "Amos—"

"Amium!" the boy stressed emphatically.

"Okay, Amium," Cory said. "Where did you say your vehicle was?"

"Over there," Amium waved again. He cocked his head to one side and said, "You don't listen very well, do you?"

Cory shook his head, smiled, and said, "My mother tells me that all the time. Come on; let's take you back to your family."

Amium smiled, and said, "My mother says the same thing." He giggled a musical cascade that filled the air around them. "I can find my way. It's around there, and under the trees. I know where it is."

Thomas finished tying his shoes and stood up.

"All the same, Amium," Cory said, stressing the boy's name again, "I think we'd better walk with you. Besides, I want to see how you got a vehicle down into this canyon. We've been searching for a way in for weeks."

"It wasn't *that* hard. We come here sometimes to check on things. Father is the caretaker, you know. And, I don't want to go back just yet," Amium said, all in one breath. "I want to play by the lake a while."

"You can come back," Cory coaxed. "You're not supposed to be swimming alone, anyway. That's not smart, and your father wouldn't approve. Come on. Let's go meet your father."

"This should be interesting," Thomas agreed.

"Yah," Cory nodded, then coaxing. "Amium. Show us where your father is."

"It's over this way," Amium said, turning reluctantly, and walking down along the edge of the water. "I don't have to go back yet. And I know about not swimming alone. I'm not stupid, you know. My brother and sister were with me when we were swimming. Where are you from, Cory?"

"We're from the town," Cory said. "What about you? What are you doing up here?"

"Father had an errand. I told you he was the caretaker. We came along to help. Mother said it would be good for us to spend time with him. They talked about it for a while, and Mother said it would do Father good, too. Is your mother like that? Mine sure is. We live in a city. It's big, and there aren't places like this there. This is great! I don't know about your town. Is it a big town?"

"Not really," Thomas answered. "Are we going the right way?"

"Yes, we are," Amium said, suddenly forceful. "I don't know if he'll even want to meet you. I told you, we weren't supposed to interact."

"Okay," Cory said patiently. "But you've already interacted. So, now you have to tell your father about it. You wouldn't want to tell him a lie, would you? We'll just let your father know it wasn't your fault. That's okay isn't it? You just keep walking. We'll follow you."

Amium shrugged, and continued to walk down toward the lake. Cory followed and Thomas fell in step behind them.

"You're just like my big brothers," Amium said sullenly. "They order me around a lot, too. They have to do what Father says, but they can order me around. I have to do what *everyone* says, and I don't get to order *anyone* around. That's not fair. Besides, this was supposed to be a fun trip."

"You can still have some fun," Cory said. "Besides, how often do you get to meet new friends?"

His face brightened, and he said, "That's right! Cory and Thomas! Thomas and Cory! I have two new friends!"

They went down the rocks, and followed along the shore. Cory sensed they were going in the direction the boy had waved. There was not much land between the lake and the cliff face. It shouldn't be easy to miss someone else in the canyon. Yet, they had. A cool breeze was beginning to blow off the water now, and they were rested after their naps. Neither of the older boys spoke. They followed the younger one, who seemed to have no lack of things to talk about.

"My father was in the military a long time ago," he said. "That was when he was young. I wasn't born yet. He's old now. He says he's too old for all that military nonsense. Anyway, his eyes have gone a little bad, and he can't see the targets well any more. You guys listening to me?"

"We sure are, Amium," Cory said, grinning. "Your father fought in the war, then?"

"Oh, no," Amium said enthusiastically. "We haven't had a war in a long time. But we all have to serve for two years. It's the code. My brothers and I will all get to serve. It's part of our education. There was a big war a long time ago. Father says he hopes there'll never be a war again. He says that's why we serve in the military: To keep from having another war."

"Oh?" Thomas asked, a grin crossing his face.

"Sure," the boy returned, still walking. "No one will start any trouble with us as long as we're strong. Anyway, that's what Father says. Are you going to serve in the military?"

"I hope not," Cory said softly.

"We will if we have to," Thomas added, seeing the boy glance back.

Amium seemed more satisfied with Thomas's answer, and said, "Good. Anyway, that's why we're here. They gave Father an errand, and so he came."

"The military?" Cory asked.

"No. The council," Amium returned, picking his way along the rocks.

"Survivalists," Thomas whispered to Cory. "I've heard about these people. They look for places like this to live, and wait for the end of the world. They have a lot of guns and stores of food, and just wait for trespassers and blow them away. I think we'd better go the other way."

"We're bringing 'em back the kid," Cory returned. "Besides, we don't mean any harm, and we're just a couple of kids ourselves."

"All the same," Thomas said, letting his voice trail off.

"Even if that's so," Cory suggested, "they can't settle in here, no matter how much they want to. This is national forest land."

"You tell 'em," Thomas returned sardonically.

"What's the easiest way out of here?" Cory asked Amium suddenly.

"In our vehicle," Amium called back. "How did you guys get in here?"

"We came up the waterfall," Thomas answered.

Amium stopped, and turned toward them.

"The waterfall?" He asked, incredulous. "I wouldn't have tried that. Father says that's the way the people used to come in and out of here. But that was a long time ago. He says the ladder is old and worn out and dangerous. He told me to stay out of the spillway, too."

"We'll let your father educate us," Cory said simply.

"Maybe he'll give you a ride home!" Amium exclaimed, and turned back toward them. "He might, you know. Would you like a ride home? We've got the speeder. It's not slow like the family transport. You'd like it."

"We live in the town just below," Cory explained. "Besides, Thomas' Jeep is parked at the bottom of the ramp. We can get home okay. I'll just be happy to find an easier way in here."

"A Jeep?" Amium asked simply. "Jeep. Jeep. Jeep."

He seemed to be trying the word out, to see how it fit in his mouth.

"It isn't much," Thomas began.

"You got that right," Cory smiled, "but it's better than what I have, which is nothing. Anyway, we have to drive it back home. Thanks, anyway."

"Jeep. Jeep. Jeep. That's okay, because I don't think Father wants to go to the town," Amium said. "You'd have to have a vehicle like the speeder to come in here our way."

"Right," the older boys chorused, smiling.

"He didn't make up all the rules, you know," the boy said. "The council made up some of them. They're the ones who said it was important for us not to interact. I suppose I won't get to come the next time. But, I do have some new friends, so it's worth it. Don't you think so? Maybe you can come and visit us sometime, and I can show you our city. You'd like it."

"I think we'd like to," Cory said vaguely. "Maybe, sometime."

"Great. Then it's settled. I'll tell Father. Our vehicle is just around here. Come on."

Cory looked at Thomas, who just looked back. The boy, meantime, crawled over a shoulder of rock, and dropped into the cleft on the other side. He turned back and stood, arms folded, waiting for his new friends.

"Well," he said loudly. "Are you coming or not? This was your idea, you know. I wanted to stay by the lake."

A deep, male voice wafted from the cleft.

"Amium. Come here."

Amium looked into the cleft, then back at his new friends.

"I think I'm in trouble," he said softly, a pained look on his face.

"You go on," Cory suggested. "Your father's calling. We'll catch up."

"You won't find the vehicle without me," Amium said impatiently.

"We'll be right there!" Cory assured him. "Go on!"

"Okay, but you won't find the vehicle without me," Amium repeated petulantly, turning and marching into the cleft between the rolls of rock. "It's sealed. In fact, you won't get to meet my father, either. He's angry, I think. I'm coming, father!"

"His father's angry, and he's pretty strange," Thomas said to Cory. "He doesn't make a lot of sense."

"I know," Cory returned. "Look around. There's no road out of here. The walls overhang everywhere. You and I looked. There's not a vehicle around that could get down here."

"A helicopter could get in," Thomas said, "but I think it'd have a hard time finding a place to land. Besides, he acts a little, well, touched. I don't think he knows what he's talking about."

"Look who's talking about being touched," Cory said. "You're the kid who's named 'Thomas', not 'Tom' or 'Tommy' or anything else. He's just a kid. Of course, he doesn't know what he's talking about. Besides, it won't hurt us to see who else is up here. Your Dad, at least, will be interested in knowing."

He started over the roll of rock, and Thomas followed. The cleft was sand filled, level, and easy walking. The sand dragged at their shoes as they stepped to the middle of the cleft. The walls rose on each side. They walked in the narrow defile cut into the sandstone, bordered on one side by the canyon wall and the other by huge boulders laid there before history began. They rounded a tight corner, expecting to see the small boy, and stood facing a blank wall of rock, rising to meet the overhanging sandstone above. There was no way out, and there was no small boy. There was no sign of a vehicle.

Cory looked at Thomas. Thomas just shrugged. They turned around slowly, studying the narrow chamber, trying to see any other way out besides the way they had come in. There was none. Cory cleared his throat.

"This is interesting," he said softly. Then he called out, "Amium!"

Moments passed, and he heard his voice echoing in the narrow canyon behind them. There was no answer.

"Amium!" The two boys called out together.

Again, the echo, and again silence followed. No answer from the boy.

"Look," Thomas said, pointing down to the sand they walked on.

Cory looked down.

"I can't be absolutely sure," Thomas said, "but I think the only prints here are yours and mine."

"That's impossible," Cory scoffed, and started back out of the cleft. "Besides, we heard his father's voice. I heard his voice. Didn't you?"

Thomas shook his head, and said, "There's that, isn't there?"

As he walked, he studied the footprints. Though uncertain in the sand, he began to believe what Thomas had argued. There seemed to be no footprints of a small boy, or anyone else besides them. They reached the entrance, and still could not detect any evidence the boy had been there.

"Keep looking," Cory said, searching the ground for any footprints.

He wanted to see which way the boy had gone. As before, he found only their prints. Down near the water he could pick out his shoe prints, and those of Thomas's shoes, and, finally, the footprints of a barefoot boy in the wet sand at the water's edge.

"Look," he said, pointing at the footprints. "At least we know it wasn't our imagination. The little kid wasn't a hallucination."

"Two people can't have the same hallucination," Thomas affirmed. "The sand in there just slides around too much to leave distinct prints. His prints are there, we just can't see them. That means his dad is real, too."

"Then, where did he go?" Cory asked.

Thomas looked around slowly, and then said, "I don't know."

"Amium!" Cory called out one last time, and heard his voice die in the canyon.

He turned to look at Thomas, who only shrugged. They walked slowly out of the cleft, and looked up and down the shoreline of the lake. There was no place to hide a vehicle in the canyon, and the boy had disappeared. They stared at each other.

After several moments of silence, Cory said softly, "I think it's time to go home now."

"I think you're right," Thomas agreed.

Without any more comment, they both started for the downstream side of the canyon, and the only way out they knew. It was getting late, and they could puzzle over the mystery of the boy later.

They took a few moments on the ledge to widen the tunnel under the rock. The work went quickly. They crawled through and walked down to Thomas's jeep. It was no more than a casual stroll to the vehicle now the work under the candle was done.

The jeep was an ugly thing Thomas had earned working for Carlos Simons early in the spring. Most of the kids in town called him "Old Man Simons". He was Mexican-American, and claimed to have fought in World War II. Later in life he settled in St. George, then in the town, with his wife and three sons. They started a mink farm when mink coats were huge in New York fashion. The farm never made more than enough to provide for the family. Later, one son died in Viet Nam defending freedom. Another was lost in the World Trade Center attack on 9/11 trading stocks and trying to tap into the American dream. An irate criminal in downtown Salt Lake City shot the last, a police officer, when he tried to serve a warrant for unpaid traffic tickets. Carlos Simons' wife died shortly after, her life drained out by the deaths of her family. Simons let his mink farm go. He got rid of the stock his son had sold him, and went into his house and didn't come out for almost a year. Then, one morning, he called Thomas' father and asked if Thomas was available for hire. Thomas' father said he was. Thomas spent a month helping the old man dismantle the mink sheds and load cages into a hired van. In exchange he gave Thomas the last thing remaining of his sons. The Jeep. It had belonged to his last son, the police officer. They'd used it to hunt together every spring. Mr. Simons said he had no use for it anymore, and gave it to him as payment in full for the work he'd done.

Thomas spent weeks getting it road-worthy, and even painted it yellow to cover most of the rust. It was the amateur paint job that made it the most recognized vehicle in the town.

Two months later, just as spring was arriving, Carlos Simons was found dead in his bed. His life had been drained out, too. He only had a few things to do before he left to be with his family. Those done, there was nothing else to keep him on earth. Doctor Lee shook his head slowly and said his heart just stopped.

Both boys were uncharacteristically quiet as they strolled down to Thomas' Jeep. Neither of them thought about the lake behind them. Both were thinking about the boy, and his mysterious disappearance.

The time spent on the tunnel had not been time wasted. They knew, without speaking, that they would use it again. They would be back. The hidden lake with its mysterious little stranger belonged to them now. They both thought about the boy, and wondered if they would see him again.

# CHAPTER 3

Both boys wanted to talk about the boy in the canyon. But there were two problems. Sometimes things happen in a boy's life that fill his imagination and seize control of his mind. Then, no matter what his desires are, he has to talk. He has to open his mouth and he becomes horrified as he listens to himself speak words he would never use otherwise. He sees his credibility seeping away. He can't stop. He has to let the conversation flow and no matter where it goes, he has to accept the consequences. It's like times when he discovers his feet have outgrown the new pair of shoes his father bought just a week ago, or he's horribly underdressed in jeans and t-shirt when he arrives at a church dance he thought was casual and all the other boys are wearing ties. The reality of the situation bursts in his mind, but cannot prevent him from feeling totally and completely foolish. In later years he will be satisfied knowing all teenage boys are just as clumsy learning how to deal with life, but at the time only embarrassment fills his soul. Both of them knew this, and both of them were unwilling to open the conversation for fear of appearing as foolish as they both felt.

Thomas started the Jeep and slammed it in gear. He turned toward the track leading down and out of the canyon. The road was rough all the way down to the highway, and they were both tired. It was a combination of the exertion in the heat breaking through the sandstone on the ledge, and the swim in the cool lake, and the nap under the warm sun. Sometimes they sensed each other thoughts. They both remained silent, lost in their own imaginations, and hoped this wasn't one of those times. The pounding of the road and the loud rumbling of the engine precluded any deep discussions. As they drove down the road, they started a couple of conversations about innocuous things, but those were destined to dwindle away with no real end beyond a pitiful silence.

"Just where did he go?" Cory finally asked loudly as they neared the mouth of the canyon.

"We were there together. I don't know, either," Thomas said, turning hard to avoid a deep rut in the road. They both bounced in their seats.

"Slow down a little," Cory suggested, tightening his seat belt.

He knew Thomas was as frustrated as he was. They had no idea how a small boy could disappear in the rocks, and they had no idea how to talk about it without feeling foolish.

"We're not going to solve anything," Thomas said, turning back onto the road. He slowed down, and said, "We'll just have to go back up there and find out where he went. There has to be something left behind. Maybe we were too brain dead to see it."

"You think we just didn't see a Jeep parked in that ravine?" Cory asked, trying to smile and failing miserably. "I don't think I was that tired. I think I would have seen a Jeep, or a road, or *something*!"

"Well, there's got to be some kind of road up there. We know that. And there has to be some tire tracks. We'll find it if we have to go clear around the lake. What do you think? Next Saturday?"

Cory was silent for a moment, grabbed the frame as they bounced over a washboard section of road, and said, "I was thinking. Why wait?"

Thomas slammed on the brakes, and the jeep slid sideways to a stop. Dust rose around the vehicle. He looked at his best friend, trying to read his face.

"What do you have in mind?" he asked.

"Well, tomorrow's out. It's Sunday. My dad expects me to be in church. All we're going to do in school this week is play. It's the last week before summer vacation. Why don't we go up Monday?"

"You think your father'll let you out of school?" Thomas asked.

"He may be the Bishop, but he's also a pretty reasonable guy," Cory returned. "What about your father?"

Thomas shrugged, and said, mimicking Cory's inflections, "Well, he may be the Sheriff, but he's also a pretty reasonable guy. What's the worse he can say?"

They both chorused, "No!" and laughed loudly. They were tired, and the laughter was a little too loud, a little too forced. But there was a release of tension they both felt. They each took a deep breath. They were confused by the disappearance of the small boy. They wanted to solve the mystery. They were ready to take on even their fathers.

Thomas pulled his foot off the brake, and touched the gas pedal. He turned the Jeep back onto the road and toward the highway.

The Jeep rounded the shoulder of the last sand hill and broke free of the canyon walls. The valley opened up below them. The town was just a little to the right. The highway was less than a hundred yards below. The dirt road became smoother, and the last few seconds were almost pleasure by comparison with the rest of the journey. The soft dust rose in a cloud behind them. They both took a deep breath as the tires rolled out on the smooth pavement of the highway.

The drive through the town was familiar. Cory grew up there. Thomas had been there since second grade. They walked every street in the town before Thomas got the Jeep. They both relaxed completely for the last few minutes of the ride, letting the wind cool them. They wound through the residential section until Thomas pulled into Cory's driveway. He turned the Jeep off.

"It's a good feeling," Cory said, as he got out of the jeep. "Even if someone else knows a better way to the lake, we still did something pretty amazing."

"I know," Thomas returned. "You want me to pick you up for church tomorrow?"

"Sure," Cory said. "See you then. Thomas, where do you think...?"

"We'll talk about it tomorrow," Thomas almost snapped, starting the Jeep up and backing out of the driveway. "Right now, I need a shower, and a change of clothes. Maybe I'll fall asleep watching TV."

Cory laughed and watched as Thomas drove down the street. He turned the corner without stopping, and was out of sight. Cory breathed deeply, still smiling, and turned toward the house. He picked his bicycle up off the side lawn. He'd seen it the second they'd pulled up in the Jeep. He made a mental note to talk to his little brother about borrowing things. He pushed it into the garage and hung it on the hooks on the wall. He looked around at the other bikes there. They were part of his family's recreation. Sometimes they rode the back roads together. He walked out of the garage, and went in the back door of the house. He wondered if Thomas was as tired as he felt.

His mother was in the kitchen. He felt himself filled with the very aroma of her existence. He smelled the steam from the potatoes boiling on the stove, and the mellow aroma of the chicken roasting in the oven, and, finally, the faint waft of the lilac perfume she always wore. He looked at her. She was a short woman, with auburn hair cut short and arranged around her round face. She wore an old dress, slightly faded. But her carriage and demeanor made it obvious she was in charge of the house. Every move she made, every nuance of her being shouted authority. Cory knew it wasn't the dress. It was the way she was. It was her domain. In a world that laughed at domestic tasks, she reveled in her realm. She smiled as he came in.

"Your father wants to talk with you," she said warmly. "I suppose you knew about the dance being canceled tonight."

Cory smiled back, and said, "I didn't, but it doesn't matter. I'm too tired to go out anyway."

"Up the canyon again?"

"Yes'm," he said, continuing through the kitchen. "We finally found the lake."

"Well, you should have washed your clothes in it," his mother called after him, staring at the dust he was tracking across the floor. "Come back and sweep this up when you've changed."

Cory turned left at the hall, and knocked gently at the first door. His father called out, and Cory opened the door.

The office was small, just large enough for two chairs, a bookshelf and the computer desk. His father was sitting at the computer typing.

"Hi, Cory," he said, motioning gently to the chair. "I was just putting the meeting schedule together for next quarter. If I can finish it tonight Brother Hansen can take it down canyon with him Monday and get the copies made. Boy, you're covered in dirt. What have you been up to today?"

"We finally got to the canyon today," Cory explained. "There's a lake up there, and some steps cut into the rock wall, and a waterfall. It's pretty neat. I want to take you and Mom up there and show it to you."

"Sounds good," his father said. "However, if there's any climbing involved, you know your mother can't go. Not with her legs."

"There may not be," Cory continued. "I think there's a road into the lake. You've lived here all your life. Have you ever heard of a road up on the slick rock?"

"No, but that doesn't mean it isn't there," the man returned. "I spent a lot of time up there when I was younger, but there are still a lot of things I don't know about the slick rock. I don't think anyone knows all there is to know about this area. This lake of yours sounds like something that's been hidden a long time. I've never even heard of it. But, if there's a way to it, I'll bet Kevin Vinson knows about it. You know how much he likes to fish. He knows every fishing hole in a hundred-mile radius, and most outside that."

"I'll ask him tomorrow," Cory said. "Dad, we met a boy up there. We worked for weeks trying to find a way in. Finally, today, we dug under the candle above the grove."

"The candle? I really wish you'd be more careful," his father said, leaning forward. "That boulder's been there most of a thousand years or more. But it's pretty precarious. You know we don't even picnic underneath it. There's no telling when it might turn loose and drop to the canyon floor."

"We were careful," Cory assured his father. "We dug between the cliff and the rock, and just dug out enough to get under it and to the other side. Anyway, we found a waterfall in the cleft. You know, most of the water just sinks in the cleft. Only a little makes it out to dribble down the cliff. And we found a ladder cut into the wall. Someone used the canyon a long time ago. Then, up at the lake, we found this boy. He was about Russell's age. He was wearing a swimsuit and must have been playing in the lake. I know he had someone else close by because he talked about his family and how they didn't like him to swim alone. He said they got there in their vehicle. I guess they had a four-wheeler or something. Anyway, when he went to lead us to where they were, we lost him."

"You lost him?"

"We lost sight of him around the rocks," Cory explained. "When we tried to catch up, he was gone."

"Gone?"

"The path ended at the cliff face," Cory went on. "That lake is surrounded by overhanging cliffs. We looked around for a road of some kind, but there wasn't anything like that up there. Everything that's not overhanging is pretty much straight up and down."

"That's interesting," his father said. "So, you know this boy got down to the lake somehow. He says they got there in their vehicle. But he disappeared when you tried to follow him. That's a story for your journal."

"You got it," Cory smiled. "Anyway, Thomas and I were thinking about going back up there Monday. I wanted to run it by you and see what you thought."

"What about school?"

"It's the last week, you know. Monday will be a play day. In fact, all week will be play. We've already turned in our books. There aren't any assignments due. They're mostly practicing for graduation. Seniors are the only ones need to worry about that."

"Well, if you go back up there take a good look around," his father said.

"We will," Cory returned. "We'd like to find that road if we can."

"There may be other things, as well," his father said, leaning forward. "If there are steps cut in the wall, then the ancient ones may have lived up there. You may find Anasazi ruins, even some artifacts. If you do, take care to leave them undisturbed until the archeological department at the university has a chance to look at them."

"Sure," Cory said.

"I just thought of something else," his father said softly. "What if this strange boy's vehicle was a helicopter?"

"It's pretty hard to hide a helicopter in a canyon that small," Cory answered. "We thought about that. I don't even know if you could fly one in there. I'm surprised they hid a four-wheeler in there. It's a good-size lake for this area, Dad. But the canyon walls are wrapped in tight around it, and everywhere you look it's straight up. The water is cool and deep. It's great swimming, but there's not much room for anything else. We'll find the road on Monday, I guess."

"You probably will," his father said. "Okay. You can take Monday off. But, be careful. There's something else I wanted to talk to you about. Mrs. Smith needs some help."

Cory realized his emotions showed on his face.

"Oh, relax!" His father chided. "You know that flower bed of hers? Well, she wants to plant some day lilies there. She found out we were thinning ours out, so she asked if she could have some. I'm afraid I promised you'd plant them for her."

Cory thought a moment, and asked, "When did she need it done?"

"Well, we don't want to leave the plants out of the ground very long," his father returned. "Maybe you could do it Monday morning before you go up the canyon. It'll only take you twenty minutes or so. With Thomas there to help you can finish in half the time."

"Okay," Cory relented. "We'll do it before we go. It'll be cool that early anyway."

"Good," his father said, putting his hand on his son's shoulder, then lifting it gingerly and dusting it off. "Now, I've got work to do and by the looks of things you have a shower that's waiting for you. In fact, I suggest a long shower and a complete change of clothes."

"Sure," Cory said, smiling. "Thanks, Dad."

"Oh, and Cory."

"Yes, Dad?"

"The dance has been canceled. They're not sure the new varnish on the recreation hall floor is dry enough yet."

"Thanks, Dad," Cory said, smiling.

He left the office, and closed the door quietly behind him. He walked down the hall to his room. He knew he'd have to shower before his mother would let him sit at the table for dinner, and a shower sounded good.

Thomas drove home down Placer Street, counted two blocks and turned left again. His home was on a short street only a couple of blocks from Cory's. He was happy to see the large weeping willow that stood in his front yard. He parked in the gravel on the right side of the driveway and went into the house.

The cool air from the swamp cooler surrounded him. He realized how warm it had been outside, and was grateful to be in out of the heat.

His mother was working at the stove. One pot was boiling; another just beginning to steam, and the kitchen was filling with good aromas. She looked up as he walked in.

She was just forty, and slim. She moved with short, quick motions. Her hair was a deep bronze color, and tied back out of her way. There were a few streaks of gray, but she refused to color it.

"You've gotten some sun today," she said softly. "Did you have fun?"

"We were up the canyon," Thomas returned, getting a glass and filling it at the sink. "We found the lake up there and went swimming. Is my face red? Mom, you talk with most of the ladies in town. Have any of them ever mentioned a lake up above the cliffs?"

"No," the woman answered, shaking her head casually. "You've been obsessed with that lake ever since you helped find that scout troop. I'm glad you finally found it. Now you can think about something else, like, maybe, mowing the lawn."

"I will Tuesday," Thomas said. "But, have you ever heard of a lake up there?"

"No. But, they say there are a lot of small canyons and folds up in the slick rock. Obviously, anything's possible. Go ask your father. He's the one who knows the canyons. He's out in the living room."

"He's home?"

"Yes, but he has to check back in after dinner."

"I didn't see the patrol car when I came in," Thomas said casually walking toward the living room with his glass.

"Karl Rosen took it down canyon to check out the reservoir," his mother answered, continuing with her dinner preparations. "His cruiser is over at Lucky's getting the oil changed."

Thomas nodded, and said, "Okay. See you in a minute, Mom."

It wasn't often his father was home, even on Saturday. There was always something going on in the town that needed his personal attention. His deputies were competent, but he made the whole town safe. Most of the people in town voted for him. They knew he'd do the job right. Thomas was proud of him.

"Dad," he said as he entered the living room.

His father picked up the remote and muted the television as he came in. He looked up.

"Hi, son," he said. "I understand you've been doing some digging up in the canyon."

"That's right," Thomas said, sitting opposite his father on the couch. "How did you know?"

He was used to his father knowing everything happening in the town. It'd been that way since they moved in. It was why the people voted him in as sheriff when Sheriff Miller had his first heart attack.

"A town this size can't keep many secrets. You know that. Besides, that Jeep of yours is pretty hard to miss. You be careful. The sand up there is pretty loose. It could be dangerous."

"We're done," Thomas said. "We got through."

"Through where?"

"Well, there was that boulder on the ledge. You know; the one they call the candle. It's up above the grove."

"I know it. That thing split from the top of the cliff hundreds of years ago," his father said. "It's just freak accident it didn't fall into the canyon. It just clings to the cliff face there like some kind of vulture waiting to pounce down. Most of the old timers think it's there till the end of time. I suspect it wouldn't take much to drop it into the canyon."

"Well, we dug under it to get to the other side of the ledge," Thomas said. "Dad, we found a lake up there. Remember the lake I said I saw when we were searching for those scouts?"

"Yes. As I recall I told you it was probably just a seasonal puddle," the man said, sitting up. "I gather it wasn't."

"No. It's a full-blown lake. It's not very big, but it's there all year round," Thomas said. "It's large enough to be a lake, not a pond. What I want to know is whether you know of anyone doing any exploring up there."

"Exploring? What kind?"

Thomas sniffed, and said, "Well, I don't know. Maybe archeology or geology. I don't really know. You see, we tried for weeks to get into that canyon, and we couldn't find any way in. Then, when we dug under the boulder, we found a passage that led to a waterfall. That's where the water from the grove comes from."

"The water that comes down the cliff face there is hardly a waterfall," the sheriff said quietly.

"I know," Thomas answered. "The waterfall is twenty feet back in the crack in the cliff. Most of the water drops in a pool and disappears. We think it goes underground. We found handholds carved into the waterfall, Dad. Someone had used the canyon a long time ago. But we thought we had found the only way in."

"Okay. I follow you so far. Maybe the Anasazi or Navajo used the canyon before. That's not unusual down here. If that's true, we ought to get the university to send someone over to check it out. That is, if they haven't been up there already."

"Yes. Well, there was this boy in there," Thomas continued. "He was young, maybe only six or eight. He wasn't dressed for hiking. He was wearing a swimsuit. In fact, he was wet, like he'd already been swimming. He didn't wear shoes, so someone had to be close by with his clothes. That's what we thought, anyway. I mean, we worked for three weeks trying to find a way into the canyon, and he was already there acting like he was on a picnic and it was an everyday thing for him to be there. He was kind of strange, and said his father and a brother and sister were up there with him. We tried to find the way he got into the canyon, but we couldn't. Cory and I had to come out the way we went in."

"Why didn't you just follow the boy? It seems to me that would've answered your question."

"We were going to," Thomas said softly, "but he went around a large rock and disappeared."

His father sat forward, and said, "That's a little vague."

"I know. Well, he went into a fold in the rock, and when we tried to follow, he was just wasn't there," Thomas said. "I think we found his footprints, and maybe a lot of others, but the fold ended in a rock wall with no way out."

There was another moment of silence. After a few seconds his father said, "There was no way out you could see. It's obvious you missed something. You know, a barefoot kid can climb out of just about anything. Remember when you were that age."

Thomas smiled, and said, "I do. Well, maybe. We were tired. Maybe we weren't thinking clearly. At the time it seemed like magic."

"Well, he's probably having a laugh right now about how he fooled two teenagers twice his age. I wouldn't worry too much about it. He said his father was up there with him?"

"He did," the boy answered. "We heard him call to the boy, but we never saw him. It sounded like his voice came from where the boy went."

"And you're sure you didn't recognize him? Of course, you didn't. You know all the kids in the town. Well, to answer your question: I don't know anyone doing any kind of exploring up in the slick rock. Most of the University people would check in with me before going up there anyway. And, even if you didn't find it, there must have been another way into the canyon. It's really as simple as that. What made you think of the University?"

"That's easy," Thomas said. "He said his father was a caretaker, and he had an assignment from the council."

Sheriff Brady thought a moment, and said, "That's interesting. Can you think of anything else that might give us an idea where they came from?"

"Not really," Thomas said. "I thought we'd get some answers from his father when we met him, but, like I said, the kid disappeared. It was all so strange. We thought we'd been the only ones up there and then there was this kid. We worked hard to get up there, and he just strolled in. A kid. Anyway, I just thought you'd want to know."

"I appreciate that," his father said quietly. "By the way, do you know where my crowbar went? I was looking for it this morning."

"We had it with us," Thomas admitted. "It's in the Jeep. That sandstone isn't exactly easy to dig through. I'll put it back in the garage."

Thomas's mother stepped quietly into the room. Thomas liked the way she walked. Unlike her other movements, her walk was quiet and assured. She seemed to glide into a room silently.

"Brady," she said softly, "It's time to wash up for dinner. You, too, Thomas. After dinner you'd better shower and change. And I think you ought to wash what you have on, too."

Thomas smiled, and said, "Yes'm."

Brady said, "On our way, Macey."

"Dad, we want to go back up there Monday," Thomas said.

"What about school?"

"The seniors are practicing for graduation," Thomas answered. "There won't be anything for us to do. We'd like a chance to find that road. We already tried from up on the slick rock. We thought we'd find it from inside the canyon."

"That's okay with me," Brady said quietly, "but there are two things. You have to clear it with your mother first. And I want you two to be careful up there. If you run into any of those old-time Indians you let me know."

"And, Dad, I'm going to Church tomorrow with Cory," Thomas added.

He waited for a response from his father. There was none. Instead, his father simply got up. He towered over Thomas, but was far thinner than his son. His face was sharp and angular, and he was fond of attesting he was glad his son had his mother's looks. He put his hand around his son's shoulder, and they went up the stairs to wash up.

# CHAPTER 4

S unday was church. Church was the only thing that separated the two boys. Cory went to church because he enjoyed going to church. It would have been the same even if his father had not been Bishop. Thomas, on the other hand, only attended occasionally. He went to church because Cory would be there. It had been that way since they were in second grade, one enjoying, and one tolerating, one leading and one following. It was almost the only time they were apart.

Joseph Smith, the founder of the church, was a boy of fourteen when he became troubled by the myriad of teachings by the ministers close around his home. Cory thought about that as he sat at the sacrament table. A boy younger than he was had the courage to read John's promise in the Bible and pray about which church was true. He wondered if he had that kind of courage.

He wondered what it meant to have that kind of courage, the kind Joseph Smith had. He breathed deeply and wondered.

It amazed Cory that people of such divergent beliefs and morays would single out one church not dissimilar from their own to be the object of incredible persecution. Nevertheless, it culminated in the martyrdom the prophet. Yet, the church went on and grew because people believed in what he had taught them. Faith, individual agency and love.

Cory believed it deeply, too. He knew Thomas wasn't sure, and he simply followed Cory. In the great plan of things, it just didn't matter as long as they were best friends.

Sunday was church. Thomas sat near the back of the chapel and waited for the service to end. Thomas's parents were LDS, but had not been active since early in their marriage. His father simply quit attending. For a while Thomas's mother attended alone, and then she began to stay home with her husband. That's the way it happened. Thomas was not sure why. He never questioned it. He just accepted it. His father just didn't see the value of church. Thomas didn't, either. But, Cory was there, so he went just to be with Cory.

Cory loved the stories, stories of heroes from the Bible and Book of Mormon, and stories of heroes in modern times. They were stories of ordinary men called to do remarkable things. There were the modern prophets, from Joseph Smith to John Taylor, David O. McKay, Spencer W. Kimball and Gordon B. Hinckley. He knew them all. Each had a message to teach. Each taught him through the words they spoke, and through the words they left behind.

Thomas listened to those stories, too. But they were just stories, tales from a book. He never really thought about those men as real men. He never really wondered about them.

When the sacrament was over, and the cloth placed reverently over the used trays, Cory and Ramon sat on the bench behind the sacrament table for a moment. The bishop stood and publicly thanked the congregation for their reverence during the service, then released the members of the Aaronic priesthood, the boys and young men who had helped with the sacrament, to return quietly to sit with their families for the remainder of the service. Cory stood, and he and Ramon stepped down from the front of the chapel to sit with their families as well.

Thomas sat at the back of the chapel. He felt alone. His father was cruising along the quiet roads around the town, or picking up phone messages at the office. Sheriff Brady did not want to schedule his men for Sunday duty. He wanted them home with their families. At least, that was what he said. Thomas sniffed. Mom stayed home because she didn't want to go to church alone. That was what she said. Thomas came to church, but only because Cory was there. But he stayed home often enough.

Sometimes he thought about the Savior. Sometimes he wondered why that Savior allowed himself to be hung on the cross. He didn't understand that. He wondered if He were so powerful why He didn't just take over the world and make everyone be good. Be good. He wondered what "be good" really meant. He wondered what "sin" was, and why "sin" was so abhorrent to God, and why "righteousness" was so important. He wondered what "righteousness" was, and looked up to see Cory coming down the aisle toward him.

Cory stopped a moment at the bench where his Mother sat with his younger brother and sister. He reached out, and their hands met. Their eyes locked for a moment as he nodded slightly toward the back of the chapel.

His mother let her eyes drift back slightly, not enough to see Thomas, but enough to let Cory know she knew he was there. She nodded, smiled, and pulled her hand back to lie in her lap again.

Cory walked back to sit with his friend.

Bishop Morris smiled down at him from the stand. Thomas realized it almost as if he knew what he was thinking. The Bishop was okay. He remembered what it was like to be young. Thomas wondered, for a moment, why Cory got the Bishop as a father, and he got the Sheriff. Maybe he'd be more like Cory if the Bishop was his father.

He sighed, and rested his elbows on his knees. He wanted to move, to be free, instead of tied to the bench.

He glanced over at Cory, and was amazed. His friend was listening raptly to every word the speaker was saying. He seemed to find the subject exciting, and all Thomas wanted to do was nap. Cory looked at him when the speaker made a particularly important point. His eyebrows rose as if to say, "Did you get that? That's important!" But Thomas' mind had been wandering, and he missed it. He smiled vaguely back, and Cory turned back to the front.

After what seemed like an eternity (and Thomas reflected on that: If this is what eternity was like, he wasn't sure he wanted to go there), the Bishop got up and thanked the speakers. He announced the closing song and prayer. Thomas sat up and picked up the hymnbook. He was anxious to go.

Cory shared the book. For him it seemed like only a few minutes. He knew it had seemed a lot longer for Thomas, and he wished he could fix that. He said a silent prayer that he could find a way to help, then joined in the song. He bowed his head for the prayer, and, after the "amen" got slowly to his feet. He looked down at Thomas, and realized he didn't get much out of the meeting. He looked bored.

"Come on," Cory said softly. "Kevin Vinson is out in the foyer. We need to talk to him."

Thomas let his eyes roll, but he followed Cory out of the chapel. He knew Kevin, and liked him.

Kevin was the town handyman and one of his father's deputies. He did the jobs in the town no one else knew how to do. He was tall, and thin, and wore a beard kept cut short and even. The sun had burned his face countless times, and left its indelible mark. His skin was almost like leather.

He saw the boys approaching and turned to greet them.

"How's it going, guys?" he asked.

His voice carried a kind of twang, almost Appalachian backwoods drawl, but, to his own admission, he'd never lived outside of the state. He smiled warmly, and reached out a hand. Both boys shook it.

"So, what can I do for you?" he asked.

"I was wondering," Cory said. "You know every fishing hole in this area."

"Well, all 'cept one," Kevin said.

"All except one?" Thomas asked.

"If'n I knew 'em all," Kevin said, the corners of his mouth twitching into a gently smile, "then I wouldn't keep lookin' for the one jus' a mite better'n the last one I fished. Why? You guys plannin' on doing some fishin' this summer?"

"You already showed us some pretty good spots," Cory said, smiling back. "No. What I was wondering is if you ever heard of a lake up on the slick rock. You know, hidden in a fold up above the cliffs."

"You mean up Taylor Canyon?" Kevin said. "Naw. There ain't nothin' up there but a few puddles in the folds. Certain there ain't nothin big enough to grow a decent fish."

"You sure?" Thomas asked, realizing what Cory was asking.

"Well, I was sure til a momen' ago," Kevin returned. "Now, I'm thinkin' you foun' somethin up there, or you wouldn't be askin' like that. Did you find one?"

"We sure did," Cory said, grinning. "It's about the size of the lower reservoir. I don't think it's ever been fished."

Kevin smiled broadly, and said, "If I ain't fished it, it ain't been fished. Where is it?"

"Well, we get in from just above the grove," Thomas said quickly. "But we think there's an easier way to get to it. We wanted to know if you'd ever heard of it."

"No. I ain't heard of it," Kevin said, his eyes growing bright. "I think I'd like to, though. When you gonna take me up there?"

"Soon," Cory said. "Real soon. Promise. But we have some things to do first. Thanks, Kevin. Come on, Thomas. Let's go to Sunday School."

The people of the ward were still standing and talking. Many of them only saw each other on Sundays. The work week kept them all busy. Church provided them with a chance to socialize and catch up on the news. The crowds were beginning to break up and file off into various classrooms for Sunday school.

"I like Kevin," Thomas said as they walked down the hall. "I think he'd like the lake as much as we do."

"You know it," Cory said. "Dad said if he didn't know about the lake, no one did. Now, if no one but us knows about the lake, where did that kid Amos come from?"

"His name was Ammon," Thomas responded. "No. That doesn't sound right, either. I don't know. But, I'll tell you, I'm more interested in where he went. He disappeared awful quick. My dad says a barefoot kid can climb out of just about anything. He said the kid is probably having a good laugh about fooling a couple of teenagers."

"Probably," Cory agreed, turning into the classroom for Sunday school.

Brother Terrance, recently from England, taught a lesson on the destruction of Ammonihah. Cory listened, and enjoyed it. Thomas merely endured it.

"The Lamanites did not destroy cities," he said quietly, in his usual teaching style. "We've seen it time and again to this point. They took over a city. They killed only those that opposed them but kept the city intact and utilized it and their new slave population to provide food and wealth for them. That was what they were into.

"However, in the case of Ammonihah, they moved in and killed every man, woman and child in the city. Why?"

"Because they wanted to," Ramon answered.

There was some laughter in the class. Thomas looked around at the young men and women in the class, most just older than he was. They were all interested, it seemed, in the lesson. He mentally shrugged. The greatest mystery in church to him was that anyone actually enjoyed it.

"No," Cory said, just to his right. "Alma had prophesied that if they didn't repent, they would be destroyed."

"Right!" Brother Terrance said, pointing directly at Cory. "Alma promised them, through prophecy, that they would be destroyed. Could they have prevented their destruction?"

"They could have repented," Lori said quietly.

Thomas looked over at her. He was surprised at how lovely she looked. He would like to have gone to a dance or two with her, but she was always staring at Cory. He shrugged. He was happy with Wendy. He even believed love was growing between them. Cory couldn't see what he was missing. He didn't even know Lori had a crush on him. It was obvious to everyone but him. That was the way he was.

"Right, Lori," Brother Terrance said. "Okay. Now we come to the big question. Why did the Lamanites level the city? Why didn't they just take possession of it? That's what they'd done to every other city they encountered, wasn't it?"

"Yes," Cory said, "but Alma had prophesied the *city* would be destroyed. That came from God, and God doesn't lie."

"Right again," Brother Terrance said.

Sunday school was less than an hour long. Immediately following Sunday school, they went into priesthood meeting. Thomas felt like he was having a meltdown being over-exposed to gospel teaching. Cory still looked fresh and excited. He wondered why.

He was relieved when Brother Gardner was absent. Brother May took the lesson, and it was mostly a talk session. Most of the talk among the deacons, teachers and priests strayed far away from the subject of the lesson. He liked Brother May. He let them wander through the lesson instead of hitting gospel principles too hard. Thomas drifted into his own thoughts. He wanted the day to be over. He at least wanted church to be over. At least at school they had some fun.

The meeting block finally ended. Thomas breathed a sigh of relief. The boys drove home quickly, and returned to their casual clothes. By mutual, unspoken, agreement Thomas appeared at Cory's door only twenty minutes later.

Cory met him there almost before he'd had time to knock. They walked past the Jeep parked in the street, and continued down the street.

Cory's mother shouted from the door, "Dinner is in one hour, young man."

"I'll be back," Cory replied.

Sundays were comfortable days. They fit into a regular pattern, each like the one previous, each predictable. Even on weeks when Thomas didn't go to church, the walks together were predictable.

The mountains were beautiful in late spring, with snow at their summits, and the purple drifting down to the reds and oranges of the sandstone cliffs. Below that was the green of the trees and grass. It didn't take long for the subject to turn to the mysterious boy.

"I asked my father," Thomas said quietly. "He said he never heard of any roads up above the cliffs. It's too rough, with too many obstacles. The kid must have been camping out with his family. So, despite what we've all thought, there has to be a road of some kind up there. But, how did a stranger find it? We couldn't find a way in, and we looked for weeks. And Kevin's never ever heard of the lake."

"I know. I feel kind of stupid about the whole thing, too. And, where did the kid go? He just disappeared into thin air," Cory said softly.

They both stared up at the red cliffs north of the town.

"Where did he go?" He repeated more softly.

"We'll probably kick ourselves when we find out," Thomas said, equally softly. "It's like watching a card trick. You know there's some trick to it, but watching it you don't have a clue, and it's amazing. You try to work it out and you just plain can't. Then when you learn the trick it's so simple you feel stupid for not figuring it out before."

"I know," Cory said.

The subject seemed to grow stale, and they turned to more pressing matters. The graduation dance was, indeed, a pressing issue. They talked about arrangements for the dance. Of course, Thomas would drive. He was the one with the vehicle. They'd meet at seven, and go to pick up their dates. Thomas knew who he was taking. It would be Wendy. It had been Wendy for some months. Before that it had been Marion. He never had trouble finding the right girl to date. With Cory it was different. He was still thinking. He thought, maybe, Karen again. But he wasn't sure. He said so.

"Well, young man, you'd better get sure pretty quick," Thomas said, with a deep, semi-serious tone in his voice. "You have to ask someone soon or you won't have a date. They'll all be going with someone else."

"Don't worry," Cory said quietly. "I'll ask Karen. She'll go with me. Come on. Let's walk through the park."

He turned and started across the gravel parking lot of the town park. It was mostly associated with the elementary school. The school was bordered by three of the town's streets. The park was tucked in between the school and the river. The chain link fence that bordered the road was old, twisted and rusty. The bowery over near the river had seen better days. There were picnic tables scattered across the lawn, and they, too, were old and worn. But the park was clean. The town maintenance crew kept the garbage cans empty. Regular work parties by the citizens kept the grounds attractive. As they started across the lawn three boys stepped out from behind the clump of cottonwoods near the bowery.

Cory and Thomas slowed slightly, and turned to walk toward them. They both recognized them. It was Calvin Franklin and the Coopers. They were the local "element". They were always on the edge of some kind of trouble. They tried out new things, experimented in ways to push the limits of propriety, opinion and decency. Their latest adventure had been cigarettes. Somehow, they could get them any time they wanted, and they were seen around the town smoking and acting defiant and tough. Cory and Thomas could see smoke around them now, and knew they were sharing a pack. They weren't advanced enough to be able to get a pack for each of them. None of them worked, so the price of a single pack was dear to them.

"Hi, guys," Calvin said as they approached.

He held up a cigarette, lit and trailing smoke, as if to welcome them. Mostly, they knew, he wanted to draw attention to the fact he was holding what he considered a mark of rebellion.

"You want a light?" he asked.

Thomas shrugged, and said, "No, thanks. How are you guys, today?"

"Doin' fine," Franklin said smoothly, taking a long drag on the cigarette and trying to hide the cough. "We're just hangin' out. How's the Sheriff's kid doin'?"

"Not bad," Thomas said.

Franklin didn't say anything to Cory, but acknowledged his presence with another drag on the cigarette, and a curt nod. Cory saw Thomas's nose twitch as some of the cigarette smoke wafted over him. He half smiled, and looked at the Coopers.

Calvin Franklin was big, built like a football linebacker. In fact, he was on the football team before the coach kicked him off. His newly acquired habit threatened to influence other members of the team. He was graduating with his class, but they all knew it was his mother who'd pressed to keep his grades just above failing. At that, it was a near thing. He mostly carried a scowl, more pronounced since his mother died the year before. It was almost as if he were expecting a fight from the next person he met. At one time or another he'd beaten up almost every kid in town, including the both of them. Then he suddenly mellowed four years ago. Thomas and Cory knew why, but no one else did. Beating up kids, especially younger kids, did not seem to interest him the way it once had. No boy in town wanted to challenge him. So, he'd struck an uneven, uneasy truce with most of the other boys.

The Coopers were a different matter. There didn't seem to be an original thought between them. They were a year younger than Franklin, a year older than Cory and Thomas. Hank and Howard were twins. They didn't look much alike. Hank was bigger, though not as big as Calvin, and Howard was shorter, stockier. Both wore their hair nearly shaved all year round. Neither spoke much, but seemed content to be in the presence of their mentor. They smiled and their dirty teeth leered out between their lips.

"Thought we'd take a walk," Thomas said pleasantly. "Anything happening?"

"Not much," Franklin said, and his shadows nodded agreement. "I can't wait to get out of this town. Nothing ever happens around here. I'm sick of it."

He flicked the remainder of his cigarette across the lawn. It was only half burned, but he was trying to show off. At a signal Howard Cooper pulled out the pack and offered Calvin another. He took it, and Hank lit it with more flair than necessary.

"It'll be good to be gone," Franklin continued, drawing the smoke deep into his lungs. "I understand you two've been doing some excavating up the canyon."

He pointed vaguely toward the canyon.

"News travels fast," Cory said quietly, slightly amused.

"It's a small town," Calvin said. "Too small. What you been doing?"

"Trying to get that boulder up canyon to drop off the ledge," Thomas lied quickly.

Neither he nor Cory wanted Calvin or the Coopers in their canyon. None of them were much into hiking, but they might want to hang out at the lake if its uniqueness suited their fancy.

Calvin considered the prospect, and said, "You know what I think? Dynamite. Two sticks ought to do it. Plant it about shoulder high. Light the fuses. Then run like hell. That'd do it. If you want, I could get you some."

Thomas swallowed quickly, and shook his head. It was a farming community. Dynamite was not hard to get if you were an adult and had some real use for it. None of the farm supply houses in the south part of the state would sell Calvin Franklin explosives. In spite of that, he knew Calvin would make good his word if Thomas simply asked.

"No," he said, smiling. "That's okay. I think we'll just let it stay where it is for now. Are you going to the dance Friday?"

"It's the graduation dance," Calvin said coolly. "Of course, I'm going. Me and Ruby have a understanding. She's with me."

"Good. We'll see you there," Thomas said. "We have to get home for supper. Goodbye Hank. Goodbye Howard."

The Coopers nodded, smiled again, and mumbled something. Cory and Thomas walked back to the river.

"You let me know if you want that dynamite," Calvin called after them.

"You'll be the first to know," Thomas shouted back.

They walked down along the river. It wasn't a large river, no more than 20 or so feet wide, and less than hip deep in most places. Upstream, where the valley spread out, it branched into a number of smaller streams, wandering across the flats and creating a maze of small channels bordering small, swampy islands. Kevin Vinson loved that area. He caught large fish in there. Most people couldn't even get a bite. They'd leave with nothing to show for a day of wading but muddy clothes and mosquito bites.

The boys were silent now, as they walked downstream, past the streets that simply ended at the riverbank. A few blocks and they turned right, and onto the street Cory lived on. They stopped by Thomas's Jeep, and stood close together, neither speaking for a long time. They'd said everything they'd wanted to say.

"I won't be back over tonight," Thomas said quietly. "Pick you up at eight?"

Cory knew Thomas was aware they held family home evening on Sunday Evening. Cory invited him often, and Thomas declined just as often. There was a tension there that was hard for Cory to understand. He breathed deeply, and nodded. He opted not to extend another invitation, knowing he was reserving the right to invite him again, later.

"I have to go over to Sister Smith's house," Cory said, and reached out to slap Thomas gently on the shoulder. "I need to plant a few day lilies. It won't take long. Pick me up there."

They parted. Cory stood on the front lawn until the Jeep disappeared around the corner. Then he turned and walked toward the front door. He could smell dinner even before he grabbed the doorknob, and he realized how hungry he was.

# CHAPTER 5

Cory woke up early. It was like any other school day except he wasn't going to school. He was going to plant lilies.

He grabbed a couple of slices of toast, and headed for the door.

"I'm going over to Sister Smith's," he shouted over his shoulder.

His father came out of the hall, still tying his tie.

"The bulbs are on the planting table in the garage," he said. "Are you coming home before you head for the lake?"

Cory paused a moment, looked back at this father, and said, "No. I think we're both excited about trying to find out what's up there. Thomas is going to pick me up at Sister Smith's. Do you need us to stop back here first? We can."

"No. Not really. You just be careful," the bishop said. "Let me know what you find."

"I will," Cory smiled. "And, Dad: Thanks."

The bishop nodded, smiled back, and turned back toward the hallway.

Cory only had to walk down the block. The box of bulbs was too small to be a burden, and the morning air was still cool.

Sister Smith's house was bigger than most of the houses on the street. It was dark brick, and had a large front porch. A large window was on the left of the wide front steps. Smaller windows on the right opened into the dining room, which Sister Smith seldom used.

The driveway was two concrete tracks that led back to the garage. Grass grew between the tracks. The concrete itself was broken and, in some places, almost degenerated back to gravel. The garage itself matched the house. It was the same dark brick, the same peeling white trim paint. The garage door had a series of windows about head high running across it.

Cory grasped the handle and lifted the door upward. After a moment of hesitation it rotated on the hinges and the whole door swung up to the ceiling inside. The left side of the garage was piled with possessions collected over eight decades of life. These were relegated to the garage because there was no better place to put them. He had cleaned out the right side, somewhat, to allow him to store the gardening tools he used whenever he visited Sister Smith. A 1957 Nash Rambler was stuffed in toward the back of the garage. He washed it for her twice, but she never drove it. He grabbed a shovel, a hand trowel and his gloves, and turned back toward the front yard. He deliberately left the garage door open.

The small garden around the large globe willow was particularly bare, and he knew that's where Sister Smith would want the lilies. She was fond of flowers and liked color in her front yard. He enjoyed planting things that grew, and was particularly fond of Sister Smith. He picked up the box of bulbs, and dropped them near the garden. Then he began to turn over the bare soil with his shovel. He knew Sister Smith had taken at least a week to clear the little plot of weeds.

As he worked he heard the front door open, and close quietly.

"Good morning, Sister Smith," he said, looking up at the slender old lady.

She was a small lady, with a froth of silver hair piled neatly atop her head. Her face was covered with wrinkles, both of age and wisdom. She bore a pleasant smile, and her eyes flashed warmly as she observed the boy working.

She wore a dark dress. Cory reflected that he'd never seen her when she wasn't wearing a dress. He doubted she owned a pair of pants. The dress was old, but clean and neatly pressed. She wore flat shoes, black leather, and white ankle-length socks. A string of pearls, which Cory suspected were real, were around her neck. She had taken the time to put on a touch of lipstick, even at this hour of the morning, when many other women were still asleep.

"And good morning to you, young man," she returned, smiling.

She stood at the top of the stairs watching him work for several minutes. Then she took hold of the rail and descended one stair at a time. She walked across the small yard to the shade of the willow, and picked up a lawn chair. She brought it back, set it near the garden, quietly sat down and straightened her dress.

"So, tell me about this lake you found up the canyon," she said without preamble.

Cory was used to her blunt questions. She had once explained she was too old to waste time with small talk. He finished the digging, and laid the shovel aside.

"Thomas saw the lake when they went up canyon looking for that Scout troop that got lost up there last month," Cory answered directly, amused that she had heard about their find. "He thought we could get there if we dug under the candle."

"Dangerous," Sister Smith commented bluntly.

"My dad thought so, too," Cory responded, laying out the bulbs where he wanted them. "These are bright yellow, and the ones in back are orange and red. Will that be okay?"

"You have good color sense," the woman complimented, smiling.

"Well, we tried to get up there by riding around the slick rock above the canyon on our bikes, but there were too many folds and deep crevices scoring the rock every which way. So, we went back to the candle Saturday, and spent most of the day digging under it. The lake is tucked in above the grove."

He planted several bulbs during his talk, and a couple more before Sister Smith spoke again.

"What did you find up there?" She asked finally.

Cory felt tenseness in her that he had not felt before. He glanced back at her. She was sitting rather formally, her back straight, and her eyes on him. Her mouth was a thin, straight line across her lower face.

"A lake," he said simply, wondering at her demeanor.

"A lake?" She asked simply. "Nothing more?"

"There was a waterfall where the lake emptied into the crevice above the candle," Cory said softly. "There was a stone ladder there that led up to the lake. Dad says the early American Indians must have used it at one time. Sister Smith, what's the matter?"

"Nothing more," she said with finality, and her shoulders relaxed. "I'm okay, young man. I was just hoping..."

Cory turned around to face her. He was concerned.

"What were you hoping, ma'am?" he asked quietly.

"I was hoping you found something else up there," she said, then breathed deeply. "You didn't. That ends it. So tell me about the lake you found."

It was as if she'd dismissed the incident. She was moving on to something else now. Cory was still worried. He planted the last of the bulbs as he told her about finding the lake. He told her how beautiful it was, and the cool water, and the overhanging cliffs. He gathered his tools together, put them in the empty box, all except the shovel, and sat on the ground at her feet. He waited a while before he spoke again.

Then he said, "We found a young boy up there."

Sister Smith leaned forward, and asked, "Where? Up at the lake?"

Cory nodded, and told her about the boy, and said, "We don't know where he came from, or where he went. We heard his father call to him, but we don't know where his father was, either."

Sister Smith nodded, listening intently.

"You were hoping we found something else," Cory said softly. "Please tell me."

Sister Smith was quiet for a few moments, as if she were trying to make a decision. Then she nodded again, and smiled.

"I'm going to tell you something I want you to keep as a trust," she said. "I don't want to start the rumors about my grandfather all over again. For a long time, the town believed he was insane, that he was, well, a little crazy. Some thought he was a liar. He wasn't. But he's been gone for a good long time and he entrusted his story to me. I think I can entrust it to you."

Cory nodded, and said, "I'll keep your secret."

Sister Smith nodded, and said, "When my grandfather was no more than a boy, probably younger than you are now, he would go up that canyon exploring just as you and Thomas do. He loved the canyon. That was back when the mines up at the top were just beginning to be worked. There was gold up there then, you know. And silver. The town became profitable for a decade, maybe more. Most of the gold then began to go out of state, and the town profits dried up. That's another story, for another time.

"One day my grandfather came back into town excited and with a tale so fantastic no one would believe it. He found something up there no one had ever seen. He was adamant. He was not known to prevaricate. However, without proof the townspeople called him a liar and a vagabond, and he was disgraced. After a while he just let it drop. No one would believe him, so he quit trying. Unfortunately, the damage was done. His reputation was ruined. As he grew to a man, he had a hard time making a living in the town. For a while no one would hire the crazy boy. Eventually things began to blow over, and, for the most part, people forgot about the incident. He bought a small mine at the top of the canyon, and struck a large vein. People forgot about his earlier claims to have found something and accepted him as one of the rich miners. Many years later he told me the story. He made me promise to keep it safe and secure. I was just a young girl then. I've kept it all these years. I've not told a soul until today."

There was a long pause. Cory was afraid she had changed her mind about telling him. He waited and watched. Her eyes grew dreamy, as if she were staring into the distance and could see something beyond everyone else's vision.

"What did he find, Sister Smith?" Cory asked quietly, gently.

"It was a castle," she said softly, her voice touched with awe.

"A castle?"

"A castle," she repeated as if she were trying to convince herself as much as Cory. "He told me there were windows and walls and rooms. There were so many rooms you couldn't count them all. He wandered and explored for several days before he left the canyon."

"This... castle... was in the canyon?"

"No. Not in the canyon. He found a side canyon, a fold similar to the one you described to me, up on the slick rock," Sister Smith said. "He said there had to be a connection with the canyon, but he never found the connection. He entered the castle from up above."

"From above? You mean, up on the slick rock?"

Sister Smith smiled warmly, and said, "He said he found a secret cave, an opening with carved steps leading down into the cleft where the castle was. He said it was a chance thing. There was a fold in the rock that looked like a dead end, but when you stepped closer a passage opened up leading down. Stairs."

"And he went back for several days?"

"No." The old woman's voice carried a sense of finality. "No. He stayed up there for several days. His parents, my great grand-parents, were frantic.

A search party from the town looked for him. They never found him. They were sure he'd been dragged off by a bear or mountain lion. They'd pretty much given up hope.

"Then, on the fourth day he walked back into town as if nothing at all had happened, as if he had only been gone a few hours."

"Bet he was grounded," Cory said ironically.

"He was punished," Sister Smith affirmed. "He told his parents about the castle. They didn't believe him, of course. It was too fantastic. Everyone in town knew the slick rock. They hunted up there to feed their families. There was the mystery of where he'd been, of course. He wouldn't change his story about the castle. There was also the mystery about how he'd stayed well fed and well-watered in the slick rock."

"He wasn't hungry?" Cory asked.

"Of course, he was," Sister Smith laughed. "He was a boy, remember. Boys are always hungry. However, he'd suffered no ill effects for lack of food or water. When asked, he said there were still gardens growing there. He talked about the water pouring through the canyon, and how it was shunted off for irrigation and culinary use. It was all so very logical. Still, they didn't believe him."

"Why didn't he just take them up there?" Cory asked.

"That's an interesting question," Sister Smith returned, leaning forward. "He did."

There was a long silence.

Finally, Cory said, "Then, they knew, didn't they?"

"My grandfather took them up on the slick rock to where he knew the entrance was," Sister Smith said, a touch of mystery entering her voice. "It wasn't there."

Cory shook his head, and said, "How could that be?"

"You know the slick rock," the old woman returned. "You know it exists only to fool you when you least expect it. Remember that my grandfather was just a boy at the time."

Cory was silent for a moment, then said, "That boy we saw disappeared right under our noses on Saturday. And the lake has been hidden up there for centuries. No one ever knew it was there. Still, it's a shame there was never any proof."

Sister Smith straitened her dress again, and sat back with a satisfied smile on her face.

"Oh," she said, "there was proof. The town simply chose to ignore it."

She reached into the pocket of her dress and pulled out a small cloth bag. It was black velvet, and closed with a drawstring. She placed the bag in her lap and placed a hand on either side of it as if guarding it.

"I will show you this proof, Cory, but you must promise to keep it a secret. You cannot tell anyone. Do you understand?"

Cory was struck dumb. She never called him by his first name. He was always "Brother Morris" or "young man". He nodded hesitantly.

"You must tell no one," she repeated.

"Thomas is my best friend," Cory said softly. "We don't have any secrets."

"Then you must tell him," Sister Smith affirmed. "You cannot keep secrets from your best friend. You may tell your parents. But you mustn't tell anyone else. Tell no one else, Cory."

Cory nodded and said, "I promise."

The old woman carefully began to untie the draw string. She opened the bag with an air of familiarity. She'd looked at what was in the bag many times before. She knew what was there. She gently shook the bag and a shiny yellow medallion dropped heavily into her hand. She raised her eyebrows, held out her hand to Cory.

"You can take it," she said softly. "Look it over. This is my grandfather's proof. He was there."

Cory took the medallion and felt its weight. It was metal, probably gold, he realized. It wasn't perfectly round. The edges were rugged, as if cast by someone with only primitive tools to work with. It was almost the size of his palm, and nearly half an inch thick. He rolled it over in his hand and studied the piece.

The front was cast with characters and figures Cory knew he recognized, but couldn't quite remember from where. The back had been etched, carved into more characters that couldn't be anything but writing. Old writing.

Then he remembered where he'd seen the figures on the front side, the stylized panther, the flattened pyramid.

"Mayan," he breathed. "Wow. Is it a form of money? The gold alone must be worth a fortune."

"It's not money," the old woman said firmly, "nor would I ever sell it. The early Americans didn't use coins. It's a medallion. It may have religious significance or was a badge of office of some kind. There is no hole, so it wasn't worn around the neck. I've studied artifacts from the Americas my whole life, Cory. I have rooms full of books in that house behind me. I've never, never found anything that is remotely like what you hold in your hand."

"It may not be money," Cory breathed. "But it's still worth a fortune."

"It is worth much more to me," Sister Smith said.

"Did he show this to the town?"

"He tried," Sister Smith said, holding out her hand. "They decided in their wisdom it was a gold nugget he'd spent the four days hammering into shape. I told you there was gold in the mines in those days. Since he'd found it, and taken such pains to work it into shape, they let him keep it. But they didn't consider it proof of anything except his desire to show the townsfolk a bunch of fools."

Cory handed the medallion back to her, and said, "Thank you for showing me that. I will keep your secret, Sister Smith. I'm sorry we didn't find the castle your grandfather found. I really wish we had."

Sister Smith's voice returned to normal almost instantly as she put the medallion back in the velvet bag and tied the draw string.

"I told you because I knew I could trust you, young man," she said. "As for finding the castle, well, someone will find it some day. I believe it's there. I know my grandfather was an honest man. There is one more thing, Cory. Some day I will return to our Father in Heaven. I suspect that day is rather sooner than later. I have already written this medallion into my will. It is for you. My lawyer has it all arranged. No, don't argue. It is decided.

"My three nephews will divide almost everything else, but this is for you. You remember that and don't let them cheat you out of it."

She patted her lap.

"Perhaps I will tell you why some day," she said smiling at the blank look on his face. "However, for now you'd better put the tools away. If I'm not mistaken your friend Thomas is driving around the corner to pick you up now."

She stood up, and quietly returned the lawn chair to its former position near the roses. Cory picked up the tools and started toward the back of the house, waving at Thomas driving up the street as he did so. Then he looked back at Sister Smith.

She was slowly climbing the porch stairs. She caught his eye, smiled and patted her pocket. She raised her eyebrows and mouthed, "Shhhhhhh."

She went into the house and closed the door quietly.

Cory stood a moment, then checked Thomas' progress up the street, and ran to put the tools away.

# CHAPTER 6

ory looked down at Thomas, and shouted, "There's not a lot down there. Come on. We've got the whole canyon to explore!"

The waterfall echoed in the chamber. Thomas was less than twenty feet below, but he still had trouble hearing what Cory had shouted. It didn't matter, though. He knew what his friend wanted. He studied the wall a few more minutes, satisfied there weren't any more surprises left by the previous users, and looked up.

"There's nothing else down here," he shouted back up at Cory. "There are just the holes in the wall."

"What are you looking for?" Cory shouted back down.

"I thought there might be something else down here," Thomas shouted back. "I thought there might be some pictographs or something. There's nothing."

He looked up, and could see Cory standing next to the waterfall. He waved.

"Come on up," Cory shouted, and punctuated his words by swinging his arm in a wide motion.

Thomas stuck his hands in the holes and stepped into the first one with his foot. The climb was easier than the day before. He knew where he was going, and that made the difference. He looked up at Cory when he reached the half-way point. His friend was smiling down at him.

The cool water splashed around him. They'd discovered there was no way to scale the falls without getting wet. But, even in May, the weather in the southern part of the state was hot, and dry. They lived in a desert, and learned to adjust to the summer heat. The ride up the dirt road had been warm, and they'd arrived at the top of the ledge sweaty and ready for the cool water of the falls.

In a few moments he stood beside Cory, and turned to stare down into the cool darkness.

"I was hoping we'd find some other signs," Thomas said. "I mean, someone used this canyon a long time ago. I thought they'd leave something else behind."

"Maybe they did," Cory said, raising his voice slightly to be heard over the falls. "Just not here. Let's go find that road."

Together they walked out into the small canyon. The sun was bright, and the water looked cool, but they'd already determined they'd look for the road first, and then swim. Instead of wading out into the lake, they turned to the side and skirted the shore, walking, at first, directly under the overhang of the cliff.

"We ought to give it a name," Cory said as they climbed over the rocks.

"It probably already has one," Thomas said cynically.

"Don't be ridiculous. Nobody knows about this place but us."

Thomas stopped, and waited for Cory to turn toward him.

"Right," Cory said after a moment.

"He really was here," Thomas reminded his friend. "You know it, and I know it. We don't believe in ghosts. The question is: Where did he go?"

"Up the canyon," Cory said simply, turning around and walking around the lake again.

It didn't take long to find where they'd swum Saturday. They hadn't been far past the entrance of the canyon. Most of the lake trailed ahead of them. They explored the cleft where the boy had disappeared. It was as they'd left it. It was still a dead end. It was still empty of any evidence the boy had actually been there. This time they looked for a way a small boy could have climbed out. The rocks were steep, and the cliff unassailable. There simply wasn't a way out.

"Dad said a barefoot boy could climb out of almost anything," Thomas said quietly, trying a couple of times to find a foothold in the steep rocks. "But no one could get out of this."

"Okay," Cory said, patting the rock. "Let's forget this for a while. Let's keep going. We need to find out how the boy got down here."

They went back to the lakeshore, a matter of a dozen paces or so, and skirted the water, exploring every crevasse and corner they could find. The cliffs surrounding the lake were no more than a dozen yards from the shore. There wasn't much to explore. At the foot the lake emptied into the waterfall chamber. The stream they had tried to explore over a month earlier fed the head of the lake. The crevasse in the wall gushed water that tumbled over the rocks to splash into the still lake. The watercourse looked as twisted and convoluted from below as it had from above. They climbed up the rocks to see into the crack, and realized there was no passage there. The path the stream took was so narrow and tortuous no human being could squeeze through, not even a small boy. They knew, also, that if they had found a way down the course from above it was likely they'd have been trapped, with no way to go forward, and no way back up the stream.

The overhang all around the lake was impossible to climb. There were no breaks in the wall except the entrance and exit of the stream. The way they had come in was the only way they could find in or out of the canyon.

It took about an hour to completely circle the water, and return to the rocks where they had first met the strange boy only a few days before. They sat in the sun, and were very quiet for a while. Then Cory stood up, quickly changed into his swimsuit, and walked toward the water.

Thomas followed him. It had been Cory who had insisted they bring their swimsuits. After all, the boy had talked about his father, and his siblings, being there with him. If there were any chance this was a public lake they wanted to be prepared.

They swam for a while, and returned to the rocks for the sun. Neither of them felt as totally free as they had the week before. Neither one said anything more about the boy, though he was not far from their thoughts.

They lay in the sun, letting the warmth sink into their bodies. It was funny how different the sun felt after swimming. After a long while Cory interrupted the quiet solitude.

"There is only one way into this canyon," he said, speaking straight up into the sky.

"I know," Thomas said, equally softly.

"My dad says there aren't any roads up on the slick rock," Cory continued.

"My dad said the same thing," Thomas returned. "You saw the way he was dressed. He wasn't a hiker, or an Indian ghost. Indians don't dress that way. And he wasn't far from his family. We heard his father's voice."

"Then, what? Where did he come from? Where did he go?"

Thomas thought a while, and then said, "I don't know. Hey. It's spooky, right?"

"Yah. Twilight Zone," Cory mumbled.

He hadn't believed in ghosts or monsters in an awfully long time. He felt uncomfortable not knowing about the boy, or where he had gone.

The conversation lagged, and he relaxed in the summer sun. Cares seemed to drain from him, and he felt himself drifting into sleep. Just on the edge of sleep, when things are floating half in consciousness, half in the dream world, Cory suddenly woke up. He was alert and wide-awake. He sat up and opened his eyes.

Sitting on the rocks, a dozen or so feet away, was a boy. It wasn't the boy they'd met on their last trip. This boy was, maybe, fourteen years old. He was dressed in white pants and a white shirt. The shirt was long-sleeved, and loose, with no buttons. The sleeves ended slightly opened. The pants seemed to be of the same material, and matched for color. He wore leather sandals. His black hair was long, and curly. His blue eyes sparkled as he watched Cory. He smiled at Cory, white teeth flashing in his deeply tanned face. He held up one hand in a shy greeting.

"Hi," he said softly.

"Hi," Cory said, mimicking the boy's wave. "Thomas..."

"What?" Thomas asked sleepily.

Then, sensing the tension in Cory's voice, he sat up. He stared at the boy.

"Hi, Thomas," the boy said, smiling. "I knew you guys would be here. Thank you for your help."

"Of course," Cory said softly. "Where's your little brother?"

"He's in trouble. Father wouldn't let him come this time," the boy said. "He would have been okay if he kept his mouth shut. He kept talking about your shoes. I think Father would have let it pass, but finally he had to do something. So he confined him to his room for the day."

"Harsh," Thomas breathed.

"Oh, he has plenty to do," the boy said. "He has to finish his studies before next exam period anyway. And he has his own Kumba game."

"Kumba?"

"Oh," the boy said, "don't worry. He plays pretty good. I like to challenge him sometimes. He can almost beat me. Trust me. It's not as much a punishment as it sounds. Besides, I enjoyed watching him talk about his new friends."

"Right," Cory said. "Who are you?"

"You know who I am," the boy said evenly. "I'm Tobias. Amium is my brother. You know that, don't you?"

"We met Amium," Cory conceded, emphasizing the name and trying to burn it into his memory. "He left a little abruptly."

The boy smiled, and said, "And he was pretty spooched when you couldn't find him."

"Spooched?" Cory asked.

"You know. He giggled and laughed for a long time," Tobias said. "He thought it was a pretty good joke to play on you."

"Where did he go?" Thomas asked.

Tobias let the smile drain away, and said, "Into the vehicle. You didn't know, did you?"

"We can't even find a road down here," Thomas said evenly. "How did you get down here?"

Tobias face grew stern, and he said, "You're from here, aren't you?"

It was more statement than question, as if he'd realized something he hadn't known until that moment.

"Of course," Cory said. "Where else? Where are you from?"

Tobias shook his head and started to get up.

"Well, I think I have to go now," he said quickly, brushing the seat of his pants off.

The pants were cut to match the shirt. He presented an almost homespun look. There were no buttons or snaps anywhere, and the pants were held in place by a simple drawstring tied in front. They were loose, but not baggy. The sandals were tied on the side with thongs.

"No. Wait a minute," Cory said quickly, stepping toward Tobias.

The boy's face grew white, and he stepped back.

"I have to go now," he repeated. "I think I've made a mistake. I'm so sorry."

Cory could see the boy trembling. He took a deep breath.

"He's scared," Thomas observed, speaking softly.

"I know," Cory returned, holding his hands at his sides deliberately. "I didn't mean to scare you, Tobias. Look, we have to report to our parents, too. In fact, we're going to leave in a little while ourselves. We just wanted to talk a while. That's all."

The boy relaxed a little, and said, "No, really. I have to go. I thought..."

"You thought?" Cory asked, letting his voice lead the other boy along.

"Well, I thought," Tobias stammered. "You see: I have some friends. I wanted to play a trick on Amium, and so they said they would do it for me."

"You thought we were your friends?"

"I know my friends," Tobias said flatly. "I thought they sent you, friends of my friends. I wanted to play a trick on Amium. I thought it would get Amium in trouble, and it did. We're not supposed to interact with the locals. But you really are locals, aren't you?"

"We have smallpox, right?" Thomas said evenly. "Amium said something about not interacting with locals, too. Look, all we want to know is how you got down here. We don't mind climbing up the waterfall. But it'd be nice to drive the Jeep up here."

"You can't," Tobias said.

"Then how did you get your vehicle up here?" Thomas asked quickly.

Tobias sniffed, and took a deep breath. He was clearly agitated. Cory thought he'd seen the same look in the pig they'd greased down for the school field day several years before. That hadn't ended well for the pig. Nor had it ended well for the organizers of the activity. He wanted this to go better for the boy.

"I know you're scared," he said quietly. "You want to run away. You came to find us. Remember that. Maybe you thought we were someone else. But you came to find us."

Tobias nodded, and said, "I think I'm in pretty big trouble, too."

"Maybe we can help," Thomas said, stepping forward.

Tobias moved like a spring suddenly released. He turned on one foot, and was off across the rocks like a scared jackrabbit. Cory and Thomas glanced at each other, and Cory darted after him.

The difference in ages should have given the advantage to Cory. He found quickly it didn't. The boy had a head start, and increased it as they ran over the rocks beside the lake. He reached the crevasse, the one the younger boy had disappeared in two days before, and stopped to look back. Cory slowed slightly, which, he realized later, was a mistake. Tobias turned and jumped into the crevasse.

"Wait!" Cory shouted after the boy.

He slid up to the edge, stopped and looked down into the sandy bottom ten feet below. The boy was gone. He looked both ways, and groaned.

"Twice in three days," he said, berating himself. "The first one you can't blame yourself for. But you knew this could happen! You let him bolt! What is the matter with you?"

He decided there was no use climbing down into the cut. He wouldn't find anything more than they had Saturday. He turned around, reluctantly, and walked back toward the beach they'd once claimed as their own.

He stood, frustrated for a few moments, watching Thomas tie a shoe. He had waited, determined not to follow after them.

"He's gone," Cory said evenly.

"I know."

Cory nodded, and said, "Pretty smart boy."

"Not that smart," Thomas said softly. "He thought we were someone else. Where did he go?"

"Twilight Zone, Thomas," Cory said softly. "It was the same place his little brother disappeared. There's something about that crevasse that gives me the creeps."

Thomas sniffed, rubbed his nose a moment, and said, "Why is that? Because kids keep disappearing in there and we can't figure out how? I've got an idea. Let's go home. It's getting late."

"It sure is," Cory conceded, a touch of irony in his voice. "We really ought to give the crevasse the once-over, just for old-time's sake."

"You really think we'd find anything new?" Thomas asked, tying his other shoe. "We've looked it over twice now. A third time won't help. Come on. Get dressed."

"Maybe not," Cory conceded, reaching for his clothes. "You're probably right."

He dressed quickly. Then both boys began the hike toward the falls.

"Maybe they are," Thomas said, almost to himself.

"Maybe they are what?" Cory asked, slipping between the cattails at the opening of the cleft.

"Ghosts," Thomas returned. "I mean, they show up, then disappear at will. Maybe they're just ghosts."

"I don't think a ghost would be scared of us," Cory said, leaning over the waterfall. "I think a ghost would try to scare us. I guess I'll go first."

It was probably that he was thinking about the boys, and their spontaneous appearance and disappearance. Whether he gave himself to the fall, or the fall simply took him he never really knew. He put his foot into the first step below the edge, and reached out to grasp the corresponding handhold. He felt the sandstone crumble under his hand, and instead of reaching for another before his balance was too far-gone, he simply looked up at Thomas. He saw in Thomas's face pure terror, and felt the fear grip him.

Thomas watched, paralyzed, as his best friend seemed to gently slip backwards into the dark of the falls. He caught his breath, frozen in time, wishing he could reach out and catch him, and knowing all the while it was already too late.

"Cory!" He shouted, for lack of anything else to shout.

But Cory was already gone. The dark surrounded him, and the falls hid his landing.

Cory watched as the falls suddenly rose around him, and Thomas disappeared behind the overhang. Somewhere, in that instant of flight, he knew there was going to be a hard landing. He didn't have time to process the thought. He thought about Thomas disappearing, and wondered, for one brief instant, if that was how the boys had done it. Maybe they were still there, and he and Thomas had moved.

He hit, and the breath left him. He couldn't breathe out, or in, he couldn't move, and blackness surrounded him.

He drifted half-awake for an instant and saw an old man leaning over him. He couldn't tell what the man was doing. He couldn't feel his arms or legs, and he was groggy. It was dark, and everything was blurred. The old man stared into his eyes a moment, touched his temple with something very warm.

"You'll be fine," the man said. "You'll be fine. Lay still till your friend comes. Now, I have to go."

Cory started to drift again, and the man moved out of his range of vision. He could see Thomas climbing down the face of the cliff, and knew from his movements he was trying to hurry. He turned to see where the man was, but he was gone. He smiled wryly to himself.

"Just like the kids," he thought, and lost consciousness again.

When he woke up Thomas was by his side. He could see the look of worry in his friend's face. He tried to smile, but the pain in his head stopped him.

"Cory! Oh, gosh, Cory! Are you all right?" Thomas asked. "Cory, talk to me. Come on, don't move! You could be hurt."

"No, I'm okay," Cory said, slowly becoming aware of his surroundings again. It hurt so very much to talk. "The old man. He was here just a moment ago. He said I'd be all right. Did you see him?"

"No," Thomas answered, a touch of concern in his voice. "What old man?"

"He was dressed like Tobias," Cory answered. "He did something. He touched me here."

He felt his temple. It was still warm.

"He said I'd be all right," he continued. "You must have seen him. He was here only a moment ago. You were climbing down."

"You fell," Thomas said. "All I wanted to do was get down here to you. I didn't think it would do you much good if I fell on top of you, so I was being careful. I'd have a comfortable landing, but you might not like it."

Cory smiled. If Thomas were joking, then he knew things weren't that bad. He struggled to sit up, but Thomas held him down a moment longer.

"You sure you're okay?"

"Yah, I think so," Cory said softly.

Thomas helped him to his feet, and support him a moment.

"Just a little dizzy," Cory laughed gently. "Come on. You sure you didn't see the old man?"

"You had a bad fall," Thomas said. "It must have scrambled something up there."

He patted his head, and Cory winced. His whole head was tender. It throbbed with every movement.

"Careful," he said quickly, pushing his hand away.

"I want to look at that when we get out of this dark," Thomas said.

"What about the old man?" Cory asked.

"I think you were dreaming," Thomas said simply. "You were completely unconscious when I got to you."

"I guess we both dreamed the kids," Cory said, half angrily. "Come on. Let's go home."

Thomas put his arm out to help, and Cory brushed it away. He walked toward the light, and the ledge in the outer canyon. He felt the warmth of the sun as he stepped from the crevasse, and stretched his arms. His shoulders were sore, and, he thought, if that were the worst damage done by the fall, he was pretty lucky.

"Judas, Cory, you're bleeding," Thomas breathed.

Cory felt the pit of his stomach turn, and he looked over his shoulder.

"Where?" He asked.

"Take off your shirt," Thomas ordered. "Quick."

Cory peeled off the shirt. He pulled it gently over his head. His temple still throbbed. Thomas searched his back, then held the shirt and looked at it.

The shirt was covered in blood over the left shoulder. The blood, diluted by the water, had soaked down the sleeve and the back, making it look even worse.

"But I can't find where it came from," Thomas said, running his hand over Cory's shoulder.

"My head," Cory said softly. "The old man did something here."

He touched his temple, and winced. It was still tender.

Thomas lifted the wet hair there gently. He breathed deeply, and whistled.

"You have a scar here, but your hair is bloody all around here," he said. "I didn't know you had a scar. There's no cut or scrape of any kind."

"I don't have a scar," Cory returned. "I've never cut that side of my head."

"You have one," Thomas said. "It's a pretty good one. You have a pretty large knot here, too. You landed pretty hard. I'm surprised that's all you got."

"Okay," Cory said, feeling a lightheaded again. "Give me back my shirt. I think we ought to get back to town."

Thomas nodded, and helped him with his shirt. Together, Thomas shadowing Cory all the way down the ledge, they made it back to the Jeep. He helped Cory buckle in.

"I know how to do that," Cory protested, but he let Thomas finish.

Thomas jumped in and started the Jeep.

"You ready?" He asked.

"You never asked before," Cory said, leaning back in the seat. "Just don't hit too many bumps. I think I'm going to have a headache."

Thomas nodded, and backed the Jeep up onto the dirt road. He started down toward the town. As they reached the crest where the road dropped toward the town, Thomas turned around and looked back. He slammed on his brakes.

"What's up?" Cory asked lazily.

"Someone was up on the ledge, near the boulder," Thomas answered. "He's gone now."

Cory smiled at his friend, and said, "It's the old man. I told you."

"Right," Thomas said, looking back at Cory. "You okay?"

"I'm fine," Cory said, smiling and feeling a little silly. "I'm really fine. Just a little dizzy."

"No, you're not fine," Thomas said, worry in his voice. "Don't worry. We'll be down in a few minutes."

He glanced at Cory as he put the Jeep in gear and began to inch down the road, over the ruts and bumps. He watched Cory for any sign his friend was in trouble. Cory smiled stupidly at him, his eyes slowly beginning to glaze over in sleep.

"Cory, stay with me," he snapped.

"I'm here, Thomas," Cory replied, his voice lilting slightly. "I'm here, old friend."

"The old man you saw," Thomas said, trying to keep Cory's attention. "You think he was the boys' father?"

"Not at all," Cory said, letting his head roll with the bumps. "He was too old. Maybe he was their grandfather. Maybe he was their great-grandfather. Maybe he was..."

"That's all right, Cory," Thomas cut in. "Just stay awake. We're almost there."

Cory felt the world slip away, and he closed his eyes. He didn't even hear Thomas shouting at him. He relaxed into a deep, dreamless sleep.

# CHAPTER 7

ory became aware suddenly. He felt suffocated for just an instant as things around him came into focus. A light was in his eyes. Like coming out of a deep sleep, being wakened by a shock or loud noise, he jerked, and tried to sit up.

"Stay still, Cory," a calm voice broke through.

The light moved, and the doctor's face filled his vision. Cory relaxed, and laid still. His memory was fuzzy, and fragmented. He was at the lake. Then he was in the Jeep. Now he was here. How had he gotten here?

He knew the doctor's office. He'd been here many times as he grew up. First it had been Dr. Parker. The old doctor had treated most of the people in town for many years. When he died Benjamin Lee had taken over the practice, and had moved it from the frame structure in the middle of town, to the old brick and concrete union hall on the west end. Cory remembered when he was seven, going to a new doctor to get stitches in his knee and the comforting demeanor of the new, young doctor.

"What happened?" He asked. "Doc...what am I doing here?"

"How much to you remember?" The doctor asked, leaning close, and shining the light into Cory's eyes again.

The oval shape of the instrument filled his vision, the light shining at him from near the center. He could see the lens the doctor was looking through just above the light source. The doctor turned the wheel in the instrument, and the light changed intensity.

"I don't know," Cory said softly.

He searched his memory. He was telling the truth.

"What's the last thing you do remember?" The doctor asked.

"Not much," Cory replied.

The doctor moved slightly, and the light switched to his right eye. For a brief instant he saw Mrs. Compton busy at the counter in the small examination room. She glanced his way, and smiled briefly.

He remembered Mrs. Compton working with Dr. Parker years before. And he had not known her by any other name. He wasn't sure she had a first name.

All that aside, she had presided at the illnesses and injuries of most of the people in the town since long before he was born. She had the doctor's phone forwarded to her home in the evenings. She was the one who decided if the doctor should be disturbed, and when he should not be. And she was always right.

He never knew her to have a husband, but the "Mrs." was always attached to her like an earned title. She handed the doctor a tissue, and turned and walked out of the room.

"Tell me what you do remember," the doctor said softly, retreating slightly.

Cory breathed deeply, and started to sit up.

"No. Stay down for the moment," the doctor said, again softly. "Just tell me what you remember."

Cory relaxed again, breathed deeply and said, "I was at the lake with Thomas. We were coming down the cliff. I...I think I must have slipped. It's kind of like a dream. I saw Thomas staring at me. He was falling away from me. I guess I must have been falling away from him."

"Okay," the doctor said. "What happened next?"

"No. He definitely wasn't falling," Cory said softly, closing his eyes to think more clearly. "I'm sure it was me."

"Don't go to sleep on me," Dr. Lee said casually, exploring Cory's scalp with his fingers. "Don't move your head. Just lie still. Lie very still. Do you understand?"

"Of course I do," Cory replied, equally softly. "Am I hurt?"

"Well, I don't think so," the doctor replied. "I just want to be careful for the moment. What do you remember next?"

Cory thought a moment, and said, "I think I blacked out. I don't remember landing."

He touched his temple, and said, "There was an old man. He had white hair. He touched me here. His touch was warm, almost hot."

"You sure that wasn't Thomas?" The doctor asked.

"No," Cory said. "I could see Thomas coming down the ladder."

"The holes in the cliff?"

"Yes. Thomas told you? Somebody cut the ladder into the cliff a long time ago. How long have I been...unconscious?"

"You haven't been," the doctor replied. "At least, you haven't been completely unconscious. For the most part, you've been awake nearly the whole time. At least, your eyes were open and you seemed to function. You were pretty foggy. You couldn't answer questions. Your lights were on, but you weren't at home. That's why all this is important."

Cory nodded, but the doctor put his hand on his forehead to keep his movement curtailed.

"I'm sorry," he said softly.

"Go on," he coaxed. "You were telling me what you remembered."

"I remember being in the Jeep," Cory said. "Thomas buckled me in. We stopped and looked back. There was someone up on the ledge. Thomas saw him, too. It must have been the old man."

"Okay. Next?"

"Nothing, I guess," Cory said softly. "Just here. That was just a couple of minutes ago."

"Do you remember what you said when your parents brought you into the waiting room?"

Cory thought a moment, and said, "No, I don't."

Mrs. Compton entered the room, carrying a large envelope. Cory recognized the x-ray packets. He'd seen them many times before, but only twice did they carry films of him. He was ten when he broke his ankle and eleven when he sprained his wrist falling off his bike.

The doctor slid the films out of their packet, and stuck them sharply into the holder at the top of the viewer. He threw the switch. The light behind the white glass shuddered into life. The films jumped out at them. He was staring at his own skull.

"You think I fractured my skull?" He asked.

"I think you shook something up pretty good," the doctor said softly. "Mrs. Compton, do you see this?"

"That's just a shadow," the nurse said confidently. "That's a shadow, too. I don't see anything there. Do you?"

"No," the doctor returned.

His finger traced down the back of the skull, and followed the spinal column as far as it was visible. He tapped the last vertebra a couple of times, and then nodded to Mrs. Compton.

"Thank you," he said to her.

She switched off the light, and gathered the films.

"Okay, Cory, you can get up now," the doctor said, turning toward him. "Slowly. That's it. Don't make and sudden moves."

"I feel fine," Cory said softly, a little dizziness spreading through him as he sat up.

He realized for the first time he was in one of the doctor's examination robes, the ones that were completely open in back. He stretched it to cover as far down his thighs as he could.

"What's the prognosis?" He asked.

"You're going to live, I think," the doctor said, running his fingers through Cory's hair again.

When he touched the left side, above his ear, Cory winced. It hurt.

"A little tender there, is it?"

"No kidding," Cory answered.

"I'm not surprised. You have a pretty good goose egg. That will go away in a day or two. There was a lot of dried blood in your hair on that side of your head. But I can't find any other injuries, young man. I suspect you've been pretty lucky. I've examined you a hundred times. I don't remember a scar here."

"I don't have a scar on my head," Cory said stolidly.

Mrs. Compton stepped in, and said, "Your phone call, Doctor."

The doctor nodded, and said, "I have to take this, Cory. You go ahead and put your clothes on. Mrs. Compton, will you..."

He glanced at Cory, and said, "Never mind. I'll have his father come in and help. Stay here till he comes in, please."

Mrs. Compton smiled knowingly, and turned toward Cory.

"How long have I been here?" Cory asked, trying to keep his tone conversational.

Mrs. Compton began to straighten up the pile of damp clothes on the chair.

"A little over an hour," she said.

"An hour?" Cory asked. "Mrs. Compton, I can do that."

"No, you can't," the nurse returned, folding the pants neatly, and laying the underwear carefully on top. "You're to remain calm and still. The doctor said so."

"What happened to my shirt?" Cory asked as she began to fold the t-shirt.

The whole left side was stained deep brown.

"That's what we'd like to know," Mrs. Compton said.

"It was awfully muddy up there, but I didn't think I got that muddy," Cory suggested.

"No. It's blood," the nurse said. "It's your blood."

"Where am I cut?" Cory asked softly, carefully running his hands through his own hair.

"You're not," the nurse said softly, folding the garment, and laying it on the pile.

"Then, how..."

"We don't know," Mrs. Compton said, turning toward him. She laid her hand on his, and said, "Doctor Lee is the most thorough doctor I've ever worked with. I helped him with the examination. You're not cut anywhere. There's no place the blood could have come from. But the fact is it is your blood. I tested it myself. Now, you didn't lose enough to be dangerous. That's hardly a spoonful. But the doctor is going to want you to be very quiet for the next few days. He may have some other orders for you. And he may want you to be seen at the hospital in St. George tomorrow. For tonight, I think he'll just want you to go home and rest quietly."

"But I'm not really tired," Cory said.

"That's all right," Mrs. Compton said warmly. "You'll do as the doctor says."

Mrs. Compton was finished speaking. She was like that. When she finished, she simply turned off, and the conversation was over. She'd always been like that. The door opened and Cory's father stepped in.

His father's face was washed with worry, but the worry drained away when he saw Cory sitting up. He smiled, a warm, comforting smile, and held up a grocery sack.

"Thought you could use something dry to wear home," he said.

"I sure could," Cory returned, sliding off the examination table.

He caught himself on the edge of the table and stood there a moment. He tugged at the gown, looked up at Mrs. Compton, who was studying him carefully.

"How do you feel?" She asked, her voice filled with concern.

"I'm fine," Cory answered, then, with some truth, "just a little dizzy."

"Take it slow and careful," the nurse ordered. "Bishop, I'll be out in the hall if you need me. You call, okay?"

Then she was gone.

Cory felt his father's arms wrap around him. There was moment they were close, then the man stepped back.

"We were worried," he said, handing the sack to his son.

"I'm sorry," Cory said, opening the sack and pulling the clothes out.

He began to dress, keeping one hand on the examination table. He didn't want his father to know just how dizzy he really was. As soon as he had his pants buttoned, his father opened the door and signaled to the nurse. Almost immediately his mother came in. She embraced him, as well.

"How do you feel?" She asked, echoing her husband.

Cory nodded carefully, feeling the stiffness in his neck as he pulled on a t-shirt, and said, "I'm okay, Mom. I really am."

"Well, we'll see," she returned. "Let me help with those."

Cory found himself pushed up on the table again. His mother knelt at his feet. She stretched each sock and gently drew them over each foot.

"I can do that," Cory said weakly.

"Nonsense," his mother said firmly, smoothing the sock on each foot.

She opened each shoe and slipped them on his feet.

"I did this for you a long time ago, when you were little," she said. "Once more won't hurt either one of us."

She looked up and smiled. It was that radiant, warm, thoroughly happy smile he liked. She was happy with the world, with herself and with everyone around her. He realized there was only one thing that could break that happiness, that complete joy, and that would be if he insisted on putting on his own shoes. He relented, and glanced up at his father.

His father smiled, and shrugged.

The doctor came in carrying a prescription pad. He glanced down at Mrs. Morris, and half smiled. He was used to parents pampering sick kids. He set the pad down and began to write.

"I just talked with the neurologist in St. George," he said softly. "We both agree there's nothing to worry about right now. I suspect the blood on his shirt was nothing more than a nose bleed. That wouldn't be unexpected, considering the fall this young man took. The water from the stream simply cleared his nasal passages and washed his face off. As for the rest, concussion, head trauma, but I think he'll be all right. I'm sending the films down to St. George by courier tonight. If there's anything else I'll let you know."

"Thank you, Doctor," Mrs. Morris said quietly.

"Not at all," the doctor said, turning toward Cory. "Follow the end of my pen. No. Don't turn your head."

Cory followed the pen with his eyes. He wondered what the doctor was looking for.

"For tonight, don't let him be alone," the doctor said. "I don't want him to go to sleep until after midnight. You get to stay up with him. I want you to wake him every hour for the rest of the night. If he doesn't wake up completely, or if he's having too much pain, you let me know. This prescription is for pain medication. It'll take care of anything normal. Anything more, anything that the prescription doesn't cover, you call. Mrs. Compton will relay the call, and I'll be there. Oh, and keep him home from school the rest of the week."

"The rest of the week?" Cory exclaimed.

"That's right," the doctor said, turning away.

"The graduation dance is Friday," Cory almost begged. "You can't keep me home from that, can you?"

"We'll see," the doctor said, opening the door. "If you do as you're told between now and then you'll probably get to go. I want to see you here tomorrow afternoon. Got that? Stay home, and stay quiet. No video games. You can watch movies or read books. Okay?"

Cory nodded, and said, "Okay."

It wasn't much of a sacrifice. He didn't like video games, and he loved to read.

"Good," the doctor said. "I would like to see your parents a moment. Mrs. Compton, will you take young Mr. Morris out to the waiting room?"

Mrs. Compton waited until everyone in the room was out before she entered. She quickly put the damp clothes into the paper bag, including his wet sneakers. Then she reached out to help Cory off the table again.

He let her take his arm this time, and she ushered him out into the hall. There was a jog, and another door. Then they were in the waiting room.

The room was dark. It was late afternoon, long past time any patients would be waiting to see the doctor. Thomas jumped to his feet the second Cory entered. His eyes glistened, and his breathing was shallow and quick.

"You okay?" He asked, his voice husky and unsure.

"You saw the old man," Cory said.

Thomas nodded, and said, "I was scared, Cory. I was really scared."

"I guess you did okay," Cory returned, moving closer to his friend. "You got us down safely. I don't know if I could have."

"You could have done better if I fell," Thomas said, and breathed deeply. "I'm sorry I yelled at you on the ledge."

Cory shook his head, and laughed softly.

"I don't remember, Thomas. I don't remember anything. Not from the time we started down the ladder at the waterfall. But I remember the old man. I know he was there."

"That's okay," Thomas said. "Listen, I want to tell you something."

"Sure."

"Don't you ever, ever scare me like that again," Thomas said carefully, a catch in his voice. "If you do, you'll have to look for a new best friend. I won't put up with it."

Cory smiled and held Thomas's shoulder for just a moment, and then the boys embraced. Cory felt Thomas shaking and knew the last hour had been harder on his friend than on himself. After a moment they parted, aware of Mrs. Compton. She was busy straightening the magazines in the rack. She looked up a moment, and then continued with her work.

The door opened and Cory's parents came in. Cory's father was smiling, his mother looked more relaxed. The doctor followed them partway into the room.

"Until tomorrow, then," he said softly.

"We'll be here," Cory's father said. "How do you feel, son?"

"I'm okay," Cory returned. "I'm not as dizzy any more, but my head hurts a little."

"We'll get the prescription filled on the way home, just in case the pain gets worse," the Bishop said, holding up the prescription. Then he turned toward Thomas.

Thomas's lip began to quiver, and he said, "I'm so sorry, Bishop."

Bishop Morris stood directly in front of him, and said, "It was an accident. You had no part in that. But you did bring him home safely."

He reached out and put his arms around the boy.

"Thank you for bringing our son back to us," he said, hugging Thomas.

Cory saw the tears in his friend's eyes as his father released him. He turned away to hide his face, and wiped his eyes quickly.

"You're welcome," he almost whispered. "Well, if you're going to be okay, I guess I'll head for home. I know my folks will want to know how you're doing."

"Give them our love," Cory's mother said.

"I will," Thomas said. Then he said, "Bishop...I need to talk to you."

"Of course," the bishop returned. "Tomorrow?"

"Tonight, if you can," Thomas said softly.

"Come over to the house tonight, then," the bishop said. "We'll go into the office."

"Thank you."

They all left the building. As they left, Mrs. Compton locked the doors behind them and returned to the interior to whatever work she had to do to finish the day.

Cory climbed into the back seat of his father's car. He looked over at Thomas, climbing into his Jeep. For just an instant he looked so very much alone, and so very lonely. Then he was gone.

# CHAPTER 8

ory sat in the corner chair of the living room reading quietly. He glanced down at the plate on the footstool, the remains of a light dinner his mother had made. She was in the kitchen cleaning up. He could hear every move she made, moving pans, loading the dishwasher, opening cupboards. The kitchen door, which could swing both ways, was propped open with a kitchen chair. His mother came to the door.

"Are you finished with your plate, dear?" She asked softly.

"Yes, ma'am," Cory said, leaning forward.

"You stay put," she said, shooting across the room to retrieve the plate. "You're supposed to be resting."

"And not sleeping till midnight," Cory reminded her. "Mother, I'm fine. I have a headache, but other than that I'm okay. Honest."

"I have no doubt you are," she said, pausing to look down at her son. "But we're just going to be careful for a few days, okay?"

"Sure," Cory answered. "But I'm not an invalid."

"You are for tonight," the woman answered, turning on one foot and crossing the room again. She didn't give him time to argue. She just retreated to the kitchen with his plate.

Cory, alone again, looked down the hallway.

Thomas had arrived during dinner. He looked Cory over, with some relief, and had gone with Bishop Morris into the small office.

"We won't be long," Cory's father had said.

But they had been. Almost an hour had passed, then another. There seemed to be no movement down the hall. His mother put the younger children to bed. Cory waited.

He knew this interview wasn't with Mr. Morris, his father, but with Bishop Morris, the bishop of the ward. The length of the interview puzzled him. Thomas had not seemed to have any real desire for religion. He knew, regardless, that all he could do was wait.

He heard the office door open, and decided not to stand up. He was curious to know the content of the interview, to know what they had talked about for so long. He also knew Thomas would tell him. They had no real secrets between them.

Thomas came down the hall first, followed by his father. Thomas looked calmer than when he had arrived. His father looked warm and happy. Cory laid the book in his lap. His mother continued her work in the kitchen, offering a brief, quiet "Hello" to Thomas as he passed the open doorway.

Thomas came across the room, straight to him, pulled the footstool up and sat down directly in front of him.

Cory smiled and said, "Hi."

Thomas sat still, staring directly into his eyes. Cory waited for his friend to speak. Thomas looked a little hesitant. Cory looked up. His father smiled, and went into the kitchen with his mother. They were leaving the two alone. Thomas rubbed his hands, and then cleared his throat.

"I just want you to know that I'm glad you're all right," he said quietly. "And, I'm glad you're my friend."

"Me, too," Cory returned, more to fill the dead air space than anything else.

Thomas looked down at his feet. After a moment he said, "I'll let you know what's happening in school. I'll be over as soon as I can after school. Okay?"

Cory nodded. He wanted to ask Thomas what he had talked about with the bishop. Thomas didn't seem ready to reveal what had taken place in the office.

"Good," Thomas said. "Good. Then, I guess, I'll see you tomorrow."

Cory breathed deeply, and said, "Are you okay?"

Thomas looked into Cory's eyes, and said, "I am now. I'll see you tomorrow."

There was a long silence. Then, without another word, Thomas slowly got up. With a kind of gentle wave, he turned and walked out the door.

"We'll be at the doctor's tomorrow afternoon," Cory said quickly.

Thomas looked back, and said, "I know. I'll catch up to you somewhere. Good night."

He looked back one last time before the door fully closed, and smiled.

Cory took a deep breath. His father walked quietly into the room as Thomas left. He was smiling broadly.

"What's happening?" Cory asked his father.

"You know I can't tell you," the bishop said. "But it's good. He'll tell you when he's ready. Just be patient."

"I don't know if I can be that patient," Cory said softly.

I t wasn't that she didn't like Ramon. She just didn't think they had strong feelings for each other. More than anything else she wanted to feel strongly about a boy. Of course, when Ramon asked her to the dance, she knew she wasn't going to stay home from the best dance of the year on a technicality. She accepted his invitation. Ramon wasn't a bad date, just a bland one.

Ramon was a friend. Plain and simple. She agreed to go out because she hoped, deep down, something more would develop. It didn't. She was beginning to think all boys were alike, and maybe she'd have to settle for friendship. Maybe that's all love really was.

She thought about her name. Lorelei Bennett. Not a bad name for a spinster. "There goes Miss Bennett, the town spinster. She's never married, you know. She couldn't find the right one." No, it wasn't a bad name at all. But, she didn't want to be a spinster.

She wanted to meet someone special. She wanted to see a boy across the room and know, really know, that he was the boy that would be hers forever. She didn't feel that with anyone, and she was beginning to wonder if she ever would.

The closest she'd come to that feeling was with Thomas. But he was an item with Wendy. They went everywhere together, did everything together.

She was jealous when she saw them sitting close together at the graduation dance in the school gym.

Then she smiled. She knew she wasn't jealous because Wendy had Thomas. She was jealous because they had each other.

Thomas had been trying to get her to go out with Cory Morris. She knew Cory. Everyone in town knew Cory. He was the Bishop's son, and usually was at the bottom of most of the good times. He'd been the one who organized the huge water balloon party the second day of school. And he'd been the one put on probation. Again.

Lori smiled at that.

Cory was immensely popular. She wanted to go out with him, maybe, but she wanted a boy who would be hers alone. The competition was just too active around him.

She looked over at Ramon, and smiled weakly. He looked back, and returned the smile. It was obvious to her he'd misinterpreted her smile, taking it for something deeper than friendship.

"I had a good time tonight," she said, and knew it was true.

She was surprised at how flat her voice sounded. It wasn't a lie, but her disappointment was also bleeding through. The dance was nice, and the refreshments okay. Besides, most of the school was there. The quiet time down by the reservoir was okay, too. Kids joked about it a lot, but the police departments from two towns patrolled the place regularly. The reservoir was always so crowded there was no privacy at all, no danger of doing anything you shouldn't. Everyone just sprawled out on the lawn and watched the stars and talked.

She thought about talk. She didn't like the same things Ramon did. He talked about things that were totally uninteresting to her. It didn't matter how hard she tried to be interested in the conversation, it generally deteriorated to boredom. In fact, she thought, most of the time she was bored when she was with him.

"Stop the car," she said suddenly.

Ramon looked at her, and his face reflecting his confusion.

"What?" He asked.

"Oh, Ramon, if you say 'what?' one more time tonight I think I'll scream. Just stop the car. We have to talk."

"About what?"

Lori half smiled, and said, "About you and me, Ramon."

"It's late and dark," Ramon said quickly, slowing the vehicle, but not stopping. "It's less than three miles to town. Why don't we stop at the Frosty Freeze? We could talk there."

"No, Ramon. No good. We have to talk about this now. Do you understand?"

Ramon shook his head and said, "No. I don't. You want to stop here? We're in the middle of the highway. I mean, are you nuts or something?"

"Not here," Lori said. "Look, take that side road. That one right there! Come on, turn!"

"Don't be silly," Ramon said. "That's government property. They'll arrest us and throw us in prison up in Salt Lake."

"Not for federal offenses," Lori scoffed. "You'd go to some federal prison. Leavenworth or somewhere like that. Turn, Ramon. Right now."

"Up there?"

"We're not going all the way up, Ramon. Just get us off the road a few feet so we can talk. We really need to talk."

Ramon smiled weakly, and touched the brake.

"Okay," he said. "Let's stop."

He pulled on to the dirt road. The car was bounced in and out of the ruts, and scraped bottom twice in a hundred feet. Ramon stopped the car, and stared at the sign framed by the headlights,

Stop!

US Government Property!

No Trespassing!


Ramon turned off the headlights and looked at his date. She was tall, a little taller than he was, and very blond. Her skin was smooth and flawless. She held her head just right, and half smiled. She was pretty, but that was all he could feel.

"Okay," he said. "You wanted to talk."

Lori breathed deeply, and said, "Okay, Ramon, here's the thing. I like going out with you. Whenever you come over and invite me out, I'll go with you. For now."

Ramon shrugged, and said, "What's that supposed to mean?"

"Just that I don't love you," Lori said, then added quickly, "but I like you. Not like, you know, boyfriend-girlfriend. I just like being with you."

Ramon was quiet a long time. He could hear the little noises the engine made as it cooled off. He tried to think of the proper thing to say.

Finally, he said, "Why are you telling me this?"

Lori thought a moment, and responded, "I didn't want you to think there was anything romantic between us, Ramon. I wanted you to know if there was another girl you found attractive, I wouldn't be jealous. I just like you for a friend."

"You have a lot of friends, don't you?" Ramon asked.

"I've hurt your feelings, and I didn't want to," Lori returned. "Look, if you want me to get out and walk back to town, I'll understand. I just wanted to be fair to you. You're spending a lot of money on me, and you might have a better chance with someone else."

"I don't want you to walk back to town," Ramon said, shaking his head. "I don't want any other girl. I just want you."

"I know. I'm sorry."

Ramon nodded.

"Well, I guess it's back to playing the field," he said softly. "I'm sorry, too, Lori. I thought we could have something special."

"That's what I want. I want something special. I don't know why, but you aren't it. It's not you. It's me. Do you understand?"

"Yes. Friends. Just friends."

He became quiet. Lori stared ahead of them. Even in the quarter moon she could see the long winding road climbing the rising hills ahead of them, then cutting across the face of the cliffs. Near the top of the mesa it disappeared into the black slash of an arroyo. She could see headlights coming out of the canyon. One, two, three vehicles headed down the long road, maybe two miles away. But they were coming down.

"I've hurt your feelings," she repeated. "I'm sorry."

"No. It's just that I'm always a friend. I never get to be a boyfriend. Well, except for Millie Norwood. We maybe had a chance, but she moved clear to New York City."

"New York City?"

"Yah. Her dad got a job back there last year. Remember? I don't know. What's wrong with me?"

Lori smiled, and said, "The same thing that's wrong with me. We both want something that we'll never have with each other. We'll find it. I have to believe that. Look. There are some jeeps or something coming down from the base."

"I saw them," Ramon said, reaching out and starting the car. "Maybe I should stay here and let them arrest me. It'd be kinder than living."

"You're kidding, right?"

"Of course, I'm kidding," Ramon said, backing the car out onto the highway. "I'll live. And if you still want to go to the region dance next week, I'll take you. You want to go to the Frosty Freeze?"

"Sure," Lori said, looking behind them as they accelerated up the highway toward town.

"Don't worry," Ramon said. "They're not after us. We didn't do anything wrong. Besides, they'll never find us once we get to town."

Lori nodded.

The lights of the town were around them before Ramon said anything more. Lori noted with some concern that he kept looking in the review mirror. She looked over her shoulder. There was no one there.

"You have to be home by 12:00, right?" Ramon asked after a bit.

Lori nodded, and then said, "Tomorrow's Saturday. You know my father and curfews."

She knew better than to make her father wait. He was the only one in town she didn't try to get around. At least, she didn't try to get around him in the usual ways. She smiled to herself.

"No problem," Ramon said, swinging into the Frosty Freeze. "It's still early."

The Frosty Freeze was old, built when their grandparents were kids. It had changed owners at least four times, but the Warrens had owned it ever since she could remember. None of the larger chains had even expressed an interest in their small town. To get a Big Mac and fries required a 70-mile round trip. So, the Frosty Freeze remained the sole source of fast food for the whole town.

VerDean was the matriarch of the Warrens. She was a grandmother, tall, lanky, wrinkled, and prone to chewing gum and bad language. She was also the Freeze's most prominent waitress. She was there most days, and every night. She laughed at their jokes, put up with their noise, and took their orders. When the mood struck her, usually when some of the kids were too loud, too obnoxious or too profane, she would even throw one or two of them out. She always followed up with a call to the parents of the offenders. She knew everyone in town, and they knew her.

There were some cars in the lot. One Lori recognized, but chose to ignore. The Jeep was a fixture around town. It was Thomas Brady's, the sheriff's son. He'd be there with Wendy.

She got out as soon as Ramon stopped the car. Ramon jumped to get ahead of her, and grabbed the door. Lori smiled at that. He was always a gentleman.

Before she went in, he said, "Look, whatever happens, I want you to know I like you a lot. But I never really felt like trying to steal a kiss or anything. Maybe it's better we're just friends."

"Sure," Lori said softly. "Friends."

She couldn't help feeling disappointed. She wanted to find something that she knew just didn't exist with any of the boys in town. She had hoped that she would learn to love Ramon. Five dates, and there was still nothing there. She wasn't even sure if she'd recognize love if it ever really did happen.

"Well, let's go inside," Ramon said, squeezing her hand.

The lights were bright, and there were the usual greetings from school friends. It was Friday night, after all, and the dance was over. Cory Morris was already in the corner booth with his "group". She saw Thomas Brady and Wendy Turner, and Calvin Franklin. They were the "in" group in town. Cory's dad was Bishop in the ward, and Thomas's dad was the sheriff. Calvin, well, Calvin was a kind of groupie. He hung out with Thomas and Cory, but only when the Coopers weren't around. Or maybe Cory and Thomas hung out with him. He was a senior and two years older than they were. Wendy Turner was interested only in Thomas. She went where he went.

Cory had dated most of the girls at one time or another, but had never settled on one. It looked like tonight he was with Karen Bringhurst. He almost seemed to shine in his white shirt, white tie and white slacks. He always stood out among the crowd, and Lori couldn't help noticing him.

"What do you want?" Ramon asked.

"Just some fries and a Coke," Lori said, gazing around the half-dozen booths, trying to find someone to sit with.

She knew she didn't want to be with just Ramon while they ate. It would be a little too painful for both of them. Then she smiled. Marion Kenley was in the booth next to Cory's. It was perfect. She could talk to Marion and her date... Jarrod Whitehead... and ignore Cory at the same time.

"Here we go," Ramon said, carrying the tray. "Where should we sit?"

"How about with Marion and Jarrod," she said, trying to make it sound like it was a hard decision.

Marion greeted Lori warmly. Marion was the Laurel Class president in church. They had been best friends when they were in junior high, but they'd grown apart since she started going out with Jarrod. Lori smiled, and returned the greeting, and slid into the booth next to her. Jarrod greeted Ramon and moved over for him.

Ramon ate slowly, trying to match pace with Lori. Based on their newly formed agreement, he was sure she would want to go home early. He didn't want to finish before she did, nor did he want her to have to wait for him. He, too, wondered why he couldn't find a girl as closely matched as Wendy was to Thomas. He went everywhere with her.

Meantime, Lori had turned around and was hanging over the back of the seat to talk to the group behind them. It was with some satisfaction Ramon noticed she was talking to everyone except Cory. At least Cory was in the same canoe. Neither of them could find the right girl. But, Cory seemed to enjoy dating different girls. Ramon wanted to find one special girl.

Lori smiled warmly as the conversation developed. Wendy was her good friend, too, and had been over at her house for sleepovers with Marion and the rest of the girls. She knew when they were together they drove her father crazy, but she loved it.

"Did you see the moon tonight?" Wendy asked.

Lori grew a little irritated. She'd seen it, all right. And it hadn't generated the romantic mood she had expected. It was probably that, more than anything, which spawned the talk earlier with Ramon.

"We were down by the reservoir," Wendy said, smiling at Thomas.

"Ramon and I stopped there, too," Lori said, almost defensively.

"Oh, great!" Wendy giggled. "Did he give you his ring? He said he was going to."

Lori looked back at Ramon, and saw him stare down at his fries, flushing. So, Ramon was telling the truth. He hadn't felt it, either. She sighed, and turned back around.

"We talked about it, and decided we wanted something else," Lori said. "We're just good friends, and I don't think the moon is going to change that. I'll see you two in church Sunday."

She started to turn away, but her eyes caught Cory staring at her. Their eyes met for the barest fraction of a second, and she was sure there was a spark. She turned away quickly. She didn't believe it had happened.

"I want to go home now," she stammered, and immediately hated herself for it. "Ramon, are you ready to go?"

Ramon nodded, and said, "Absolutely."

They smiled, laughed, and said goodnight to everyone. Then he slid out of the booth, and helped her out. They slipped through the crowd to the door.

It seemed like the ride home only lasted a few seconds. They didn't speak at all. When Ramon pulled up in front of her house, he leaned over toward Lori. For a second she thought he was going to kiss her.

Instead he said, "Cory was watching you pretty close tonight."

Lori shook her head, surprised he'd noticed, and said, "That's just your imagination. I think you might be just a little jealous."

"It's not jealousy," Ramon protested. "If you can find someone, then maybe I can. Lori, maybe you ought to talk to him at least."

"Maybe I will," Lori returned, sure she never would. "Listen, Ramon, thanks for the evening. I'm sorry I blew it for you."

"We blew it," Ramon said. "There's someone for us, Lori. I know it. I guess it just takes a little more time for us to find them. In the meantime, I still have my ring, and you still have a date for next weekend."

"Thanks," Lori said genuinely, sliding out of the car.

As she turned to slam the door, Ramon said, "If Cory asks you to the dance, say yes. You have to see if what I saw was imagination or not. Okay?"

"I have a date with you, Ramon."

"Don't worry about me. I'll get by. Call me and let me know."

Lori slammed the door, and Ramon pulled away from the curb. She watched as he drove down to the end of the block and turned the corner. With an ache in her heart she turned toward the house and started in.

"Oh, well," she said softly.

The moon was nice, even if she didn't have a boy to share it with. She'd go in and spend the rest of the evening with her father. She didn't like that, particularly as a fall back, but it was better than nothing.

She heard a whimper as she stepped up to the porch. At first, she thought of a puppy, but it was fuller, more like a child. She stopped and listened. It was a child, and not far away.

There was a large lilac bush on the east side of her yard. Her father had insisted it grow wild, and had refused to have it trimmed. It took over the yard from the corner near the road to halfway back to the house. He prided himself on the fact he had successfully shielded the empty field on that side of the yard. When it bloomed it became a mass of purple, and the sweet smell wafted through the house all through spring. The whimpering was coming from there.

Lori stopped near the bush and gently lifted the branches. She peered into the darkness, lit slightly by the quarter moon overhead. A boy cowered on the ground, struggling desperately to stay hidden in the shadows.

"You! Come on out!" Lori said, not too gently.

The boy tried to shrink further back under the bush. She saw the effect she had on him. He cowered deeper against the main group of trunks. She took a deep breath.

"Come on. I won't hurt you," she said more gently.

He looked up, and she realized she wasn't dealing with a small child. The boy was, perhaps, fourteen or so, only a couple of years younger than she was. His face was dirty, and tears glistened on his cheeks. His eyes were deep and dark, and his head was covered with thick, curly black hair, longer than the boys in town normally wore. Still, he didn't move.

Lori shook her head, and said, "If you really want to stay there, I guess you can. But maybe I can help. Whatever's wrong can't be that bad."

She dropped the branch and turned away. She'd taken two steps when she heard a soft voice behind her. She looked back.

"Please," the boy said, standing, but still half concealed by the bushes.

She could see he was nearly as tall as she was, but his face seemed so much younger. He wore a simple white pullover shirt, but fully cut. It wasn't a t-shirt. The cloth weave was much courser. His pants looked like they were cut from the same material. Both were dirty, smeared with the common red soil found all around the town. Grass stains marked his knees.

"You and Cory Morris have the same taste in clothes," she said casually. "What's wrong? How can I help?"

The boy shook his head, and wiped at his eyes.

She wanted to walk away, unsure what to do with a teenage boy crying in her front yard. Something held her. There was a look in his face that softened her resolve. He looked like he'd suffered immeasurable loss. With that was the look of fear.

"What do you need?" She asked softly, as gently as she could.

"They took my sister," the boy said.

Lori stepped back toward him, and said, "Who? Who took your sister?"

"The men in black," the boy said, frightened. "They all wore black."

Lori held out her hand and the boy stepped into her arms. He melted against her and trembled. Lori felt a cold shiver up and down her spine. Where in this town were there men in black? Where were the men who would take a girl? Any girl? And, for what reason? She stared around at the dark, and shivered again.

# CHAPTER 10

Lori looked down at the boy, and began to feel a little uncomfortable. She liked being close to boys, but it was usually her choice, and this one was a little young. There was something that yanked at her heart, though, and she just waited for him to quit shivering. It was a warm night. Something must have really frightened him.

"Come on," she said quietly. "Let's go in and see if my father can help."

"No," the boy said quickly, pulling away.

He wiped at his face and stared up at her.

"Who are you?" he asked.

Lori smiled gently, and said, "I should be asking you that question. You're in my yard, you know."

She could hear the barest trace of an accent in his speech. Yet, his English was perfect. Maybe his parents were foreign, and he spoke their native language at home. That would explain it. It would also explain why she couldn't place the accent, though she usually had an ear for such things.

"I'm sorry," the boy said with resolve. "They were all around us, and I was afraid. I think I should have tried to save my sister, but they took her away too quickly. They were adults, and I'm not supposed to talk back to adults. This was different, but it happened too fast. They put her in a vehicle. I don't think they hurt her, but they took her away. She was crying and reached out to me, but I couldn't help. There were too many. When the others tried to take me, I ran."

Lori could see he was getting agitated.

"Okay," she said. "Okay. I'm Lori Bennett. What's your name?"

"Tobias," the boy said, breathing slower.

"Good. Now, what kind of car did these guys have?"

"There were three, I think," the boy answered. "Maybe there were four. The men were all wearing black. It was a uniform, I think. There were many of them, ten or more."

He held up his hands, his fingers spread, as if trying to be sure Lori knew exactly how many he was talking about.

"And they all had weapons, I think," he added. "Some had long weapons that fired many shots quickly, others smaller weapons they held in their hands."

"The cars," Lori prompted. "You said they put your sister in one of the cars."

"They had vehicles. Yes. They were black as well, with large wheels. They weren't skimmers or flyers. They traveled on the ground."

Lori smiled, and said, "Not likely around here. Sounds like Broncos or Rovers. But, why were there three or four of them? Are you sure there were three or four?"

"Yes. They were wide and flat, and high off the ground. The lights on the front were partly covered, but I could see them well enough. And I couldn't see in. I can see in most of the... the cars around here. Their windows were black. Just black. They threw my sister in. I couldn't see her anymore."

"A lot of black," Lori said, trying to decide how much she was going to believe. "How many men did you say there were?"

"There were three, maybe four vehicles, all alike," Tobias repeated earnestly. "There were at least this many men. Ten."

He held up his fingers again, and Lori let her breath out slowly.

"This doesn't make sense," she said. "What kind of trouble are you in, Tobias? Who would want to take you or your sister away? Look, did Wendy and Thomas put you up to this? Is this some kind of joke?"

"Joke? No, it isn't a joke," Tobias said hotly, emphasizing each word. "All I want is my sister. They have no right to take her."

"They have no *reason* to take her," Lori returned. "Come on. We're going to talk to my Dad, and then we'll go over to Thomas's house. His Dad's the sheriff. He'll need to know about this."

"Sheriff?"

"Policeman," Lori explained. "Law officer."

"Oh," Tobias said. "Sheriff. Okay." He seemed to study the word, then asked, "Will he help?"

"Don't worry. He's a good guy. He'll help. He may be the only person in town who can."

She turned and started toward her house. She turned back suddenly. The boy jumped back, startled.

"Look," she said evenly, anger growing in her, "if this was cooked up by Thomas or Cory or anyone else as some kind of practical joke it isn't funny. I want you to know that."

"I told you it wasn't a joke," Tobias almost shouted. "The men were your people. You know where they took my sister! I just want her back!"

"I'm supposed to know everything?" Lori snapped. "You just go back under the bush there and play your little games. I don't think I want to be part of this anymore. I don't know who put you up to this, but the fun is over, and you can go back and have a good laugh at my expense. Stupid Lori believes anything. Well, it stops right here. Good night."

The boy didn't speak. He just stared at her, his mouth hanging open slightly.

Lori was angry, and she wasn't sure why. She believed the boy, and that bothered her. She felt like she was being incredibly gullible. The boy's story was too fantastic to believe. She didn't want the other kids in town laughing at her. Yet, deep inside she still believed, and that made her angrier.

With deliberate control she turned and walked toward the house. Halfway there her heel stuck in the turf and she almost stumbled. She realized she'd been emphasizing each step of her departure by stomping, and that impaled her heel in the grass. Her "high heels" weren't very high at all, and the heels were wide, so it had taken some effort to jam her heel into the ground.

She stooped to free her shoe.

"Look, Tobias," she said softly, turning back. "I'm sorry. Let's tell my father about this. He'll help."

The boy was gone. Then her eye caught the headlights of a car moving down the block toward them.

Probably the neighbors, she thought.

She was standing, one shoe on, and one off, scraping dirt off the heel of the offending shoe when she noticed the growl of the engine. It grew louder as the vehicle approached. It had to be a truck engine, but the lights were too low, and too far apart. And they had shades on top to shield them from above. It wasn't a normal car.

The vehicle pulled even, growling, and slowed to a crawl. For a moment it paused in front of her house. It seemed to be weighing whether to spring onto the lawn or to continue hunting. The moment passed. It chose to continue. It moved on, marking its new territory with a low, throaty growl. It seemed to be daring someone to question its right to be there.

Lori felt her heart pounding.

The vehicle was low and wide, but held high off the ground by the tires. She knew the car. It was a Hummer, the kind the military used. But this one didn't look military. It had no insignia, and it wasn't camouflaged. It was painted black. And the windows were tinted black.

Lori sucked in her breath. The boy's description was still fresh in her mind. He'd talked about black vehicles and men dressed in black. She looked around for the boy again. She couldn't see him.

"Dad!" she shouted as she ran to the door, one shoe on and one shoe off.

Her father opened the door as she reached for the knob. There was no mistaking the look of concern on his face.

"What is it, Pumpkin?" he asked as she threw herself into his arms.

"There was a boy, and a car," she spurted, trying to explain.

It had seemed so logical in her mind, but she realized as she said it how silly it sounded. Her breathing was fast and ragged.

Her father wrapped his arms around her, and pulled her into the house. He pushed her behind him. He looked up and down the street before he shut the door. The vehicle was gone, well up the street and out of sight. The boy had disappeared in the dark. There was nothing left of what she'd seen to show her father.

She stared up at him. He was a tall man, thin, slightly balding in front. He had a touch of gray at the temples. In all he seemed plain, ordinary. Now, as she looked up at him, his arms around her, she felt his strength.

He'd been waiting up for her. He always did. She tried to pretend she didn't like that, but she enjoyed having him there when she got home. Tonight, she was grateful.

"Okay," her father asked quietly. "Tell me what's going on."

"I just got home a few minutes ago," Lori explained, "and I heard someone crying in the lilac bush."

"Crying?"

"Yes," she said.

She quickly explained the encounter with the boy, and the Hummer prowling past.

"I heard the engine," her father said quietly. "I was hoping Ramon wasn't driving some kind of souped up pickup. I was coming to the door to see when you shouted. Where is this boy now?"

"I don't know. He was gone when I turned around."

"Let's go take a look. Maybe he just ducked back into the lilac. Black Hummer? I don't think I've ever seen a Hummer around here any color. I know the military uses them, but they're standard military colors. You know...khaki or brown."

They went out on the front lawn, and stood in the cool of the night. The tall man stood near the porch, well back from the foliage, and motioned for Lori to move toward the bush. He looked around, searching for anything out of the ordinary. Everything seemed to be normal. The things his daughter had told him made him a little nervous, and cautious. He moved carefully, his muscles tense.

Lori felt his tension. She edged toward the lilac, tension building up in her as well. Then she stopped.

Further down the block, near the corner, she could see a man. He was more shadow than real. Even under the street lamp he was impossible to see clearly. He wore black, and Lori could see a lump at his hip. She decided it was a gun.

"Dad..." she said quietly.

"I see him," her father returned, moving calmly to her side. "I don't recognize him. Do you?"

Lori shook her head. She was aware her father couldn't see the movement. She was also aware the question was more rhetorical than anything else. She knew her father well enough to know he wasn't really looking for an answer.

"He's not trying to hide, is he?" Her father said softly.

Suddenly he looked up, and pointed at the stars.

"What are you doing?" Lori asked, confused.

"I'm letting whoever that is know we don't care whether he's there or not," her father returned. "He can't hear what we're saying, but he can see what we're doing. Young man, are you still in my lilac bush?"

There was a long moment of silence, and Lori could hear her own heart beat in her ears. She started to speak, but was cut off.

"I'm here," a hoarse whisper wafted from the bush, and the branches started to move.

"Don't come out," her father said quickly, turning Lori away from the bush to point to another set of stars. "Stay still and listen. It would seem there are some strangers running around here tonight. Lori tells me they may be looking for you. I don't know what they want with you, and she says you don't know, either. However, I don't like it when someone comes into my town armed. I don't think Sheriff Brady will like it, either. We're going walk over to the driveway very slowly. Do you understand?"

"Where the... car is?" the boy whispered.

"Yes. Now, as we walk that way, we're going to block that man's view, and I want you to follow the fence line to the back yard. Climb the fence and circle behind the house and meet us by the car. Can you climb a fence?"

"Yes, sir."

"Good," Bennett said softly. "Don't worry, there's not much back there to stumble over. Just meet us by the car, and stay low and out of sight. I know you're frightened, and I don't blame you. I'm asking you to trust me. Do you think you can do that?"

There was a moment of silence, then the boy said softly, "Yes, sir."

"Good. Now, just do as I say, and we'll try to get you to Sheriff Brady's. You'll be safe there, I promise."

"My sister," the boy said plaintively.

"We'll deal with that as soon as we get to the Sheriff's house," Mr. Bennet said.

The lilac rustled slightly, and Lori knew the boy was getting ready to move. She wasn't sure if he was going to do what her father asked. He'd seemed more like a scared rabbit earlier. She thought he might just try to get away on his own instead of staying with her father and her. She wasn't even sure what she wanted him to do.

"We're going now, youngster," Jacob said softly. "You just do what I said."

Jacob squeezed his daughter's shoulder, and glanced at his watch.

"Let's just walk casually toward the car, now, Lori," he said softly, gesturing once more toward the sky as if continuing their conversation about the stars. "As long as we move slowly, he shouldn't suspect anything."

"I'm not sure I want to go," Lori said frankly, much more softly. "I'm really scared."

Jacob whispered, "I won't leave you alone here. Not with that gentleman down on the corner. Besides, the boy knows you, and he may still be a little leery of me. I know he'll feel more comfortable with you along."

"Okay," Lori said, walking across the lawn slowly with her father.

She tried to ignore the man on the corner, and found that the harder she tried the harder it was to pretend he wasn't there. She looked over her shoulder once, and nudged her father.

"The boy is gone," she whispered. "I saw him run past the corner of the house. I hope that guy didn't see him, too."

"I saw him. The man on the corner is a little further away. But I wish the boy were wearing something besides white. Even with a quarter moon his white clothes shine in the dark. It would be better if the man on the corner were wearing the white. Just get in the car."

"White seems to be in fashion tonight," Lori said softly. "Cory Morris was wearing all white, too."

"Yes. Well, he's not trying to hide in the dark, is he?"

Jacob ushered her around the back of the vehicle and into the front. He opened the back door, and pretended to be shuffling around in the back seat. There was an almost oppressive silence in the darkness. He looked around nervously, and glanced at his watch. Then he saw the shadow move. He motioned with his hand, and the boy was past him into the auto.

"Stay on the floor," Jacob warned as he slammed the door. "We'll be away from here in a few moments."

He slid behind the steering wheel, started the car, and backed out of the driveway. It all seemed to be one fluid act. He deliberately drove past the figure on the corner. He looked the man over carefully as they drove by.

He could see little more than from his front yard. The man wore a black jumpsuit with no insignia, and had a weapon strapped at his waist. He wore dark glasses.

Dark glasses at night bothered Jacob. He had the irresistible feeling the man was hiding something more than just his identity. As they passed, the man pulled a communication device from his belt and spoke into it.

"That doesn't thrill me a bit," Jacob said softly. "What's your name, youngster?"

"Tobias," the boy whispered.

"Of course," Jacob said. "Lori told me. I just forgot. You can speak up, Tobias. They can't hear you in here. Do you know who these people are?"

"I do not," Tobias answered firmly.

"Lori said they took your sister. Why?"

"I don't know that, either," Tobias returned. "We were waiting at our vehicle. It was... broken. Our Father was on his way to help us. Then the men arrived, and they caught my sister and threw her into their vehicle."

The boy's voice was filled with emotion, and he faltered.

"Like the Hummer that passed on the street a few minutes ago?" Lori asked.

"Yes," he choked out. "That was one of them. They had no right to take my sister."

"She was older than you?" Jacob asked.

"No. Younger. She was very frightened. She cried out to me, and I couldn't help her. They may be hurting her! They had no right to take her!"

"Who was driving your vehicle, Tobias?" Jacob asked casually.

"I was," Tobias choked. "I think I did something that broke it."

"Possibly," Jacob returned. "Tell me, son: Did you have your father's permission to take the car?"

There was a long silence from the back of the car, then a sob.

"No," the boy said simply. "Father was very angry about that. But he was coming to help. Now I've lost my sister, too."

"Calm down, son," Jacob said warmly. "We'll help you. The first thing we need to do is find out who has your sister and get her back. Then we can find out who they are and what they think they're doing. Sheriff Brady will help with that."

He turned onto the main street of the town. The stores and shops, the few there were, were all closed up now. The only thing in town with significant lighting was the Frosty Freeze. They passed by, and Jacob shook his head.

"It's after eleven. Don't those kids ever go home?"

"It's closer to midnight," Lori said softly.

"Well," Jacob said. "Tonight doesn't seem to be a good night for partying."

"I don't think the rest of the kids have a clue what's going on," Lori said wistfully.

She wished she were still innocent, too.

"We've got some trouble up here," Jacob cut in suddenly.

Ahead, about half a block, two Black Hummers had pulled into the road facing them, their headlights dimmed. They faced the Bennet's car, one in each lane. They effectively blocked the road.

Jacob slowed the vehicle to a stop. There was no movement from the Hummers.

"I don't think this is a good thing," he said half to himself.

He flashed his lights to bright, then back down again. The hummers didn't move. He flashed once more, with the same results.

"I think our friends in the Hummers suspect who our passenger is," he said. "I want you to stay down, Tobias. Lori, try to look calm."

"Is passed out calm enough?" She asked.

Jacob put the car in reverse and began to back up slowly. The Hummers suddenly began to move. They followed, keeping the same relative distance between them.

"Lori, dear, I haven't felt afraid until now," Jacob breathed. "I think it's time to improvise. I'm going to pull into the Frosty Freeze, and circle the building. When I get in back, I want you and Tobias to jump out and get inside. You'll be hidden from our friends in black for only a few seconds, so don't dawdle. Find your friends and hide in the crowd. Do you understand? Have you got that, Tobias?"

"Yes, sir," the boy responded.

Jacob was even with the entrance to the Frosty Freeze parking lot. He slowed to a stop. Trying to appear casual, he shifted into drive, and pulled into the lot of the burger stand. The Hummers stopped a hundred meters up the street. Seeing a wider window of safety than he'd expected Jacob pulled around the building. He stopped for a few seconds in back. The boy was out before he could look back. He grabbed Lori's hand through a partly open door and pulled her out. Jacob reached across and yanked the door shut behind her. The two paused. Tobias pulled Lori away from the car.

"Good. Very good," Jacob muttered, pulling forward again. "Now let's hope they'll follow the car."

When he reached the street he turned left, away from the Hummers, and picked up speed. He knew how to get to Brady's by going through the residential area. Unless they knew the town better than he did, they couldn't stop him. But the black hummers still frightened him. And he was worried about the kids' safety.

When he glanced in the rear-view mirror, he could see only one of the Hummers. He took a deep breath and turned right on Woodruff Avenue. He had to get to Brady fast.

Lori felt Tobias grab her hand, and recognized the protective nature of his grasp. He started to pull, and she yanked back gently.

"The back door," she whispered harshly. "There! It's always open!"

Before she got the last out, Tobias was already dragging her toward the entrance. The smell of rotting food was around the back door. The dumpster was close and the early summer sun had done its duty to the leftovers that were stored there between trash pickups. The old battered screen slammed behind them, and the short, dark hall opened quickly into the kitchen.

"Hi, Lori!" the cook shouted.

Max had graduated the year before, and was just waiting for classes to start over at the college in Cedar City. He was always friendly, and attached to Rachel Covens.

Lori breathed deeply. Those two sentences seemed to always go together with the boys in the town. He's friendly and he's attached. Pick any two names. She followed Tobias through the kitchen.

VerDean turned around when she saw Lori push out of the kitchen toward the dining area. She slapped her hands on her hips, the stub of a pencil sticking out from between her fingers, and whistled.

"Geese, Louise!" she said. "Hey, Lori! That one's a little young even for you, ain't he?"

"He's my cousin," she said weakly as they passed the older lady.

She saw Thomas and Wendy still in the corner booth, and pulled Tobias with her down the row of booths. Thomas looked up at them and then stared at the boy.

"Hi, Lori," he said. "Hi, Tobias. What are you doing here?"

Cory immediately turned around, and smiled at Lori, then looked at the boy.

"You have a habit of disappearing fast," he said. "Where did you go the other day?"

Tobias said quickly, "These are your friends?"

"It's a small town," Lori snapped. "You've met? Look, we... I need your help. There are these guys..."

"Guy trouble is your middle name," Cory cut in, only half smiling at his insensitive joke.

Lori grimaced, and said, "I'm not kidding. Tobias, I could use a little help here. What's wrong with you, Wendy?"

Wendy had started to open her mouth, but gasped instead. She stared past Lori, toward the main entrance. Lori turned around.

Five men had entered, spreading out to cover both the front and back entrances to the diner. They all wore black jumpsuits and dark glasses. They had weapons strapped to their waists, with several other utility pouches strapped to the same belt. They wore black berets. One, the apparent leader, had a headset on with a tiny microphone suspended at his right cheek. They stood as if they were waiting for something.

Only a dozen or so teens were still in the diner. They turned, almost as a unit, to face the intruders. The noise level dropped immediately. The room became silent. Lori pushed Tobias behind her. Thomas, sensing her attempt to protect the younger boy, reached out and pulled him into their booth, pushing him all the way to the back. Then he stood to provide a shield for the boy to hide behind.

"What's going on?" he whispered.

"I wish I knew," Lori almost cried. "I don't know who they are, but they seem to want Tobias for some reason. They grabbed his sister a while ago. We need your dad, Thomas, but we can't get there. They blocked the road."

"What do you want?" VerDean asked, stepping out from behind the counter.

"Two teens came in here a few minutes ago," one of the men said casually. "We just want to talk to them."

"The place is full of teens," VerDean said. "They come in and out a lot. Why don't you take off your sunglasses so we can see your faces? Then order something. This is a restaurant, not a public park."

"These two, a boy and a girl," the man said carefully, "came in through the back entrance."

VerDean smiled, and said, "Then I can help you."

Lori felt her heart skip a beat.

"No one came through the kitchen, but kids are all the time ducking in to use the restroom. They leave it a mess. I get to clean up after them. Lord knows I don't have anything else to do."

The leader nodded to one of the others. He paired off, and the two went into the kitchen.

"You just wait a minute!" VerDean snapped.

"Ma'am, just stay put," the leader said evenly. "We have every right to search this place, and we will do it. When we find what we are looking for, we'll leave. Not until."

The two who had gone through the kitchen came back, and shook their heads. The leader keyed the microphone, spoke softly into it, and waited a moment. He looked around the room.

"Not you, old lady, or the cook," he said softly. "But the girl looked like you."

He pointed directly at Lori. She shrank back against the wall. Immediately the teens around her filled in and half hid her from the gaze of the leader. Lori stared around at her friends.

"Max," VerDean ordered, "go in the office and call Brady."

"Don't call Brady, son," the man said evenly, letting his hand drop casually to the handgun sheathed at his side. "He's the local sheriff, I would guess. We don't need him. Now, your name is 'Lori', isn't it?"

Lori wanted to hide behind the wall, but there was nowhere else to go. She simply stood stiffly, waiting for something else to happen.

"Where's the boy?" the man said simply.

There was silence through the room. Only the sizzle of hamburgers forgotten on the griddle broke it. Lori glanced at the booth, an almost involuntary action that filled her immediately with regret.

The leader keyed the mike again, said something, waited, and responded. He looked directly at her. His mouth was thin, his jaw tight.

"Your father was wrong, little girl. We heard your conversation with the boy in the car. Every word. We don't want to hurt you or the boy. In fact, we don't want you at all. Just the boy. Come on out, boy. We know you're here. You can't hide from us anymore."

There was a dread silence again.

"You can't just come in here—" VerDean started. Her eyes flashed.

"We can," the leader said evenly, pointing directly at the waitress. "You don't want to go there, lady. You will lose. Just leave us to our work and we'll be gone. Boy! Come on out or I will send two of my men to get you. Now!"

Lori glanced at the booth again, and saw Cory getting up. She felt a wave of horror sweep through her. She knew the men would eventually come back and grab Tobias, but she didn't want to think Cory would betray her or the boy!

"Why won't you leave me alone?" Cory shouted as he got up. "What have you done with my sister? I want her back!"

The leader spoke into the microphone again, then said, "Come over here, boy, and we'll take you to her. That's all we ever wanted to do."

"You'd never be able to find me if you didn't have my sister," Cory shouted. "I had to stay close to her!"

"Come on out now. It's over. We have some men who want to ask you a few questions. That's all."

Cory crawled over the boy, and pushed into the aisle next to Thomas. He stood there a moment. Then he cleared his throat.

"These people all know you're taking me," he said. "They all know you have my sister. They'll tell everyone, and they'll get the Sheriff to come after us."

"By that time we'll be finished, and you'll be free to go anyway," the man said. "Come on, and let's get this over with."

"What if they won't let you take me away?" Cory asked.

"They don't want to get involved," the man said harshly. "They really don't."

Cory looked around and shrugged.

"You're probably right," he said quietly.

"White shirt and pants," the leader of the group said quietly. "That's not a good outfit for someone trying to hide."

Cory looked down at his pants, and said, "Yes. Well, I had a date tonight."

"You've got a different one now," the leader said. "Come this way."

Lori was the only one who saw Tobias start to stand up, and Cory's hand pressed against his face pushing him back into the booth. Thomas shielded the action from the strangers, and Lori from the other teens.

"Thomas, tell my father," Cory whispered, then stared directly into Lori's eyes.

For a fraction of an instant she was sure they were the only two in the restaurant that night. The feeling ended, and Cory walked toward the front of the diner where the men stood.

Without formality, two men flanked him, and took him by the arms and half pushed, half carried him out the doors. The others followed. Lori ran to the front doors, and got there in time to see the men almost throw him into one of three Hummers in the lot. The men climbed into the vehicles, each apparently pre-assigned. The leader crawled into the same one Cory was in. The Hummers growled out of the lot in convoy fashion, the leader's vehicle in front, and headed west down the main street of town.

"Cory!" Lori shouted.

Somewhere in the background she was aware of squealing car tires. It wasn't from the black hummers.

The Hummers drove into the darkness, growling their way down Main Street, daring anyone to get in their way. At first only their taillights were visible, then even those swept out of sight around the curve down near the lower bridge.

# CHAPTER 11

Lori heard the squeal of brakes, and saw her father throw open his car door. He jumped out, and watched the last of the Hummers disappear up the street. His face reflected his fear.

"Daddy!" she cried.

"Lori!" he shouted, running toward her.

He gripped her in a tight embrace.

"Only one of them followed me!" he said. "I thought they might have gotten to you, and I couldn't get back here!"

The kids in the diner were beginning to emerge. Thomas moved close to Jacob, and put a hand on Lori's shoulder. Tobias pushed through the gathering teens and stood beside her.

"Tobias!" Jacob exclaimed. "You're still here, too! Then they didn't find you!"

"Yes, they did, Daddy," Lori explained. "They wanted Tobias in the worst way. They were mean. They demanded we give him to them."

"But they left," Bennett said, confused.

"They got what they wanted," Lori said. "They got one of the boys. They only thought it was Tobias. Daddy, they knew what I looked like, but they didn't know what he looked like. They only knew he wore all white. They never got a good look at him."

"Then, who did they take?"

"Cory," Thomas said simply. "He kind of let them believe he was Tobias. You know Cory. He always wears white to the dances. It's kinda his thing. We have to get to his father."

"No. We have to get to your father first. VerDean, I need your phone!"

"Sure thing, Mr. Bennett," VerDean responded as she held the door for him. "I think Max has him on the line right now."

Some of the group followed him into the diner. Others milled around outside. Max handed the phone to Jacob as he entered the closet-sized office. Jacob looked back at Lori, and held the receiver to his ear.

"Brady! I know. I was here. Look, there's not much time to explain, but there's a group of paramilitaries roaming the town looking for a boy. They're mean, and they're armed. They got Cory Morris by mistake and are headed west toward the highway. They're driving black Humvees. There are at least three of them, maybe four. No. I don't know. Brady, be careful. The kids said they don't mess around. I'll be there as fast as I can."

He slammed down the receiver, and pointed at Thomas.

"You call Bishop Morris and tell him we'll be down the canyon. Brady will block the road. He's on his cell phone, coming up canyon. They can't get by him, and there aren't any other roads till the old Iron City cutoff. I'm going to get out there as fast as I can. Lori, you stay here with Tobias."

"No," Lori said, following her father to the car.

She jumped in, and Tobias was in the back before Jacob could put his key in the ignition.

"I don't have time to argue," Jacob snapped.

"You don't," Lori agreed. "So, you'd better go."

Jacob scowled, and said, "You always choose the wrong time to be stubborn. Okay. Buckle up. Both of you."

He turned out of the parking lot and put his foot down on the accelerator. They sped down Main Street toward the river, over the west bridge and up the long slope to the highway. Jacob wasn't inclined to obey the speed limits. He was filled with a sense of urgency, and a fear it might already be too late to help Cory.

They came over the crest of the hill where the main road meets the highway. Jacob ignored the stop sign, and turned onto the highway. The tires screamed in protest, but Jacob pushed his foot as near the floor as he dared. He knew the road, knew where the tight curves were. He prayed Brady could stop the convoy of Humvees.

They rounded the point of rock. Jacob breathed deeply, and slowed down. A mile ahead, down the slope, the flashing lights of the sheriff's car greeted them. Three black Humvees were pulled up. They seemed to be waiting for something. The sheriff's car was parked, angled across the road, blocking it. He'd picked Grover's stream for the roadblock. The road narrowed at the bridge. The ground around the highway was marsh for a quarter mile either way. Only a fool would drive off the blacktop there. The Humvees waited, their motors growling in the darkness.

Jacob slowed, and angled his car behind the rear Hummer. He wanted to pin them in. With the marsh on both sides of the road, his car behind and the sheriff's car in front, the black vehicles had no place to go. He opened his door slowly.

"You two stay in here!" he ordered, and stepped out of the car.

He slammed the door to draw the attention of the men in the black vehicles. He strode to the front of his car, standing just left of the front fender. The rear Humvee was no more than 10 meters in front of him. He put his hands on his hips and waited. He was content for the moment to let Sheriff Brady handle the situation.

Lori opened her door quietly and stepped out to stand beside her father. Tobias joined her only a moment later. She glanced at him. He looked nervous.

The sheriff stood just in front of his own car door with a shotgun cradled in his arms. He waved casually at Jacob. He stepped toward the lead Humvee, and stood so his badge was plainly visible in the shielded headlights of the vehicle. He lowered the shotgun slowly, and smiled.

"We seem to have a problem here," he said evenly. "I don't suppose you'd like to step out so we can talk."

The Humvees were idling, their lights framing the Sheriff. Each one emitted a low, throaty snarl. They seemed content to wait. Their engines growled in the darkness.

The lead Humvee began to pull forward slowly, snarling, challenging the sheriff. Sheriff Brady stood his ground. He acknowledged the movement by raising his shotgun slightly, pointing it directly at the driver's window.

"What is it doing?" Lori asked. Her voice was tense.

Jacob glanced at his daughter, and said, "I told you both to stay in the car. They're calling his bluff."

"What if the sheriff moves?"

"They could push the sheriff's car off the road, maybe. They just don't know Brady. He doesn't bluff. This could get ugly, Lori. I wish you and Tobias would get back in the car."

"This is scary, Dad!"

"I know. It would be nicer if we knew who they were and what this was all about. Get back in the car, please."

Neither Lori nor Tobias moved. She felt his hand grasp hers suddenly, and she glanced over at him. His face was tense.

"Someone might get hurt because of me," he almost sobbed.

The Hummer was nearly to the sheriff's knees. The sheriff remained firm, but Lori could see he was going to have to step back.

"I told you to get in the car," her father said absently.

"What's going to happen?" Lori asked.

"That's up to them," Bennett answered. "Right now it looks like they expect Brady to get out of their way. Brady won't give in. You know him. Like I said, this could get ugly if they don't decide to talk things out. Let's hope they're more willing to reason than fight."

Headlights came up behind the sheriff's car, and Lori took a deep breath. The Humvee threatening the sheriff hesitated, and stopped. The lights blazed from the tractor of a semi-trailer rig. The rig was shiny red paint and polished chrome. For a moment Lori thought it was normal night traffic on the highway. Then she recognized the vehicle. The tractor reached the sheriff's car, and pulled sideways on the road to match the patrol car. It was there to help.

"Well," Jacob Bennett said softly, "they won't push <u>that</u> off the road."

The passenger door of the tractor opened, and someone stepped out, hidden behind the sheriff's car. He came around the front, and, for a moment, was spotlighted in the Humvee headlights.

Lori recognized Calvin Franklin. She never liked him much, but she was elated to see him. He strode to the sheriff's side, and stood there, hands on hips, waiting. For the first time she noticed he was taller than the sheriff. Brady said something to him, and he smiled and shook his head firmly. The sheriff said something else, and Calvin pointed with his thumb.

A huge hulk of a man came around the front of the rig. He was easily four inches taller than the sheriff, and twice as heavy. He was a larger version of the boy. He carried a huge club that reminded Lori of an oversized baseball bat. She knew the man, though she'd never spoken to him. Everyone in town knew Carter Franklin, Calvin's father. He was on the road most of the year, but the roar of his rig could be heard all over town whenever he was home. He took a place next to his son, and simply nodded to the sheriff.

The sheriff spoke to both of them again, his voice still drowned out by the engines of the Humvees.

Carter pointed at the nearest vehicle, and, in a voice loud and resolute, said, "There ain't no way they're comin' in here and takin' our boys like this. Calvin and I aren't gonna allow it!"

The sheriff looked a little angry, and said something else.

"Well, you may be in charge," Carter roared, "and I ain't gonna tell you you ain't. But, it's our town, too. We have a right to be here. And you better stop that thing right there!"

He pointed directly at the lead Hummer, with the club. It had started inching forward again.. With a sudden yell, he stepped to the side of the vehicle and swung the club in a huge arc, smashing it hard across the windshield on the driver's side. The club bounced off, but the Humvee stopped. Carter raised his club again, and swung. A second dull thud broke the growl of the Hummers, but no glass shattered. Carter raised the club a third time, threatening. After a moment the Humvee slowly, almost imperceptibly, backed away.

"That was for good measure," Carter shouted, tapping the windshield with the club. "You don't know what trouble is till you tried to cross a picket line I'm walkin', friend!"

He stepped back to his place beside his son and the sheriff. Lori felt the tension in the air.

Sheriff Brady said something to Carter. He replied with a loud, throaty laugh. Calvin joined in, mimicking his father. Lori wondered if they knew how much alike they were. Carter raised the club and waved it at the Humvee immediately in front of him, taunting whoever was inside. Calvin shook his fist, and made an obscene gesture. The sheriff said something, and Calvin laughed. It grew silent again, except for the growl of the Hummers.

The door of the middle Hummer opened and one of the men stepped out. Lori recognized the man who had been giving the orders at the Frosty Freeze. He still had the communicator on his head, and he spoke into the microphone before he addressed Sheriff Brady.

"What can we do for you, Sheriff? We weren't speeding, I trust," the man said evenly.

The humor in his voice seemed artificial and shallow. Brady waited a moment before he responded.

"You weren't speeding," he affirmed. "I am pleased that you are concerned about our local laws. That will make dealing with our problem easier."

"We don't want to interrupt the life in your small town," the leader returned. "Let's cut to the chase. This is our jurisdiction. We are acting within our legal mandate. Will you let us pass?"

"I don't know who you are, or why you think this is your jurisdiction," Brady said evenly. "I don't know anything about your mandate. You have made a mistake, however. I'm told you have the son of one of our citizens in your custody. We would like him back now. That would start things off in the right direction."

The leader looked confident, but he glanced into the vehicle. He keyed his mike and turned away from the sheriff to talk into it. He found himself facing Jacob.

He took a long, even look at Jacob. Then he looked over Lori and Tobias. He paused a moment staring at the boy. He leered at Lori's father, almost as if issuing an unspoken challenge. It was clear he now recognized Tobias, and was fully aware of the error he'd made. His smile was cold and accusing. Lori shivered.

The leader turned smartly and faced Brady again.

"Sheriff, as you said, you really don't know who we are," he said, his voice veiling the true message he seemed to want to convey. "You shouldn't try to push your small-town vigilante group at us like this. We haven't kidnapped anyone. The boy is under arrest, and that is the end of the matter."

"Even if you did have jurisdiction you should recognize the fact that Cory Morris is innocent of anything but poor judgment," Brady said, shifting his weight to bring the gun full to bear on the leader. "The point is, you are in violation of the law and I have a sworn duty to uphold that law. And I am sworn to protect the citizens of my town. I want the boy."

"I am in command of this elite group," the man boasted. "Our job gives us broad latitude in dealing with certain situations. Our orders come from the highest level."

"Would that be the President?" Brady asked. "I'm sure he would want to ensure the safety of every citizen. I still want the boy back. And, just so you will know, I don't really care where your orders come from."

"You should know I have 10 highly trained armed men in these vehicles. In fact, that's the most important thing you need to know right now. We could keep the boy if we wanted to, and you couldn't do a thing to stop us."

Lori saw the flash of headlights on the leader and his black vehicles. She turned as another car pulled up behind her father's. The door swung open and Bishop Morris stepped out. Thomas jumped from the passenger side of the vehicle. He ran to Lori's side.

"What's happening?" He almost whispered.

"It's a standoff," Lori returned equally quiet.

Bishop Jonathan Morris pulled a long-barrel hunting rifle from the back seat and stepped away from the vehicle. His face was taught, he jaw set.

"Brady," he called across the Hummers, "I'm told these men have my son."

"They have, Bishop," Brady returned.

From somewhere down the highway toward town a siren began to wail.

"This is the boy's father," Brady explained. "You might want to explain your jurisdiction to him. I don't think he'll want to listen, though. He only wants his son back. That siren would be my deputy with a squad car full of reserve deputies. I don't like repeating myself, but you still have not explained why you're here or why you want the boy. We want him back. Then we will discuss who you are, who you want and why you think you have jurisdiction. This is not a good place to start a war. I wouldn't want to have to explain why people got hurt on my watch. I hope you feel the same way."

The leader shifted his weight, and glanced back into the vehicle. He keyed the microphone and spoke quickly into the instrument.

The rear doors on the first Humvee began to open. Brady immediately pulled his shotgun to his shoulder. Jacob Bennett stepped back, shielding his daughter, Tobias and Thomas. Jon Morris focused on the Humvee. Carter Franklin edged forward, holding his club high, waiting for the first man to step from the vehicle. Lori gasped.

"Don't do this!" Brady snapped. "Right now, right here, this is a hostage situation. You will be the first one I shoot!"

"We are from the government!" The leader shouted angrily.

"I don't know that," Brady snarled. "You haven't identified yourself. You have no insignia on your vehicles or your uniforms. You have one of our children in that vehicle of yours. You've made overt threats to an officer of the law!"

"At ease!" The leader shouted loudly, as much to Brady as to his men.

The Humvee doors closed immediately.

The leader turned around slowly. He glanced at Jacob and Jon, nodded at Lori and Thomas. His eyes rested on Tobias again. Then he turned back toward Brady.

"No, Sheriff," he said quietly. "We won't press this issue tonight. Your deputies are getting closer, and my men don't want to hurt any of the locals. It may well be that we do, in fact, have the wrong boy."

"Good," Brady said, dropping his shotgun slightly. "My name's Brady. I am the sheriff. You?"

The leader breathed deeply, nodded and said, "Remmick. Major Remmick."

He placed a great deal of emphasis on the rank.

"All right, Major," Brady said quietly. "Now, let us have the boy."

Remmick smiled wryly, and said, "You would be a good soldier."

"I was," Brady returned. "Twice. The boy."

Remmick nodded, and reached into the vehicle. He pulled Cory out, holding him by his necktie. He said something to him, and waited for Cory to nod. Then he released him. Cory started to walk toward Brady, his feet a little unsteady. Brady held up his hand.

"Go to your father, son. We'll talk later."

Cory said, "Okay," and turned.

He looked relieved to see his father standing next to Jacob Bennet. He walked past Remmick toward his father. He gave the major a wide berth. When he reached Jon Morris, they embraced.

"You're making me old before my time," his father said softly.

Lori and Thomas closed around him, but kept their eyes on the major and Brady. Tobias merely stood back and watched.

"I don't suppose you would come quietly if I arrested you, Major," Brady said, still holding his shotgun toward the officer.

The major shook his head, smiled wryly again, and said, "I don't suppose I would."

Brady waited a moment, then said, "Well, as I said, people could get hurt. It's not worth that much to me to push the issue at this point. We have our boy back, and I can file a report with your commanding officer. That presupposes you will tell me where you are stationed."

The major smiled. He seemed to be enjoying the exchange with the sheriff.

"We're temporarily deployed," he answered. "We're currently stationed at the Hurricane Mesa installation."

"That's the weather station up on the mountain," Brady said. "What's an elite group doing at a weather installation?"

"Oh, we like the weather," Remmick answered, a snarl in his voice.

"Well, don't kick up any more storms around here," Brady said. "If you have issues, or need anything in our town, you come to me first. Do you understand?"

"I do," Remmick said, opening the door of his vehicle. "Sheriff, you understand that this posse of yours could hardly make a difference. We have a mission to finish, and you've only delayed it. We'll be back."

"Not like this. Not again," Brady warned. "If you would like to work through channels, I would be happy to cooperate totally. But you won't do this again. Not in my town."

The major smiled. It was a hollow smile, devoid of humor. He stepped into the Humvee with one leg, holding the door and leaning out.

"By the way, Sheriff," he said with some emphasis, "*your* jurisdiction ended about a quarter mile east of here."

"State law grants me broad authority when chasing a felon," Brady returned. "Besides, *our* mandate gives us authority throughout this canyon. Do you want to make it an issue?"

"As I said," Remmick cooed. "We won't do that tonight. Later, perhaps. Tell the boy, Tobias, if you do see him around," at this he glanced back at the boy, "that we still have his sister."

"She's here?"

"No," Remmick said simply. "She's already back at the base. You produce her parents and we can talk about her release."

There was almost a lilting tone in his voice, a kind of taunting meant not only for the sheriff, but for everyone else within earshot.

Brady remained silent.

Remmick shut the door behind him.

Tobias bolted, running toward the Humvees, but Jacob Bennet, Thomas and Cory all grabbed him.

"My sister!" He shouted.

"Now's not the time," Jacob said. "Settle down. Let's give Brady a chance to work. He's already performed one miracle tonight. He may have another one up his sleeve. Son, settle down. Brady can do this for you."

Brady turned toward his car to move it, but the leading Humvee didn't wait. The vehicle jumped to the right, barely missing the Franklins. Calvin jumped, dodging the left front fender. Carter swung his club in a mighty arc, catching the side window of the vehicle. The window responded with a dull thud, but the Humvee kept going.

"Step out here! We can finish this right now!" Carter shouted.

Calvin brushed his pants, and looked angry.

The vehicles, each in turn, leapt into the marsh on the right side of the road, and plunged through the deep water and mud. Mud splattered all around them as they surged ahead. They crossed the stream in turn, leaving behind a deep mud furrow, crossed the marshy area on the opposite bank, and lunged up the shoulder of the road. The first Humvee fishtailed onto the blacktop, even though it wasn't going particularly fast. The second followed suit, and the third slid on the lubricating mud the other two had laid down, straightened, and followed. Brady watched their taillights disappear in the dark.

"Well," he said, walking toward Jacob, Jon and the youngsters. "That was exciting. Are you okay, Cory?"

Tobias broke free of the three holding him, and stepped close to Lori. Brady watched with interest, smiled, and turned back to Cory.

"They were a little rough," Cory said, rubbing his shoulder.

"I'm not sure your father appreciates 'they were a little rough' after your fall Monday. Are you okay?"

"I'm fine," Cory said, glancing back at his father and smiling. "Where were they taking me?"

"The major said they were attached to the weather station. I'll find out about that. Did he say anything to you?"

Cory shook his head, and said, "No one said anything until he pulled me out of the Hummer. You know, once they lock the door you can't get out until they want you to. Child proof locks. When he pulled me out, he said he could throw me in jail for twenty years for lying to him. Then he said he'd be back."

"He won't throw you in jail for that, son," Brady said evenly. "You did a brave thing tonight, but it was a little foolish, too."

Cory nodded, and said, "I know. But I figured if they took Toby, we'd never see him again. He disappeared on us once. I wanted to find out where he went."

Brady nodded, and looked at the boy.

"So, you're the boy from the canyon," Brady said quietly.

"One of them," Thomas affirmed.

Tobias looked uncomfortable, and slid closer to Lori. Brady studied him for a few seconds.

"Those men won't hurt you," Brady said softly. "You're safe with us. Understand?"

Tobias nodded, but his face was still drawn with worry.

"They still have my sister," he said weakly. "My father will be very upset."

Brady looked at Cory.

"I saw in one vehicle as we passed by," Cory said. "There was no one else in that Hummer except soldiers. She could have been in the lead Hummer."

"I doubt it," Brady said. "Tobias, I got Cory back. They thought he was you, but I got him back. I'll get your sister back, too. Bishop, take your son home and put him to bed. He's had a pretty busy week. I'll get Ben Hart to set up a watch at your home. You'll be safe there. They don't want your boy. They want this one. Karl Rosen is parked at the junction. He'll follow you home. Love those white slacks, Cory."

"They saved Tobias," Cory said casually.

He smiled at the group, but no one smiled back. Thomas edged toward him.

"I'm getting tired of you trying to get yourself killed," he said.

"It only happens when I'm with you," Cory replied, turning toward his father's car. "Well, looks like I'm going home now. I promise, Thomas, the next life-threatening situation that comes up is all yours. Right now, I think I just want to get some sleep."

Tobias reached out and touched Cory's arm. Cory paused a moment.

"Thank you," he said quietly.

"You're welcome," Cory returned, smiling. "We need to talk, but not tonight. I'm going home to bed."

Jon Morris held out his hand and clasped Brady's firmly.

"Thank you, Sheriff," he said. 'Thank you for getting my boy back. You did something very brave tonight."

"I did my job," the sheriff said firmly, quietly. "Go home now. I know your wife will be worried sick. We'll talk tomorrow. Jacob, would you please take this youngster to my house? We're need to find out a few things."

"Certainly, Sheriff," Jacob said.

Lori watched the bishop follow his son toward the car. Thomas walked along with them. She watched Cory. Her breath suddenly came short and fast. For an instant, as he turned to get into the car, their eyes met. For the second time that evening she felt a strange stirring in the pit of her stomach. Her cheeks flushed, and she looked back at Tobias.

"It seems we'll get a chance to visit the sheriff tonight, after all, Tobias," Jacob said wryly. "We all want to know who you are and why the military is eager to arrest you. Shall we go?"

His words were punctuated by the huge diesel exploding to life. The shiny tractor backed up, giving the sheriff room to move his car. The sheriff climbed in, waved at the semi. The air horn blasted, and Brady smiled. He started the patrol car, jammed it into gear, and slid around the semi rig. He gunned the vehicle. He wanted to see where the Humvees went, and they already had a head start.

Jacob waited until Lori and Tobias were both in the car before he opened his door. He watched the taillights of the bishop's car disappear around the curve toward town. He climbed in and started the vehicle. It hummed to life.

"Buckle up," he said. "Both of you."

He turned the vehicle around and started back toward town. Carter Franklin fell in line behind his car. He found the presence of the huge rig calming. The huge grill filling his rear-view mirror made him feel safe.

Brady's home was down a side street near the middle of town. Jacob pulled up in front, and the Franklins parked across the street. The bishop's car was just turning the corner, heading home. Thomas was waiting on the porch.

The hiss of the air brakes broke the quiet of the night. Carter dropped out of the high cab with the ease of years of experience. He carried his club. Calvin rounded the front of the rig and walked beside his father. They followed Jacob, Lori and Tobias up to the door.

"Sheriff has me restricted to certain streets in town," Carter said loudly as the approached the house. "Tonight I think he'll be glad to have me here on his street!"

Thomas turned the knob to open the door. The sheriff's wife pulled the door open, and out of her son's hand.

"Come in," she said, a touch of worry edging her soft voice. "I've been expecting you. Brady called over the radio and said you'd be coming. He didn't say what was going on, just to make you comfortable until he got here. Hello, Carter, Calvin. Welcome. Lori, Jacob, please, all of you come in. Sit down. Thomas, we'll need more chairs. Get the ones from the dining room. I'll get something to drink if you'd like. I have root beer."

"That's fine," Lori said quietly.

Franklin looked like he'd prefer something different, but all the men passed on the drinks. Tobias looked up at Lori, and nodded when asked. Macey Brady went off into the kitchen to get the refreshments.

The living room seemed crowded, especially with both Franklins present. They milled for several minutes before anyone began to sit down. Thomas bounded down the stairs, three at a time, and landed at the foot. He carried his tennis shoes and was pulling his shirt down as he landed. He'd changed from his white shirt and slacks into jeans and a t-shirt while everyone else was milling.

"We'd be best outside," Franklin finally said gruffly.

Jacob started to get up, too, but Franklin said, "This is our turn. The Sheriff will want to be talking to you, so stay inside. Don't worry. We'll cover things out there. Whoever they were, they aren't stupid enough to come back here tonight."

"They're military," Jacob said. "There's an oxymoron in there somewhere. So, stay alert, and be very careful."

Franklin nodded and left by the front door. Almost at the same time Macey Brady returned with cans of root beer. She passed them out.

"I knew you'd want one," she said to her son.

"Right," he returned. "Cory's all right, Mom."

"I know," Macey said. "Your father told me. I don't know anything more than that."

"I'm sure glad it all turned out all right," Lori breathed. "That was pretty tense. Cory's sort of a hero, I guess. He let them take him instead of Tobias. This is Tobias. Your Dad was great, Thomas. He just stood there, blocking the road, and wouldn't let them pass while they had Cory. I think he was real mad."

"He gets that way, sometimes. But they wanted you, Tobias. Who are you?"

Tobias looked up, and half smiled.

"I'm Tobias," he said softly, slightly amused by the question.

"So, Toby, what do they want with you?"

"I don't know," Toby said, accepting the nickname without question. "We weren't bothering anyone. My sister and I were just waiting for my Father up there," he waved vaguely, "and they came and took her. They would have taken me, too, if I hadn't run away. I came down into the town to get help. But I was scared, and hid. I guess I'm not very brave. Then I found Lori. Then Jacob took us to the Frosty Freeze, and I saw you."

"Why the Frosty Freeze?" Thomas asked.

"That's a story in itself," Jacob answered. "I wanted to come here, but there were Humvees all around. I've never seen that many in one place before. They blocked the road, and I thought the kids would be safer in a crowd than with me trying to outrun them. So I left them there. I guess it worked out okay, but Cory could've been in big trouble. That was my fault."

"Nonsense," Macey said vehemently. "You were doing what you thought was right."

"The question is: What are we going to do?" Thomas asked.

"You're not going to do anything," Brady said, walking in at that moment.

"Did you find out who they were, Brady?" Jacob asked, standing.

Toby was studying the can Macey had handed him. He was watching Lori drink, and didn't seem quite sure how to get at the soda inside. Thomas took it from his hands, popped the top, and handed it back. He took a sip, his eyes lit up, and he started to drink deeply.

"I followed them to the base road," Brady said. "Two of the Humvees drove on up, but the third stopped at the bottom and four men piled out, fully armed, and set up a guard post. I'm telling you, Jacob, they're just plain out of control. The military comes into *my* town and rousts *my* people. They don't even try to identify themselves, and they kidnap one of our kids to boot. I have to report this."

"They have my sister, too," Toby reminded him. "They took my sister, and they still have her."

Brady looked down at him, and breathed deeply.

"I know that, son, and I promised you I'd get her back. What is your name?"

"Tobias."

"Toby," Thomas corrected.

Toby looked up at the older boy, caught his smile and smiled back. He was beginning to look comfortable among the strangers.

"Is there a last name?" Brady said softly.

Toby shook his head slowly, and said, "Ben Salah."

"Okay," Brady said. "Tobias Ben Salah. Everyone sit down. I want each of you to tell me what you know about what's happened tonight. I just want to hear your version, not what you think someone else will tell me. And the rest of you keep quiet. Tobias... Toby, since this all seems to be about you, maybe you should start."

Toby breathed deeply, and began to speak.

"We took my Father's vehicle and I broke it," he said softly.

"You're too young to drive," Brady said softly. "I can understand why you're frightened. That's another issue, though, and probably best left between your father and you. Let's just get through the rest of this. Was it an all-terrain vehicle or just a normal car?"

"All terrain?"

"Yes. Could it go off road, or was it a road-type vehicle?"

"Oh. It didn't need the road," Toby returned. "I couldn't get it operating, and I thought the best thing to do was to call my Father. So, we did. He said to stay with the vehicle, watch after Anisha, and he'd come and get us."

"What caused the accident?" Brady asked.

"I don't know. A flash, then something from the top of the mountain flew right at us and hit us."

"A rocket? You mean a rocket hit your car?"

"Yes, I think. I was blinded for a moment, and I crashed into the rocks."

"Those jerks shot at a couple of kids?" Jacob snapped. "Brady, it seems the military is a little trigger-happy."

"You must have been in a restricted area," Brady said softly. "That base has never been a high security area before. Of course, things have changed since 9-11. They seem to have an elite group up there now. Didn't you see the signs?"

"There weren't any signs."

"The boy took his dad's SUV, and went joy-riding in the hills," Jacob said. "I don't think he'd have been paying any attention to any signs. That still doesn't give them the right to shoot at him. That also explains why they don't want him to get away and tell anyone else. Things could get a little hot for them. Go on, Toby. What happened next?"

"We were waiting, and then the vehicles arrived," the boy said. "You called them 'Humvees'. Then there were men all over, and they grabbed Anisha, and they tried to grab me. I shouted, but they didn't listen. One had a weapon and fired at me, so I ran."

"He shot at you?" Brady exclaimed.

"Not at first," the boy said. "When they thought I would get away they did. I think they wanted me to stop, but I was scared and kept running. Then I found Lori."

"Oh, wow," Thomas said softly. "I understand why you were scared of them."

"They have my sister," Toby repeated. "I'm more frightened for her."

"For what it's worth," Brady said, "I'm sure they're military. I don't understand the clandestine clothing, or the lack of insignia. I don't even understand the sudden high security status up there. But I'm pretty sure they are ours. So, I don't think they'll want to hurt your sister. I think she's safe enough. How old is she?"

"Just younger than me," Toby sniffed. "Can we get her back?"

"Yes," Brady said emphatically. "But we won't be able to do anything before morning. I'll make some calls then. I promise. I want to hear the rest of this. Lori, tell me from your point of view what happened. You seem to be the next one involved."

Lori shook her hair, aware it was snarled and unkempt from the night's activities. She took a deep breath and told him what had happened to her that evening, including feeling Thomas and Cory had been playing a joke on her by planting Toby in the bushes back at her house.

"I'm really sorry about that," she said softly, holding her hand out toward the boy.

He touched her fingertips with his, and smiled shyly. Thomas smiled broadly at her suspicions.

When she was finished, Brady breathed deeply.

"Have you got anything to add?" he asked Jacob.

"No, just that leaving the kids at the Frosty Freeze didn't work," Jacob returned. "I thought they would avoid going into a well-lit, crowded place. You need to know that one of the Humvees followed me, and there were three pulling away from the Frosty Freeze when I got back."

"That's four," Brady reflected. "Only three went back up to the base. Hon, call the Bishop, and tell him there's another Humvee roaming around. Use the radio and tell Ben to be real careful, too. I told Karl to cruise around the town. Tell him, too. Thomas, they don't want you, but they might come back for the boy again. Go tell Carter to be careful. Tell him to keep that club of his real close."

Thomas nodded, and said, "You want to give him one of your shotguns?"

"He won't take it," Brady said. "He prefers the intimacy of his club. He's walked too many picket lines. But you can offer."

Thomas smiled, and went out the front door. Calvin jumped up from the couch and followed.

"Okay, this is the situation," Brady said after a moment. "Toby and his sister trespass on government property. The kids take their dune buggies up there a lot, and the worst they get is a warning from the guards, and sent home. They confiscate a vehicle once in a while, but it's all military guidelines, and the guards wear regulation military uniforms. The vehicles are returned through channels.

"So, tonight, Toby and his sister stray up there. Maybe they have something special going on. It's primarily a weather station, but it's possible they're doing other things up there now. Maybe the base has been turned over to some top-secret arm of the military. Maybe the new commander is a martinet. In any case, someone up there is just a little trigger happy, and blows the kid's car away. The kids are lucky to be alive.

"But, that's not enough. They think the kids have stumbled onto something they're not supposed to know about. Or they just want to protect their reputation. So they want to take them into custody and question them, maybe threaten them. Maybe they want to detain them for a while until things cool down. I don't know. Anyway, they go about it with the finesse of a sledge hammer. Is that about the way it looks to you, Jacob?"

"Just about, but there are a couple of things that don't quite add up," Jacob answered. "You and I have gone up there a time or two. I never saw any rockets up there. But, if they had rockets, and if they fired the rocket by accident, why go to these lengths to cover it up? The military has made mistakes before."

"I don't know," Brady said, thinking his way through carefully. "If all this happened close to the way we've worked through it, then the kids are, indeed, really lucky to be alive. Toby, I'm sure they won't hurt your sister, but I think we'll keep custody of you till we can contact your father. As for the military, maybe they'll come to their senses. Everyone in town knows who you are now. That should provide some protection for you. They can't make you disappear as easily as they could earlier. It would be pretty hard to keep you a secret. How do you feel about that?"

"I don't want to go with them," Toby hummed. "They frighten me."

"I don't blame you. I wouldn't, either. Did you see anything out of the ordinary tonight?"

"You mean, before or after they shot at me?" Toby said quietly, smiling weakly.

"He could tell us," Thomas said wryly from the door, "but, of course, then he'd have to shoot us."

"I would never shoot you!" Toby protested indignantly.

"Relax," Thomas soothed. "It was just a joke."

Brady wiped his face, and said, "Not too funny right now, Thomas. Well, Toby? Did you see anything strange?"

"Nothing," Toby relented. "There were just a few buildings, some lights, fences and lots of rocks."

"You were close enough to see the buildings?" Brady asked, incredulous. "I'm not surprised they got a little excited. But, as far as we know, it's still only a weather station. What could you have possibly seen? Okay, then, you definitely created a problem. But it's not nearly as big as the military apparently thinks it is. We can work it out. I don't want you to worry. I'll call Salt Lake tomorrow and see what kind of help we can get down here. The more people know about this, the better chance we have for a quick resolution. In the meantime, Toby, you'll stay here. Let's call your father right now and tell him where to find you."

Toby looked up from the root beer can, and said, "My communication link is in the vehicle. Do you have one?"

"I have a telephone," Brady said softly, "and a police radio, and a CB."

"Father doesn't have a telephone. We can't reach him that way. I don't think he'll be monitoring your radio frequencies."

"How else can you contact him?"

"Just the communication link," Toby said softly, sounding a little depressed.

"What about your mother? Can we call her?"

Toby looked up, pain showing in his face.

"Not without the communication link," he said softly.

"You don't have a phone at home?" Thomas asked, incredulous.

Toby shook his head, his eyes watering up.

Thomas shook his head, as well, but in disbelief rather than consternation.

"Well, we can't go back up to your vehicle," Brady said. "They'll be watching it like vultures. I'd be surprised if they haven't already impounded it. Your father will just have to find you here. The sheriff is the first person in town he'd go to for help, and that's me. When do you expect him to arrive?"

"He had to make arrangements," Toby said quietly. "He said he'd be here by morning."

"Okay," Brady said. "In the meantime, Thomas can make up a bed for you in his room, and we'll keep a guard on the house. Jacob, I think you'll probably be all right at home now the boy is with us. Lori, you did a good thing tonight, too. I'm proud of you. For now, try to get some sleep. We'll get to work on this first thing in the morning."

"Okay," Jacob said, rising. "You want me to take a turn on guard?"

"Absolutely not," Brady said emphatically. "I don't think they'll pay any attention to you now that you're out of the loop. They'll see you come home without Toby and will probably only watch your house for a day or two. They won't want to kidnap the whole town. But I don't want Lori home alone. That's pretty good advice for all of us tonight. Buddy up with someone and don't go anywhere alone until we sort this out. And get what sleep you can. If you can."

"Okay," Jacob replied, walking out the door. "You're probably right about the sleep part. I'll check in tomorrow. I'll take a few days off, so I can help where ever you need me."

"I appreciate that," Brady said.

"No problem," Jacob responded. "My boss has been trying to get me to clear my vacation off the books for a long time. This is a good opportunity."

"Good night, Sheriff," Lori said quietly, following her father.

"Lori," Toby called out, more like he was trying to remember her name than calling to her.

"What?" Lori said warmly, turning back.

"I've never had a girl hug me back before," Toby said softly, his cheeks coloring. "When I first met you I hugged you. I was scared and you hugged me back. Thank you."

"My pleasure," she said, smiling, and turning away.

She felt her cheeks flush slightly, too. As she turned back toward the street she gasped.

A black Hummer was cruising very slowly past the house. Carter Franklin was holding his club menacingly. He breathed heavily, and grinned broadly. Lori stared at him, and was reminded of the Viking movies. She knew Toby would be safe at the sheriff's house.

"Sheriff," Jacob said.

"I saw it, Jacob," the sheriff said softly. "Go on home. We'll be fine here. Carter, I'm going to spell you in two hours. Karl will be back later and spell me. Carter, I appreciate what you did tonight. I couldn't have done a thing without you there."

"I know," Carter said, grinning.

"How much damage did you do to their windshield?" Lori asked.

"It was bullet proof glass," Brady said. "At best, a few minor surface cracks."

"I didn't break through," Carter said, still smiling, and swinging his club, "but they'll have to replace it. They'll have to replace the side window, too."

The sheriff nodded.

"Toby, you stay out of sight," Brady warned. "Inside."

"I'll get something warm to drink," Macey Brady said.

"Cold, dear," Brady said, and settled in for a long night. It was nearly 1:30 already.

The black Hummer crawled by again three minutes later, slowly. It picked up speed when Carter walked off the porch toward the road, carrying his club. Brady sipped the cold soda his wife had brought, and smiled at Franklin. For the moment he felt he had everything under control.

# CHAPTER 12

Sometime during the night Thomas got up to use the bathroom. He stopped at the top of the stairs, not surprised to see lights on downstairs. He heard his father's voice, then his mother responding. Somewhere in the conversation he recognized the voice of Karl Rosen, his father's deputy. He walked slowly down the stairs. He got to the bottom and stared around the room. Four men, besides his mother and father, were talking. Karl was there, and Kevin Vinson. He recognized Ben Hart and was relieved to see Carter Franklin in the room as well.

"My boy can take care of himself," Carter was attesting. "Give him a club and no one will stand up to him. He takes after me."

"Don't think I don't appreciate that," Brady said, setting his soda down on the coffee table. "However, he's still just out of high school. I'd prefer to have adults doing the guarding."

"I prefer you not make this an issue," Carter said evenly. "He's old enough to join the Marines. They're recruiting him pretty heavily. He should be old enough to stand shoulder to shoulder with the rest of the men in the town."

Brady thought a moment, then said, "Then I won't question your judgment. Just make sure he's with one of the older men, Carter."

"I agree," Carter returned, smiling. "They may need his help."

"So that's the whole of it," Brady said to the others in the room. "You all know as much about this as I do. I'd like your input."

Carter looked up, saw Thomas, and said, "Your son's no slacker, either, from what I hear. He could help."

"I want the kids kept out as much as possible," Brady said, still unaware of his son's presence.

"I hear he bested my boy not four years ago," Carter pressed, this time nodding at Thomas, a slight smile playing across his face. "I suspect it took both him and the Morris boy. Calvin was pretty big even back them. Calvin would never talk about it. You know my boy."

The comment brought up unhappy memories of the fight they'd had. Thomas remembered it had been pretty one-sided at first. Calvin did walk away with a bloody nose and a scraped fist and a new respect for the younger kids he'd been fond of bullying. After the fight, a friendship grew between Calvin, Cory and him.

Brady turned and saw his son.

"We're just going over what our next step should be, son," he said warmly. "You okay?"

Thomas nodded, and said, "I just heard voices."

Brady nodded, and said, "It's late, son. Try to get some sleep. I'll catch you up on anything that happens in the morning. Nothing much will happen tonight anyway."

Thomas nodded, smiled weakly at his mother, and turned to go back upstairs. He visited the bathroom, then stepped around Toby sleeping on the cot and crawled back into bed. He'd tried to give up his bed, but Toby wouldn't have it. He settled for the sleeping bag and an extra pillow on a camping cot. Thomas stared down at the stranger in his room, and was aware the boy was awake staring up at him. Neither spoke. After a while Thomas drifted off to sleep.

He woke up early. It was just beginning the get light outside. The blue pre-dawn light filled his bedroom. The red numbers on the clock told him it was only 5:00 A.M. He rolled and looked at the boy on the cot.

Toby was laying on his back very still. He was breathing shallow, his hands folded over his chest. His eyes were open.

"You're scared," Thomas said quietly.

"For my sister," Toby returned softly, without moving.

Thomas breathed deeply, and said, "If anyone can get her back safely, it's my father."

Toby blinked, and asked, "What if no one can get her back safely?"

Thomas understood, and was quiet for a few moments.

"Did you sleep at all?" he asked.

"No. You did."

"Not much," Thomas said. "You're not what you seem."

"What do I seem?"

"I don't know. You're not from around here. You speak very well, but I bet you don't know the language half as well as you want us to think you do. You speak another language at home. Where are you from?"

"Sometimes it seems like a long way away," Toby said softly. "I wish I was there now. This is all my fault. If I'd stayed home this wouldn't have happened."

"I understand. What do you want to do?"

Toby thought for a moment, and said, "My father will look for me at my vehicle. That's the last place I was. If those men are there, he could be in trouble. I have to go to him."

"You can't. They'll get you, too."

Toby nodded, and said, "Maybe. Your father and his men are almost as bad as the men in black. I'm a prisoner here just like I'd be a prisoner there. I can't go to my father, or try to find my sister."

"Your father will come here," Thomas argued. "My father just wants to keep you safe. The guys we're dealing with can be rough. You heard Cory last night. Let my father do what he knows how to do. He'll get your sister back."

"He might, but I don't think I can wait to see. I'm going to get dressed and go up to where I left my vehicle. Thomas, I have some things there that will help my father find me."

"They won't help against the army," Thomas said. "Toby, don't be stupid. You can't pull a weapon on those guys. They'll blow you away."

Toby was quiet for a while. Then he said softly, "Thomas, do you pray?"

Thomas didn't answer right away. He thought about his answer for a long time.

"Not a lot," he said thoughtfully. "Not before last Monday. Something happened, Cory got hurt. I was really scared. I prayed then."

"What happened?"

"Cory fell at the water fall. He was hurt. I was so scared I could barely think. But I thought to pray," Thomas returned. "I didn't really know what I was saying. I just talked to God like he was really there."

"He is always there," Toby affirmed. "I know about Cory falling. My father told me. We prayed for him, too."

Thomas suddenly felt the boy knew what he was talking about. He wanted to tell him everything he felt, everything he learned.

"When I thought nothing could get worse a strange feeling flooded through me," he said. "I can't explain it. I don't even know what it was. I felt like everything was going to be all right. It was kind of a warm feeling here," he touched his chest, "and it spread all over me. I was still scared, but I knew it was going to be okay. I've been praying a lot since then."

"Father has us pray every night and every morning," Tobias said quietly. "We bless our food, too, and pray as a family. But our personal prayers are where we talk to God. I've been praying all night. I believe he wants me to do something more than just wait here."

"How do you know that?" Thomas asked into the dark.

Toby was quiet for a long time. Then he said softly, "I can feel it here," and he touched his chest. "Thomas, will you help me?"

Thomas thought about it for a long time. Then he said, "My father will kill me."

"Mine already has reason enough to be very angry with me," Toby said simply, accepting Thomas's metaphor for what it was. "If you can take me back to where my vehicle was located, we can contact my father. I can tell him where I am. He'll come for me. He might even be there now. Then we can go and get my sister together."

"Sounds like your father is pretty resourceful," Thomas said quietly. "What will you do if I don't help?"

"I'll go back there without you."

"I could wake the whole house," Thomas said. "My father would even put you in the cell down at the office. He'd call it protective custody. He'd keep you on ice until your father got here."

Toby rolled over toward Thomas, a funny smile on his face, and said, "You wouldn't have any fun doing that. Let's get your friend Cory and go find my father."

Thomas suddenly smiled, feeling the adventure ahead, and said, "Okay, let's go find your father. Only one thing, Toby: No weapons. Okay?"

"No weapons," Toby agreed. "We don't use weapons."

The boys got up and dressed quickly. Thomas looked at the sandals the younger boy was wearing. The rest of his clothes, though dirty, would be fine. The sandals would not be practical.

"Here's a pair of my socks," he said, throwing them at Toby. "I have a pair of shoes you can wear. If we have to do some hiking, or running, those sandals won't work."

Toby nodded, but said, "They worked well enough last night."

He watched Thomas slip his shoes on, and mimicked his actions. In a few minutes they were ready to go.

The hallway was empty. Thomas expected it to be. The stairs presented a minor problem. Some of them squeaked, but Thomas knew the worst ones. He pointed them out, and stepped over then. Toby followed his lead.

Karl Rosen was sitting on the sofa in the living room. His head was resting on the back of the sofa and he was fast asleep. Thomas slipped down the hall, walking quietly, with Toby right behind him.

The back door complained as they opened it, and both boys held their breath hoping Karl wouldn't wake up. The silence in the living room told them they were still safe. They shut it as quietly as they could and stepped out into the back yard. Thomas's jeep was there, waiting patiently. His father's patrol car was gone.

"Dad must be at the office," Thomas whispered. "That's a break for us. He usually blocks me in."

"On purpose? Doesn't he trust you?"

Thomas looked at Toby, realized the boy was being ironic, and said, "I haven't taken his patrol car out for a joy ride yet."

Toby nodded, accepting the backlash in the spirit it was given.

The jeep was old, and had rust spots everywhere. Thomas had tried to repaint it a bright yellow, but the rust had eaten its way through again. The back was open, the front covered only by a makeshift canvas he'd attached between the top of the windshield and the roll bar. The roll bar and the lights across the top of it were new. He'd installed them himself. The lights didn't work quite right, but he was sure he was only a wire away from making them all work perfect.

"Are you sure operating this is safe?" Toby asked.

"It'll get us there and back." Thomas said. "This vehicle is a classic."

He slapped the hood.

"I wouldn't hit it too hard," Toby said.

Thomas glanced at the younger boy. Toby's grin told him everything he needed to know.

Thomas walked down the driveway until he could see around the corner of the house. There was no guard there. His father must have thought the proximity of daylight would protect them from the men in the black Humvees. He smiled and turned back toward Toby.

"Help me push my jeep into the road," he said, releasing the emergency break, and unlocking the steering column. "We'll coast down the hill and start it at the bottom."

Toby looked puzzled, then smiled.

"We don't want to alert the others," he said.

"Right," Thomas returned.

Together they pushed the jeep backward down the driveway and into the street. They jumped in, and Thomas let it coast silently down the half block to the stop sign. There he turned the ignition key, and the motor turned over.

"It works," Toby said, smiling.

"Of course it works," Thomas said.

"I wasn't sure it would," Toby said.

"Next stop is Cory's place," Thomas said, ignoring Toby's remark.

They were silent as they cruised down the street. Thomas turned at the stop sign, and then again at the next street. They stopped halfway up.

"Cory's is the third house up," Thomas said. "We'll walk from here."

Toby looked amazed, and said, "You've done this before."

Thomas smiled. He was amazed the boy caught on so quickly. But, then, he'd stolen his own father's car just the night before. He shook his head and realized Toby was just a younger version of him. He led Toby around the side to Cory's window. He put his finger to his lips, and leaned close to the screen.

"Cory!" he whispered.

"I'll be right out," Cory whispered back almost immediately.

Toby raised his eyebrows, but followed Thomas back to the jeep. In less than a minute Cory joined them there.

"I couldn't sleep," he said softly.

"You got quite a scare last night," Toby admitted.

Cory glanced at Thomas, then back to Toby, and said, "It wasn't the 'scare'. Those men weren't going to hurt me. I mean, really hurt me. Thomas, do you know what we're doing?"

"What we always do," Thomas said. "We're finding something to make our parents worry about. Get in, and let's get out of here before we have an attack of reason and change our minds."

"Little boys in the back," Cory ordered, jumping into the front seat. Toby climbed into the back quickly, and Thomas pulled away, swinging into a "U" turn and heading back the way they had come.

They cruised down the main street of town. At the intersection with the stoplight Thomas pulled up short. The light was green, but he waited anyway.

"That's my dad's patrol car," he explained to Toby, pointing to the squad car parked in front of the sheriff's office. "There's no use trying to get caught, so I think we'll go around the block."

That said, he turned right and drove through the residential streets behind the office. As they pulled back up to the main street he slowed down. There was no activity around the office, so he pulled out on the street and drove toward the edge of town.

Cory, who was used to their covert operations, breathed deeply, but Tobias smiled. He was happy. They were finally doing something to free his sister.

"You're not from here," Thomas said. "Since the first place you found in town was Lori's place, I thought the best place to start to retrace your steps would be there."

"Good thinking," Cory returned.

"It's okay," Toby said. "I followed a track down from the hills. Up there. Go between those escarpments."

"Taylor Canyon," Thomas said. "I thought so. That's where we first met you. But, that's a ways from the military base."

He turned toward the highway. Suddenly he slammed on the brakes. Off to one side, wearing blue jeans and a t-shirt, was Lori. She'd seen them coming up the street and was already walking out to meet them.

"We ought to go," Cory said suddenly.

"No," Toby insisted.

"You're going up to his car, aren't you?" Lori said as she got closer.

"Yes," Thomas admitted.

Cory slapped his hand over his face.

"I'm going, too," She said decisively.

She started to climb into the back of the jeep. Toby smiled, holding out a hand to help her.

"No way," Cory said evenly. "Look, this could be dangerous."

"More dangerous than last night?" she asked. "I'm going."

"She's going," Thomas repeated, smiling. "We have a full crew now."

Cory groaned as the jeep picked up speed toward the highway.

Lori leaned up between the front seats, and said softly, "Besides, you wouldn't want me to call the sheriff and your father and tell them exactly where you three are right now, would you?"

"She would, too," Thomas asserted. "Your father doesn't know you've gone, either, does he?"

"He thinks I've gone for a short walk," Lori responded defensively.

"With the stuff that happened last night I can't believe he just let you go for a walk," Cory said.

"Well, he did," Lori said. "Sort of."

"Your father was still asleep, too," Cory concluded. "We're all going to be in a lot of trouble. You all know that, don't you?"

Thomas turned over the bridge and on to the main highway. He turned right, toward the cleft Toby had indicated. Two of the boys were very familiar with the canyon.

"Well, we should be back in an hour or so," Thomas said after a time. "We're going to see if Toby's father has arrived, and try to contact him if he hasn't. He's apparently got some kind of specialized radio or something. This is the way, right, Toby?"

"Yes. Up there."

Thomas turned off the main road, and up the dirt road toward the cleft. He was glad that they were going to be farther away from the base than he at first had thought. He liked the adventure, but mitigating the risk was good, too.

"Do you know this area?" Toby asked.

"We've been up here a few times," Cory said, shoving Thomas playfully.

"Hey! Do you mind? I'm trying to drive here!" Thomas shouted.

Toby smiled, and said, "My vehicle was above a valley, a place where the canyon opened up. There were trees, and an old building below on one side."

"The mission," Thomas said. "What were the army grunts doing around the old mission?"

"I didn't know there was a mission up here," Lori said.

"It is, and it isn't," Cory responded. "It's not like an old Spanish mission or anything. About a hundred years ago or so a religious splinter group tried to set up a commune up there, but it didn't fly."

"From what we've been told, they had some pretty strange practices," Thomas continued. "They believed in plural marriages, but that's true of a lot of fundamentalist groups. The men had total control over everything. The women were expected to keep quiet and obey the men. They, at least, got that right."

"Hey!" Lori snapped.

Cory laughed, and said, "They had a prophet, of sorts. He was more interested in his own welfare than in theirs. His biggest concern was power. When he said 'jump' they asked how high on the way up. He totally controlled everything and everyone."

"I hate the part about the men having total control," Lori said.

"I knew you would," Cory replied, still smiling.

Lori flashed a scowl his way, then asked, "What happened to them?"

"They faded away, like most fundamentalist groups," Cory said. "When their 'secret practices' become known they have trouble gaining converts, and the core of people eventually drifts apart. The leader, a man named Isaiah Robertson, was supposed to die and come back resurrected. That was supposed to signal the start of the millennium. After listening to his promises for a number of years, and living under his rule, they decided to hurry things up a little. They were a little tired of his promises not being fulfilled. So they took him to the top of one of the cliffs and threw him off. I guess they wanted to get a jump on the millennium, or see one promise fulfilled. They were disappointed."

"Rumor has it he didn't really want to go over the edge," Thomas laughed. "But, over he went."

"Did he get resurrected?" Lori asked, an ironic tone in her voice.

"He didn't move a muscle after that," Cory said. "When he didn't get up off the rocks and start walking around they sort of decided he wasn't a true prophet after all. There was a trial that lasted months. Several of the women were key witnesses, and four of the men went to prison. The group broke up, and the commune disappeared. The only thing left is the old mission. It looks more like a broken-down motel than anything else, though."

"It's just around the corner," Thomas said. "Look. There it is."

They bounced over a low hill, and the canyon opened into a small valley, just like Toby had described. The remains of an old building were tucked away in one corner. Cottonwood trees surrounded it. The dry streambed meandered through the trees, then wound back against the east cliff face before it followed the canyon back down toward town.

"Sometimes in the spring there's water in the creek," Thomas said. "This is a great place to picnic. It was really a pretty good place to set up a small town. The well still has some of the cleanest water around. The town's hooked into the well for part of its water supply."

"I didn't know that," Cory said.

"My dad brought me up here to inspect the well head a couple of times," Thomas said. "The concrete shack off to that side is where the well used to be. The pipes are under ground. There's a pump, but most of the year the water flows by gravity down to the treatment plant."

"Hmmmmm," Cory mussed. "You learn something new every day. What's the well like?"

"It's just a concrete building, with a concrete floor," Thomas responded. "The pipe loops out of the floor, out the wall, then back into the ground. Nothing to see. Dad helped an electrician replace the pump when I was in sixth grade."

"What's up there?" Lori asked, pointing up canyon.

"More of this," Cory said. "The canyon pinches off after about ten miles or so, and the road ends in some old played-out mines. Hey, bug, where's your car?"

Toby pointed to where the sand formed a huge spill as it poured from a funnel in the cliffs above. It came to within a few feet of reaching the top of the cliffs, with more sand filling the depression above.

"How did you get up there?" Thomas asked, pulling the jeep off the road under the cottonwoods.

"That's where we hit the rocks. Can we get up there in this?"

"Not a chance," Thomas responded. "Were you up there to begin with?"

"Of course," Toby said. "The Hummers came from up there, too. I got away from them because I jumped off the cliff, and they couldn't follow me. I ran down the sand, then down the canyon."

"It didn't take them long to catch up," Lori said softly.

"They probably know this area better than we do," Cory said ironically, climbing out of the jeep. "Well, let's hike. How far up is the car?"

"Just over the lip of the escarpment," Toby returned, starting up the sand.

Lori got out and followed reluctantly. She looked around to see the sun just touching the tops of the cliffs further up canyon. It was going to be a hot day. Climbing in the cool morning shadows was nice, though. It felt good to be doing something other than waiting.

Their feet sank ankle deep in the sand, and they all had sand in their shoes and socks before they'd gone a dozen steps up the steep incline. It only took twenty minutes to reach the cliff, and they found a crevasse that gave them access up the last ten feet. When they got to the top they turned around and surveyed the valley behind them. The sun sprayed them from the east, turning the ground and everything around them golden red. Below the canyon was still bathed in cool cobalt blue. Even the mustard yellow jeep, so small below, had a distinct blue cast.

"Up here," Toby said, climbing on up.

They reached a place where another ridge jutted up out of the sand at right angles to the canyon. The ground was firmer, so it was less tiring trying to walk through the sand. Sagebrush and a few other desert plants spotted the landscape.

"There are tracks everywhere," Cory commented. "Those are Hummer tire prints. Look at the knobs on the tires. Over here are some footprints, and then, over here..."

He stopped. There was a line of indentations in the soft sandstone. He'd seen marks like them before, when he'd been out target practicing with Thomas and his father.

"You weren't kidding," he said softly. "Thomas, they did shoot at him. Look. These were automatic weapons!"

"I know. Toby, where was your car?"

Toby looked around slowly, as if trying to get his bearings.

Then he said, "It was dark, but I think it was over there against those rocks. Yes. Look at the hole in the soil. That's where we crashed."

"That's where you hit?" Thomas said. "Look. The sandstone is smashed there. You can see the cracks. They took it, Cory. Why would they take it? Look at the way the rocks were torn up. Your car must have been totaled! Toby, you're lucky to be alive."

"Everyone keeps saying that," Toby said simply. "I couldn't get our vehicle to run any more. But, I don't think it was damaged that badly. I just couldn't get it to go. Where do you think they took it?"

"I don't even know *why* they took it," Cory said softly.

"My father said they wouldn't want anyone to know what they did," Thomas returned. "They were covering their backsides."

"There's nothing up here," Lori said nervously. "Maybe we ought to go back to town."

Thomas nodded, but Cory said, "Let's see where these tracks lead. We'll only go a little ways. We both know this isn't military land. It's part of the wilderness area. There aren't any roads up here", he flashed a stern look at Toby, "so no one should be up here with vehicles. These tracks are the Hummers. There are three or four of them. But I don't see any tire tracks from your vehicle, unless it had the same kind of tires as the Humvees."

"It only made one track," Toby said, a little irritated. "Right there!"

With a quick motion of his hand, he turned away and started down the hill toward the jeep. The shadow in the canyon was growing lighter.

"What's that supposed to mean?" Cory snapped.

"Whatever you want it to mean!" Toby returned loudly. "I told you all I know. Let's go back down. I think we need your father again, Thomas."

"Hey, guys, it's all right," Lori shouted. "Toby's right. Let's just go back. I'm feeling a little bit nervous about this. We can argue about it later."

She turned and started to follow Toby toward the cliff. Then she shouted.

"I think we're too late!" she yelled over the sudden noise.

A helicopter rose from just beyond the edge of the cliff, and turned toward them. As they froze in their tracks, it belched a line of bullets aimed to divide the area between them and the cliff. It was clearly a warning not to go that direction.

Toby backed up slowly till he was beside Lori. He reached out and grabbed her hand. Thomas and Cory ran to them. They began to pull Lori and Toby back, slowly, carefully toward the cover of the rocks.

"No one in my group would have been this stupid," a voice boomed from behind them.

Lori turned to see Major Remmick, complete with communication set and sunglasses, standing near the crater where Toby's vehicle had been. The helicopter was backing off slightly, but its guns were trained on the slope below them.

"Of course," Remmick said evenly, "we were sure *you'd* come back up here. You'll have to go with us. We have some questions for all of you."

Thomas stared down at his jeep, measuring the distance. He wondered, for a brief instant, if they could make it down the way Toby had the night before. Then he scowled back up at the leader.

"You can't do this!" he shouted. "My father will find my jeep! He'll know where we are. He'll come after you!"

"I'm counting on it," the leader replied. "Let me explain my authority to you, young man. I'm sure your father will get the message."

He spoke into the microphone, and made a motion with his hand. The helicopter turned easily, slowly, almost dreamlike, and launched one rocket. The missile, trailing smoke and fire, flew directly at the yellow jeep below. They saw the jeep disintegrate in a ball of flame and smoke. The sound of the explosion came back to them a second later. Thomas felt his cheeks flush.

"You jerk!" he shouted. "I worked on that jeep all winter to get it running! I'd like a chance to belt you just once!"

He clenched and unclenched his fists.

"I'd win," Remmick said easily. "We have places to go, children."

He raised his hand, and they heard the roar of the Humvees. In seconds three of them flew over the ridge to skid to a stop between them and the cliff face. Men in black began to pour out of them.

"We didn't have the helicopter in the right place last night," the major said. "We don't make the same mistake twice. Let my men show you our vehicles."

"I've seen them, thank you," Cory spat.

He rubbed his shoulder where he could still feel the bruising.

"This time don't overplay your part," the major returned. "Just get in."

"My father will think we're dead!" Thomas shouted.

"You and I both know your father is smarter than that," Remmick returned. "I just gave him something to think about. He will understand the message."

Toby sniffed, and said, "Where's my sister?"

"Anisha? She told us her name. You'll be telling us a lot more, too. We'll take you to her, though the reunion won't be quite what you expect. You'll like your new home. You'd better get used to it quickly. You're going to be there a long time."

# CHAPTER 13

Thomas yanked his arm away from one of the soldiers, and shouted, "You don't have the right to bother us. Leave us alone!"

"Get them all in the vehicles, and let's get back to the base," the major said simply.

Thomas felt a strong hand grab his upper arm again. He tried to yank away as he had before, but this time another soldier grabbed him from the other side, effectively pinning him between them. They half carried, half dragged him toward the nearest Humvee. He tried to see where the others were being taken. He was shoved toward the vehicle so quickly he only caught a glimpse of Lori. She was being thrust into one of the other vehicles. His next view was of the dark interior of the Humvee.

The inside of the vehicle was black, just like the outside. Everything was flat black. It gave the appearance of a dark box, or a coffin. The driver was sitting still, monitoring a dashboard of instruments. Most were normal for any vehicle. He recognized a radar screen and a computer screen, and several dials that were strange to him. Another body was thrown against him, and he turned to see Toby. It was apparent they were expected to share the seat. The center of the vehicle was taken up by a large square hump, and it was impossible to crawl over it to the other side. Remmick slid into the seat from the other side. He slammed the door, and nodded to the driver. The interior became dim when the last door closed, but the view out the windows was unexpectedly crystal clear.

The vehicle started up, and the rear wheels began to throw sand behind them as they climbed the dunes in front of them. In a few seconds they were bouncing over the terrain at a high rate of speed. Thomas estimated they were going well over forty miles per hour. He struggled to hold on, and keep Toby from bouncing into the front seat. When he saw the cliff coming at them he grabbed desperately at the seat belt. He wrapped it around both of them and managed to secure it in the lock. The shoulder harness smashed them together uncomfortably. The Hummer slid sideways, and accelerated away from the edge. He was sure he saw a look of demonic satisfaction on the face of the driver. He tried to look behind them, but could not see the other vehicles.

"Where are we going?" He asked.

The major ignored him, but turned to Toby.

"Ever since Roswell we've been trying to make some sense out of you people," he said. "First you look ghastly, then you look human, then ghastly again. What are you up too, little warrior? And just how old are you, really?"

Toby didn't say anything to him. Thomas stared from Remmick to the back of Toby's head. He held onto the harness as they bounced over some particularly rough terrain. Toby's fingers began to dig into his forearms as he struggled to stay in the seat with him.

"It's okay," the major said softly. "We can teach you how to answer questions. We've come a long way since Roswell. We already know a lot more about you than you can imagine."

"You're talking torture," Thomas spat, incredulous.

The Major simply looked bored, and said, "Well, it's not really as if he's human or anything. We can find out what's going on easily enough. By the way, I don't think you can fool any of my guards. They're trained to recognize you even if you change forms."

Thomas blinked hard. What the major was suggesting didn't make any sense at all. He tapped Toby's shoulder. Toby twisted around to look at him. Thomas raised his eyebrows slightly. Toby recognized the gesture, and shook his head. Thomas was more confused than ever.

"You've watched too many science fiction shows," Thomas muttered.

Remmick smiled wryly, and continue to watch their progress over the driver's shoulder. Meanwhile the Humvee had arrived at a long slope, covered with cedar trees. Thomas could see the base over the trees. He'd never seen it before. From the road it was virtually invisible, just the water towers and the fence along the edge of the mesa. Now he could see an organized complex of buildings and a short runway complete with hangar. The American flag, almost indistinguishable at this distance, floated gently at the top of the pole.

He looked left, and saw one of the other Humvees poised at the edge of the hill next to them. When he looked right, he saw the other one.

"Escort," he mumbled, more to call Toby's attention to them than anything else.

The leader pointed at Toby and said, "Of course. What we have here is worth protecting. We've waited a long time and spent a lot of money to get to this point, and we don't want to lose what we have."

"You tried to shoot him last night," Thomas accused.

The leader half smiled, and then said, "Expedience. A dead alien is better than none at all. However, today we have him."

"Why?"

"You really don't know who he is, do you?" the leader said.

The driver turned, and said, "We have clearance, Major."

"Proceed," the major returned casually. "It involves national security. You may find out the real story, but if you do, we're probably going to have to kill you."

He smiled broadly at his joke, and leaned back. Thomas thought it was funny last night, now it just made him angry.

"At least you could be original," he mumbled.

The Hummer lurched forward and down the slope at break-neck speed. Thomas held on to the door handle with one hand and struggled to keep Toby from bouncing around uncontrollably in spite of the shared harness. The major was taking it all in stride. He'd done this before.

They reached the bottom of the slope, and arrived at a gate in the tall, chain link fence. The gate was double, a second gate about a hundred feet inside the first, and both were guarded. On the right was a small unpretentious guard shack manned by two soldiers. Six more soldiers guarded the first gate, two outside the fence and four inside. They wore regular uniforms, a fact that brought some comfort to Thomas. There were four more guarding the second gate, two on each side of the fence.

As the Hummer pulled up, one soldier approached, and the other backed him from the fence. He tapped on the window, waited for the driver to lower it, and stared into the dark interior. He seemed agitated, stood, and marched stiffly back to the gate. At his order the gate opened slowly. The Hummer proceeded in. Thomas hoped the others were behind them.

The soldiers surrounded them as soon as they were inside the first gate, one on each corner of the vehicle. The two men in the front seat opened the doors and stepped out. Their identification was checked, and one of the guards stuck his head into the vehicle. He saw the two boys and frowned. Up to this point none of the soldiers had spoken. They all seemed to know what was expected of them. Now, however, the guard spoke.

"We cannot authorize you to bring civilians on base, sir," he said simply.

The major nodded, and stepped from the vehicle. When he was standing, he slowly took off his sunglasses. It was the first time Thomas had seen him without them. He smiled and nodded.

"You know who I am?" He asked softly.

"Yes, sir, I do," the soldier said nervously. "We have been instructed by our commanding officer not to allow any more civilians on base."

"Do you really want to challenge my authority?" Remmick said evenly.

"No, sir," the soldier said. "But, I must repeat, that we cannot-"

"We are going on base, soldier," the major said quickly. "I am giving you a direct order to let us pass. Do you understand your order?"

At a signal from the major the men from the Humvees immediately emerged and took up defensive positions around the vehicles. The gate guards immediately backed away, trying to match the black-dressed soldiers' positions. They all carried weapons and it seemed each had targeted one of their counterparts. The one talking to the major raised his hand. His men stood firm, but looked a little uneasy. Thomas saw the two in the guard shack raise their weapons and crouch a little lower in the window.

"You can't be serious, sir," the soldier growled.

"You won't interfere with my orders, or my mission here, sergeant," the major said quickly. "You may report this to your commanding officer. You tell him I will be happy to discuss your orders and your performance in this matter at his convenience. In the meantime, this is a direct order. Let us pass."

"I cannot," the soldier said firmly.

"You push this issue right now, soldier," Remmick said, "and you will never find out just how much authority I really do have. You, and your men, will be dead. My men will take this gate. Then we will pass anyway. Do you want to take responsibility for that? Make a decision, Sergeant. I will not give you a second chance."

The soldier barked a couple of orders, and two men moved quickly to his side.

"Get Captain Farris on the land line," he said decisively. "Sir, you will wait until I confirm this with my superior."

Remmick raised his hand, and one of his men raised his weapon and released a burst of shots at the top of the guard shack. The men in the shack dropped behind the protective wall. The wires from the shack were severed, and flopped limply to the ground.

"You're insane!" the sergeant shouted angrily.

"I'm going through," the major said evenly. "You have your orders. Open the gate and let us pass. Or die. Those are your choices."

The sergeant nodded at the two men, then turned stiffly and signaled the men at the second gate. The second gate began to open.

Thomas nodded slowly, and nudged Toby.

"They have a little bit of trouble up here," he whispered. "This may be worse than my father thought."

"This looks bad," Toby returned softly. "Do your soldiers always fight each other?"

"This is the first time I ever heard of this happening," Thomas answered honestly.

"Maybe now is a good time for a prayer," Toby suggested.

"Absolutely," Thomas breathed.

Toby nodded, and Thomas continued to watch the soldiers outside his window. He was more frightened than before. The situation seemed more out of control than it had. He suddenly began to see the possibility of release grow very small.

Remmick signaled with his hand, and the men in black immediately climbed back in the Humvees. The major smiled broadly as the doors slammed shut.

"I know what you're thinking," he said. "Remember that I don't need you or your friends. I only need this one. When you plan your escape make sure you decide how you will carry your friends' bodies out of here."

Thomas scowled, and said, "You're completely insane, aren't you?"

"That has been said of me," Remmick acknowledged, smiling. "Just be sure you remember that."

The Hummer moved through the second gate. The soldier from the front seat stood by the gate, an ominous reminder to the others who was in charge. The driver slowed for him, and he jumped back in as the Hummer moved past.

The roads in the compound were neatly laid out, with logs and stones marking where curbs and gutters would be in a normal town. The walks were crushed rock harvested from the surrounding hills. There were areas that should have been grass, but were simply cleaned free of any growing thing in mute imitation of a real town. The buildings, about twenty of them, were spotless, well kept, freshly painted. There was no indication anywhere what the base's function was.

They drove straight through the compound to the airfield. The runway, though short, was concrete. Two black, unmarked helicopters rested on the pad in front of the hangar. Several small planes, well marked with the usual Air Force symbols, were nearby. The distinctive decorations of the airships seemed to clash.

Where the Air Force planes seemed to be for transportation, with no visible armament, the helicopters seemed overloaded with firepower. One of the helicopters was being re-armed. Thomas was sure it was the one they'd encountered earlier. The new missile was to replace the one that had blown his jeep apart. He got angry again.

The Humvees crossed the tarmac straight toward the hangar. If there had been any doubt about their destination, it was allayed by their direct course. Thomas wondered if they were going to be loaded directly on to airships and taken somewhere else. He breathed deeply.

The Humvees rolled through the gaping hangar doors and drove almost halfway down the length of the building before they stopped. The growl of the engines echoed against the arch of the roof overhead. It was a small hangar, but was still hugely out of proportion to the small aircraft out on the tarmac. The hangar was filled with men in black, and a few in regular Air Force fatigues, packing a myriad of equipment in wood and cardboard boxes. Styrofoam chips were scattered everywhere. Everyone was moving quickly.

The major cleared his throat, and pointed at the door. Thomas pulled on the handle, but nothing happened. The door suddenly burst open, attended by one of their guards. Toby climbed off his lap, trying not to step on him. Thomas half climbed, half fell out behind the younger boy.

He tugged at the handle a couple of times, remembering Cory's description the night before, and glanced back at the major. Remmick smiled and nodded.

"They only open when we want them to," he said quietly.

Thomas stood up gratefully and stretched. His muscles were cramped by confinement with Toby mostly sitting on his lap. He looked around at their new world.

"Our new home, I guess," he mused, looking around.

The aircraft hangar doors at both ends of the hangar were wide open. A breeze blew through the interior that tended to scatter the Styrofoam around. The smaller doors at the sides were closed tight. There were no guards visible, except the ones who had escorted them onto the base, but there were none needed. The place seemed guarded by sheer numbers alone. He looked at the windows, and looked for any avenue of escape. There seemed to be no place to run.

The men from the Humvees took up pre-assigned positions around them. It was a drill they knew well. The only path open was the one toward the offices at the side of the hangar. There was a row of windows, and a door. The windows were ripple glass, hiding what lay on the other side. The pall of age hung over the building.

The major cleared his throat again.

"I saw that look, boy," he said, walking around Thomas. "You remember what I said about your friends' bodies. There is too much at stake here to worry about a couple of small-town brats who can't keep their noses out of government business."

"I don't think this is government business," Cory said as they herded him up from behind. "Don't push her!"

He shouted the last at one of the soldiers encouraging Lori to join them. Lori stumbled against Cory. Cory helped steady her, and glared at the soldier.

"What do you think this is, boy? Kindergarten?" The major asked.

"And who do you think you are, Remmick," Thomas snarled, "Adolph Hitler?"

Remmick scowled and opened his mouth to speak, but was cut off.

"What do you think you're doing, Remmick?" A voice boomed from behind them. "Have you taken absolute leave of your senses?"

They all turned. The man approaching wore an officer's uniform, clean and neatly pressed. He strode into the hangar. Two armed men flanked him; one Thomas recognized as the sergeant from the gate. He felt something volatile was going to happen, and he was scared.

"I'm doing my job, Captain Ferris," Major Remmick said evenly. "I understand you left word I was not to bring these...witnesses...on board."

"I did indeed," the officer said. "I've received a call from the sheriff of the town down below about your operation last night."

"He's small town," Remmick snarled. "He hasn't got any idea what's at stake here."

"I've also received calls from the commander of Hill Air Force Base," Ferris continued. "It seems he's a personal friend of this sheriff."

"He has no authority in this issue," Remmick returned.

"I also got calls from the Senator of this district, the governor of this state and *my* commanding officer," Captain Ferris said. "They are all telling me things I don't really want to hear. You've been doing things-"

"I know what that sheriff says I've done," Remmick cut in. "Let's get down to it. You're a captain. I am a major. You do not outrank me. I outrank you. You cannot give me a direct order. I can give you a direct order. Now, listen very carefully. I have been ordered to bring the occupants of the vehicle back for examination, alive if possible, but dead if necessary. That order comes from the *highest level*. I will use the authority that order gives me to do whatever is necessary to accomplish my mission. If that means starting our own little war here for control of this rather shabby little base, then I will do it. Captain, understand that we will win. My men are better trained, and I have an unlimited number of men to call on to augment my group. Is there anything else you need?"

Captain Ferris frowned. He waited a long time. Then he slowly shook his head.

"You've said it all," he said thoughtfully. "All base personnel working with this unit will immediately report to operations for reassignment. They will be directed to obey only my orders from this moment on. Sergeant, rejoin your men at Desolation Gate. Until further orders, you are in no way to interfere with the operations of this unit. Is that satisfactory, Major?"

He emphasized Remmick's rank in a particularly unpleasant way.

"I could still use a few of your men as we wrap up this assignment," Remmick suggested.

"No," Ferris returned simply. "You may take that up with my commanding officer, if you wish. This operation may be over much quicker than you realize."

"I see," the major said softly. "Then, we will not delay our departure any longer than is needful."

He spoke into the microphone, then looked up and said, "I will need the use of your hangar for a few more days. I hope that will not interfere with you plans."

Captain Ferris nodded grimly, and said, "For the moment. As I said, this operation may be over much quicker than you realize. You have attracted a great deal of attention down here in a matter of only a couple of weeks. I am filing a full report, and you are not being treated favorable in that report. I cannot approve of you taking children captive, Major.

The girl was bad enough. Now you've kidnapped four more children. How many more will there be, Major?"

"The children are in protective custody," Remmick corrected him.

"We call it kidnapping where I come from," Ferris rejoined. "If I had the authority, I would stop this right now and I would throw you in that brig you've so conveniently built for us. We are momentarily expecting that authority to be granted. My superiors are on their way. I hope, for your sake, that your authority is from as high as you say it is."

"It is, Ferris," Remmick said. "Trust me."

"I cannot for one instant find anything in you to trust," Captain Ferris said carefully. "But, trust me, sir. I will be thrilled to stand witness at your courts martial."

"You may have a long wait," Remmick said. "You are dismissed, Captain."

Captain Ferris stood still. Frustration lined his face. He looked at the boys and Lori. For a moment his face softened.

"I know you're frightened," he said to them. "I spoke with your sheriff last night. I'll be talking to him again in a few moments. He will tell your parents where you are, and that you are safe."

He glanced up at Remmick, and there was pure anger in that look. His face softened quickly.

"You won't be harmed here," he continued. "Look at this as a kind of adventure. We'll have you back home before you know it."

"That's sweet, Captain," Remmick taunted. "However, children, don't count on it. Captain, I dismissed you."

After a moment Captain Ferris turned sharply and marched from the building. His escort had trouble keeping up. As if at a given signal all the men in the hangar wearing regular fatigues left the jobs they were performing and followed their captain out. The hangar was left only with black uniformed soldiers.

Thomas watched the Captain leave. He could tell by his step that he was furious. He frowned, and glanced at Cory, who just shrugged. Lori had a worried, scared look, and seemed close to tears. Toby simply glared at Remmick, following every move he made.

"A little disagreement," Thomas said quietly, for no better reason than to needle Remmick.

"If you say so," Remmick said, turning away. "You four come this way."

The four prisoners were herded into the office. The room was narrow and long, with a box erected floor to ceiling in the northeast corner. Cells had been built there. Three heavy steel doors had been set in the new wall. There was a narrow slit in each door just lower than a man's face. Lori was shoved into the first cell, and Thomas and Cory into the second. Thomas looked back in time to see Toby pushed toward the third.

The cell was about six feet wide, and maybe ten long. There was a small cot on one side, and a toilet and sink at the back. Everything looked makeshift, pieced together. The cells were an afterthought, a recent addition. Sheetrock mud was still splattered and dried on the concrete floor. The walls weren't even painted.

"I hope your stay here will be comfortable," Remmick said as each of the doors was locked by one of his men. "These cells are temporary. We've prepared something a bit more permanent elsewhere. You won't be here long."

"There's only one bed!" Cory shouted. "How are we supposed to sleep?"

"I told you that you won't be here long," Remmick snapped. "I'll fly your friend out of here in about an hour. He has some people who want to meet him. You'll follow shortly after that. You'll have your own cell where we're taking you. I promise."

"Where's my sister?" Toby shouted.

"You'll be near her soon," Remmick answered, turning away. "We flew her out early this morning. You will be going where she is. If you do what you're told I may even let you see her."

Thomas, staring through the slit, saw him leave the room. Three guards took up positions facing the cells, one for each door. He saw two more guards outside the office door as it shut.

"We must be dangerous," Thomas said angrily.

The guards didn't respond.

"Are you okay, Lori?" Cory shouted through the slit in the door.

There was a moment of silence, then Lori said, "Yes. I guess so. You?"

Cory heard the catch in her voice, and knew she was crying.

"We're okay," he said, a little reserved. "Toby?"

"I'm okay."

Toby sounded angry. Cory realized he was, too.

For the first time he realized how bad the cell smelled. He heard the toilet flush, and turned around.

"The last one in here didn't flush," Thomas said, disgust in his voice. "Not much privacy, is there? Hey, Toby, what you think we ought to do now?"

Cory nudged Thomas, and said, "Leave him alone. This isn't his fault, you know."

"I know," Thomas conceded. "I could've made him stay home. It's just that I didn't expect to spend Saturday in jail. Sorry, Toby."

"It's all right," Toby answered, his voice low and reserved now. "It is my fault, I guess. I just thought we could call my father, and find my sister. I got us into a lot of trouble."

"We're here because we wanted to be," Lori shouted. "Hey, guys, do you think there's a camera in these jails?"

"I don't know," Cory said. "Why?"

"No reason," Lori returned.

They heard the toilet in her cell flush.

"Thomas, are you still there?" Lori said from her cell. "Do you think your father found your jeep?"

Thomas looked at his watch. It wasn't even noon, and he was hungry.

"You mean what's left of it?" He asked a touch of irony in his voice. "I'm not sure he'd recognize it even if he did find it. That rocket blew it to kingdom come. But, I'm pretty sure he'll put two and two together, and he'll be up here soon to see what's going on. If we get real lucky, that Captain Ferris will contact him and get us sprung before this Remmick can do anything else."

"So, we just wait?" Cory asked.

"Not much else we can do," Thomas said softly. "Toby, what will your father do when he doesn't find your car?"

"He'll go to the vehicle, not to the site," Toby said simply.

Cory looked at Thomas. Thomas simply shrugged.

"How would he know where it is?" Cory asked. "They moved it. It could be anywhere. Does he have some kind of homing beacon?"

"He'll know where it is," Toby returned simply. "I wanted to get back to it because I knew he'd go there. Now we won't be there when he gets there. We're...trapped."

"I think the correct term is 'imprisoned'," Cory said evenly, staring through the door slit. "Hey, guard! When do we get lunch? We're hungry in here!"

The guards just stared back at him. He was frustrated, and slammed his fist against the door. The dull "thud" echoed in the small room. He rubbed his hand, and sat on the bed. As an afterthought he hit the wall. A hollow "thud" filled the cell.

Almost immediately Cory looked up, and met Thomas's smile. The walls were hollow sheetrock! They'd worked on the new houses near the upper reservoir the summer before. They knew about sheetrock.

Cory pulled his pocketknife from his pocket, opened the blade and smiled. Thomas pulled out his own knife, and opened it.

Cory began to cut the sheetrock on the wall between them and Lori's cell, and Thomas began to work on the wall toward Toby.

Suddenly Lori started pounding on the door and screaming.

"There are rats in the walls!" she shouted. "You have to let me out of here! There are rats in here!"

Cory and Thomas knelt by their respective walls, holding their breath. They couldn't finish if Lori continued to draw their attention.

The soldiers remained deaf. But Lori wasn't going to let them ignore her. She pounded on her door, and screamed louder.

"Would you shut up!" one of the guards finally said.

"No! I'm going to get bitten by rats, and you just want me to be a good little girl!" she wailed. "You have to let me out!"

The outer door opened, and they heard gruff voices outside. There was a hurried, if covert, conference between the guards and whoever had opened the door. Then one of the guards crossed the room and unlocked Lori's door. He made a superficial inspection of the cell. He slammed the cell door, and jammed the key in the boys' cell.

Cory and Thomas stood quickly, and jammed their pocketknives into their pockets. With a horrified shudder, as the cell door opened, Cory realized he'd left the blade open. He felt the blade stab through his pocket and jab into his thigh at an oblique angle.

The soldier stood in the opening, one hand in his belt near his holster, the other holding the key. He looked at them suspiciously.

"You see any rats in here?" he asked.

"Just one," Thomas answered quickly. "Why?"

"How about you?" the guard asked, ignoring Thomas and pointing the key at Cory.

Cory shook his head, and stammered, "No, sir!"

The soldier stared curiously as Cory held his thigh tightly where the blade, in his pocket, was still impaling him.

"What's your problem?" he asked.

Cory glanced down and saw the sheetrock dust all over the floor, and looked up to meet the soldier's gaze. He knew in that instant they were caught. He thought about punching Lori, but realized he was just beginning to like her.

# CHAPTER 14

Brady looked up from the mug of cold soda he was drinking. Jacob Bennett slammed the door behind him as he entered. He was agitated.

"Brady, I think we still have a problem," he said.

"What's going on?" Brady asked, motioning to the chair next to his desk.

Jacob ignored the chair. He leaned over the desk instead.

"I just got up and found this," he said, sliding a paper across the desk.

The paper was a scrap of notebook paper, torn hastily from a pad. A short message was scrawled across it:

> *Dad,*
>
> *I'm going for a short walk. Be back soon.*
>
> Love, Lori

"Okay," Brady said quietly, feeling his stomach turn. "I gather she hasn't come back yet."

"No," Jacob returned. "I looked all over town. You know I'm not one to get emotional or excited all the time. But this thing last night has stretched me pretty thin. I'm worried and a little scared."

"Okay," Brady said, trying to remain calm. "Let's go find her."

He picked up the microphone for the radio and said, "Ben, are you on duty yet?"

The radio sputtered, and Ben said, "After last night? I haven't been off duty. I'll bet you haven't been, either."

Brady smiled, and said, "You've got that right. You know the Bennett girl, right?"

"I do."

"Then, cruise the town and see if she's out walking around anywhere," Brady said.

"Is there a problem?"

"There might be. Jacob is here. He says she went out on a morning walk and didn't return. She was involved in that fracas last night with the military people from the base, and I want to be sure they're not still picking up strays around town."

"Got it."

"That's 'ten four', Ben," Brady said, smiling.

"Oh, yah. Ten four!"

Brady looked up, and said, "Let's cruise around ourselves and see what we can see."

Jacob nodded gratefully, but Brady frowned suddenly.

"I don't know why," he said thoughtfully, "but I have a bad feeling about this."

He grabbed the phone, and dialed. There was a long wait before Macey picked up at the other end. Brady breathed deeply.

"Hello, Macey," he said. "Of course, I know what time it is. It's eight o'clock. Look, Macey, I want you to go down the hall and check on the boys. No, I don't think there's anything wrong. Just do it. I'll wait."

He looked up at Jacob, and smiled weakly. Almost a minute passed before the phone was picked up again.

"No, Macey, don't panic," he said calmly. "Look out the window and see if the jeep is there. It's not? Okay, good. They've probably gone touring around the town. Look, just stay tight, and I'll find them. No, Macey, I don't want you to come down here. I want you to call me when they come in. I'll have a few things to say to that son of yours when he gets back. Something like grounding and taking his jeep keys away. No, I'll handle it. Just call me when he gets in."

He pressed the receiver button and dialed again.

"Hi, Bishop, it's Brady. Yes. I want you to check your boy's room. Yes, I think so. Thomas is gone, so I have a sneaking suspicion Cory is with him. No, Bishop. Thomas has the Jeep. He would be the instigator. Well, you can talk to your boy about following his lead too quickly, but for now just check to see if he's in his bed, please. Okay, I'll hold on."

Jacob leaned forward again, and said, "You think they're all out together?"

"Probably," Brady answered. "The Bishop and I've been through this a time or two. If they're together then they're safe enough. I'm still going to take Thomas's keys away, though. A couple of weeks of walking will send a clear message. Yes, Bishop. I'm here. He's not? No, he's probably out with Thomas and the new boy, Toby. They might have Jacob's daughter with them. You know Lori. No. I'll find them. You stay there and don't worry. Call Macey if they come in. She'll radio me."

He hung up the phone, and saw Jacob relax some. He drank again from the iced soda pop, and stood up casually. He hoped he was presenting an air of calm confidence. He felt neither calm nor confident.

"Let's go see if we can find them," he said.

Jacob nodded, and said, "I agree."

They walked out to the patrol car, and got in. Brady switched on the radio, and started the car.

"Brady to home base," he said as he keyed the microphone. "Macey, are you there?"

After a few moments, Karl Rosen said, "We're here, Sheriff. Your wife is upstairs getting dressed. What do you need?"

"I want you to get your car and cruise down the canyon. Give me a call from the lower dam. We're looking for my son again. You know his jeep."

"Right. Look, sheriff, I'm sorry. I guess I was asleep, and-"

"Karl, I know my son," Brady interjected. "If you had been sitting wide awake on the foot of his bed it wouldn't have made any difference. If he wanted to get out, he'd get out. Don't worry about it. Your job wasn't to keep him in, but to be available if those military idiots came back. You did what you were supposed to do. Now go down and check out the reservoir."

"Right," Karl said, and was gone.

They drove down the main street past the Frosty Freeze. The sun was already beginning to sear the plants. It looked like it would be an unusually hot summer. Jacob looked over at the sheriff.

"You don't think they went down the canyon, do you?" He asked.

"No. Not past the base," Brady returned, turning into the west end residential district. "It's more likely they went up to the diversion dam above the railroad trestle. Look! There's the Forster boy delivering papers. What's his name? Nathaniel!"

He pulled up matching the patrol car's speed with the pace of the boy's bike. Nathaniel Forster was barely twelve. He was a small boy, almost elflike in appearance. The bicycle he rode seemed two sizes too large. He delivered to half the houses in town and never missed a paper. Brady was always sure the paper would be there before he left for work every morning.

"Hi, Sheriff," Nathaniel said, tossing a paper over his shoulder. It landed on the porch. "Did I miss your house this morning?"

"I don't think so," Brady said, smiling. "I got an early start this morning. You must have been up pretty early yourself. Am I right?"

"I'm up early every morning," the boy said, slowing to a stop.

"That's right. It takes, what, two hours to deliver all your papers?"

"Counting wrapping," Nathaniel returned. "I always deliver yours first, then I go home and wrap the rest and go out and deliver them. Anything wrong?"

"No," Brady said easily. "I was just wondering if you saw anything unusual this morning. For instance, did you see a black Hummer cruising around this morning?"

"There was one parked down near the west end of town," Nathaniel said. "My dad said not to deliver down there till the sun came up. It kind of worried him. He said if it started cruising to knock on the first door I could find and call him."

"It's a military vehicle, Nathaniel," Brady said calmly. "I just want to keep tabs on them. By the way, you didn't happen to see my son driving around, did you?"

"Well, yah. He and Cory, and some girl from the high school, and a boy I've never seen before were going up Taylor Canyon. The boy was dressed funny."

"Are you sure?"

"Sure," the boy asserted. "The strange boy wore all white. Sorta looked like he was running around in his pj's."

"No, Nathaniel," the sheriff said. "I meant, 'Are you sure it was Thomas?'"

"Yes, sir. They drove right past me, and about five minutes later I saw them go up the canyon road. You know, you can see Thomas's yellow jeep for miles."

"Thanks, Nathaniel," Brady said, letting his foot off the brake.

The car cruised forward a few feet then he stopped it again.

"Say, Nathaniel, you don't happen to know about what time that was, do you?" he asked.

"It had to be before six," Nathaniel returned. "I'd already delivered to your house. I guess you were already gone. Then I wrapped the papers and was out delivering up by the river. That's when they cruised by. The sun wasn't up yet. Are they in any trouble or something?"

"No. Just keeping track of them is all. Good. Thanks, Nathaniel."

They pulled away, and turned the next corner. Sheriff Brady pulled the microphone up.

"Karl, are you there?" He said.

"Right here," Karl said. "I just talked to a trucker down here at Irma's. You remember Brigham Hurst? He was stranded in town last winter when his truck broke down. You let him stay in the jail cell till Murphy's got it going again. He said he saw your boy driving up Taylor Canyon. He said the yellow jeep was pretty bright that early in the morning."

"I got the same story from Nathaniel Forster," Brady said. "You want to follow us up the canyon? I feel a little uncomfortable about this."

"I'll be right there, Boss," Karl returned.

Brady turned across the bridge and up on to the highway. As he put his foot down, he heard his wife.

"Brady, have you found the boys yet?"

Brady picked up the microphone, and said, "Not yet, Macey. But we know where they went. They went up Taylor Canyon. They spend a lot of time up there. They probably know every rock and bush in that canyon. They're okay. And there's no way out, so he'll have to deal with me shortly. I don't think I'm going to be too pleasant this morning. I'm going to send him straight home. When he gets there, I want you to take his keys away. He'll be expecting that."

"I wonder why they decided to go exploring this early," Macey mused.

"He probably thought he'd be home before we discovered they were missing," Brady said evenly. "Maybe the new boy, Toby, was going to show them where he went the other day. I'd bet he had a flat tire or something. You know his jeep, Macey. He's lucky he can get the stupid thing started, let alone up and back down Taylor Canyon without breaking something. We'll go up there and find him. Then, when we get that jeep back down you and I are going to impound it for a couple of weeks."

He heard Macey laugh on the other end, and he smiled weakly. That's exactly what he wanted. He didn't want her to worry. He could handle the worry for both of them.

"I don't want you to worry, either," he said to Jacob. "The situation is probably just the way I explained it to Macey. They're okay. They lost track of the time or they're just stuck somewhere."

They turned off the road and started up the winding dirt path into the canyon.

The patrol car was four wheel drive. It was necessary in the southern part of the state. He was occasionally called out to find lost hikers, or to help with injured campers. Each year hikers came into the area without any idea where they were going, and got hurt or lost on the slick rock around the town. Brady knew the road well. Only the first mile or so was bad, the rest was nearly flat, following the dry creek bed gently uphill to the end of the canyon.

First stop, he knew, would be the old mission. The boys liked to spend a lot of time there. Next would be the grove, a little further up, and the mysterious canyon they discovered only a week before. They liked to hike around the side canyons. There was an abundance of places to explore and nothing extraordinarily dangerous.

He shook his head, thinking about Cory's fall that week. That was unusual. The boys were good hikers and they knew the country. He told himself they were okay.

They bounced over the sharp rise, and turned into the flat part of the canyon, where it spread out to form the small valley the mission was in. He saw the cottonwoods and the mission about a mile away, and swallowed.

Something was putting off a lot of black smoke under the cottonwoods. It was still smoldering. The gently breeze was wafting the smoke up the canyon, so they hadn't seen it before coming into the valley. Brady knew what it was before they got halfway across the valley. The paint on the few parts lying around was unmistakable. He pulled up, a safe distance away, and he and Jacob climbed out.

"This is bad," Jacob whispered softly.

Brady could see him tremble. He had recognized the wreckage, too. Even though it was scattered over a thousand square yard area the yellow paint on the parts not burned was distinctive. Jacob began to kick through the wreckage, becoming more agitated as he did. Brady looked up, and cleared his throat.

"Leave it alone," he said softly. He said a quiet prayer under his breath.

"Where are they?" Jacob said, his voice almost frantic. "Where are they?"

"They weren't here when this happened," Brady said calmly. "Now, don't disturb the evidence. Look. They climbed up that way. You can see four distinct tacks going up that sand ridge. They went up on top. I need to get some help up here. Here comes Karl. I want you to go down with him."

"I'm going to stay here with you," Jacob insisted, a little calmer.

"Okay, but no matter what we find, I want you to stay calm," Brady said. "And, don't touch anything unless I tell you to."

Jacob nodded.

Karl climbed from his car, and surveyed the wreckage. He waited as Brady approached. He shook his head.

"What happened up here?" he asked. His voice mirrored his agitation, too.

"That's what's left of my son's jeep," Brady said quietly, unnecessarily. "They weren't in the jeep when it blew up. I don't know where they are right now, but I intend to find out. I want you to go back down and get hold of Ben Hart. He's supposed to be going down to the lower reservoir to see if the kids went down there. Don't use the radio. I don't want my wife to worry. When you find him, get him up here as fast as you can."

"Why Ben?" Karl asked. "He's kind of a wimp when it comes to physical stuff, you know."

"He was an ordinance expert in the Army for 20 years. Then he worked at Kennecott up in Salt Lake engineering their blasting in the copper pit for at least 5 years," Brady said quietly. "He knows explosives. Do you?"

"No," Karl said softly. "You planning to blow something up?"

"No. But I want to find out what blew up my son's jeep. Now, get going. Call the FBI, too. They're going to want to get in on this."

"The FBI, too?" Karl said thoughtfully. "We're going to have a lot of strangers running around for a while. You know, it takes them months to complete this kind of investigation."

"That's what I want," Brady returned. "I don't want this swept under the rug. Don't use the radio. Just the phone."

"Ten four," Karl said loudly, and climbed back in the patrol car.

He turned a large circle in the flat area, and headed down the canyon. A trail of dust followed.

"Brady!" Jacob called out. "Come over here!"

Brady walked toward Jacob, over one hundred yards from the main portion of the wreckage. He pointed into the sagebrush.

The twisted metal of the yellow hood was readily identifiable. It had been blown clear, and, though torn and mangled, was not burned. Next to it, hiding partway under the sagebrush, was a fragment. Brady knew immediately it didn't come from the jeep. It was a fin, painted dark blue, and emblazoned with serial numbers.

"Unless I miss my guess," Jacob said softly, "I'd say that's what's left of a rocket."

Brady clenched his fist, and said, "Don't touch it. Jacob, I want a round-the-clock guard on this site until the FBI gets here. No one is going to try to pretend this didn't happen."

He felt an anger crawling up inside him he hadn't felt in a long time. He wanted to unleash it on someone. The more he thought about his anger, the more vivid Major Remmick's face became.

# CHAPTER 15

"This way," Brady shouted at Jacob.

He intended to follow the tracks the kids made up the sand ridge to the top of the cliffs. The sand was loose and hard to walk in, but he trudged upward anyway. The sun was climbing higher, and the temperature was rising. Jacob lagged behind. He was intent on following, but more slowly.

Somewhere deep inside Brady kept hoping the kids were at the top. Reason told him they were already in the custody of the military group he'd dealt with the night before. The path they took was clear and easy to read. The last ten feet over the lip of the cliff was a little more difficult than he'd expected. But, for kids it would have been no problem. The trail the kids blazed through the crevasse was easy to follow. He knew they weren't trying to hide their trail. They wouldn't have felt the need. He stopped at the top and helped Jacob up. He turned and looked down.

From the top he could see the blast pattern. Black debris was blown away from the jeep toward the old mission. The hood and remnants of the jeep were in a straight-line opposite where he was standing. He looked down and shook his head.

"Helicopter," he said quietly. "I thought I heard one earlier, but there are so many coming and going around that blasted base lately I just ignored it."

"You couldn't have known," Jacob said. "The question is: Where are our children?"

"Not down there," Brady said, walking uphill again.

He found tire tracks, and the bullet holes in the rock face. He followed the tracks and turned back downhill.

"They came to here," he said softly. "They didn't find what they were looking for, and started back down."

"What were they looking for?"

"Toby's car," Brady said softly. "But all these tracks are Hummers. They're too wide to be jeeps. There's some kind of impact crater here, but there's nothing around that could have caused it. It's not a blast crater. I'm sure of that."

Brady squatted next to the crater, stood up slowly and followed the footprints with his eyes. He stared at the pockmarks in the sandstone ridge.

"Something high powered," he said, pointing at the marks. "Someone shot at our children, Jacob. I don't know whom, yet. But I'd bet a month's pay it's the same group that came into town last night."

He walked back to the tire marks.

"At least three vehicles, maybe four. The children were surrounded here," he said, pointing at the ground. "Look at all the other footprints up around here. See where the footprints end? They stop here, right at the tire tracks. They were taken into the Hummers."

"Then, they're okay," Jacob said quietly.

"For now, I think," Brady said. "I don't think those martinets want to hurt them. But that isn't the point, is it? Why are they bothering with kids? There must be more important things to worry about. All we have to do is figure out where the Hummers were going. I've got a pretty good idea about that."

He stared up the slope, and could see the tracks marking a line straight back toward the west. The weather base was west of them.

"Brady! Come here," Jacob shouted.

Brady turned and walked to the edge of the cliff. Jacob pointed down the sand spill.

"Look over here," he said. "One of them got away. He jumped over the edge of the cliff here, and ran down there."

Brady looked at the tracks, and said, "I think that's how Toby got down last night. He probably got away only because the Hummers couldn't follow him down that sand spill. The tracks are different. They're softer, less detailed. Time does that to them. The bullet marks in the wall were probably from last night, too. He said they shot at him. They were trying to warn him. If they'd wanted to kill him, he'd be dead. They didn't want him to run. The biggest puzzle here is the rocket. Why would they fire a rocket at Thomas's jeep? Did they think I was too stupid to recognize my son's vehicle? No. Remmick was sending a message to me. He wants me to think very carefully about my next move. I already have. Come on, let's go. There's nothing else we need to learn up here."

The climb down was different than the climb up. They took one step and slid two. Their legs were aching when they reached the more solid ground at the base of the slide.

Brady strode to the patrol car, relieved to be on flat ground again. He pulled the microphone off its cradle, and keyed it.

"Karl. Are you there?"

There was a moment, then Karl said, "I'm here, Boss. I got that package you wanted. We're coming up the road right now. Is there anything else you need?"

"Not right now. I'm thinking about pictures. You wouldn't happen to have your camera, would you?"

"Never leave home without it," Karl said. "Sheriff, we got a strange call a short while ago. Guy said he was from the FDEA. He was asking about the incident up there."

Brady thought for a moment, and then asked, "How did he know? We didn't know what we would find until we got here."

"I don't know," Karl responded. "He didn't say. But he said not to do anything till he got here. He said he'd be here in an hour or so."

Brady breathed deeply, and said, "Okay. Thanks, Karl. Macey, are you there?"

There was a moment of silence before Macey said, "I'm here. What did you find that the FDEA would want to know about?"

Her voice was weak, and Brady could hear the fear. He swallowed and took a deep breath.

"Fair question, Macey. I was going to keep all this from you until I knew what was going on. But I think I'd just better let you in on what's happened. First, our son is okay. He's with Cory and Toby and Lori Bennett."

"Can I talk to Thomas?" She asked. Her voice was stronger.

"No. He's not here. The military yahoos from last night picked all of them up. We'll be getting him back this morning, though. You're going to be hearing some rumors about a bomb up here. It seems the soldiers got cute and used a rocket to dismantle Thomas's jeep."

"Oh, Brady, no!" Macey said anxiously. "Was anybody hurt?"

"No, dear," Brady returned quickly. "The kids weren't anywhere around. These macho men were trying to make some kind of a point. I think Remmick was trying to tell me something. He doesn't want me meddling. I got the message, but not like he thinks. It's our kids he's got. Meddling is something I intend to do a lot of. Are you okay with all this?"

"Oh, Brady. He put so much work into that jeep. You don't think this man could hurt the kids, do you?"

"They'll be okay," Brady returned. "We have some friends coming up here to look things over. Remmick may have been trying to scare the kids, too. If I know Thomas and Cory, it probably worked, but, again, not like he thinks it did. Remmick doesn't understand our family at all. The boys will keep a low profile and do what they're told until I can get to them. Count on that. In the meantime, go ahead and listen, but don't tie up the radio with questions. I'll answer all of them later."

"Okay," Macey said weakly.

"Macey, I love you," Brady said quietly. "I need you to trust that I'll find our son and the other kids."

"I do," Macey said softly. "I'm just scared."

"I am, too," Brady admitted, "a little. I promise we'll talk later. I love you, Hon."

"Love you, Brady."

Brady slammed his door and turned. Karl skidded to a stop only a few feet away. He jumped out, with Ben Hart following close behind.

"What's so important?" he asked.

"I want your opinion of this blast," Brady said.

Ben nodded, and walked toward the wreckage.

"Thomas' Jeep?" He asked.

"Yes."

"Okay, then."

He was careful to walk around the perimeter, and study the pattern of the debris. After only a few minutes he found the hood, and the evidence there. He walked back to the patrol car where Brady stood.

"The jeep didn't blow itself up," he said softly. "It didn't spontaneously fly apart. This wasn't an accident. It wasn't dynamite or nitro glycerin. Did you see that piece of rocket by the hood? I thought so. You weren't going to tell me about that, were you?"

"Not till you'd looked around some," Brady affirmed.

"Well, it happened this way," Ben said quietly. "There was a rocket launched somewhere up there, above the cliff. I'd bet it was launched from a helicopter. It hit the engine compartment just ahead of the passenger door. The front parts of the jeep were blown that way. The back parts went that way. It's pretty straightforward. Anything else?"

Karl handed him the camera, and said, "Yes. I have a two-gigabyte memory card. I think the Sheriff wants you to use all of it."

"Get pictures of everything you think is important," Brady added. "Karl, stay here with Ben. When he's done, bag that piece of missile. He'll show you the one. Then get back down and cruise the town. I want to know if that Humvee is still around."

"Right," Karl said. "What if they come up here?"

"Don't do anything on your own," Brady replied. "Wait for backup. And hide the camera. It's evidence."

Karl smiled, and said, "I'm no loose cannon, Boss. I'll wait for you."

Jacob came back over, and said, "There's one of the wiper blades impaled in the wall of the mission, Brady. It's sticking in the cinder block like someone deliberately jammed it there. I'm glad the kids weren't close by when this happened. What did Ben say about the rocket?"

Ben looked at Brady and nodded.

Brady said, "He knows about it. We've got work to do before we go up to the base. You ready to go?"

"Absolutely," Jacob responded, walking around the car. "There's not much more to see up here."

Brady waved to Ben and Karl, and slid into the car and started it. He waited till Jacob was in and turned it down canyon. Jacob didn't speak.

He saw Brady's jaw set, and knew the Sheriff felt the same tension he did. Brady seemed to make a decision, and picked up the radio.

"Macey," he said.

A moment passed, then Macey responded, "Yes?"

"See if Carter is still in town," Brady said quietly. "If he is, ask him to meet me at the station. Macey, tell him to bring his baseball bat."

"Planning a game?" Macey asked, almost casually.

Brady could hear the tension in her voice.

"We're already playing," Brady said, turning the vehicle to avoid the deeper ruts at the canyon mouth. "It's our turn at bat."

There was silence at the other end of the line. Then Macey said, "I'll do it right away."

Brady smiled and said, "We're not going to let anyone get hurt."

"Good," she said.

Brady turned onto the highway and gunned the engine.

"In a hurry?" Jacob asked.

"Yes," Brady said simply. "Jacob, there is something else going on here that we're missing. I don't like not knowing the answers."

"That's why we elect you Sheriff every four years," Jacob returned. "We know you'll find the answers for us. I'm glad you're letting me help find my daughter. I need something useful to do. I need to help, Brady."

Brady was quiet for a few moments. They turned onto Cobalt Street. It seemed almost deserted. It was still Saturday morning, and early, only a little after ten. Brady thought about how much had happened since the night before, and took a deep breath.

"I'm going to ask you to trust me, Jacob," Brady said softly. "I think this will get worse before it gets better."

"I've never heard you question your own abilities before."

Jacob's voice was tense.

"My abilities might not be enough," Brady said. "I'm going to need a lot of friends."

He pulled up in front of the Sheriff's office. He pulled the radio mike off.

"Macey," he said.

"I'm here," his wife answered.

"I'm at the office," Brady returned. "Forward any phone calls here."

"Anything new?" She asked.

"No," Brady said. "I'll stay in touch."

He got out and walked to the door of the office. Jacob closed his car door and followed.

The office was built when mining was the main industry in the town. Local businesses had financed it, and built it. It was a strong building, entirely brick, mortar and concrete. The strength of the building stood as a reminder there were limits the miners, and the townspeople, could not cross.

There was one six-foot window, arched at the top that balanced the over-large door to the left. The door opened outward on large iron hinges rescued from one of the mine installations years before. The building, even the door, had an early twentieth century look. The hinges themselves cast a medieval aura over the building.

Brady pulled the door open and entered. Jacob followed him into the building.

A small waist high white fence enclosed the small area immediately inside the door. On the right, the office proper, three desks were arranged in a neat row. Two jail cells and a small office divided the back wall, separated by a narrow hallway.

The bars on the cells, like the door hinges, seemed over-large. They, too, had been rescued from one of the mining operations and pressed into service for the town.

The office was familiar to Brady. He was used to it. It was comfortable for him. He walked directly back to his office. He entered and continued toward the desk. Then he stopped. He turned slowly.

A man sat in the corner of the office. He was slouched in the chair and partially hidden by the low wall below the window. Brady raised his eyebrows, and the man smiled.

"I'm Boothe," he said softly. "That's spelled with an 'e' on the end."

Brady judged him to be mid-thirties. He was slender, dark. His hair was long, but controlled by a headband. He hadn't shaved for several days. His clothes were old and tattered, but clean. He brushed at his jeans and smiled up at the sheriff.

"Okay," Brady said, equally quietly. "Are you FDEA?"

Boothe grinned, displaying a mouth full of even white teeth. He shook his head.

"Not," he said simply. "I'm going to be in town a while. I'll be staying in the trailer on the old Sabey property. I just wanted to report in."

"Report in?" Brady asked.

"Convicted felon," Boothe returned casually. "Leavenworth. I'm on parole. They told me to stay here. Special request. I'll report to you twice a week, so there's not much for you to do except see I stay out of trouble."

"You have a job?"

"Not yet," Boothe answered. "People tend to trust me, despite my record. I'm resourceful. I'll get one. I hear the sheetrock plant up canyon is hiring. In the meantime, the rent is paid up for three months, and the cupboards are stocked. You can check with Mrs. Sabey. I have her number in Salt Lake."

"I have it too," Brady said evenly. "I'll do that. Is that trailer habitable?"

"Barely, " Boothe said. "The utilities are hooked up. It was all I could find on short notice, but it'll serve."

"What were you convicted of?"

"Desertion," Boothe answered.

"Desertion?"

"I was military, and I just walked away," Boothe answered. "The sentenced was 20 years. I served two. Good behavior. Judge didn't accept my excuse. No one would have. So, here I am. Not violent, or harmful to anyone close by. Not particularly proud of my actions, but no excuses."

"I'd like to talk to you about it," Brady said, "but today is not a good day. I'm involved with something a little complicated. I have some issues I need to address. We'll talk in a few days."

"Of course," Boothe said, rising.

He was taller than the sheriff, and his clothes were loose on his slender frame. He reached out and shook hands. His handshake was solid. For the briefest of moments their eyes met. His eyes were steady, and he seemed comfortable with the sheriff.

"I'll check you out in the meantime," Brady warned him, releasing his hand.

"My papers are on your desk," Boothe said, turning and brushing past Jacob. "You can make copies for your files, but I'd like the originals back."

"I'll see that you get them," Brady said as the man left.

Jacob followed the man with his eyes. He moved with an easy grace that belied his guilt. He was either innocent, or just didn't care. When the big wooden door closed Jacob turned to Brady.

"That was interesting," he said.

"Yah," Brady said softly, staring at the door as if the man might return. "Boothe."

He picked up the papers and gave them a quick glance, then set them aside. He rubbed his forehead absently.

Then he said, "I have a terrible feeling Remmick wanted to say something more with that rocket, Jacob. I feel like I'm missing something here."

The radio squawked. Brady pushed past Jacob and went directly to the console. He picked up the microphone.

"Brady," he said simply.

"Sheriff," Karl Rosen responded, "I think you need to get back up here. There's a helicopter circling the valley. They're raising all kinds of dust, and they're looking to land."

"Who are they?" Brady asked.

"The copter is black," Karl said evenly, "but there's 'FBI' in big white letters on both sides of the thing."

"How did they get here so quickly?" Brady asked, more to himself than to Rosen. He set the microphone on the desk and said, "How did they know where to go? They didn't talk to me or anyone else I know about, and we haven't known about this more than an hour." He keyed the mike again, and said, "Karl, I'm coming back up. I'll be there in ten minutes."

He looked up at Jacob, and said, "Stay here and watch the office. I want you to keep track of where everyone is. When I get back we're going up to the base and get our kids back."

"I'll be here."

Brady drove back up the canyon. He was still concerned the FBI knew where to go. He didn't take the road at the bottom of Taylor Canyon with the usual care. He drove quickly, and with little concern for the vehicle. There was something bad going on, beyond the issue of the kids, and he couldn't quite put his finger on what it was.

Somewhere over the ridge ahead he heard a helicopter. He was surprised they hadn't landed, and that added to his concern. Just before he got to the rise in the road at the head of the little valley the sound of the helicopter dimmed and died. He drove over the rise and saw the machine, rotors still spinning, to one side of the valley. It was black, bore the "FBI" logo on its side, just as Karl had described it. Brady was a little shaken to see it was heavily armed.

He picked up the microphone to his radio.

"Jacob," he said. There was no answer.

"Jacob, are you there?" he said again.

"If Jacob is at the office, I think he might be busy," Macey responded. "We have a helicopter on Cobalt Street right now."

"Whose?" Brady asked pointedly.

"They flew right over the house, Brady," Macey said. "I think they're FBI."

Brady breathed deeply, and said, "Keep me updated, Macey."

"Brady?" Jacob suddenly came on the air.

"What's going on?" Brady asked.

"We have FBI all over the place," Jacob said nervously. "They're taking over the office. You have a computer on your desk now. There's a helicopter outside in the street. No, there it goes! I think it's coming up to where you are. The man in charge seems to be a guy named Spritzky. Did you get that? It's been a little noisy around here for the last few minutes."

"Good work, Jacob," Brady said. He could hear the second copter behind him now. "You keep a tight rein on what's going on there. I'll be in touch soon. Be very careful, Jacob."

"Got it," Jacob said.

"Anything else I should know?"

"They're acting a little strange, Brady. They keep asking questions about you. And, they're wearing black uniforms."

Brady frowned. Jacob sounded worried, and he trusted the man's instincts.

"Did they show some credentials?" Brady asked.

"The head guy did," Jacob responded. "I didn't even have to ask. The rest have insignia on their jumpers."

Brady took that in and was quiet while he thought through all of it.

"Are you still there, Brady?" Jacob asked.

"Look, Jacob," he said softly. "I hope that they're here to help us. I want you to cooperate in any way you can. We want as many people in on this as we can get. That's how we'll get the kids back. There will be so much publicity about this that they won't dare keep the kids. Publicity. Macey, are you still listening?"

"I am."

"I want you to call the news stations in Salt Lake. I want you to tell them everything you know about what's happening here. They all have an investigative reporter, a consumer advocate who loves to dig into things like this. That's who you want to talk to. Can you do that?"

"Of course, I can," Macey said. "That should be fun. It'll give me something useful to do."

Brady heard the irony in her voice.

"Jacob, stay put, and let me know if there's anything they want from me," Brady said.

"Got it," Jacob repeated, sounding calmer.

"Gotta go," Brady said, as the second copter cleared the red cliffs behind him.

The second helicopter bore the FBI logo as well. It dropped down in the valley and landed back behind the first air ship. Eight men jumped out before the rotors had slowed. One wore a suit and tie. The rest wore black jumpsuits with an "FBI" logo over the left breast, and a larger version on their backs. They began unloading equipment. The man in the suit waved at Brady, and moved to meet him as he drove up.

Agents were all over the wreckage, sifting through pieces of old jeep and bagging and carrying off debris. Brady nodded to the man in the suit.

"I'm agent Spritzky," the man said, flashing a badge and extending his hand. "We're here to help where we can. Of course, an explosion makes this our jurisdiction now, but I don't want you to think we're pushing you out. You have valuable information we will need to conclude this investigation. And we, of course, will keep you informed every step of the way. You are Sheriff Brady, aren't you?"

Brady nodded, releasing the agent's hand, and said, "I am."

"Well, you looked a little confused," Spritzky said. "Give me a quick overview of what we have here."

Brady nodded, and said, "It's my son's vehicle."

"Stop right there," Spritzky said. "First: was anyone hurt in this accident?"

"No. The kids weren't in the vehicle when it exploded. Somehow I think you already know that."

"Well, we'll check that out," Spritzky snorted, ignoring the comment. "Second: If we find something that you don't want to know about your son, you know that we are bound to bring it out. We could be looking at a possible prison term. Do you want us to proceed?"

"What's that supposed to mean?" Brady bristled.

"Well, our experience has been that these kinds of things are usually drug or gang related," Spritzky almost hummed. "I understand you don't believe that's the situation here, but I want you to be sure you know our priorities."

"Is that a threat?"

"Relax, Sheriff," the agent said evenly. "We're here to help."

"This was done by the military," Brady replied, staring at the man a little askance. "There were no gangs or drugs involved anywhere. My only passion at this moment is to find five kids that are in the custody of a rogue military unit. When I get the kids back I'm going to return them to their families. Heaven help anyone stands in my way. Does that pretty well tell you where my priorities are?"

"Absolutely," Spritzky said softly. "You are certain, however, that you want us to continue with this investigation?"

Brady nodded and, deflating slightly, said, "Of course."

"If our investigation supports your story, then we'll help all we can," the agent crooned. "But, if we find something else, we'll have to bring that out, too. Now, is that fair enough?"

"Yes. That's crystal clear," Brady returned. "Look, I've always been too blunt for my own good. I've had my deputies look this site over. We know what's here. You aren't talking about...planting...evidence to protect the military, are you?"

"Sheriff, I wouldn't think of it," Spritzky assured him. "If the military is culpable in this incident, I am the first one who wants to know."

"Okay," Brady returned. "Then, let's get on with it."

"Good," Spritzky said. "I just wanted to be sure the air was clear between us. I think I would like to talk to your son."

"That's a little difficult right now," Brady said, frowning. "As I told you, the military has him in custody."

"I am aware of that. What makes the military think they have a jurisdictional mandate here?"

"You tell me."

"No, Sheriff. You tell me," the agent said. "I'll take notes."

He pulled out a notebook, and looked expectantly at Brady. Brady stared evenly at the man, then finally relented and gave him a brief account of what happened the night before. Spritzky listened without taking a single note, despite his pad and pen. He asked a couple of questions, but seemed totally disinterested in the details. As Brady talked, he watched men circle the site and photograph everything in the area. Others took measurements. Still more continued to bag debris and carry it to the waiting helicopters. In less than ten minutes Brady was finished, and one of the agents brought a large evidence bag up to Spritzky.

"What do we have here?" he asked, examining the fin in the bag.

"This is the only hard evidence," the agent said softly, handing Spritzky the bag. "Everything else is conjecture and speculation."

"That was in the care of one of my deputies," Brady said.

"We had to coax him to give it up," the agent said. "He's a good deputy, simply obeying orders."

"Look at that!" Spritzky said. "It's just a fragment, but it does prove someone with access to military weapons blew up your son's jeep. It might be traced. We'll take this. Are you sure this is everything?"

"We will be shortly," the agent answered.

Spritzky handed the fragment back to the agent. He wrote a quick note in his book, and turned back to Brady.

"You believe your boy is on the base, then?" Spritzky asked.

"I'm sure of it," Brady answered. "I was going up there with some of my reserve deputies to see about his release. You showed up just as I was organizing the trip. I have a feeling I should invite you to come along."

"I will," Spritzky returned. "We have some more work to do here, but let me see if I can get clearance to join your party."

"Well, don't make too much of it," Brady said evenly. "I'm going down to pick up my deputies now. I don't think there's anything more to do here."

Spritzky went to the copter and crawled up into the front. Brady could see him speaking over the radio. The conversation got a little animated a couple of times. Brady drifted toward the helicopter. None of the agents paid any attention to him. He ran his hand along the side of the machine. For a moment it brought back memories of Afghanistan, Kuwait and Iraq. He brushed the logo, and frowned. Spritzky finished with a nod, and climbed back down.

"I relayed what you've told me to my superiors," he said. "I have been authorized to be part of your group. Knowing the military, it would probably be best if we approached them by land. I don't want to have a FBI chopper shot down over a misunderstanding. My superiors have indicated it would be better if I were to take charge of this mission. You and your deputy are more than welcome to join us. I would recommend we don't take any others. We don't want anything to go wrong because someone gets a little nervous."

Brady nodded, and said, "Do you have enough men?"

"I have twelve that can be spared," Spritzky answered. "That's enough for a show of force, but not enough to be really threatening to the military. Let's drive back to town in your vehicle. My men can use a few minutes to clean up here. They'll meet us below. We'll need your car to get to the base, anyway."

Brady looked around at the men covering the explosion site, then back to Spritzky.

"Okay," Brady agreed. "Let's go."

They climbed into the patrol car, and Brady started it and drove down the canyon.

"I have a couple of questions, if you don't mind," Brady said as they drove.

"Of course," Spritzky returned.

"You seem awfully anxious to get involved with what could be construed as a local affair," Brady said. "We made a call, and you were here in two hours with over two dozen agents. You knew right where to go to find the site of the explosion without checking with anyone in the town. When we called, we didn't even know there had been an explosion. You're anxious to confront the military up at the base."

"You want to know why, and you don't know how to ask," Spritzky returned sardonically. "You wouldn't believe that we just want to help the locals protect the freedoms guaranteed by the constitution. If you did, it would be a lot easier."

Brady shook his head.

"Then let's just say that there have been some unusual activities in this area of late," Spritzky said. "It's been our assignment to try to keep tabs on what's going on and report back to our superiors. So, we've been close. As to the explosion site, well, we knew about the explosion long before you called. We knew where it was, and we were already putting together a team. Your call simply changed the timetable a little."

"How is that?"

"As I said," Spritzky returned. "We were on our way even before you called."

"That sounds like a lot of people are involved," Brady commented.

"There are enough," Spritzky acknowledged.

"This won't escalate to shooting or anything, will it?"

"No. I think I can assure you that it won't."

Brady nodded, and turned hard onto the highway. He wanted to get his son back and to get this incident behind him. But he had a bad feeling about the involvement of Spritzky and his men. Spritzky had done nothing to assuage his suspicions.

# CHAPTER 16

T he soldier stared at Cory. Thomas stepped in front of his friend, and smiled. "Cramp," he said quickly. "He gets charley horses when he hikes too much, and the hike up those cliffs a while ago was just enough to do it."

"You need to exercise more," the soldier suggested sourly.

"Sure. You want to let us go out to the track?" Cory asked.

"Not likely," the soldier said, stepping back out of the door, and slamming it.

They heard him open Toby's cell door.

Toby said quickly, "No rats in here. Sorry. I'd be happy to catch a few for you if I see any. How do you normally prepare them for lunch?"

The guard slammed the last door hard and returned to his post across the room. Sheetrock dust filtered down from the ceiling and the walls vibrated.

Thomas smiled.

"Toby's a quick thinker," Thomas whispered. He glared back at Cory. "What is the matter with you? You want to get us shot?"

"My knife," Cory whispered back, grimacing. "It's sticking in my leg. Oh, man, that hurts!"

Thomas's mouth dropped open, and he said, "What can I do?"

"Nothing," Cory stammered. "No, don't touch. Just let me do it."

He held his thigh with his left hand, and reached into his pocket with his right hand. He pulled the knife out with a quick jerk, then gingerly handed it to Thomas.

"Take this," he said, leaning back against the wall.

He unbuckled his belt, unsnapped his jeans, and peeled them down to the wound. He released the pressure, dropped the jeans, and grabbed his thigh again.

"There's no blood on the blade," Thomas whispered.

"There sure is on my hand," Cory said. He reached out and grabbed a wad of toilet paper from the roll, and raised his hand long enough to stuff the paper under it. Thomas saw the blood smeared there, and breathed deeply.

"We need to see how bad it is," he said, kneeling. "Come on. Move your hand."

Cory nodded, and released the pressure. Immediately there was a small stream of blood welling up out of a half inch slit in his thigh. Cory daubed at it with the paper, and spread the edges of the wound to let it bleed.

"Your knife wasn't sterile," he said. "Unless we want to let them know we have knives in here, we're going to have to take care of this ourselves. It's pretty small. I don't think a doctor would take the time to put a stitch in it. Here, wash it off now in the sink."

Cory nodded, hobbled to the sink, and washed his leg. Then the two of them worked out a bandage with a strip torn from the sheet on the cot and toilet paper stuffed under it to provide pressure to stop the bleeding. Cory pulled his pants up and secured them.

"Next time, close your knife," Thomas whispered, and turned to work on his wall.

Cory nodded and returned to his side of the cell. He continued to carve away at the sheetrock, and in a few seconds was able to push the panel in, and then pull it out of the hole. There was enough room between the studs to let them crawl through, but he still needed to cut through the second sheet lining Lori's cell. He started to work on it, and looked over his shoulder at Thomas. He was just pushing the first panel in on his side of the cell. They'd have access to Toby's cell soon, too.

Suddenly Lori screamed and began beating on the door.

"Oh, no," Cory groaned.

Thomas turned and sat on the floor.

"You have a great girl friend," he commented.

"She's not *my* girlfriend," Cory snapped. Then he smiled, and said, "But that gives me an idea."

"Let me out!" she repeated. "There are rats in these walls! I can hear them!"

The guards ignored her.

"Did you hear me? There are rats in the walls! If one of them bites me, my father'll sue you!"

"We went in there once," the guard said harshly. "There aren't any rats in the walls. There aren't any rat holes, either. Shut up!"

No response. Cory waited until he heard the springs on her cot squeal, and he started to cut the sheetrock again. Thomas had retreated to their cot and waited for Lori to calm down. Almost immediately Cory heard the springs on her bed creek again. He stopped.

"Lori, dear," he said loudly, "I just wanted to tell you that our date last night was really special."

He waited and held his breath. Thomas's eyes grew wide. The silence in the cells was almost complete.

After what seemed like an eternity, Lori said, "It was for me, too, Cory."

Cory winked at Thomas. He knew she got the message.

"I know you were pretty mad at me when I suggested we go up to the mines to watch the moon rise," he said.

"I was," she said softly. "I'm not anymore."

"Well, it's just that my grandfather used to work in those mines, Lori," Cory continued. "I wanted to show you some of the tunnels he'd dug himself."

"It was late, and it wasn't the tunnels you wanted to show me," she returned. "Maybe you should try again, when we get out of here."

"That's a promise," Cory said.

He glanced over his shoulder at Thomas and smiled.

"She got it!" he whispered.

He went back to work on the wall and in a few seconds, Lori was helping him pull the piece out of the wall into her cell. She poked her head through and whispered, "Hi, guys!"

"You nearly ruined it!" Cory whispered.

"Next time you plan an escape let me know ahead of time," Lori returned sharply. "You nearly scared me to death!"

Thomas let his breath out slowly, and turned to work on Toby's wall. The outer door opened again, and he heard Remmick's voice. He jumped on the cot, and Cory pushed Lori back into her cell.

"Stand in front of the hole," he whispered.

She nodded, and he stood, concealing the hole he'd created. Thomas piled the blanket up on the end of the cot to hide the hole he'd been digging through the sheetrock.

"We're ready to leave," Remmick said to the guards. "We'll take the boy with us in the first copter. The second will be loaded with our equipment. The third will be ready to go in less than half an hour. The other three will go in that one, with you. I don't want anyone talking to them. You are personally responsible for getting them to me. Open the door, and let's get the alien."

They opened the door to Toby's cell, and there was the sound of a scuffle.

"We have your sister," Remmick said coldly. "We are going to take you to where she is. How you get there is up to you. You can arrive in good shape if you behave. If not, well, that's your choice. Now, you may not care for yourself, but do try to think of her. So, how is it going to be? Easy or painful?"

Toby said quietly, "Easy, I guess."

"Good choice," Remmick said. "At least you understand English. Bring him along."

Cory realized immediately that Toby had deliberately distracted Remmick's attention. Remmick didn't check on them, so their attempt to escape was still hidden. Thomas checked the office, and saw it was empty. All the guards had gone with Remmick to guard Toby.

"Why would they need so many men to guard one boy?" he asked.

He jumped to the wall. In seconds all three of them were crawling through into the cell Toby had vacated. The door to his cell had been left ajar!

They scooted across the floor as quietly as they could. Cory opened the outer door just a crack. They peered out through the slit. Many of the soldiers were climbing aboard a large copter just outside the hangar doors. They could see Toby inside the sliding door, his face masked with fear. Remmick sat between the boy and the door, his hands busy with Toby's wrists.

Cory felt a surge of anger as he realized the major was handcuffing Toby to himself.

A second copter was being loaded with boxes. A third, smaller than the other two, was still being fueled. Two escort ships were preparing to take off, ostensibly to guard the major and his prisoner in the larger ship. Two men were peeling large white letters off the side of one of the machines.

They pulled a large white "F" off, carefully peeling it down, and threw it on the ground.

"We need to get into that ship," Cory pointed at the cargo ship.

"No," Thomas said quietly. "We need to get back to town."

"If we do make it back," Cory said softly, "then we won't have a clue where Toby is. They can deny ever having heard of him. This is the government, Thomas. They can do whatever they want."

Thomas said quietly, "Maybe we should split up. Some of us go down to the town; the others get aboard the cargo carrier."

"We can't split up now, Thomas," Cory said. "We have to stick together. We have to try to help Toby!"

Thomas thought a moment. Cory was making sense, but he still had a bad feeling about it.

"Okay. That ship," he said finally.

The hangar was emptying rapidly. The three fugitives slid out of the office, and crawled along the line of Hummers toward the hangar doors. They hid behind a haphazard pile of empty boxes and watched the almost frantic activity outside. The soldiers in black seemed to be in a hurry. Toby sat in the larger ship. He looked alone and frightened. Remmick sat next to him with a satisfied smile playing across his face. The boy was now firmly chained to the major. They could see Captain Ferris across the tarmac. An armed escort stood next to him watching the proceedings.

Cory shuddered, and said, "They don't really care who they hurt."

"Maybe if we could get to Ferris, we'd have a chance," Thomas said.

"You heard them argue. He doesn't have the authority to take us back from Remmick."

"He hates Remmick. He'd try if we gave him half a chance," Thomas argued.

"Then Toby would be gone," Cory said. "Same result. We have to follow Toby, and we have to try to do it without losing our freedom to act."

Thomas nodded, and knew Cory was right. There seemed to be something wrong with his logic, but he couldn't see what it was.

Two guards walked back toward them. The three scrambled to stay hidden behind the boxes. The guards passed on by without any indication they knew they were there. For the moment they felt safe. Cory could hear one of the copters revving up for takeoff.

"We have to get out there," Cory repeated. "We'll lose our ride if we don't."

"Right," Thomas returned, speaking louder now because of the noise. "But, how?"

"Maybe we could help," a voice from behind them said loudly.

They turned to face the muzzles of two M-16s. The guards leered down at them over the top of the rifle sights.

# CHAPTER 17

B rady pulled up in front of his office, and got out of his car. The agent, Spritzky, got out, too. Brady stared at the painted area marked off in the middle of the street. An agent stood at each corner protecting it. They were directing cars to turn around and find other routes. The street was blocked off. He shook his head in disbelief.

"It looks like a war zone," he said softly, addressing Spritzky. "I know this is important for you, for whatever reasons. I don't really care as long as I get my son back. But the town still has to live, in the meantime. I don't suppose you could move those things out of the street."

"We won't be here long enough for it to be an issue," Spritzky said smoothly. "For the moment we need to keep things as compact as possible."

"There's the park two blocks that way," Brady suggested.

"No. There are some tall light poles that don't look too substantial," the agent said. "They might blow over and that would cause you more grief than just rerouting your traffic for a few minutes."

"You're right. How about the schoolyard at the end of the block? No one will be there till Monday, and we could post reserve deputies to keep the grounds clear for you."

"We probably wouldn't feel comfortable with your deputies guarding our equipment, Sheriff," Spritzky said. "I don't want to be difficult. I really don't want to be. We'll stay here for the moment. I thank you for your concern, however. Now, I have some things to go over with my men. I'll meet you inside."

Brady nodded slowly, and went in. He stopped to study the thing his office had turned into. There were boxes everywhere, and a computer on his desk. An agent was busy using the keyboard. He looked up, and nodded to the Sheriff. Several others were running wires across the floor.

"I'm afraid your land lines are tied up," the agent said. "I'm on line with Washington right now and, for some reason, the computer seems to have eaten up both your incoming lines. That can happen when we're setting up a remote office like this."

"Not surprising," Brady returned sardonically.

He turned and immediately bumped into another one of the agents.

"Excuse me," he said softly, reaching down to pick up the pencil he'd dropped.

"No problem," the agent said, moving on.

Brady found the microphone for the radio on the floor next to the desk. He keyed the mike, and said, "Macey, are you there?"

He waited a full minute before Macey responded.

"What's going on down there?" she asked. "I've been trying to call but both lines are constantly busy."

"The phone lines are down, Macey," Brady told her. "I'm back in town now. We're going to go up and get the kids in a few minutes. The FBI people will go with me. I don't think the military will be able to hold them any longer."

He gripped the microphone tighter and prayed she'd believe him.

"Good," Macey said softly. "I've been trying to call Salt Lake like you asked, and I can't get an outside line. Long distance seems to be completely tied up. That's pretty strange, isn't it, Brady?"

Brady glanced at Spritzky, who'd just entered the office.

Spritzky held up his hands and said, "That's not us. We only disrupted your office lines."

Brady nodded, and said to Macey, "Keep trying. I'm going to get the kids now."

"You be careful, though."

"You know me," Brady said.

"I know you. That's why I told you to be careful."

"I will," Brady returned. "Karl, are you out there?"

"Just coming out of the canyon now, Boss. Ben's with me."

"Get down here. We're going to need your vehicle."

"I'm on my way," Karl returned.

Brady set the microphone on his desk, and turned to Jacob.

"Your truck would be helpful," he said. "We want to take as many deputies up there as we can."

"If I go, you can use it," Jacob said firmly.

Brady shook his head, and said, "I don't think-"

"This isn't going to be a shootout," Spritzky said quickly. "I just don't want anyone along who might turn it into one. Bennett, wasn't it? You come along. After all, it's your daughter up there, too. However, we might want to limit our party to a couple of deputies and my men."

He turned away and began to organize some of the men. Brady heard the helicopter landing outside. He motioned to Jacob.

"None of this makes a lot of sense," he said quietly. "Just be very careful what you say around these guys, okay?"

"What's wrong?"

"Maybe nothing," Brady said. "I just get the feeling that these guys aren't what they appear to be."

"You mean you don't think they're FBI?"

"I don't know, but if they are, they're not exactly regulation," Brady said. "Just be careful."

Karl and Ben came in, and the down draft from the helicopter nearly yanked the heavy door out of Karl's hands. Papers in the office flew everywhere. He struggled with the door, and shut it.

"The copter is back," he said.

"I know," Brady returned. "Come over here."

Karl came close, and Ben moved in closer, too.

"I want you to drive my cruiser up to the base, Karl. You'll follow me. Jacob will follow you with his truck. There will be four in your car, including the agents, and four in mine. We can get four in Jacob's truck, two in front and two in back. Even one extra deputy with us will be a comfort. These...agents...want this to be a closed party with just me and them. I don't think that ought to happen. Ben, if you don't mind, I'd like you to stay here and watch the office. I need to be able to keep in touch with the town. Now, listen very carefully."

He repeated the same warning he'd given to Jacob. Karl responded with the same questions, and Brady was quiet for a moment. The men stood, puzzled looks on their faces.

"Their helicopters have logos on them," he said softly, "but they're military helicopters. They're fully armed. And the logos are vinyl. They peel off."

"You're kidding," Karl snapped.

"I deliberately bumped into one of the agents a few minutes ago," Brady continued. "This fell off."

He held out a cloth patch with the FBI logo on it. The agents all had them over the left breast pocket. The one in Brady's hand had Velcro on the back.

Jacob grew angry and started to turn.

Ben said softly, "They're spending a lot of time setting up that computer, Sheriff. If I'm right, it'll never work. They've got it all hooked up wrong."

"What do you mean?" Karl asked.

"It looks to me like they've deliberately disconnected the phone lines," Ben said softly. "And the computer isn't connected to the phone lines. It seems to be completely stand-alone. The communication port isn't connected to anything. The wire just trails off across the office. And they don't need all that wire. It's just a ploy to waste time and look busy."

"I agree. However, it doesn't matter who they are," Brady said quickly, "or what they're doing as long as we get the kids back. I mean all the kids, including Tobias and his sister. That's what we want, isn't it?"

Jacob nodded vehemently, and Karl said, "Right."

"Good. Ben, if I'm right as soon as we leave all these others will get on board a helicopter and leave as well. They'll head up Taylor Canyon and circle way around to arrive at the base unseen. If that happens, key the microphone and tell me anything you want about the Jeep wreckage. Got that? You other two, I just wanted you to know what was happening. Remember our goal is to get the kids back. Nothing else matters. Just be careful. Okay?"

Brady looked at the cloth logo, and examined it carefully. He didn't feel good about anything that was happening now.

"Just keep this to yourself until we get the kids back," he reminded them. "Remember: All we want is the kids. Let's go."

He shoved the insignia into his pocket as he walked toward the door. He was more worried than he had been the night before. Things were moving more rapidly than he ever could have imagined. The whole world was looking differently than it had 24 hours before. He glanced back at his men. They were all following him.

They went out and found the vehicles already loading. Brady got in, with Spritzky riding next to him. The back was packed with three agents.

"I apologize if it's a bit cramped," Brady said, pulling away from the curb and turning around.

The copter was an imposing beast in the middle of the main street. He didn't like the airship in the middle of town, especially considering his dark feelings about the men that surrounded him now. If he was right the remaining 'agents' in town would board the copter and be gone a few minutes after they left.

"The men have had to put up with much less comfortable accommodations," Spritzky returned. "In any case, it's only seventeen minutes to the main gate of the base. We'll be there before they have time to be uncomfortable."

Brady looked at him, and nodded. He drove the road out the west end of town in silence. He continued to think about everything the man had said.

They passed the stream where they'd confronted the military unit the night before. The mire was marred by deep muddy tracks from the hummers. He glanced at Spritzky and though he saw a wry smile curl his lips. He took a deep breath.

"Sheriff," the radio blared. "Are you there?"

Brady picked up the microphone, and said, "I'm here, Ben. Did you need something?"

"Yes. Look, I just wanted to tell you the blast pattern around your son's Jeep indicates he was almost empty. There wasn't much of a secondary explosion. I don't think he had any gas in that thing. He may not have even had enough to get him back down the canyon."

"Thanks, Ben," the Sheriff said, and glanced at Spritzky. "He's always been careless about his fuel reserves. I appreciate the information."

He felt his stomach tighten.

Spritzky said, "Your men are thorough."

"They are," Brady said, turning on the dirt road leading up to the weather station.

A black Hummer was parked across the road, blocking access to the base. Brady pulled up short, and looked at Spritzky. The large man climbed out of the car.

"Come with me," he said.

Together they approached the black vehicle. Brady was a little uncomfortable in the company of the FBI agent. One of the soldiers approached them. He thought he saw a look of recognition wash over the soldiers' face. As quickly as it was there, it was gone. He stiffened and nodded as if to greet them.

"We're going up to see the commander of this base," Spritzky said simply. "I am with the FBI. Here is my identification."

He turned and started back toward the sheriff's car. Brady stood easily beside the door. This was the first test of the agent's authority.

"I'm sorry," the guard said easily, "but we're engaged in top secret exercises up there. We're not allowing anyone access at this time."

"You check with your commander," Spritzky said, turning back toward the soldier. "He'll clear us. We can wait."

"But not too long," Brady murmured.

"I'll check on this, sir," the soldier said, "but I can assure you there isn't much chance. Our instructions were clear."

"You do whatever you have to do," the agent said evenly.

The soldier went back to the Hummer and took the radio microphone out. There was a lengthy conversation. Brady stretched to try to hear what was being said, but was too far away. The soldier, sensing his interest, turned his back and continued talking. He seemed to be answering questions and giving information. Finally, after what seemed a long time he read the identification over the microphone. Then he nodded, and replaced the microphone. He walked almost casually back to them and handed the identification back to the agent.

"You are cleared to go up," he said. "We'll move the vehicle."

At his signal, one of the soldiers started the Hummer and pulled it back. Spritzky looked over at Brady, smiled and raised his eyebrows. Then he got into the squad car.

Brady climbed back in, and rammed the gear lever into drive. They had wasted nearly 15 minutes at the checkpoint. He believed more than ever Spritzky wasn't with the FBI. They started up the dirt road.

The first quarter mile was rough, but once they passed the "no trespassing" sign the road was well cared for, and almost pavement smooth. It seemed as though the first section was deliberately roughed up to discourage casual sightseers. They climbed across the face of the cliffs of the mesa. Near the top they turned into a gully, originally a gash cut by water flow from the mesa above. They drove up what amounted to a steep ramp. The road leveled suddenly as they crested the top of the mesa. A gate barred their progress a hundred feet ahead.

It was a perfect place to put the gate. Anyone trying to gain access would be stopped by the steep walls of the gully. There was nowhere to go except back, or straight ahead. And a few well-armed soldiers could hold off an army.

Brady noted the tracks of a number of vehicles joining the road from the right. The tracks went across the mesa and up into the lower foothills to the east. Not every vehicle climbed the cliff road to gain access to the base.

The soldiers here were in regulation fatigues. Two were outside the gate, four inside, and another two inside a guard shack on the right of the gate. A second gate barred access a hundred feet inside the first. There were four soldiers there, as well.

Brady noted damage on the guard shack, and the wires tied off to the mast. Make-shift repairs had been made to them. He realized with a jolt that they had been shot apart. There were bullet holes across the top of the shack. The holes were concentrated at the point the wires were damaged. The destruction looked fresh and deliberate. Certainly the repairs to the wires were only stop-gap recently completed.

The agent stepped from the vehicle and approached the guards, just as he had before. He spoke quietly, extended his identification as before, and, as before, the soldier accepted the credentials, and passed it to the men in the guard shack. One of them immediately picked up a microphone and spent several minutes speaking.

Brady stood by the door as Spritzky walked back toward him. He could hear several helicopters warming up. They were very close, but he couldn't tell exactly where the sound was coming from. He stood patiently. Spritzky merely smiled at him.

A moment later a soldier, wearing fatigues, drove up to the inside gate in an Air Force Jeep. Brady reflected at how normal Air Force blue seemed after all the black vehicles he'd seen since last night. When the other soldiers turned to speak to him he held up his hand and shook his head. He parked at the center of the gate, and sat in the vehicle silently. He seemed to be waiting for something.

Brady took a deep breath, wondering what kind of hurdle the newcomer was going to provide for them.

"This may take some time," Spritzky said reassuringly, glancing at the new arrival. "They just don't seem to be in much of a hurry. It is just a matter of time, however. My authority comes from the highest level."

Brady suddenly frowned, and said, "I've heard that before."

Spritzky just shrugged, and said, "I can assure you we'll get in."

"Spritzky, what's going on around here?" Brady asked suddenly. "You're not FBI, are you?"

Spritzky looked amused, and said, "What makes you think that?"

The sound of the helicopters suddenly grew very loud, and Brady looked up to see a convoy passing overhead. The airships were black. He felt a shiver run down his back.

"It's you," he said simply. "You don't follow normal procedure. You got past the black guards below without any trouble, but they took their time. We're wasting more time here. I've been up here before, and my uniform and ID has been enough to get me in almost immediately. The uniforms your men wear are black. You were smart enough to put FBI logos on them, but you weren't smart enough to put them on permanently. The copters you fly have peel off logos on them as well. And the FBI doesn't arm their helicopters like yours are armed."

He pulled the logo out and held it so Spritzky could see it, but not close enough so he could take it.

"This fell off one of your 'agents'. Your phrasing about certain things is identical to the way Remmick talked last night," Brady continued. "You knew it was Jacob's daughter that was in custody. I didn't tell you that. You knew the distance between the town and this base, and you've supposedly never been here before. Now, I'm going to ask you again: What's going on?"

"Nothing you could do anything about," Spritzky said, growing suddenly very cold and advancing toward the sheriff.

"Sir!" the guard from the gate shouted at him.

He smiled grimly, turned on his heel and walked to the gate. The guard said something, shaking his head emphatically. Spritzky only nodded confirmation, and took his credentials back. He dropped them in his pocket. Then he walked back to Brady and stood menacingly in front of him.

"This part of the game is over," he said. "I want you and your men out of the vehicles. We'll be taking them back down to the highway. We have a flight to catch."

"No," Brady said evenly, feeling his anger rise, "you can walk back down."

Spritzky raised his hand, and the men were out of the vehicles, all weapons aimed at the drivers. Brady raised both hands immediately.

"Take them," he said quickly. "Take them. Jacob. Karl. Get out and let them have the vehicles. Quickly."

Karl was out fast, keeping his hands raised in the air. Jacob was slower, but didn't bother to raise his. He glared at the agent who slid into the driver's seat of his truck.

Spritzky slid into the driver's seat of the sheriff's car and the doors started to close behind him. He smiled coldly at Brady.

"What was all this about?" Brady asked. "Why all this charade?"

"To keep you busy," Spritzky answered. "You already figured that out. There was an added bonus. You now have no evidence. In fact, your son's vehicle is buried where no one will ever find it again."

"If you didn't want anyone to know, why did you blow it up in the first place?"

"Major Remmick wanted to send a clear message," Spritzky answered smoothly. "Did you get the message, Sheriff?"

"I got two messages," Brady said evenly. "The first was that Remmick has no honor. He only looks at the end, never at the cost."

"And the second?" Spritzky asked.

"That he's afraid of someone," Brady answered. "With all your bravado, so are you. Now tell me: Where is my son?"

"He's up there right now," Spritzky said, pointing to the western sky. "He was in that convoy you saw. We just needed to give them time to get off the tarmac."

"Where are they taking the kids?" Brady demanded.

"Sorry. That's classified. He'll be returned, though, in a while. We don't really want him. We don't want the other teens, for that matter."

"That begs the question," Brady said angrily.

"Perhaps to keep them busy, too," Spritzky returned. "I don't really know. Maybe they know something. Maybe they don't know they know something. It's all part of the game, Sheriff. But if our leader is right, the two brats from the crash site could be worth millions for each one of us!"

Brady reached through the window and grabbed Spritzky's tie. He yanked him hard against the window. Overhead a single helicopter circled and headed west.

"I'm not amused, Spritzky," Brady snarled as two guns were immediately pointed at his face from inside the car. "All this was for *money*?"

"What else is there?" Spritzky said. "Sheriff, I would be very careful right now, because I promise you my men will shoot to kill."

"I'll make you a promise, Spritzky," Brady said. "If anything happens to my son, or any one of those kids, I'll come looking for you and I'll kill you. I swear I will!"

"You're getting a little close to the edge, Sheriff," the man said quietly. "One word from me and you're a dead man."

Brady breathed deeply. He struggled to control his anger. He let the man go.

"I mean it," he said evenly.

"I'm sure you do," Spritzky said, smiling again. "You just saved your life, Sheriff."

He nodded, then backed the car up against the embankment and turned to follow the other vehicles down the gully.

Brady stood with Jacob and Karl alone in front of the gate to the base. He suddenly felt hollow, empty. He'd known there was something going on, but he hadn't expected it to end this quickly and with such finality.

The soldiers stood as if not knowing exactly what to do. Brady walked toward the guard, and the guard stepped back.

"That's close enough, sir," he said firmly, bringing his rifle up to a ready position.

It was enough to scare Brady. He stepped back, and looked from Jacob to Karl. They were having as much trouble accepting what had just happened as he was. He watched the last of the vehicles, his own patrol car, disappear around the edge of the gully.

"Is the whole blessed military in on this conspiracy?" Brady snarled at the guards.

"They're gone, sir," the soldier shouted back through the gate.

"Not everyone is in on the conspiracy, sir!" The soldier in the jeep shouted. "Captain Ferris wants to speak with you. Soldier! Get them in here now!"

The soldiers moved quickly, and began opening the gates. Brady stood still for only a moment.

"Get up here now, sir," the soldier shouted. "We don't have a lot of time."

Brady dodged the gate posts, but approached the jeep and the soldier cautiously. Jacob and Karl were close behind.

The soldier breathed deeply, and said, "You don't have a reason in the world to trust me. But I just got you in this base, and I've been ordered to take you to my commanding officer. We are regulation; the group you have been dealing with commandeered our base two weeks ago. Captain Ferris has been doing everything possible to find out who they are and where their authority comes from. He's had no success. They're gone now, and we can act, but we don't have much time. Please, get in."

Brady nodded, and jumped in the front. Jacob and Karl climbed in the back.

The soldier backed the jeep away from the gate, off the road into the cedars, then slammed it in first gear and roared onto the road and toward the compound.

"I'm Sergeant Ryan Nichols," the soldier said. "I can tell you a few things you don't already know. Your children were brought to this base earlier this morning. They were taken aboard that helicopter convoy a few minutes ago."

"Where are they going?" Brady asked.

"Unknown," Nichols responded. "However, Captain Ferris can give you more information. I was told to tell you everything I knew for sure, but to defer to him on the things I didn't."

Brady was familiar with the base. He'd come up to spend time with the commanding officers before. They seemed to change at regular intervals. He'd not met Captain Ferris.

The base hadn't changed in the eight years since he'd first been invited to tour it. The hangar on the right was the same, and the rocks lining the road hadn't changed. He breathed deeply and wondered, fleetingly, what else this day could offer. It wasn't even noon.

"Over there," the soldier said, turning toward a building and slamming on the brakes.

The soldier climbed from the jeep, and waited. Brady followed, glanced back to see Karl and Jacob still close behind. They walked up to the officer waiting on what was a close imitation of a sidewalk.

"Thank you, Sergeant," the officer said. "You're Sheriff Brady. I talked with you earlier. I'm Captain Adrian Ferris. Now, hold on. I understand your problem, and I am working to solve it. First, we have to talk."

"First let's get my son and the other kids," Brady said evenly. "Then we'll talk."

"That's impossible at the moment," Captain Ferris returned. "They are no longer here. The helicopters you saw a few moments ago took them away. However, the welfare of your children is top priority. I'm doing everything I can to get them back."

"Where were they taken?" Brady snapped, advancing on the Captain.

"I don't know, but I've been working on this situation since our phone conversation this morning. It would be better if you just trusted me for now. We could work more quickly if we worked together. You and your friends come to my office and we'll see what we can do."

"We've been helped all morning, Captain," Brady said evenly. "I'm afraid we're a little tired of the help we've been getting. What do you have to offer?"

"I'm sorry I wasn't there to help before," the captain returned apologetically. "I was doing what I could, Sheriff. I tried to keep the kids off base so you could recover them. That failed, so I tried to keep them here. I'm sorry that failed, too. I'm sorry about all this. It's bad business all the way around. However, I'm not out of options yet, and neither are you."

Brady turned to Jacob, and said, "They're gone. This officer wants us to trust him after all we've seen the last few hours."

"I do wish you would," the Captain said. "I have access to resources that could be of service. Now, I'm going to tell you something I shouldn't, but I believe you have a right to know. We have a serious problem with a military faction that seems to report to no one. I've been working around the clock for several weeks to find their chain of command. I've been unsuccessful so far.

"This... faction... believes they have a mandate that allows them broad latitude to complete their mission. That includes arresting and imprisoning civilians when they believe it's necessary."

"Just what is their mission?" Brady asked. "Kidnapping children? Spritzky, the man masquerading as FBI said they expected to collect millions for each of them. Is it ransom they're after? Nobody in my town has that kind of money!"

"No. It's not ransom," the Captain said quietly. "They want to acquire, and retain a bona-fide UFO. From what you just told me, they expect to sell such a vehicle and its occupants, whether dead or alive. They think they shot one down last night up on the ridge about eight miles east of here. They believe at least one of the boys they imprisoned here today, and the little girl they captured last night, was on that craft."

Brady stared at Jacob, and together they said, "Tobias."

# CHAPTER 18

The guards hadn't been fooled. Cory rose slowly, helping Lori up. One M-16 in the hands of a psychotic militant would have worried him, but two made his stomach quiver. He was more aware than he had ever been before that a small slip of a finger could end their lives. He shuddered involuntarily, but managed to keep a blank face.

Thomas stood, raising his hands above his head.

"Be real careful, guys," he said softly. "We won't give you any trouble."

The guards smiled.

"Right idea," one said. "You know where the cells are."

They marched back to the cells. They heard the helicopters leave the pad. Cory breathed deeply, and glanced at Lori and Thomas. They knew Toby was gone.

The guards pushed Lori into Toby's cell.

"It looks like you've found a way to get around in there, so pick the one that suits you. You two stop where you are."

Cory and Thomas turned toward the guard.

"Over here, hands against the wall."

One guard stood with his rifle pointed at them, the other proceeded to search them, one at a time. He found their knives, keys, and the little bit of money they each carried. He got their wallets, and their watches. He turned their pockets inside out, and left them standing against the wall.

"Well, I certainly feel silly," Cory said.

"You'll feel a lot worse if you try that again," the guard said harshly. "Now, get in the cell. And behave yourselves."

"You can't be that angry," Thomas said evenly as they pushed him toward the cells. "After all, the first order of business for a prisoner of war is the escape."

The soldier sneered, and said, "You're not a prisoner of war. We will shoot you if you try that again."

They felt the door slam behind them. The walls rattled, and dust filtered down from the ceiling. Lori sat on the edge of the cot, tears in the corners of her eyes. Thomas turned toward the door, and slammed his fist against it. Cory only smiled.

"They took everything," Thomas said grumbled.

"Not everything," Cory responded, whispering.

He smiled, and carefully pulled a pair of fingernail clippers out of his mouth. He displayed the prize to the other two.

"You're insane," Thomas whispered hoarsely. "You're going to get us killed!"

Even with his protest, Thomas felt a resurgence of pride. The clippers were more than just a means to escape. They were a symbol of their individuality, independence and defiance. Cory had managed to retain something that belonged to them.

"Relax," Cory said. "I don't care how secret their operation is, they won't kill us. They can't afford the paper work or the investigation. They know your dad is looking for us right now, and they know he won't stop until he finds us."

"Mine won't stop, either," Lori said adamantly.

"Right," Cory said, "and neither will mine. The point is it's our duty to try to get out of here, just like you said. You watch them. When they're gone, let me know."

"It's comforting to know our safety lies in the paperwork," Thomas said sardonically, and peered out the slot in the metal door.

The guards were already gone. It was as if they didn't believe they could escape again, or that they were daring them to try. He nodded back to Cory. Cory opened the clippers and started to wear a line into the outside wall of the cell with the lever of the clippers. True to form, the outside wall was sheetrock, too. They hoped it would be their path to freedom. It was a lot slower than the knife, but it was working.

"They're back," Thomas choked out suddenly, stepping back from the door as quickly as he could.

"Let's go, children," the guard said almost casually, unlocking the cell door.

Cory barely had time to stand up. The guard threw the door open and took only a second to assess the work Cory had done on the wall. He made no attempt to hide his anger. He held out his hand, and Cory backed up a step. The guard became enraged immediately.

"Look, little boy, you have never been through a strip search before," he said savagely. "We take your clothes and examine them one inch at a time. Then we explore every body cavity you have, and we do it right in front of your friends. We've been trained in this procedure, and we are very good at it. You make the choice, but do it quickly. We have a flight to catch."

Cory was angry, but, after a moment, relented. He stepped forward and laid the clippers in the guard's hand. The guard tossed them behind him angrily. They clattered across the concrete floor.

"Anything else?" he asked.

Cory shook his head submissively.

"What about you two? You have as much to lose as he does."

"Nothing," Thomas assured the guard.

"Just this," Lori said, pulling a rat-tail comb and a nail file out of her pocket and handing them to the guard.

The guard held up the nail file, and said, "This is a lethal weapon. We've been trained to kill with less."

He threw them behind him. They bounced across the floor to join the clippers.

Then he said, "Your ride is ready. We'd have tried to escape, too, children. We would have succeeded. I don't want any more foolishness, do you understand?"

"You're as bad as your boss," Thomas muttered.

"And you're in my custody," the guard snarled. "Don't forget either of those facts. You know where the copter is."

Cory nodded, and walked past the guards holding Lori's hand. Thomas followed them. They were ushered out of the hangar. It had become almost totally deserted in the few minutes they'd been in the cell. The helicopter's rotors were already revving up.

Captain Ferris still stood across the tarmac. Cory wondered what he was watching for. He looked toward them, and, Cory was sure, made eye contact. But the message eluded him. The Captain looked away, toward one of his escorts. He began to carry on an animated conversation with the man. Almost immediately the soldier left at a run, and headed down the dirt street toward one of the buildings. He secured a Jeep, one painted traditional Air Force blue, and drove away at a high rate of speed. Cory felt a sharp nudge in his back and picked up his pace.

They all ducked as they approached the 'copter. They climbed up in back with seven or eight other soldiers, all in the black uniform. The guards followed them in. The door slid shut with a sickening finality. The guard signaled with his thumb that they were ready to go. As the copter lifted off the tarmac, soldiers on either side of them strapped them into the safety harnesses.

The flight immediately promised to be boring. Cory couldn't see out the windows, except for occasional view of the ground when the copter banked hard. He couldn't even tell which way they were headed, though he had a vague feeling they were flying west. The soldiers settled back. They seemed ready for a long flight. Their guards relaxed some, but still kept a wary eye on the three. They were almost a half hour into the flight before anyone spoke.

"You left our stuff back there," Cory accused.

Thomas knew he was just trying to break the monotony. He tried to catch Cory's attention, but Cory was staring intently at the guard who had searched them. It didn't matter. The guard didn't respond.

"You left my watch and my wallet," Cory repeated. "If they get lost, I'm going to hold you personally responsible."

The guard still ignored him.

Cory shrugged, and said, "He's deaf, guys."

The soldier Cory had spoken to said quietly, "You ought to remain silent. It's a long drop out that side door. No one would ever find you. Major Remmick would give me a medal."

The rest of the flight was in silence. Cory exchanged glances with Lori as often as he could. He was worried about her. She seemed constantly on the verge of tears. She sat, most of the time, with her face buried in her hands.

Thomas leaned his head back against the wall of the copter and tried to sleep. At least, his eyes were closed. He wanted to respond to Cory, but he didn't know what the guards would do. Besides, there was nothing he wanted to say in front of the guards.

Nearly two hours later Cory felt a change in their flight attitude. He could see mountains coming up in the windows, and knew they were lower to the ground than they had been. They flew like that for about a half hour, changing direction frequently, and changing altitude at irregular intervals. He could feel the copter climb or drop down. Sometimes the course or altitude changes were sudden and dramatic. Then, abruptly the copter dropped straight down. Cory felt his stomach roll over. Lori and Thomas felt the same thing. There was a bump and a settling as they touched down. The flight was over.

The soldiers got up. Both sides of the copter opened, and the soldiers filed out, jumping down under the still-rotating blades of the machine. Cory felt the strong hand of his guard guiding him to the tarmac. The hand never left his shoulder even as they jumped. He stood in the bright sunlight and looked around.

He felt like he'd stepped into an oven. The heat was oppressive. His eyes adjusted to the bright sunlight and their surroundings began to swim into view.

Five Hummers were on the tarmac directly ahead of them, all black, all identical to the ones they'd dealt with back home. Beyond the Hummers a hodge-podge of buildings marched across the flat land. He saw several satellite dishes some associated with buildings, others standing on their own. Behind them the land rose toward black, razor sharp mountains. To the right the black ground gave way to flat white sand that stretched a couple of miles toward low, harsh mountains. To the left the tarmac ran toward huge hangars. He thought he could count four. The heat made the buildings and landscape beyond seem to swim in an almost fluid dance.

Ahead, and directly around the buildings, roads seemed to have been laid out in a haphazard manner. Left, beyond the hanger, were more mountains, rocky and black as the ones to the right, but closer and more forbidding. The only green seemed to be a few sparse Joshua trees dotting the landscape.

One soldier nudged him toward the vehicles. He glanced back, blinking. The soldier's face was expressionless.

He realized he lost sight of both Lori and Thomas. He turned, desperately searching for them. He suddenly caught sight of them to his right. They were being herded toward the vehicles. They were being separated. Cory felt fear grip his stomach. The realization they were far from home was just beginning to sink in.

The heat bounced off the concrete as he was pushed toward the open vehicle door. He crawled into the dark interior of the Humvee. The soldier behind him slammed the door. He realized the vehicle was air conditioned, and he sat back and let the cool air wash over him. He'd begun to perspire heavily in the few minutes they'd stood on the tarmac.

It was too dark to see the interior at first, but the darkened windows allowed an almost unobstructed view outside. The helicopters were on the tarmac in a close group. The one they'd flown in still had it's doors open as soldiers unloaded equipment. The others, he hoped, were the ones that had taken Toby away.

Maybe, he hoped, Toby was here, too. Maybe they would be reunited.

He could see the flat valley stretch out beyond over what must have once been a lake. The imposing mountains rose on the far side. He realized that, where ever they were, they were completely isolated.

The cool air inside the vehicle was welcome. Cory struggled to make out as much detail about the base around them as he could. He had no doubt the base was military. He was totally disoriented. He had no idea which way was north. The sun was almost directly overhead and offered no help whatsoever.

He tried to look out the back window to see the vehicles Lori and Thomas had been pushed into. The black windows precluded seeing inside, especially in the bright sunlight. He turned back around and sighed.

The Hummer suddenly filled with three soldiers, one in each of the remaining seats. The one who assumed the driver seat snapped the seatbelt with familiarity and ease, as did the other two soldiers. Cory immediately fumbled with his own restraint trying to get it fastened. He remembered the ride earlier that day.

The vehicle suddenly lurched forward and sped across the tarmac. A quick glance assured Cory the other Hummers were following in line.

They jogged slightly left and popped out on a concrete roadway. Cory recognized it as an airplane taxi way. He was not surprised. The base had a long runway running at an angle to the path they were on barely a quarter mile to the left. They followed the taxi-way a short distance past the hangars he'd seen, then jogged to the right, then left and onto a road facing a number of buildings on the right, still traveling the same direction. They approached a larger, rather important looking building. Cory could see some kind of insignia on the font, but before they got to an angle he could read what it said the Humvee lurched to the right and darted down a roadway between the buildings.

Parking lots bordered most buildings. More hangars lined the runway on the right. Soldiers in uniform, along with a few civilians, stopped to watch them pass. Some seemed to show open animosity. Whatever the base was, whatever its purpose, Remmick's unit didn't seem to be any more welcome than they had been up on the mesa back home. Cory felt both cheered and worried about that.

They reached the end of the narrow roadway. Without stopping or slowing the driver turned left. If he was correct, Cory felt they were traveling the same direction they'd begun a few short minutes before. They were passing a large building on the right, and smaller buildings on the left. The latter appeared to be barracks of some kind. They were laid out in neat rows, each long and narrow and identical to the building next to it. There were more than he cared to count.

They reached the end of the new road, and the Humvee lurched right, then left almost immediately. The quick jog in the road threw Cory off balance and he banged his head against the door window. If the soldiers noticed it, they paid no attention.

They passed several more rows of barracks on the left, a couple of buildings on the right. Then, ahead, three dark buildings, lined up at right angles to the barracks, drifted into view. They were surrounded by a high chain link fence. From the glass isolators top and bottom Cory guessed the fence was electrified. They turned off the main road and pulled to a gate bordering the side road. The signs on the gate said it all.

DANGER

20,000 VOLTS

SECURE AREA

NO ADMITTANCE

The words were clear, large, bright red on a white background. The signs were new, as was the fence. The buildings, on the other hand, looked old beyond comprehension. They seemed nothing more than tar paper and wood shacks despite being as large as the barracks next door.

Two soldiers, dressed in black, stood behind the gate. They seemed to communicate through headsets like the one Remmick had used the night before. After a moment the soldiers stepped forward and pulled the gates open.

Cory took note. They had to turn the fence off to provide entrance. He smiled at a piece of information he felt would come in handy some time.

The buildings were nearly 200 feet long. The Hummers drove through the gate and to a door midway across the side of the first building. They turned a tight 180 degree turn and stopped one behind the other, with Cory's side facing the building. Cory didn't have a chance to breathe before his door flew open and a soldier stood next to him motioning him out of the vehicle. He fumbled his seat belt open, and stepped out. The ride had been only a few minutes, not nearly long enough to cool him off completely. The heat from the asphalt hit him in the face. He struggled to breath.

The soldier motioned him toward the door. As he approached the three steps leading to the door he glanced back. The doors to the other vehicles were being opened as well. Lori was being helped out of the vehicle directly behind the one he'd arrived in, and Thomas was climbing out of the third vehicle. He was taking his time, and the soldier seemed to be permitting this small expression of independence. The soldier next to Cory tapped his shoulder and pointed to the door. Cory acquiesced.

He reached for the handle, but the door opened without his help. He stepped into a ten foot by ten-foot entrance hall, bound by a second door ahead, and a black window on the right. All he could see was his own reflection. The second door seemed to be iron, with large hinges and huge rivets. Two soldiers stepped in with him. One pulled an ID badge from his breast pocket. There was a flash of light inside the black window. Cory thought he saw a shadow moving behind the black glass, but he wasn't sure. The outer door jerked closed, and there was a loud snap. Then the inner door released with a clang and swung open slowly.

Cory looked back to see if there was any movement behind him, but the outer door remained closed tight. He was pushed into the next room and the inner door, fully six inches thick, swung closed slowly.

It was dark and musty, but only by comparison to outside. The lights were fluorescent, and old, bare. He was in a large office of sorts, with many desks filling the central space. Most had computers, which clashed with the ancient look of the desks. Some of those were wood, but many were metal of a type Cory had seen in town, in the doctor's office. Desks were stacked two deep against the wall, obviously not needed. There were typewriters with open keyboards piled on the discarded desks, unused and discarded as well. The soldiers, many men, but some women, were busy at the computers. No one looked up as they entered.

Cory was herded into the aisle between desks. It ran the length of the office space. A wall at either end, seemingly equal-distant from the central door, ended the office area. In each, centrally located, was an un-imposing door. Cory was pushed toward the one on the right. As he walked, he noticed no one looked up to watched him pass. He felt more alone than he'd felt in a long time.

As they reached the door the large entrance behind them activated again. Cory turned to see the metal doorway swing open, and Lori was pushed into the room. She looked at him, her eyes red with tears, and started to walk toward him. Immediately a female at the nearest desk jumped up, and herded her toward the door at the other end.

"Cory!" she shouted.

"Lori," Cory said softly.

At that moment the soldier reached out, grabbed the door, and yanked it open.

Cory's eyes had become adjusted to the fluorescent lighting. He was shoved through and the door closed behind them. He was led into a plain room with a single beat-up wood desk and a computer. A heavy-set soldier sat at the desk, dressed in the same black uniform as the others. No insignia.

"How do you tell who outranks who?" Cory asked, angry at not being allowed to help Lori.

The guard nodded to the man behind the desk, turned and went out the way he came in. The man at the desk looked up, and grinned. There was no comfort in that grin.

"Name," he said simply.

"Why?"

The man scowled and bellowed, "Name!"

"Cory," Cory answered nervously.

"Surname," the man said, typing the answer into a computer keyboard.

"Morris," Cory returned. "What? Am I being booked?"

"Sex," the man said.

"Male," Cory returned, shaking his head. "Duh!"

He was having trouble believing this interrogation.

"Age," the man said.

"Sixteen," Cory returned. "Where are my friends?"

"Address," the man said.

"No," Cory said firmly. "No. I'll exchange an answer for an answer. I answer one, and then you answer one. Deal?"

The man stood, and started to lean forward, then thought better and sat down slowly. He typed a few words on the computer and sat back, smiling congenially at Cory.

The door at the opposite side of the room opened, and a guard came out. Without warning, he grabbed Cory by the back of the neck and started pushing him toward the door.

"Hey!" Cory shouted.

The soldier grabbed his arm as well, and Cory was powerless to resist. They entered a hall that was brightly lit. A shelf was on one side, about waist high. There were two frosted glass plates set in the middle of the shelf. The soldier took Cory's right hand and placed it flat on the right plate. Before he could walk behind him, Cory put his left hand flat on the left plate. The soldier nodded. Immediately a bright light flashed through the plates. The light died and the soldier took him by the neck again.

"Just tell me what to do," Cory said. "I understand English."

He was pushed down the hall to another door. The door swung open, and Cory noticed the small lenses above the door. There were three of them.

"Cameras?" he asked, pointing up.

The soldier pushed him along. This time they were in a smaller hallway with a window and counter on the right. A soldier was on duty there. The one that accompanied him turned immediately and went back out.

"Shoes," the soldier said curtly.

Cory blinked, and said, "What?"

"Give me your shoes," the soldier repeated.

Cory nodded, and sat down on the bench opposite the window.

"At least you speak English," he said as he untied the laces.

"In a moment I will ask you to stand in front of the glass panes to your left. You will be photographed from front, back, above and below at the same time. You will stand in the anatomical position as depicted in the diagram immediately to my right."

Cory glanced at the picture. He handed the shoes to the soldier. The soldier immediately dropped them behind him. There was a dull, metallic thud.

"Socks," he said.

Cory nodded, and stripped the socks from his feet.

"Do you understand the instructions?" the soldier asked, as if it were a memorized script. "I can repeat them in a number of other languages if you prefer."

"I understand," Cory said somberly, handing his socks over.

He used the socks as an excuse to get close enough to see the soldier was sitting in an almost empty cubicle, no more than five feet square. There was a door to the left, and no other opening. A large garbage can lined with a black plastic bag took up a large portion of the space in the room. He dropped Cory's socks into the can.

"Shirt," the soldier intoned.

"Am I going to get any of my clothes back?" Cory asked.

"Shirt," the soldier said a little more forcefully.

Cory stared at the picture again, and noted the stylized picture was of a naked man. It was not entirely anatomically correct, but the general idea was portrayed well enough. He swallowed hard and stripped off his t-shirt.

"Pants," the soldier said, dropping the shirt behind him.

Cory nodded, nervous now, and embarrassed. He stripped his pants off, and handed them to the soldier, who dropped them in the can.

"Remove the bandage," the soldier said.

Cory looked down and realized he still had the makeshift bandage on. He untied the cloth and pulled the toilet paper from the wound. It stuck some, but he got it all. The wound was small, just like Thomas had said, and had sealed itself. There was some dried blood around it, but he felt nothing more than slight tenderness at the actual sight.

The soldier held out a box, and Cory placed the bandage in the box. The soldier immediately disposed of the material behind him.

"Shorts," he said.

Cory felt his cheeks flush, and looked back at the diagram of the man.

"Shorts," the soldier repeated.

Cory said, "I usually like privacy before stripping down."

The soldier hit a button on the counter. The door beyond the glass panes virtually burst open. Another soldier stepped partway in. He stood there, his very presence a threat. He didn't move, but Cory knew he would if necessary.

"No," Cory said softly. "It's okay. I can do this myself."

The soldier in the window nodded, and the other soldier disappeared.

Cory stripped his shorts off, and handed them to the soldier in the window. He stood close to the counter, taking advantage of the concealment it provided. The soldier deposited them behind him. Before he turned around he was giving more instruction.

"Stand between the glass mirrors with your feet in the white circles," he said, again as if reading a script. "Face the right wall; place your hands in anatomical position. Do not smile or bare your teeth. Stand straight and do not move."

Cory did as he was told. Almost immediately a flash blinded him. He was blinking and trying to clear his eyes when the door opened again and the soldier from moments before entered. He motioned. Cory stumbled through the door.

"I want to thank you for your help a moment ago," he said wryly as he passed.

The soldier ignored him.

He was in a shower room. There were two shower heads, one on each side of the hall, and drains below. There were no handles, and Cory wondered for an instant how he was supposed to turn them on. As he stepped in front of the nearest shower head, it came on. He was washed with cool water. He let it run over his face and down his back.

"Use the soap from the dispenser and thoroughly cleanse yourself," the soldier instructed.

"I usually shower alone," Cory complained, pressing the dispenser and receiving a handful of green liquid.

"So, do I," the soldier said softly, and turned as much as he was able, and stared at the opposite wall. "Use the soap in your hair, ears, feet. Everywhere. Avoid your eyes. It will burn."

Cory rubbed it into his scalp and was surprised at the tingling he felt. Within a few seconds the tingling turned into a distinct burning. He rushed to rinse it off. The small cut on his thigh seemed to be on fire. He scrubbed with water quickly to get the soap off the wound.

"It won't do physical damage," the soldier advised, "but it's best to scrub thoroughly and rinse quickly."

Cory nodded, and said, "You're almost human."

The soldier only pointed at the lenses above the next door.

"This is a high-security area. You can't go anywhere without surveillance. Are you finished?"

"Yes," Cory answered, rinsing all over one more time to be sure he'd gotten all of the soap off.

The soldier pointed, and Cory walked toward another door. This one opened, and he entered a room similar to the one he'd been stripped and photographed in. The door closed behind him, and he stood at the window dripping.

A soldier appeared after a moment, and handed him an orange towel. He accepted it gratefully and dried himself. The soldier was there for a moment, then gone, then back again.

Cory wrapped the towel around his waist, and said, "Where to now? That way?"

"Return the towel," the soldier said.

Cory unwrapped the towel, threw it at the soldier and snapped, "I knew it was too good to last."

The soldier put it behind him, and immediately held out a pair of boxer shorts, colored day glow orange, like the towel.

"You like bright colors," Cory said.

He smiled gratefully and slipped into them quickly. He felt more comfortable. He glanced down at his wound and noted it was clean and looking good.

"Through there," the soldier said, pointing vaguely.

Cory walked through the door feeling better. The next room was small, but it was lined with medical equipment. An examination table was in the middle. After a minute a man in a white coat came in.

"I was beginning to wonder if anyone wore anything but black here," Cory said.

"Sit here," the man said, indicating the exam table.

The man punched, prodded and poked his way through a thorough, but somewhat standard physical exam. Cory realized the doctor, if that's what he was, was simply doing a job. He was being efficient, not providing a service. Cory felt the lack of rapport or even a hint of care or concern. He felt like a piece of meat in a butcher's showcase.

The doctor made some notes at a computer terminal built into the wall. When he was done, he came back and looked at the small wound on Cory's thigh again.

"How was this done?" he asked simply.

Cory explained the circumstances surrounding the injury, and what he and Thomas had done for it. The doctor nodded, poked at the wound a few times. Satisfied, he turned his back to Cory. When he returned he was carrying a syringe full of white fluid.

"This will prevent infection," he said.

Without waiting for Cory to reply, he rubbed Cory's thigh with an alcohol swab, then jabbed the syringe into his leg. He pulled back on the plunger, then injected the viscous fluid. Cory felt the pain, and gritted his teeth. When the syringe was empty, the doctor pulled the needle out. He wiped the small dot of blood away with another swab.

"You're finished," he said without emotion. "Go through there."

Cory nodded, approached the door and waited a second till it opened. He felt a lump in his thigh where he'd received the injection, and rubbed it as he walked through.

He was back in the small hall again, or, at least, it seemed like the same little hall. The window was on the right, and a soldier, dressed in black, was handing him a bright orange bundle. Cory took the package and unrolled it. It was a jump suit. He quickly put it on.

At first, he was surprised it fit, then he realized he'd been under surveillance, dressed and not, since he arrived. He'd have been more surprised, he reflected, if it hadn't fit.

The man next handed him a pair of orange socks. He slipped those on, too. Then the soldier, again without speaking, handed him a pair of bright orange canvas shoes. He slipped them on. They had no laces, but it felt good to have shoes on again. He was dressed, even if the outfit wasn't one he'd have picked out at Walmart. He followed the gesture and went through the doorway and found himself in a plain room with two chairs.

Remmick sat in the chair facing him, a twisted grin staining his face.

# CHAPTER 19

The captain's office was small, but well furnished. The walls were wood paneled, and the desk solid oak. Captain Ferris sat in a high-backed chair with the windows behind him. He motioned for Brady to sit down, and had chairs for the others brought in. Brady sat on the edge of his seat. He was anxious, and unsure what the captain would tell him.

"I have been in contact with my superiors," the Captain said quietly. "Sheriff, this base is just a tracking station, a relay point for information from our satellites. Most of the information received and forwarded from here is sensitive. Security is an issue. That's why we keep a low profile. This location was picked because of the clear air, the lack of serious atmospheric disturbance for the majority of the year, and it's accessibility to major freeways and major military installations."

"Nellis," Brady said.

"Nellis and Hill," the Captain agreed. "Two weeks ago, the troops that have been harassing your town arrived. Yes. 'Harassing' is an accurate word. At first, they were transparent. They went about their business and didn't bother our operation at all. Then Remmick came to me with requests for manpower and other resources. His requests became demands. He simply took over my command. I began requesting backup at that time. Up to this moment I have received only perfunctory acknowledgement of our problem. I escalated my requests, and provided information on the activities of the group, but until yesterday found myself out on a limb alone."

"They are not your men," Brady summarized.

"They most emphatically are not," Ferris returned. "I could have played the upper hand and forced a confrontation, but I believe that would have escalated to armed conflict. My soldiers are well trained, but it should be obvious even to you we would not have stood a chance against them in any kind of armed conflict. Our soldiers are supposed to be on the same side. There are processes to take care of issues like this. I believe, also, some of your children could have been injured. I wanted to avoid that at all cost."

"Thank you, Captain. Whose men were they?" Brady asked, emphasizing each word.

"They belong to a group whose existence is apparently top secret," the captain responded. With a wry grin he said, "I cannot find anyone who will acknowledge their existence."

"They weren't keeping it a secret last night," Brady growled.

"No, they weren't," Ferris said. "I'm sorry they've treated you and your children in this fashion. It should not have happened. I assure you it will be corrected."

"Don't apologize," Brady snapped. "Just tell us where our children were taken."

"We don't know yet," Ferris returned. "We are tracking the first group. I've secured the cooperation of several commands to do this. The 'copter carrying your children will likely be going to the same place the first group went. I have a 'copter following them, as well, just to be sure. We should be receiving word soon. As soon as we know where they've gone, we'll take whatever steps necessary to recover your children."

"We will want all the children, including Tobias and his sister," Brady said. "I hope you understand that."

"Of course," the captain said.

"This whole thing is beyond belief," Brady intoned. "There are so many things going on that are wrong I can't even sort them all out. At this moment I can tell you that I have never been so angry with anyone in my life!"

"I understand," Captain Ferris said softly.

"I also think you are out of line when you can see something going on that's implicitly wrong and do nothing," Brady said angrily.

"I have told you what my motives were," Ferris said directly. "It may or may not have been the right decision, but that is the way I saw the situation. I believe it was in the best interest of your children to handle it the way I did."

"And you let them take my children," Brady snapped. "I want to know the minute you hear anything. I'm going to make a few calls of my own. I have to get back to town."

"You're welcome to the outer office," the captain offered. "I will continue to work from here. And I can keep you apprised of my progress."

"I need to be close to my wife," Brady said. "That's her son they have in those helicopters, too. I want a radio patch directly from you to me. You know the frequencies I use. I want you to keep in touch every second of the day. If you hear anything at all, I want to know about it. Do you understand? And we all need a ride back into town."

"I'm taking care of all that as we speak. Is there anything else I can do?"

"I'm sure I'll think of something. Jacob, when we get back to town, I want you to go back to the mission and see what they left of the jeep wreckage," Brady said. "Karl, I want you to find our vehicles. We know they didn't take them out of town. They met the helicopter somewhere. Then spread the word. We need to have a town meeting and see who has favors they can call in. We're going to need all the help we can get."

"Your vehicles are being brought up to the base," Captain Farris said quietly. "They were left at the bottom of the access road. They'll be here any moment."

Brady and the captain stared at each other for half a minute.

"Captain," Brady said evenly, "I would make sure I pulled all the strings I could. We are going to do everything in our power to blow this wide open. It is my intention to have this incident on national news before the day is out."

The Captain looked up, and said, "I understand. I fully expect a formal inquiry into this matter. I expect I will be called to testify, as will you and your officers and the parents of the children. I just thought you should know."

"I just want the children back," Brady snapped.

Brady exploded out of the office. He had a lot to do, and he was going to need a lot of help. He wasn't looking forward to telling Macey their son wouldn't be home for a while.

# CHAPTER 20

Remmick motioned toward the chair, and said, "Sit down."

"I'd rather not," Cory returned. "Why am I here, and what do you want?"

"Sit down. You're here because you conspired with a known enemy of the United States," Remmick said. "We have a few simple questions to ask. Then you are free to go home."

"Yah? How will I get there?"

"We will provide transportation."

"Where are we now?" Cory asked evenly.

"Where do you think you are?"

"I'm getting tired of asking questions that never get answered," Cory said angrily. "We were minding our own business and you guys come up and take us prisoner. Then you get chapped if we aren't entirely cooperative. What's the problem? Why can't I get a straight answer?"

"You can," Remmick replied. "But, let's go back to your original premise. When you checked in you said, 'A question for a question. I answer one, and then you answer one. Deal?' I'll make that deal with you. When did you first meet the alien?"

"Who is the alien?" Cory asked.

"Okay. Me first. You call him 'Toby'. That's cute. It's sort of like 'ET'. When did you first meet him?"

"Last night at the Frosty Freeze. He came in just before you got there."

"That was when you decided to take his place, right?" Remmick asked.

"It was a spur of the moment thing," Cory responded, shrugging. "I don't like bullies, and he looked like he needed help. Where is he? And where are Lori and Thomas?"

"They are being processed, like you," Remmick said softly. "What made you want to put yourself in danger to save him? He was a stranger to you."

"I don't like being pushed around. I told you, 'I don't like bullies.' I didn't think he would like 'em, either. Why do you want him? You said he was an alien. Is he an illegal immigrant or something?"

"Two questions again," Remmick said reflectively. "Okay. He's from much further away than you could ever imagine. He piloted a ship over our protected air space. We shot it down last night. It crashed where we picked the four of you up today. That surprises you? I see that it does. What did he tell you about why he was here?"

"He said he'd taken his father's four-wheeler without permission and wrecked it," Cory returned. "You have his sister. What happened to his car?"

"He actually wanted you to believe he drove here in a car?" Remmick said, smiling.

"He called it his 'vehicle'," Cory said softly, thinking back to his conversations with Toby. "I thought he meant it was a car."

"Well, we have his 'car', and his sister. He'll be reunited with the girl when it is convenient. However, the vehicle will remain in our custody. He actually called it a vehicle?"

"Yes," Cory said thoughtfully. "There's only one thing I'm really sure about, though. I think you've been smoking more than tobacco, Major. There has to be a little funny rope in there someplace."

"Cute. However, I've seen his...vehicle."

"I don't suppose you'd prove it to me," Cory said softly. "Show it to me."

"No," Remmick said firmly. "National security. You're old enough to understand that. Did anyone else know where he was going? I'm thinking, maybe, friends, or family."

Cory thought a moment. He ran through his mind what he should and should not say. He didn't trust the man sitting in front of him. He wasn't sure how the information would be used. Lying, on the other hand, could be just as damaging. If Remmick believed him instead of Toby he could keep digging, and Toby wouldn't even know what the right answers were.

Finally, he said, "No. But, if he is an alien, don't you think he might have friends, family, a father, a bloody armada ready to come in here and blow you away?"

"Your father can't help you," Remmick said coolly. "You really don't think his father can help him, do you?"

"My father's not from Alpha Centauri," Cory returned. "Are you sure I can't get a look at his space ship? I mean, you really want me to believe you, don't you?"

Remmick thought a moment, and said, "What if I offered you a deal?"

"What kind of deal?" Cory asked skeptically.

"I can see you don't like being lied to," Remmick said, leaning forward. "We don't, either, especially where national security is concerned. Here's what I have in mind: We'll let you visit with your alien friend. We'll eavesdrop. You pump him for information about who he is and where he came from. We're most interested in flight capabilities and weapon strength and such. Now, if we get some good information from him without too much trouble, I will give you a personal guided tour of his... vehicle. Not only that, I'll see to it you get home in time for the dance Friday night."

Cory thought a moment, then said, "The dance was last night. How about this? Let me talk to my father. Let me tell him I'm okay and that he doesn't have to worry."

"We've already talked to him in person," Remmick returned. "We've explained the situation, and he agreed that we have to take this one step at a time. However, if it looks like you're making progress by tomorrow, I'll let you call him tomorrow evening and spend, say, a half hour on the phone with him."

Cory's eyes narrowed, and he said, "Okay! When do I get back with Toby and Thomas and Lori?"

"Very soon for Thomas and Lori," Remmick said quietly. "It may take a while to process Toby, however. There are certain...tests...that we have to do first. Physical exams. You know."

Cory suddenly flared, and said, "Yah, I know! You want me to believe that you really care about my friends and me and all you care about is finding some kind of alien from space. You don't even care who you hurt along the way. I got that right, didn't I? You even lied about talking to my father. He would never agree to leaving me here! So, what's in this for you? You want your name in the news? Major Remmick captures a space alien! Don't forget to tell them he's barely a teen ager and it took two regiments to catch him. I'm not going to answer any more of your questions, Major. I want a lawyer."

"You really don't understand your situation here," Remmick returned, standing. "You will stay here until I say it's time to send you back. You could be an old man by then, boy. There won't be any lawyers, and there won't be any rescues. If you don't cooperate, we'll find out everything we need to know without your help, and you'll still be sitting here when that town you came from dries up and blows away."

"At least I'll be able to look at myself in the mirror," Cory spat.

Remmick turned and walked out the door. Cory looked up at the three lenses above the door. One was video. What were the others?

He didn't have too much time to wait. Almost immediately the door opened again and two soldiers entered, both armed. Cory stood as they approached. One grabbed his arms and yanked them behind him.

"Hey!" he complained. "That hurts!"

The soldiers didn't respond. One soldier wrapped a plastic band around his wrists, laced it through itself and pulled it tight. Immediately Cory felt his circulation cut off. The second knelt and put a similar band around each ankle, lacing them through each other. He was effectively hobbled. He could walk in a fashion, but he couldn't run. He looked up at his guards and sneered. He could feel his hands growing numb.

"It takes two of you to beat up on me?" he asked. "How many of you does it take for the girl? Three or four? You're real brave. America's finest."

He put as much derision as he could in his voice, but the soldiers, again, didn't respond. Instead, they pushed him toward the door Remmick had used. Cory thought about this, and realized he'd come through a single corridor where each door led to another and another until he ended up in this last room. The others, if being 'processed' as Remmick had claimed, would be going through the same experience. Lori had been pushed toward the other side of the building. Maybe Thomas would be following him through this side. He wanted to leave some sign he'd been here ahead of them, but he couldn't think of anything he could do. The door opened and he was shoved through.

He hobbled as best he could into a large square room. The pale white light of the fluorescents refused even to cast a shadow. In the center of the room was a broad concrete stairwell with stairs winding down into the darkness. He was herded toward a desk at the head of the stairs.

The broad, flat desk held several computer screens. The soldier behind the desk was armed. He looked up, his face impassive, as they entered. Cory sniffed as the guards pushed him to the front of the desk and held him immobile.

"D block," the soldier holding him said simply.

The one behind the desk nodded, typed something on the computer keyboard, and motioned toward the stairs.

Cory found himself being pushed toward the stairs, toward the darkness that seemed to lie below. When he reached the head of the stairs, he was surprised to find the darkness he'd envisioned below was only a trick of the light. The stairs were well lit, just slightly darker than the office above. He reached for the rail, but was frustrated by his secured hands. He stared at the first step, then at his ankles hobbled and, for a moment, wondered if he could negotiate the stairs without falling. The soldiers ended his wonder quickly as each took an arm and half herded, half dragged him down. The bands around his legs tugged and yanked at his ankles.

The bottom of the stairs was a room similar to the one above except bars covered one end. The bars were thicker than the ones in the jail cells Thomas' father had, and they were closer together. They seemed to be more like a solid wall than cell bars.

He was pushed to the door, and they waited.

He could see soldiers in the short hall, each working at computer terminals. The one closest to the door looked up, almost smiled, and punched buttons on the computer. A loud clang rang through the small space, and the door slowly swung inward.

"Reporting," one of Cory's guards said simply, pushing Cory ahead.

"Good," the one at the desk responded. "D block, right? They're waiting for you."

Cory jumped as the heavy barred door clanged shut. He stood facing a second door, just as imposing. This one also opening inward, and he was herded through. His guard left him there, and stepped back through the bars. The door swung closed slowly, but the clang was loud and frightening. A soldier stepped out of a side room before he had time to worry, put a hand on his shoulder and guided him down the hall.

They walked ten paces till they arrived at a heavy metal door. The door buzzed, and his guard guided him through. This hall ended with three metal doors, one in front and one on each side. They turned left, the door buzzed, and they entered a kind of alcove office, with a console and two more guards. One came around and took possession of him. The first retreated.

He was frightened now. He was being led through level after level of security, and he was beginning to realize that any kind of escape was going to be impossible. He stared around at this last room. It was 20 feet across, and was octagonal. Each face of the octagon seemed to be a cell door. All of them were steel, some had a single 6" square pale green glass window in the center of the door. The console was in the center of the room and seemed to be a monitoring station. The guard sat with monitors wrapped around him, a display of lights, all green. He wore a headset with microphone, talked quietly into the microphone, but continued to stare at the screens in front of him. A second guard was roving around the perimeter moving quietly from door to door. He looked toward them as they entered, and immediately stood at attention.

The monitor in the center looked up, and said, "Ten."

The guard nodded. The monitor pushed a button, there was a loud metallic clang, and a door across from them opened. One of the lights on the panel turned red.

Cory glanced around quickly, taking all the details he could remember. There were eight sides, eight doors, six with windows, two without. One he'd come through, the other had a large letter 'H' on it.

The guard took him across to the open door and pushed him in. His hand became very heavy on his shoulder, and Cory was forced to bend over. He immediately felt something metallic forced between his wrists. It was moved expertly, and his hands were free. The blood rushed into them, and Cory gasped with the pain. He began to gingerly rub his wrists.

The guard stooped and with two quick motions cut off the leg restraints. He carefully picked up the plastic pieces and left the room with them. As

Cory turned around, he could see the rover standing stiffly, weapon ready. A few seconds passed as the guard cleared the door, then it began to swing slowly shut. It sealed with a clang. Cory suddenly felt isolated again.

He stood in the center of a concrete cell. There was a bed on one side, separated from a toilet by a small, waist high wall. Built into the top of the toilet was a small sink with a faucet. He could see he would be required to straddle the toilet to use the sink. Above the sink was a metal mirror with a narrow, attached shelf. A plastic cup, a toothbrush and small tube of toothpaste occupied the shelf. There was a small bar of soap, still wrapped. Everything was brand new, as if they had been waiting for him.

The cell expanded toward the head of the bed, where the pillow was. High up, near the ceiling, was a narrow horizontal window through which most of the light of the cell entered. The bed itself was a simple mattress on a raised pad of concrete. No hiding place underneath.

Cory jumped up on the bed, and stretched to look out the window. He could just reach it by pulling himself up by the window ledge. He stared out and his hopes dwindled.

First, the window was too small to crawl through, even if he'd been able to break the thick glass laced with steel wire. Second, the window was at the bottom of window well. He had no idea how deep the well was. The concrete reflected the sun's rays to the bottom of the hole. Cory's heart turned cold, and he slid back down onto the bed.

He felt alone now, more alone than he'd ever felt before.

"I'll give you tonight to think about whether you want to cooperate or not," Remmick said suddenly.

Cory jumped and looked toward the door. He ran over and stared through the window. The rover was still walking slowly around the outside edge of the room, and the monitor was still wrapped in his panel. There was no one else there.

"You won't find me out there," Remmick said, his voice betraying some amusement. "I'm in my office. I can hear everything you say, and I can watch everything you do right from my office. Even at night. Now, I want you think about that. You will be under my watchful eye from this moment on."

Cory saw the three lenses in the doorway now. As he looked around, he saw a similar set of lenses above the window. He felt his face flush, and he stood facing the door.

"Why three lenses?" He asked loudly. "What kind of camera is that?"

"Temper, young man," Remmick returned. "Nothing you say or do will make any difference in your length of stay here until you begin to cooperate."

"I don't think I want to cooperate with you," Cory mumbled softly.

"Then you'll never get out," Remmick said. "Think about it, son."

"I'm not your son!" Cory shouted.

He grabbed his shoe and threw it at the lens array above the door. It hit with an almost silent "thwap", and fell harmlessly to the floor.

Immediately the door clanged, and swung open, and the roving guard dropped to one knee with his M-16 leveled at Cory's chest. Cory jumped against the wall as if a physical force had thrown him back. Fear rushed through his gut like lightening exploding through a dark sky. He held his breath and stood perfectly still. After an eternity the rover stood slowly, and pulled the rifle up toward the ceiling. The door swung closed with a harsh clang.

Cory struggled to slide down the wall and onto the bed. He was breathing very hard now.

"You really shouldn't tease the guards," Remmick said from the speaker. "You've learned that they have no sense of humor, and they don't care about you one little bit. They won't put up with any nonsense. You're not at home where a spanking will get you off. You screw up here and you could be dead. Remember that, son."

Cory put his face in his hands, felt the flow of tears, and said softly, "I'm not your son."

# CHAPTER 21

Thomas woke up to a high-pitched tone from the speaker. He could see the two sets of camera lenses, one on each end of his cell. They were a part of his daily life now. They were always present. But he hadn't found the speaker, even though it was equally a part of his life. For some reason it had been well hidden.

Probably, he reflected, to keep an inmate from tearing it apart to silence it.

He rolled out of bed. It was still dark outside. The window was still an orange void. The mercury vapor lights somewhere outside filled the window well at night. The light high on the wall was always on. He had no control over it. He'd had to learn to sleep with it on.

He picked up his jump suit and held it under his arm. There was no reason to dress. He picked up his socks, but slipped his bare feet into the canvas shoes. He tried carrying those once, and learned quickly the guards frowned on not wearing them. He didn't understand that, either. The floors were universally smooth concrete. He waited behind the door. Four days of the same routine creates an impression. He wondered how many more days he'd have to endure it. Somewhere his father was working to rescue him. He knew that, but he was getting impatient. Each day it was harder to believe in his father's rescue.

The door clanged and swung open. The monitor sat with his eyes glued to the screens in front of him. The rover stood to one side, his rifle held close in and ready. Neither had spoken since the day he'd arrived. He was sure they had been changed, but he'd never seen that happen. Every morning it seemed to be the same two guards. They motioned to let him know where to go.

Without speaking he walked around the room to the door almost opposite his. He passed four doors that looked exactly like the door to his cell. He was sure they were other cells, but he'd never seen any evidence there were other prisoners housed in this section besides himself. The door with the large 'H' clanged and opened. He entered. The door clanged shut behind him. He dropped his jumper and socks in the bin on the left, slipped out of his shoes, then slipped out of his shorts.

"Black and orange," he said softly as he threw them into the bin. "Someone here must really be into Halloween."

He stood in front of the single shower. The water turned on automatically. He let the water run over him. He used the green, burning soap to clean off. He worked quickly, and rinsed thoroughly. He stepped back and walked back to the bin. A towel was waiting on a shelf there. He dried off, and threw the towel in the bin. His new clothes were neatly folded on the shelf. He dressed quickly and slipped his shoes back on. They were inflexible about cleanliness. He wondered how long he was expected to wear the shoes before they replaced them.

He'd never seen anyone else's clothing in the bin. He'd never gone to the shower to find the floor wet, indicating someone else had preceded him. He was reasonably sure that every suit of clothing he'd been given was brand new, that he was the first to ever wear it.

The shower area appeared more private than the one where he'd been checked in. At least, a guard didn't stand next to him and watch. But he remembered the ominous conversation with Remmick the day he'd arrived, and had seen two sets of lenses in the shower room. It was impossible to move without being seen. He chose to ignore the fact he was being watched. It was the only way he could hold onto a sense of reality.

He remembered the intense feelings of paranoia that had swept through him the first full day he was shut in.

The door clanged open on cue, and he walked out into the central area. The guard no longer needed to indicate which way he should go. He walked quietly back to his cell. He waited outside until the door opened, and entered. He found his breakfast tray on the bed.

The food was uniformly bland. There was something that looked like eggs, but didn't have any flavor. There was something that looked like sausage, but tasted like cardboard. And the milk tasted like water.

He finished quickly and placed the tray back on his bed, then went to the door. The door clanged, and opened, and he walked out. The guard stood behind him, indicating by his presence the incorrect direction to walk. He walked around the circle, passing three more cells, to the short hallway he arrived in. The door clanged open, and he entered. The door behind clanged closed, then the door directly to the right clanged open. He breathed deeply and walked into the small exercise room. He glanced back at the ever-present guard.

In the four days he'd been there, he hadn't seen another person except the guards. They didn't speak to him. Once when he tried to walk around the central area the wrong way the rover had dropped his rifle off his shoulder, stepped into a defensive posture, and had simply said, "No." Thomas knew the word, and respected it. He had tried to do exactly what was expected of him from that moment on.

Now he was expected to spend about an hour out in the exercise room. There was a weight station, brand new, and a treadmill, also brand new. He didn't know much about how to use either, but he'd figured it out. He began to work the weights as he had the last few mornings. It wasn't what he really wanted to do, but it was much better than sitting in his cell. After one hour the door clanged open. The exercise period was over. The guard stood back away from the door. Thomas thought about trying to talk with the guard, looked at the stern face, and decided against it. He was hot and sweaty, and wanted another shower, but he knew that wouldn't happen until the next morning. He entered the short hall. The door shut behind him, and the door in front opened. He went in and turned immediately toward his room. The door clanged and he went in.

The bed had been changed. He didn't know who did that, just that it was done daily. The tray was gone. The soap on his sink was new, the toothbrush new and the roll of toilet paper new. Why someone took such pains was beyond his ability to reason out. He merely accepted it, and sat on the edge of his bed. It was time for Remmick's daily call.

Right on time Remmick said, "Good morning, Thomas."

Thomas remained silent. He didn't even look up at the lenses any more.

"Okay. Then let us talk about something that may interest you. I am arranging for you to visit with your friends."

Thomas looked up now and waited.

"I thought you would react with a little more excitement," Remmick said.

"All my friends?" Thomas asked.

"Of course, all your friends," Remmick assured him.

"When?"

"Maybe this afternoon," Remmick said quietly. "I don't know. There is so much paperwork to do, and arrangements to me made. You could help out, of course."

"Go away," Thomas said, and put his face in his hands again.

There were a few moments of silence. Then Remmick said, "You don't believe I can do that."

Thomas remained silent.

"I need your trust, Thomas," Remmick insisted.

"You promised me a book if I did what I was told," Thomas said. "You promised me a television in here. You promised to let me call my father.

You promise to let me spend time with my friends every morning. None of that has happened. You promise a lot, Remmick."

"Okay."

That was it. The daily interview was ended. Thomas felt a deep darkness gathering in his chest. He wanted to cry. In fact, he had cried twice, once the night he'd arrived and once last night. The cameras recorded it all. He didn't care anymore.

Now the day would pass slowly. His only indication of time was watching the subtle changes in the light through the window. It would gradually brighten, then slowly fade toward evening until it snuffed out altogether. Still, even at night, there seemed to be an orange glow in the window well. Thomas thought about the street lamps on the freeways down canyon. There was no other indication that time passed at all.

He spent his time the first couple of days in a kind of bored euphoric state. There was nothing to do, nothing to read, nothing to write with. After two days of total boredom he tried to break the day into blocks. He found that was easier to think about than to actually do. His watch was gone, and he had seen no clocks anywhere in the cell block. The boredom grew oppressive.

He tried to remember what life had been like before the cell. After two days the memories became blurred, dim. And what he could remember hurt. He stopped trying to remember his father, the town, Cory and Lori. He turned his mind to another task. He tried to remember everything he could about his pre-school years. He tried to remember everything he could about elementary school.

He assumed it was noon, or close to it, when his lunch was brought by one of the guards. He ate slowly, stretching the time out as long as he could. It was the same as breakfast. There were things that looked like food, but Thomas believed they were only pretending. The things on his tray had no flavor. When he was done the guard came and picked up his tray. It was all efficient and colorless, like the food itself.

Sometime in the late afternoon he was taken to the exercise room again. He walked on the treadmill for a while during the afternoon sessions. Mostly he tried to find anything to break the sterility of his new life. The guard simply turned as the door clanged and allowed Thomas to exit. He glared at the guard as he passed, and thought he saw a leer flutter over his face. It was there, then gone. When he got back to his room his dinner tray was on his bed. It was colorless, odorless, and he stretched his dinner out as long as he could.

After dinner he watched the light in the window change, dim, grow distant. He thought about junior high school. He thought about senior high school. Soon the light in the window well was almost gone. The light faded to dim orange. A guard picked up his tray.

The electric light in the cell never went out, but it was dim when the sun filled the window well. As the sunlight faded he simply got used to the lower light level. Sometime later (he never knew exactly what time it was) he would fall asleep. Later he would get up, take off the jumper, and climb into the bed. He would go back to sleep. He would wake to the high-pitched tone in the speaker system in the morning. The day would begin again.

There was time to pray, too. He'd prayed a lot since he'd been in the cell. He told God everything he could about the situation he was in. He prayed sitting on the edge of the bed, and lying down. He'd prayed on his knees at the side of the bed. At first he'd been self conscious. Praying was a new thing for him. And there were the cameras. But his need was great and he got used to the cameras. He had decided it wasn't any worse having Remmick see him pray than having him see him do other things. For the first time in his life he tried to talk to God. He was afraid he wasn't being heard sometimes. Other times he felt the warm glow in his chest and he knew someone was listening besides Remmick. He was sure at those times that everything would be all right.

On the fifth morning he was sitting on the edge of his bed having his morning discussion with God. He was speaking quietly, almost silently. What he had to tell God was private and for His ears only. Suddenly there was a clang from the door and it swung open slowly. It wasn't time. He was sure he hadn't been in his cell long enough for lunch time. The light in the window well hadn't peaked yet. He stood slowly, waiting to see what was going to happen. This was different, and he felt a tingling of excitement in his stomach. Something different was happening.

The roving guard stood back and simply motioned with his hand. Thomas followed his instruction and walked slowly, carefully out into the central area. The guard backed away, and Thomas walked forward. He didn't know what was happening. The guard made a simple motion, and Thomas circled the room to the door he'd originally come in, the one that led to the exercise room, and beyond, freedom. The door clanged open. He was in the hall near the exercise room. He looked back once. The guard was following him. He followed the hall forward, hearing the door shut behind him. When he reached the second door, it swung open, and he walked through. A second guard stood halfway down the hall. Thomas walked toward him, glancing back at the guard following him. The guard followed silently. As he approached, the door to the guard's right opened. Thomas nodded and turned and walked in.

The room wasn't large, but it was apparently meant to be some kind of gathering room. There were several tables, including a ping-pong table, and a number of benches. Tables and benches were all molded as part of the floor. The walls were uniformly gray, and the light from the ceiling was no better than anywhere else in the prison. Thomas walked over to the first bench and sat down. He scanned the walls, and found the sets of lenses, four of them, one set in each wall.

Suddenly the door clanged open again, and he stood up. Lori stood in the doorway. She saw him and stared in disbelief. Tears began to spring to her eyes as she walked slowly, hesitantly toward him.

She was wearing the same uniform he wore. Her hair was tied back by plain black ribbons. She was scrubbed clean, wearing no makeup, and Thomas had to concede she was pretty even without the makeup. She walked closer to him, holding out her hands as if afraid she'd encounter some obstacle that would keep them from meeting. As their hands touched, she simply stood with tears flowing down her cheeks.

"Thomas," she said softly.

"Hi, Lori," Thomas said quietly, holding her hands.

She leaned close and threw both arms around him. He held her, sure that he needed the feeling of warmth and love as much as she did. He felt his eyes begin to water, and he couldn't talk. He could feel her silent sobs as she held on tight.

The door clanged again, and they reluctantly broke their embrace. They turned to face the door. Cory walked in, dressed identically to the two of them. He stood just inside the door with a weak, unbelieving half smile on his pale face. Then he walked forward, toward them. Without hesitation, Lori moved toward him. They met at midpoint and wrapped their arms around each other. Thomas stood, waiting, for a few minutes, then approached. He placed a hand on each of their shoulders. They were both shaking.

"I've never seen anything as beautiful as you," Cory said softly in Lori's ear.

"Me, too," Lori choked out.

"You're both beautiful to me," Thomas said, sniffing.

The two opened their embrace and let Thomas in. They stood hugging for a long time, just to feel someone warm. When they finally broke apart there were tears running down all their cheeks.

Thomas looked around furtively.

Then he said, "Remmick can hear everything we say. Be careful."

"Of course," Cory said.

"There is no privacy," Lori said, shuddering. "Even when I'm alone, I'm not alone. I have the creeps all the time."

"I know," Thomas said softly. "I know. What did you tell him, Lori?"

"Everything he wanted to know," Lori cried. "Remmick said I could go home if I told him everything, so I did."

"What about you, Cory?"

Cory smiled, and said, "I only told him what I had to. I didn't volunteer any information. I didn't give him much."

Thomas looked up, and said, "Remmick, it doesn't work. She told you everything, and Cory told you almost nothing. And, Remmick, I lied to you. I made up things to tell you. We're still prisoners. You haven't kept your word to any of us. You hear me, Remmick?"

After a moment the door opened, and Remmick walked in. He wore his black jumper, his sunglasses, even in the dim prison, and his headset. He was speaking into the headset as he slowly, almost casually, approached them. He looked at each of them.

"Now you see I can keep some promises," he said, a wry smile breaking his face. "I see you can be sly in your own ways, too."

"That shouldn't surprise you," Thomas snapped. "I want a lawyer, or I want to walk."

Remmick nodded, and said, "You won't get a lawyer, and you certainly won't walk. Even if I let you out, which I won't, it's a long way back to town."

"You promised to take us back," Cory shouted.

"Don't get too loud, youngster," Remmick warned. "You know what happens when you get too loud."

"Where's Toby?" Thomas asked. "Where's his sister?"

"They're where they need to be right now," Remmick returned. "Now, let's get right down to it, shall we? First of all, I need help to get certain information from Tobias and his sister. Neither one of them will talk to me, you know. They won't even talk to each other because they know I'm listening. Maybe they're communicating telepathically. I don't know. The girl, well, she's getting sick. She won't eat, and she doesn't sleep much. Maybe there's something else she needs. We don't know what it is because she won't talk. Maybe it's a kind of homesickness."

"So, let her go home," Cory snapped.

"We will. Eventually. Right now I need some answers, and I can't let either of them go until I get them."

"Why?" Lori suddenly snapped, clenching her fists and approaching Remmick. "What is all this about?"

"It's about protecting our homeland, our planet, our very existence," Remmick intoned. "Don't you understand? We need to find out why they're here. They could be planning invasion, or annihilation of the human race. We need to find out."

"They seem pretty human to me," Cory said. "I don't think they would want to be annihilating themselves. Besides, we know why they're here. Toby took his dad's car, and went for a joy ride. Oh, I know. You say it was a space ship. But nothing else you've said has been the truth, so that's probably a lie, too. That's it. End of story."

"That's not it," Remmick said stiffly. "I can see this is not the time to talk to you about it. Maybe in a few days you'll be more cooperative."

Remmick turned stiffly and walked toward the door. The door complained with its customary clang as it opened.

"Is that what this is all about? Making us cooperate?" Thomas shouted at his back.

Remmick ignored him and walked through. The door shut.

The three friends stood for a moment. They turned together.

"We may not have much time," Thomas said suddenly. "Remember we are all in here together. Do anything you can to try to make things seem as normal as possible. Say your prayers night and morning. Yes, Cory, I have been praying. Don't look so shocked. When we get out of here, I want to talk to you about that. Use the sun to tell time. Divide up the day in time blocks and live by them. Lori, ignore the camera lenses in your cell. If you don't, you'll go crazy."

The door opened. They all looked over at the guard entering. The guard was female, and she pointed directly at Lori.

"Oh, no," Lori whined.

"Lori," Cory said gently, holding both her hands in his, "we'll get out of this, I promise. I won't leave here without you. Remember that I'm very close. I'll be thinking about you twenty-four hours a day. Say your prayers, Lori. It helps."

He glanced at Thomas as he said this, and saw a slight smile on his friend's face.

The guard slapped the stock of her rifle, and stomped her foot. Lori felt the tears again, and turned toward the guard. Before she could go Cory pulled her close and held her in his arms. She could feel his breath gently against her cheek. When he released her, she let one hand trail behind, touching Cory's fingertips as long as she could.

Cory started to follow and the guard brought her rifle down immediately to point directly at Cory's face. Cory stopped, and backed up slowly. The guard resumed her position and ushered Lori out.

Cory felt his heart break as he saw Lori turn for one last look as she went through the door. The door closed, and she was gone.

"How are we going to get out of here?" Cory asked, turning toward Thomas.

"We need some help from outside," Thomas said morosely. "Remember every minute, every second, that we're all in here together. And remember that I'm thinking about you and Lori, too, just like I hope you're thinking about me. Cory, it's the only thing that will keep us sane."

The door opened. Cory glanced over his shoulder as the guard entered.

"I'll be saying my prayers," he said.

"I am, too," Thomas said, looking at the guard. "I wasn't kidding, Cory. Don't look so shocked."

Cory smiled.

The guard pointed, and Cory shook his head vehemently.

"We have names," he said loudly. "If you want one of us to go with you, pointing won't do."

The guard brought his rifle down and pointed it directly at Cory's chest. Cory swallowed hard.

"That'll do it," he said softly.

"I think so," Thomas replied. "Go on, before you get yourself into trouble. Don't push them, Cory. I don't know if they'd actually shoot us or not, but I don't want to find out."

Cory nodded, and said, "Me, either. Goodbye. I'll see you soon."

Thomas watched him leave, and stood in the middle of the room waiting. He knew it was only a matter of minutes before they came to get him, too. The door opened, and the guard came in.

Thomas followed the guard's signal, and walked through the door. It shut behind him. They retraced their steps back through the doors and back to his cell. As his cell door slowly shut behind him, he took a deep breath. His lunch tray was there. He ignored the tray, sat down, and then lay back on the bed. He felt like crying, but fought it off. He stared around at the drab walls. He fixed his eyes on the ceiling.

He said a short prayer for his friends, all of them. He felt the warm feeling again. It helped.

The sunlight in the window well was nearly at its brightest. It was time to think about elementary school. He tried to fall deep into his memories. It was hard to concentrate now that he'd seen Lori and Cory again. He couldn't think straight.

He sat up and pulled the tray into his lap. He played with what looked like chicken nuggets with gravy. There was no taste. He chewed slowly trying to find some flavor in the meal.

With a brief flash of insight, he realized that was what Remmick had intended. After being with his friends, being in the cell was even harder to bear. He felt a hard lump growing in his throat.

An eternity seemed to pass and the door opened again. It was time to go back to the exercise room for his afternoon workout. He got slowly off the bed, and felt the hard knot in his throat. He wondered where his father was, and the wondering hurt.

# CHAPTER 22

rady looked up from his desk and said, "What?"

As soon as he spoke, he knew he'd been too harsh. He'd been irritable and rash for four days. He leaned back and shook his head. He felt tense and angry, and he over reacted at the slightest provocation. He was sorry, and smiled weakly as a partial apology. He breathed deeply.

The man in front of him wore white pants, and a simple white shirt that reminded Brady of something. His hair was full, and also white. His eyes were deep blue. A small smile washed across his face.

"I'm sorry," Brady said. "That was uncalled for. I've been under some stress lately."

"I understand," the man said calmly, the smile remaining.

Suddenly Brady felt the tension drain away. There was a calm feeling growing in his chest that he hadn't felt in days. He breathed deeply again and felt the muscles down his back relax.

"That's better," the man said, smiling gently. "I have come to ask for your help. You are in a unique position to provide the help I need."

"Of course," Brady responded, more composed this time.

He looked up at the man. He felt a calm assurance waft over him, and breathed deeply.

"Did...did you do something?" He asked.

The man thought a moment, then said, "I just arrived."

Brady shook his head and felt the calm waft over him again. He suddenly realized he was feeling the influence of the stranger standing in front of him. He'd met a few people in his life whose presence, by their nature, affected those around. With a wry smile he thought of Remmick and the opposite affect he had on people.

"How can I help?" He said simply.

"I have been searching for my children," the man said softly.

Brady stood up quickly, and said, "You're Toby's father?"

He suddenly remembered the way the boy had been dressed that night almost a week ago.

The man thought a moment, then said, "Tobias is my son, and Anisha is my daughter. I was told you could be of some help."

"I'll do what I can," Brady said solemnly. "I'm looking for my son, as well. There are two other children involved. Please sit down, Mr...."

"I am Salah," the man said, running his hand through his shiny white hair.

The man was tall, and in spite of his white hair did not look older than mid-forties. His simple pants did not seem to be supported by a belt. His long-sleeved shirt had no buttons. It hung out at the waist. He reached for the back of one of the office chairs in front of Brady's desk.

"I think I will sit down, thank you," he said softly. "I have been trying to find my children for several days, and I am very afraid they are in peril. A man in your town directed me to your office. He had confidence in your ability to help."

"Who was that?"

"You have met him. His name is Boothe."

"Boothe?" Brady asked. He remembered the man, and said, "I only met him a few days ago. I'm afraid I haven't gotten back to him. We have some things to discus. How did you meet him?"

"He is aware of your preoccupation," Salah said simply. "He is content to be patient until your current problem is solved. I have known him for some time. When my search seemed fruitless, I sought him out. He was of great help, but implored me to seek your assistance. I hope that was not an impropriety on my part."

"No," Brady said quietly. "That's okay. As I said, I don't know Boothe very well yet. We've not had time to talk. Let me get some information from you, uh, Salah. What's your last name?"

Salah nodded, and said, "We should take the time to get acquainted, Sheriff. I understand that. However, my desire is to recover my children. My one fear is that there may be a limited amount of time to do that."

"They are being held by a military unit," Brady responded, feeling the man's frustration, and feeling frustration of his own. "Despite what we both may be feeling right now, I believe all our children are quite safe. I believe, also, they are quite frightened. Please be assured I have help, and we're doing what we can to find them. We'll get them back where they belong."

Salah smiled weakly, and said, "I understand. It is not my nature to act in inappropriate ways toward those around me. However, I feel impulses in me that I've not felt since I was very young. I do not like feeling desires to harm others."

"You want to punch someone's lights out," Brady almost shouted, his fists tight on the desktop. "Trust me. I know the feeling."

Salah nodded, the weary look draining slightly from his face.

"I need to make a report," Brady said apologetically. "I need to be able to account for all the children. Till now I didn't know where Toby belonged. Please help me here."

He pulled out a sheet of paper.

"I need your name and address, in the very least. It would help if you had some I.D."

"You are a careful man," Salah returned. "I have to be honest, and you have to trust that I am who I say I am. I am Salah ben Malachi. As I said, I did not meet Boothe on the street. I sought him out. I have been staying with him these four days."

"How do you know Boothe?" Brady asked, writing things down.

"We have known each other for a few years," Salah answered. "I'm afraid it was at my suggestion he surrendered and was put in prison."

"You know about that, too?"

"I was there. I met him in another land. He'd walked away from his military unit. I let him wander with me for several days while I did my research. He talked a lot, and I let him. I suggested it was time for him to go back. He was put in prison."

Brady shook his head, and said, "We can talk about that later. Toby didn't have the same last name."

"He is ben Salah," the man responded. "It is our custom to take the name of the father as our surname. My father was Malachi ben Raphael."

Brady nodded.

"When you're not here, where do you live?" He asked.

Salah shook his head, and said, "Here is where the trust comes in, Sheriff. I live further away than you can possibly imagine. In fact, the journey here covers many thousands, many hundreds of thousands of miles."

Brady sat still for a long time. He had stopped writing. He met the calm, easy stare of the man in front of him. The deep blue of those eyes absorbed him, and the steady stare. After a few moments he balled up the paper and tossed it in the wastebasket.

"Toby didn't steal your car for a joy ride, did he?" Brady asked.

"It wasn't a car," Salah affirmed.

"Off-road vehicle," Brady mussed. "Your son said it didn't need roads. It didn't occur to me it might not need the ground."

"Only to land," Salah said.

"He told me, but I just wasn't listening. I made some assumptions that Tobias was just a little boy. I should have listened more carefully. I'm sorry."

Salah smiled.

Brady thought a few moments, and said, "You probably don't have identification, either."

"Not that you would recognize," Salah responded.

Brady was quiet for a few moments. He studied Salah's face. Salah smiled gently, waiting patiently.

"You're asking me to believe something I've wanted to believe since I was a child," Brady said easily. "You're not from this world?"

"Oh, we're from this world," Salah said, amusement touching his voice. "We could not return otherwise. However, we left a long time ago. We've never been far away, but we've never been so close as we are now. My people are extremely anxious for a reunion. It will come soon. Some have no patience and cannot wait."

"Your son."

"My son, among others," Salah responded. "What can we do about our children? We teach them to think independently, but we are surprised, sometimes upset, when they do."

Brady nodded, and said, "I can understand Remmick's reticence to give up your son, though I'm still not sure what he wants with mine. Maybe he thinks they know more than they do. I don't know. I don't know where they are, Salah, and that's what frightens me most."

"You wish to be close to your son," Salah affirmed, "to protect him. I understand. Your military has taken over. At this point in time they have control, and that bothers you."

"It does, indeed. They won't give that up easily, either," Brady breathed. "What does your vehicle look like, Salah?"

"I'm afraid it's a rather ordinary looking sphere," Salah responded.

"But they saw it flying," Brady almost laughed.

"I'm afraid when it is flying light bends around it and it begins to look more like a disk."

"Or a saucer. All of this makes a lot more sense now. They shot at it with a missile. Toby was unable to control the ship, and he crashed. That was up on the shelf, above the cliffs. The boy and his sister are probably lucky to be alive at all. Remmick and his crew show up. Instead of refuge, which they should have found, they find danger, and abuse."

Salah looked worried. Brady breathed deeply.

"Let me tell you what happened the night your son came to town," he said.

He quickly told Salah everything he knew. Salah was quiet.

When Brady finished Salah said, "When I get him home, I won't have the heart to punish him. He's been through a punishment more severe than I could ever invoke. I do thank you for your courage in trying to protect my son."

"Don't mistake courage for stubborn rage," Brady said. "I was upset they wanted something I didn't think they had a right to. I can understand how he saw the buildings now. He was flying above them. Of course, he would seem a threat if they picked him up on radar. I just don't know why Remmick's group was there at all."

Salah nodded, and frowned.

"I'm afraid that was my fault, Sheriff," he said sadly. "We've been making some maintenance trips. We, my family and I, are caretakers of the canyon."

"The hidden canyon," Brady said, "the one that Thomas and Cory found."

"That is so," Salah returned. "I was teaching Tobias to fly. He made some erratic moves that I'm sure your sensors, your radar, picked up. The military probably traced the origin to this area and set up a watch as near as they could. We weren't coming back for a while. It didn't matter to us. They would have become tired and bored and would have gone away after a few weeks."

"But Toby decided to try some flying on his own," Brady concluded.

Salah nodded.

"He came back here because he knew the area," Salah affirmed.

"What's so special about the canyon that it needs a caretaker?" Brady asked.

"It is a special place," Salah answered, holding up his hand. "Some of your ancestors held it as a sacred place. We, my family and I, have been watching over it for many generations."

"Well, we have a lot more of the puzzle," Brady said, breathing easier. "They took your ship, too, you know. I'm sure of that. You will probably want to recover that as well."

"My vehicle is not a large concern," Salah responded. "I can retrieve than any time I desire. It is my children I am concerned about. It will be more difficult, and more dangerous, to bring them back to safety."

"Mine, too," Brady said. "Still, if we knew where they took the ship, the vehicle, we might have an idea where they took the children."

Almost instantly a broad grin flashed across Salah's face.

"I know where the vehicle is," he said quickly. "As you,, I believe our children are there, as well."

"Where?"

Salah shook his head, and said, "It's not that easy. I have another ship. I can go there if I wished. However, they are watching the skies very carefully. Even with stealth they would see me. I would not have a chance to help the children if they are there. More than that, I could fly directly there, but without some common reference I would not be able to explain to you exactly where they were. I will need land vehicles. I need some local maps to show you where they are. I will need all your help to protect them once they are free."

"I have resources available right now," Brady answered, grinning broadly. "This rogue group will have one base of operations. We just didn't know where that was, so we couldn't do anything."

Brady reached in his drawer and threw a road map of the state on the desk. Salah stood and unfolded the roadmap and laid it out. It took him a few moments to determine the orientation, but he got it as Brady moved around the desk to stand beside him. Salah puzzled over the map a long time, then shook his head.

"Where are we now?" He asked after a time.

"We're here," Brady said, pointing to the black dot on the road. "This is I-15 running the length of the state. North, here, is I-70. This is Lake Powell."

"The big lake," Salah said. "I'm familiar with it. There's another down here."

His finger traced the Colorado River off the map.

"Lake Mead," Brady acknowledged. "It's bigger than Lake Powell."

Salah nodded, and said, "This is the canyon. This is the military base up on the mesa. Why does the map end here?"

He pointed to the western edge of the map.

"That's where our state ends," Brady answered. "They're outside our state?"

"Political boundaries," Salah mussed. "Yes. They are this far again this direction. You have another map?"

"Not of Nevada," Brady returned, thinking. "The library will have one. Come on."

Brady strode out the door, heading east along the sidewalk. Salah matched his pace, the two almost marching toward the corner structure. Salah seemed familiar with their destination.

They used both doors to enter, each pulling open one side. The interior was dark after the summer sun outside, but not too dark to see the green banker's lamps spaced evenly on the hardwood tables, or the rows of shelves full of books stretching floor to ceiling. Nor was it too dark to see Lucinda Merit jumping up from behind the librarian desk in the center of the entranceway. She leaned quickly across the counter and stared at the two coming in the door.

She was a middle-aged woman, hair slightly graying. She was thin and her face angular. Her eyes were bright and flashed at the two entering the edifice. It was clear she held the ground they walked on sacred, and her domain.

"Good afternoon, Sheriff," she said cordially. "And good afternoon to you, too, Mr. I Don't-Have-An-Address."

It was hard to miss the scowl in her voice.

Brady glanced at Salah, who smiled.

"I was doing some research," he said, almost embarrassed.

"He asked for help," Lucinda said evenly, her sparse frame almost shaking, "but he wouldn't apply for a card. He said he didn't have an address."

Brady smiled, almost laughed, and said, "We need the best maps you have, Lucinda. It's very important."

Lucinda nodded, glanced at Salah, then back to the Sheriff.

"Back here," she said, walking out from behind the counter. "Not a lot of people use them. The university in Cedar City donated them, of course, when they got their new library. They're old, but they're topographical and very accurate."

She let them to a back corner, and opened a closet door. A large frame took up most of the closet space. A large bundle of maps was hung on the frame, 5 feet wide, 6feet tall, bound at the top by a heavy metal runner. There were at least two-dozen maps in the bundle.

Brady stepped forward and grabbed the frame. The whole thing rolled out as he pulled it. He could feel the weight. Lucinda stepped back watching as Brady pushed it to where they could access the maps.

Brady studied the first map, raised an edge and tried to look at the second. He tried to find somewhere to put the first map, but found the whole set up awkward and hard to handle.

"This won't do," he said quickly, grabbing one side of the supporting bar. "Help me, Salah."

"Oh, no," Lucinda began. "You have to leave them on the stand, Sheriff,"

Brady smiled, and said, "Lucinda, you have no idea how important this is. Please move so we can get these out where we can look at them."

Lucinda squeaked another objection, but moved out of the way quickly.

Brady lifted one side of the bundle, and Salah the other. They yanked the maps off the frame and carried it between the bookshelves to the tables in the central area of the library. Brady smelled the dust of a hundred years float around them as they walked.

When they got to the table, he turned to lay the maps on the hard wood surface. Lucinda squealed, and rushed to retrieve the green banker's lamps on the table. She wasn't quite successful. Brady and Salah took the huge bundle of maps and dragged them onto the table.

"This is most irregular!" She shouted as another green table lamp skittered off the table and shattered on the floor. "Gentlemen! Gentlemen!"

Her bun was coming untied as she rushed around to rescue what she could of the broken lamp. Her movements were quick, sharp. Her every motion expressed anger at the situation.

Brady rolled the top map over the backside of the table. He looked at the second map a moment, shook his head and threw it up as well. Salah helped from his side.

"These are old," Brady said softly. "They don't even have the freeway system marked on them."

"But the towns are accurate," Lucinda snapped, "and the elevations haven't changed in the last 50 years."

"She is right," Salah said. "These will do. Next map, Sheriff. Please."

The half dozen patrons in the library had stopped to watch what was going on. Lucinda seemed agitated as the two rifled through the map bundle.

Salah started to lift the edge of the next map, stopped, and stared. He placed his hand flat on the corner Brady was trying to lift.

"This is it," he said. "It's here."

Brady watched at the man searched the area across the map.

"This mountain, here, is a landmark I recognize. Here is the small town. Not much, but there. The vehicle is here."

He placed his finger on the map. Brady leaned closer for a better look. He read the markers. It was a dry lake in the middle of the desert. Groom Lake.

"We're taking this with us," Brady said, looking up at Lucinda.

She shook her head, and said, "These cannot be checked out."

"How do you get them out of the binder?" Brady asked pointedly.

"It's permanent," Lucinda said evenly. "Sheriff, the town council…"

"The town council will back me up," Brady said, reaching into his pocket and pulling out his pocketknife. "I hate to do this, Lucinda, but we need this map, and I don't have time to argue."

He ran the knife across the top of the map in one stroke. The map, heavy, plastic coated fabric, separated from the frame and came free in his hands. Lucinda stared in shock and disbelief as Brady quickly rolled the map up.

Salah walked around the table and faced the librarian.

"Madam," he said gently. "This map will aid in the recovery of our children. Thank you."

Brady saw the woman suddenly become calm and relaxed.

"This is, as you say, most irregular," Salah continued. "No one has dared violate the sanctity of this place on your watch before. I assure you it is of vital importance or we would not do so now. While I have no address you would recognize, I can also assure you I have resources available. We will replace this whole bundle of maps before summers end with better and updated maps. The library will not suffer for our vandalism."

Lucinda nodded, quite calm now, and even proffered a smile.

"I will hold you to your promise," she said.

"I won't disappoint you," Salah returned, taking her hand momentarily in his.

He turned and walked out with Brady.

"I can't replace those maps," Brady said. "I don't have the budget."

"I can," Salah said simply. "What resources do you have that can get us to this place quickly and unseen?"

"I have two patrol cars," Brady answered. "I have one of the Humvees the soldiers were using. They left it in town when the helicopter picked up the remainder of the men. I had it driven to a garage behind the Sheriff's office. I was expecting them to come back to retrieve it. So far they haven't."

"That will do," Salah said evenly. "Let us talk about how we can get our children back."

# CHAPTER 23

Thomas couldn't sleep well. He dozed fitfully and dreamt. In his dreams the camera eyes glowed red in the dark. Their presence was oppressive, and they seemed to be closing in on him. There was no place he could hide from them, and he tried to scream. He woke with a start. The light was on, and the camera lenses were dark. Even with the temperature control he was wet with perspiration. He threw the blanket back and lay in the room trying to cool off. When that didn't work, he went to the sink.

He straddled the toilet and splashed cold water on his face and chest. After a few minutes, wet and dripping, he began to feel better. He drank two cups of water, and went back to his bed. He lay down and closed his eyes.

Almost immediately he heard the door begin to open. He groaned and sat up slowly. What could they possibly want in the middle of the night?

He dropped his feet over the edge of the bed and stood up. Then he turned to face the door.

The man standing there was wearing the standard black jump suit all the guards wore. But he didn't look like a guard. He wore no weapon, no sunglasses, and he carried no rifle. He was tall, and his hair was white and thick. His face looked younger than the white hair indicated. There was a gentleness about his eyes that was different than the guards. He didn't move like the guards, in short, clipped exact movements. His movements were soft, non-threatening. He waited till Thomas was standing before he entered the cell.

"You will want to get dressed, son," the man said.

His voice was soft, and gentle as well. He smiled reassuringly, but his next word carried an imperative with it.

"Quickly."

"I'm not your son," Thomas challenged, and started to climb into his orange jump suit. "When will you get it through your—"

"No, son, that suit won't do," the man said thoughtfully. "You'll stick out like a full moon over Kessler. Wait a minute. Let me see what I can do."

He was gone then. Thomas stood in the middle of his cell wondering what was going on. He was still damp from the water, and he still felt overheated from the nightmare. He looked up at the lenses and wondered if Remmick was approving all this. The man came back in.

"It's the best I could do on short notice," he said quickly, throwing a black jump suit at Thomas. "I have some shoes and socks for you as well. There weren't a lot of choices. However, these should be at least a close fit. You are larger than Tobias, so I chose accordingly."

Thomas was climbing into the suit when he heard Toby's name. He turned toward the man and let his mouth drop open for a moment.

"You know Toby?" he asked, amazed.

"I am Toby's father," the man said quickly, picking up the nickname Thomas had used. "We have to go help my children. However, I came for you first. The security wasn't as high here, and I may need help with Toby and Anisha. You see, the security there is very high."

"And this isn't?" Thomas asked ironically, slipping into the socks.

The shoes were a perfect fit, as was the jumpsuit.

"How do I look?"

"That will do. We have to go now."

The man led him out into the central area. The guards were there, but they were simply staring. Nothing that was going on around them seemed to be affecting them. They stared vacantly around the room. The roving guard seemed to have part of a silly grin on his face.

"How did you get in here?" Thomas asked.

"Technology is good, Thomas," the man said. "It can be used for good things. Sometimes, of course, it has to be used for something bad, like tonight. But don't you suppose the Father of All will forgive our poor use of his blessings just this once? Come on, we must act with urgency."

"I don't know who you are," Thomas said, following him down the hallway, through doors that should have been secured but were not.

They stopped at a room with an open door, and stepped in. The walls were lined with shelves, with uniforms both black and orange, socks, undergarments for men and women, and stacks of towels.

"I found this a moment ago," the man said. "That guard back there told me where it was. Glad it was here. Aren't you? My name is Salah."

"Glad to meet you, Mr. Salah," Thomas said, watching the man rummage through the clothing.

"I am not 'Mr. Salah'. I am just 'Salah', unless you want me to call you Mr. Thomas. The girl is a little bit shorter than you. She's, what, about this tall? Good. We'll need socks for her and your friend. He's about your size? Oh, well, we'll trust that they have their correct undergarments, too. Come on, Thomas. Remember: Our opportunity will be fleeting. We must hurry."

Thomas carried the clothing Salah had picked out. They went down the hallway. All of the doors were unlocked. He tested two as they passed, and the doors swung slowly open. They crossed two more doors, and entered another central prison area identical to the one Thomas had been imprisoned in. The two guards, both female, looked up from their work and smiled broadly.

Salah moved across the central area to one of the cell doors. Thomas noted it was the same cell, relatively, he'd been kept in. It even had the number "10" stenciled above the door. Salah pushed the door open and turned quickly around. Thomas started to look in, but Salah quickly turned him away as well. He grabbed the jump suit he'd picked out for Lori and threw it behind him.

"We're friends, Lorelei," he said over his shoulder. "You know Thomas. We are here to rescue you."

"How did you get here?" Lori shouted from the cell. "And who are you?"

Her voice sounded strained.

"My name is Salah. I am Tobias' and Anisha's father," Salah said. "If you could dress quickly, we can be on our way. We are in a bit of a hurry."

Thomas found his deep voice somehow comforting. Something inside him tried to tell him this wasn't logical, that no one could walk into a high-security prison and walk out with the prisoners, but he wanted so much to believe it was really happening.

Sometimes, he thought, you just have to accept things on faith.

"I believe you had trouble sleeping tonight," Salah said, throwing a pair of socks over his shoulder. "Maybe even a nightmare or two."

"How did you know that?" Thomas asked.

"That was me," Salah said, throwing the shoes over his shoulder.

Lori shouted "Ouch!"

"Sorry, Lorelei," Salah apologized. "I had to disarm the guards, but I needed you alert. It was a difficult balance to provide for the guards and protect you. I knew it would probably cause some discomfort, but I hoped you would forgive me."

"If you are who you say you are, it's well worth it," Lori said, walking out from behind them.

Her face looked drawn, and she looked tired, but she gave Thomas a hug. He felt the fear in her as he held her close.

"It'll be okay," he said. "We're going home. We are going home, aren't we, Salah?"

"That is our plan."

He looked over her shoulder. Salah was smiling. He turned and walked quickly across the central area, and down the hall again. Thomas and Lori rushed to keep up with him.

A right turn and two more doors that should have been locked, and they were in another round area. Again the guards, male this time, just watched them and smiled. Salah led them across the room to the same cell, number ten, and pushed the door open.

Cory jumped off his bed, his mouth open. He saw Lori behind Salah and grabbed for his blanket. Salah grabbed the girl and turned her away.

"Must give the young man his privacy," he said simply, tossing the jump suit in to him. "This should fit at least as well as Thomas's here. Please hurry. We don't have much time."

"Who—" Cory said, scrambling into the black jump suit.

"This is Salah, Toby's father," Thomas said. "He's springing us! We're going home!"

"I'm in favor of that," Cory said. "But, how?"

"I don't know," Thomas said, laughing, "but this is great! Wait till you see what he's done with the guards. You're not going to believe it."

"I'm afraid they won't be very happy with us," Salah said quickly. "We should hurry while we can. Are you ready? Then, Thomas, Cory and Lorelei, come with me. Quickly. Please."

Together they walked across the central area, and into the hall. The doors were all unlocked, and they opened as they pushed through. They turned right again, and after a short, dark hallway, found themselves standing at the alcove they all remembered from several days before.

"This is the last gate," Thomas said softly.

The guards looked up and smiled as they pushed their way through the heavy barred doorway and into the foyer. The guard at the desk had the same silly grin as the others.

They climbed the spiral stairway to the alcove above. The door to the last room was closed, but Salah opened it and ushered them through the small rooms and doors Cory remembered. Door after door opened to Salah's touch.

They left the processing corridor and crossed the office area. Many of the desks were empty, but some had soldiers sitting, staring at the screens, most with silly grins on their faces.

"What did you do to them?" Cory asked, incredulous.

"Something I would rather not have done," Salah said softly. He thought a moment, then said, "It is not permanent, and it will be wearing off very soon. We must hurry."

"But the doors to the cells," Cory said. "There are supposed to be safeguards on them. No two can open at the same time. How—"

"All in good time," Salah returned. "Come this way."

They turned left to the security entrance. They could not see guards behind the dark glass on the left, but they were sure they were there. Cory pictured them staring blankly at them as they passed, just as their colleagues had. In moments they were out on the short stairway, stepping down onto solid ground in the night.

The lights around the compound were orange, and lit everything. Their shadows were weak and sprayed around them like a fan. The air was still warm. The fresh air felt good to all of them. The sky was black and shot with stars. Cory had no idea what time it was. He looked up at the fences and shuddered to think they might have to climb them to get away. Yet, he realized he was prepared to do that if necessary.

Lori saw him staring at the barbed wire at the top, and reached down and gently took his hand. Cory looked into her eyes, and felt his cheeks flush.

Salah said simply, "We need to go this way."

He led them to the right, away from the entrance gate in the fence. They followed him around the corner of the building they'd been imprisoned in.

"They didn't keep your son with us," Thomas commented as they walked.

Salah nodded, and glanced up at the full moon.

"They were special," he said. "Their prison is special. I am not sure the guards are adequately taken care of like these were. We may have to work harder to get them out. That is why I needed the three of you. The more hands there are, the easier the work is."

The pace he set was almost impossible to keep up with. They turned the corner and came face to face with a black jeep and a soldier standing to one side. Salah continued to walk swiftly toward the soldier. The soldier stood firm, blocking their path.

He took a defensive posture. He aimed his rifle at them, and said, "Halt!"

Salah stopped, looked at the soldier, and said softly, "There were several shielded rooms. I tried to pick a time when all the soldiers would be out and about. It appears I was not entirely successful."

"What is going on around here?" the soldier asked angrily. "Everyone acts as if they've gone crazy!"

"Not crazy, soldier," Salah said. "They just don't care about much at the moment. It'll wear off in a very short time, and there will be no lasting side effects. But I don't have time to talk. They need you in the prison area. The high security area has been breached."

The soldier nodded, and said, "Yes, sir!"

He jumped into the jeep. Salah stopped him.

"Please wait a moment. Would you be so kind as to loan us your transport for a while? You can pick it up down by the hangar in the morning."

"Yes, sir," the soldier returned. He jumped back out and jogged toward the processing building.

Salah smiled as he disappeared around the corner, and said, "He wasn't as affected as the others, but it was enough. I don't suppose you know how to operate this vehicle, do you, Thomas?"

Thomas smiled broadly, and said, "Do I ever! These goons owe me one of these, anyway!"

He climbed behind the driver's wheel and started the engine.

"Anybody want a ride?" He asked.

"In a moment," Salah said, pointing toward the high security fence that surrounded the second of the two buildings in the complex. "My children are in there."

Thomas turned the engine off, and climbed out.

The building was identical to the prison they had been in. Besides the fence that circled the entire compound, double fences completely circled the single building. Salah approached, then stopped.

"This fence is powered," he said, pointing out the insulators isolating the chain link from the grounded posts. "If we ground the fence, the power should burn out the transformers. I looked them over and they won't take much. Now, Thomas, I know you want to keep this vehicle, but—"

"You want me to drive it into the fence to short it out," Thomas said, smiling. He felt a surge of excitement.

"Well, yes," Salah said softly. "I would prefer it if you weren't in it. I do not wish to see you harmed. Can you do that safely?"

"Don't worry," Thomas said, "I can jump free. About thirty miles per hour ought to do it. Everyone get out of my way."

Cory grabbed his arm, and said, "I ought to do this."

"Get outta here," Thomas said. "I've seen you drive, and, frankly, it isn't a pretty sight. Besides, I owe the military this!"

They all stood back, and Thomas jammed the jeep into reverse. He drove backwards, weaving back and forth, for about fifty yards. Then he jammed it into gear, and revved the engine. He popped the clutch. The vehicle lurched ahead. As he came even with his friends, he yanked the gearshift into neutral, and rolled out of the seat. He hit the ground hard, but he didn't care.

The jeep went on, slowing slightly, but hit the fence with enough force to crush the insulators and ground the powered chain link section. There was a shower of sparks, and then it was over. The jeep burst into flame.

"That activated the circuit breakers. The fence is now unpowered. Excellent work, Thomas.Come along quickly," Salah said, pushing through the first gate.

It resisted, its frame warped by the intrusion of the jeep twenty feet away, but it broke free after some pushing. The second gate was easier. The front door of the building simply gave way at their touch and they entered an alcove with four guards standing around smiling a lot.

"Disarm them, boys," Salah said.

"Yes, sir," Cory responded, and took the weapons from each of the guards in turn, and threw them out on the tarmac.

The soldiers offered no resistance. One, smiling, turned quickly to help Cory with his task.

They went through the second door, which also gave way at their touch. They were in a large empty room. It was as if the whole of the building were gutted. In front of them was a large double cage of huge bars. Inside the inner cage a wide stair descended into the lower area. The doors stood open, the guards between the bars of the outer and inner cage stood listless and apparently unaware they were there. They went down. A large room, similar to where they had been kept, with similar surveillance equipment greeted them. Two soldiers manned the equipment, both under whatever influence Salah had used on them. The friends looked around and saw the rover standing against the wall swinging his rifle back and forth by the strap.

"Disarm him," Salah said, motioning casually.

The wall on the right was concrete, and there seemed to be no openings. On the left a large barred door blocked their path. Salah pushed it open easily. They went in, passed soldiers with the same blank looks on their faces, and walked through several doors that should have been locked, but weren't. They entered a larger version of the central cell blocks the teens had been kept in. This one had a dozen or more cells around the outside. Several doors without windows.

"The doors without windows aren't cells," Cory said.

"He's right," Thomas affirmed.

The guards at the console were staring vacantly at the monitors.

"We'll have to search all the cells."

"Cell ten," Thomas said decisively.

Salah looked at him, and nodded. They walked over, opened the cell and walked in.

The cell seemed identical in size and layout to the cells they'd all been used to. There were two lights, one on each side of the cell, and Thomas immediately saw three sets of the camera lenses, the third in the wall, and down lower.

On the bed was a young girl, maybe eleven or twelve. The blanket covered her, but she appeared to be wearing no clothing, and there was none in the cell. Her dark hair was scattered all over her head. She was lethargic, her face almost ghastly pale, her eyes not quite closed and glazed over.

"Anisha," Salah said softly, kneeling by her bedside. There were tears in his eyes.

He stroked her hair and face, and raised her to his arms. She hung limply for several seconds. Slowly she began to respond to her father's touch. As she responded, his smile grew through his tears.

"Find my son," he said to Thomas. Then to Lori, "Find some clothing, please. Lori, she does not look good in orange."

Lori nodded.

The three began to explore each door in turn. One door at a time. Thomas shouted first, and Cory ran to his side.

Toby sat on his bed, curled tightly in the corner of the wall, wrapped in his blanket, his head buried between his knees. When they entered, he looked up. At first, he saw only the uniforms, then he began to slowly recognize his friends. His eyes lost their glassy stare, and his mouth dropped open in disbelief.

The first words out of his mouth were unintelligible. Then he shook his head, and said, "Is this a dream?"

"Not unless we're all in the same dream," Thomas said. "Your father is here. He's with Anisha right now. Come on."

Toby hesitated, hung his head and said, "They won't let me have any clothes. I cannot greet my father naked."

"We're getting that taken care of right now," Thomas said softly. "I hope you like black. Cory, go see if Lori found the clothes locker. Hurry. You stay here, Toby. I'll be right back."

Thomas went back to cell ten, and burst in. Salah was sitting on the bed holding his daughter wrapped in the blanket. He was feeding her small bits of what appeared to be an energy bar. She was holding on to him tightly, and eating slowly. They were talking. Thomas could not understand the words either was using. He thought about it, and nodded.

"I found Toby," he said. "He's all right. We're getting him some clothes right now."

Salah looked up, tears still in his eyes, and said, "They did this to my children. I have never seen such inhumanity."

Lori appeared at the door with clothes, a black jump suit, black undergarments, shoes, socks, and pushed past Thomas.

She handed him clothing for Toby, and said, "I did the best I could. I hope these fit."

"Where's Cory?" Thomas asked, looking around the central area.

"He thought he heard a noise out in the alcove, and went to investigate," she responded.

Salah looked up, and a cloud passed his face. Thomas nodded, took the clothes and went back to Toby's cell.

Toby was standing, still wrapped in the blanket. Thomas handed him the boxer shorts first, and threw the rest on the bed.

"You get dressed. Hurry. I have to go find Cory, then we can get out of here," he said.

"You won't have to wait for me," Toby said quickly.

As he passed the cell Salah was in he saw Lori helping to dress Anisha. Salah looked totally out of place, and a little confused, but the girl seemed to be more alert and was even helping herself. He ran across to the short hall toward the alcove. He turned, and stopped short. He recognized the man immediately, and felt a wrench in his stomach.

Remmick stood there, one hand gripping Cory's jump suit at the shoulder, the other holding a gun next to his face. He was using Cory as a shield. He could effectively cover the area in front of him without becoming too exposed. He was pushing him toward the open area. Cory's face was frozen between fear and hate.

"You!" Remmick snapped at Thomas. "Get back! Now!"

Thomas walked backward until he was in the open space. Remmick followed and stepped out where he could see the whole area. He held tightly onto Cory's shoulder, but pointed the gun over his other shoulder directly at Thomas.

"Where are the rest of them?" He asked.

"Who?" Thomas asked softly.

"The rest of the aliens!" Remmick shouted. "You had to have help to do all this! I don't know what's going on, but it ends here! Your escape failed. You are going back to your cells."

"I'm not going back in the cell," Thomas said evenly. "That's not going to happen. So, what happens next?"

"Then, I kill you," Remmick said coolly. "You won't give me any trouble when you're dead."

# CHAPTER 24

Thomas stood as still as he could. He tried not to look frightened, but he could feel himself trembling. Slowly he backed away from Remmick, back toward the center of the area. The two guards there looked up, and each had a kind of puzzled look on their faces. Thomas swallowed.

"Salah," he said as calm as he could, "I think I've found Cory."

Salah came to the door of his daughter's cell, and surveyed the situation. He seemed to know instantly what was happening. He nodded toward Cory, and looked up at Remmick.

"When did you realize the drug had worn off?" he asked casually.

Remmick shook his head, and said, "So it was drugs. How did you do it? In the water? In the food?"

"Oh," Salah said smoothly, "in the water. Everyone drinks water. We thought it was about time the American public saw what you were doing here. There are about twelve or fourteen of us out and about tonight. I assume you've captured the others by now."

Remmick sneered, and said, "I didn't drink the water. How long does this drug last?"

"Well, the whole water supply is contaminated," Salah returned. "I'm not going to get myself killed over this. You will get very thirsty before this stuff is flushed out of the water system if you don't have the antidote."

"Where is it?"

"I have some in my pocket," Salah said easily. "If I reach into my pocket and get it, you won't shoot me, will you?"

"Move real slow," Remmick warned.

Salah reached carefully into his pocket and slowly pulled out a square cube. It was about an inch on a side, and shiny black. He held it up for Remmick to see. Then he reached over and put it on the top of the monitor panels. The guards followed his movements with a bland interest.

"It's very potent. That is enough to purify the water in the tank. Dissolve it in a gallon of water, pour it into your water tank, and it will purify your entire supply. I'll step back over here."

"What's in it?" Remmick asked.

"Common chemicals. Your chemists could reproduce it very easily, even without the formula. If you give a drop to each of the guards, they should all come around rather quickly. I just don't want you to hurt any of the children."

"You've been led down the garden path, mister," Remmick snarled, moving closer to the cube. "You and your fellow extremists don't know how dangerous all this is. We have things in that hangar that would scare you to death. If they wanted to swoop down and take over this planet, we couldn't stop them. We're trying to protect you! You only have one dozen men? You took over this whole base?"

"Well, no," Salah said quietly. "Just this section. We have allies among your troops. They are covering for us in the other sections. I would be happy to give you the names if you leave the children alone. You see, we didn't plan on any resistance. You're really quite efficient, whoever you are."

Remmick sneered, and said, "Those allies of yours will spend a long time with you in a federal penitentiary. You've violated the law in the worst possible way."

He moved closer to the cube while he talked. He held onto Cory, dragging him as he sidled toward it. He was close enough to reach out and grab it.

"Tell me, soldier," Salah said softly, "Of what value are these children?"

"The two in these cells are aliens. They're probably not even children, at least, not as we know them. These others—you stand right there, Thomas—have been keeping company with one of them. They are material witnesses. They probably know some of their secrets. We want to find out just how much they know."

"Oh, I see," Salah said, hanging his head. "What will my wife do without me? I know you can't let me go free, but could I talk to her before you imprison us?"

Remmick was standing next to the consol. He glanced at the cube. Both his hands were occupied. He realized he was faced with releasing Cory or putting down his gun. He chose to release Cory.

"You move and you're dead," he said savagely.

He reached out to take the cube. A puzzled look crossed his face as he realized it wasn't a container of any kind. His eyes darted back toward Salah. It was too late.

Salah moved like lightening. He stepped forward and slipped between Cory and Remmick. He pushed Cory away to safety, but Cory was surprised at the softness of that push. At the same time, he lifted Remmick's gun arm. Remmick squeezed the trigger, but the bullet struck the ceiling harmlessly. Salah twisted the weapon out of Remmick's hand and shoved him gently back toward the wall. He stood holding the gun by the barrel, and Remmick stood, weaponless, holding the cube.

It hadn't been a violent confrontation. In fact, both Cory and Thomas were amazed at the gentleness Salah had demonstrated. Yet, he stood holding the gun, and Remmick had been powerless to stop him.

After a moment, when he began to realize what had happened, Remmick looked up and said, "What is this thing?"

"Just a cube," Salah replied, laying the gun aside. "Call it a 'good luck charm'. It's an heirloom. I would like it back."

He held out his hand, and Remmick gave it a gently toss. Salah caught it.

"Boys, we have to move quickly now. This delay is putting us in grave danger. I don't know what we should do with this person."

"I know what to do," Cory said softly. "You've overridden the locks in here. Can you make just one active again?"

Salah nodded, and smiled, and said, "That would have unity. I take it you know this one?"

"This is Remmick," Thomas spat. "He's the one who captured us. It took about a dozen or so of his men to overpower four teenagers."

Salah's eyes narrowed, and he looked back to Remmick.

"You have not given me a reason to spare you, sir," Salah said, his voice betraying his dislike of the man. "You did not spare my son and daughter of indignities no child should have to endure. Yet, I see you would continue to plague them if I allowed you. Put him where you will, Cory. I will fix the lock. But do it quickly."

Cory shouted, "Hey, Toby! Get out here, quick!"

Toby hobbled out, still trying to put on his last shoe.

"You were pretty calm," he said to Cory. "You like being in danger?"

"Not exactly," Cory replied. "I'm just getting used to it. Lately every time I go out with Thomas I get in trouble. Let's use that cell over there. They don't monitor it regularly. It'll be a long time before they find him."

Remmick followed quietly. Salah watched him pass, a look of pain mixed with the anger in his eyes. When they got to the door the boys parted to let the major enter. He suddenly turned and tried to grab Toby by the collar. Cory kicked at the back of his leg as hard as he could, and Remmick collapsed under his own weight. As he turned, Cory released all his anger in one hard fist to the side of Remmick's face. The major tumbled over, and the boys were clear.

Meanwhile Thomas had taken the gun from Salah and had it trained directly at Remmick's head. Remmick came up ready to fight, saw the gun, and sank back to the floor. He reached out and held the door jamb for support.

"You won't use that," he said simply.

"I really don't know if I would or not," Thomas said, his voice carried anger and trembled slightly with fear. "I'm not sure you ought to chance it, though. I think I would pull the trigger if I had to. I won't go back into one of your cells, and I won't let them go back, either. You know I'll do anything, anything to get out of here."

Remmick stared deep in the boy's eyes for a moment, then said, "I see that you will. In here, then?"

He stood shakily, and entered the cell. Cory slammed the door shut.

Salah held the cube to his lips, and blew into it. The door clanged as the lock activated. He looked at the two boys.

"You are very violent," he said softly, sadly.

"Sometimes," Cory admitted.

He realized he should have felt incredibly satisfied to have had a chance to get even with Remmick. Instead he felt a little embarrassed.

"Where did you learn to fight like that?" Toby asked, incredulous.

"A bully taught me a few years ago," Cory responded. "It's a long story. Maybe, if we have time, I'll tell you."

"That's a pretty powerful tool you have there," Thomas said, pointing to the cube. "What else will it do?"

"This? It's an heirloom, as I told your friend. It's a…communication device. I have someone helping me. Come, we have to go quickly."

"That's what I wanted to retrieve from the vehicle," Toby said. "I had one just like it, only it wasn't an heirloom. It was new. It belonged to my mother. I'm afraid, Abba, I stole it when we took the vehicle."

Salah frowned, but there was a warmth there, as well.

"We'll discuss this later," he said softly.

"Salah," Cory said suddenly. "Why didn't the drugs in the water affect us, too? I drank a lot this evening."

Thomas glanced from Salah to Cory, then said, "There were never any drugs, Cory. He was playing along with Remmick, waiting for an opportunity to disarm him."

"Oh," Cory said, feeling a little silly.

"It was a broadcast," Salah explained quietly. "It was a kind of radio wave. We could target the area and put everyone to sleep, almost. It's distasteful because it removes free will for a time, and that is not a good thing. I'm sorry. I felt I had no choice."

Salah went back into Anisha's cell and scooped her up. He rushed Lori out in front of him, and the six escapees left the prison for what they hoped was the last time.

As they passed the alcove with the guards, one of the guards looked confused, and started to move toward them. The boys and Lori dodged past him, but Salah stopped, patted the soldier on the shoulder, and pushed him gently up against the wall. They climbed the straight stairway, through the bars, and out the doors onto the asphalt. The jeep was still burning, but more quietly now. The light was still orange and the air warm. They all breathed deeply.

As they paused to get their bearings, and to catch their breath, Salah pulled his cube out and blew gently on it. Immediately they heard the doors behind them begin to clang shut. The final door, the entrance, slammed exceptionally hard.

The boys watched; their eyes wide. They looked at Salah.

"I told her to be gentle," he said defensively. "You know your mother, Tobias. She has trouble controlling her temper."

"Mother is here?" Tobias shouted. "Where is she?"

Salah looked up, pointed at the countless stars, and said, "Right about there. But we still have to get back to her. It would be good if we had another jeep. Thomas, please take these to your father. I want him to see them."

He handed Thomas a plastic box about the size of a juice box. Thomas looked in and saw a number of discs. They looked like CD's or DVD's, but much smaller. He shrugged, checked the latch on the lid, and slipped it into his pocket. The pockets on his jumper were more than large enough to carry the box comfortably. They followed Salah toward the corner of the building, and the heavy, damaged chain link fence. Salah looked around the corner furtively. He almost immediately ducked back. He put Anisha down, and steadied her.

"What's wrong?" Thomas asked.

Salah's face showed worry.

"We were a little slow," he said softly. "Your jailer held us up for too long a time. The soldiers are leaving the other prison. I'm afraid it's too late to seal those doors. Mostly they are still dazed, but that won't last long enough for us to get past them. Look around the corner, Cory."

Cory did as he was told.

"That direction is north. Look beyond the lights, clear up to the ridge about three miles beyond the compound. Do you see it? It's the highest thing that direction."

"I see it," Cory said softly.

"That is your first landmark. You need to make for that point. From there you follow the road north, then east. Keep following the road, Cory. I drove down from there this evening."

"Without being seen?" Thomas exclaimed.

"I was driving one of their vehicles. They left it in the town when they departed and your father thought it would be a good disguise for me. It was. I was part of the family. No one questioned my presence. I left it just west of here. Listen carefully. Outside the gate you turn left, west. Follow the road west. It makes a jog past a storage yard. It looks like mostly old parts and worn out equipment. Keep going. Off to the left, about a quarter mile from here, you'll see a small shed. The vehicle is parked behind the shed. You must get to that vehicle and drive north to the ridge. Then follow the road. Your fathers are waiting for you in the pass. You must make it to the pass. Your fathers have some help, but you must get to the pass. Your fathers want to take you all home. We have to separate—"

"We have to stay together," Cory said firmly.

"We will have to separate now," Salah repeated, more firmly. "Find the vehicle. Don't wait for us. Get in and drive up to that ridge. We will all meet there."

"Where did you leave the vehicle again?" Thomas asked.

"The vehicle is there," Salah said, pointing toward the low mountains on the west. "Look for the shed. It is a quarter mile west and just off your left shoulder. The soldiers are already beginning to sense something very wrong has happened. Cory, you take Toby and Lori and go across the compound. Walk through the soldiers as if you are one of them and you expect them to just let you pass. They will. The gate is open now. It won't lock again until they replace it. Once you're free of the prison compound, turn west. You will find the vehicle hidden behind the shed. That's the shortest route. Stand tall, look like soldiers, and you won't be challenged. Thomas, you will come with me. I may need you to help carry Anisha. We will go this way. South. We will only be separated for a short time, Tobias. There are some things in a large building that direction I have to recover."

"Our vehicle?" Toby questioned.

Salah nodded and said, "Yes, son. We cannot leave it here."

"I'm sorry, Abba," Toby said softly, his voice cracking.

"It'll be fine, son," Salah said warmly, placing his hand on the boy's shoulder, then pulling him into a quick embrace. "Does everybody know what they're going to do?"

Everyone nodded, and Thomas took Cory, Toby and Lori's hands and said, "Be very careful. We'll see you at the pass."

"Go now, children," Salah said softly.

The three stood tall and started across the asphalt. As they grew close to the dozen or so soldiers in the compound they began to look more like just another small group of soldiers trying to make some sense out of what had happened to them tonight. Salah nodded, and turned back to Thomas.

"They have the best chance of making it to the pass where you father is waiting," he said quietly. "I'm afraid when they see the young girl with us, we will not look like ordinary soldiers."

"Then, we'll just have to stay in the shadows," Thomas said softly. "Salah, how long will the locks hold in the small prison?"

"Oh, I'm afraid they're permanent."

"What do you mean 'permanent'?"

"The doors won't operate ever again," Salah said, his voice edged with regret. "They will have to cut through them to gain access."

"All the doors?"

"All of them," Salah said softly.

Thomas grinned broadly, picked Anisha up and said, "Let's go. We have a ride to catch."

"I gave her something to eat," Salah said. "It will help her. Try to keep her nibbling at it."

"What is it?" Thomas asked as they walked.

Anisha held up part of a small grain bar.

"That looks like an energy bar," Thomas said.

"Something like that," Salah said.

Thomas looked down at the girl and said, "I need you to take a bite, Anisha. Your father said it would help you feel better."

Anisha, though still weak, was becoming more alert. She looked up at him with large, blue eyes, and half smiled.

"Who are you?" she asked weakly.

"I'm a friend," Thomas said. "Take a bite of your energy bar for me, okay?"

Anisha shook her head, saw her father right behind them, and relaxed again. She took a small bite of the bar, then she melted against Thomas's chest. He could feel her snuggling closer. He felt, at that moment, trusted and loved. He realized he would do anything he could to earn that trust.

Salah followed them along outer fence of the prison compound.

# CHAPTER 25

Cory walked tall, and strode evenly across the asphalt. He felt like the prison compound was at least a mile wide. He looked over his shoulder. Lori and Toby were keeping up. In spite of the extra hardships Toby had experienced, he seemed to have bounced back quickly.

An eternity seemed to pass before they reached the open part of the compound and could see the main gate. The soldiers, more of them now, were standing around looking confused. The gate, just beyond, was hanging open, swinging on a single hinge. Cory breathed deeply, stood tall as he could, and strode forward.

"Here goes," he said softly to Lori and Tobias. "Look confident."

They walked directly toward the milling soldiers. When they reached the outliers of the group they continued on toward the gate. The soldiers didn't pay much attention to them, and, in fact, still seemed confused and disoriented. Some were beginning to look around as if trying to figure out what had happened. The three teens walked out the compound gate and turned west, just as Salah had told them.

The compound lights were mercury vapor, but the lone light at the stop sign ahead was white and cast a lonely spot on the road. The three of them turned to look back. The soldiers were beginning to form into groups. Their movements were less than random. Beyond, just by the far corner, they could see Salah, Thomas and Anisha. They were small and very far away. Lori raised her hand slightly in an involuntary wave.

One of the soldiers pointed directly at them, said something to a companion, and the two began to move toward the compound gate.

"Oh," Lori said softly, dropping her hand quickly.

"We're going to get the Major," Cory shouted, deepening his voice. "Communications are out, and the vehicle back there is wrecked. Stay here and guard the compound."

"We don't think there's anything left to guard," one of the soldiers shouted back.

"I wouldn't want to tell the Major that," Cory snapped in his best imitation of Remmick. "Go and find out if the prisoners are still secure. We'll be back in 10 minutes."

"Yes, sir," the soldier said.

He began to organize the others and they turned toward the buildings.

Lori looked at Cory, and said, "That was wonderful!"

"I'm not going back," he returned. "You two, follow me."

There was no cover now, just the dark. They walked to the cross road and looked both ways. Cory doubted there would be traffic this time of night under normal circumstances, and wasn't surprised to see the road deserted. It went right past what he was sure were barracks or housing of some kind. To the left it shot off into desolation. He could not see any buildings for a long way, then, in the distance, lights and a group of larger structures. He breathed deeply.

"This way," he said, and crossed the road, walking west toward the black mountains.

"What if the soldiers find the vehicle first?" Toby asked.

"That's not likely," Cory said. "Besides, it's one of theirs, and they probably won't give it a second thought. Are you okay, Lori?"

"So far," Lori said softly.

"Good. Toby, how widespread is this — this — whatever your father has done?"

"I don't know," Toby said softly as they walked. "It could be very wide, but I don't think Father would want to hurt everyone. He'd try to only hurt who he needed to."

"They're not hurt, Toby," Cory said gently. "You father said it would wear off. It's already wearing off for most of them."

"They're still hurt," Toby returned. "Father is upset about that. He didn't like taking their freedom away."

"Toby, they took your freedom away," Cory reasoned.

"Neither was right," Toby said stubbornly. "We shouldn't do what they do! It's wrong no matter why we do it!"

"You're right, Toby. I'm sorry. Let's keep moving," Cory said quietly, noticing Lori putting her arm around the younger boy.

They followed the street away from the prison. They passed three Quonset-type buildings on the right. They seemed deserted and dark. Cory felt increasingly nervous in spite of the incredible joy he also felt at being free. The road was bad, in need of repair, and the dirt around was sterile, dead. They were passing the last of the Quonsets when Cory caught movement out the corner of his eye. As he turned a solder walked out of the deeper shadow by the last Quonset, his rifle ready.

"What's been happening?" he yelled.

Cory breathed deeply. He hoped communications were still down. That would still be in their favor.

"We're trying to find out," he said evenly, pitching his voice lower, still trying to imitate Remmick again. "Are you getting through this okay?"

"We're not fully awake yet," the soldier said. "We lost communications. We think the black prison was raided about an hour ago. Have you seen any strangers on base?"

"No," Cory responded. "We lost a couple of prisoners. Have you seen anyone running around in orange jumpsuits?"

"No," the soldier returned. "I've been here only about ten minutes, though."

Cory said, "Our group has several prisoners back in custody already. We're looking for the others. You know what's been going on?"

"We don't know," the soldier returned. "The doors are all screwed up. Nothing is locked down. We were all too fuzzy to even challenge anyone if we had seen them. You're with that secret group down there in section six, then?"

"We are."

"You're all pretty young," the soldier said, lowering his rifle. "Especially you."

He pointed directly at Toby. Toby stood as tall as he could.

"I'm old enough to be with section six," he snapped.

"It's a new program," Cory added. "Some of us are just out of high school. Got a problem with that?"

"Okay," the soldier said. "I'm sorry. I guess I'm just getting older. You're not armed."

The soldier seemed young, too, and he wasn't wearing black. Even in the dark his working uniform looked more normal than anything Cory had seen all day.

"Someone took our weapons," Cory responded.

"Do you think we're under attack, or is this just a prison break?" the soldier asked, lowering his weapon even more.

"We suspect it's just a prison break," Cory said, accepting what the soldier already believed. "You should stay real sharp, though, soldier. They may still be close by. This could still be something larger."

"I will. Maybe you'd better come in here and at least check out an M-16."

Cory glanced back at Lori, saw her shake her head. Toby only frowned.

"No, thanks," Cory said quickly. "We have to report back to the Major in twenty minutes. We have to hurry."

"The Major is running things himself? I guess the non-coms are still a little out of it, then. Do you know how they did it?"

"We think it was drugs in the water," Cory said, beginning to walk on. "You'd better not drink anything not bottled till they find out."

"Sure thing," the soldier returned. "Thanks. And, be careful."

"We will. You, too."

Cory breathed deeply as the soldier backed into the darker shadows again. They continued on past the Quonsets. They approached a second intersection. The pavement veered right, but Cory guided them slightly left, across the second road and past a large, open yard. It was well lit, and looked like a junk yard of sorts. He didn't recognize any of the piles of used, worn out parts. They walked quickly along, trying to stay in the shadows cast by the piles of discarded parts. Cory felt light was their worst enemy at this point in time. Lori turned and glanced back at the prison and shuddered. Cory realized she would have some particularly bad memories of that place. He stopped them when they reached the edge of the junk yard.

To the left they could see a shed maybe 50 yards away. It was across a large open space. He took another deep breath.

"You two stay here," he said softly. "I'll go make sure the hummer is still there. I'll come back and pick you up. Stay in the shadows."

He strode out across the space. It wasn't far and he hadn't seen anyone after the young soldier. He looked back and could see soldiers milling around in the prison compound, becoming more organized as the minutes passed. They weren't 400 yards away, and Cory was sure that wasn't nearly far enough for safety.

Off to the left, south and east of him, maybe half a mile away he saw a huge hangar lit up like a whole city. He could see a few soldiers wandering down there, too. They seemed to be recovering from the same thing the prison guards were fighting off. He shook his head and smiled. He wondered just what it was Salah had used to muddle so many brains.

He approached the shack, and breathed more easily. The hummer was parked in the blackness behind the small building. Salah had put it in just the right place. He smiled, then immediately dropped his smile. A dark mass stepped away from one of the shadows, rifle in hand, ready to shoot.

"Identify yourself," he said harshly.

"I can't," Cory said thinking quickly. "I feel like I've been drugged. What's going on around here?"

"That's a good question," the shadow said, stepping forward so the dim light revealed his face. His uniform was not the black jumpers Cory had become used to.

He isn't much older than me, Cory thought. He hoped he could get away as easily as he had a few minutes before.

"I need a weapon," he said. "Ours were stolen, and we don't know who took them. The Major sent me up here to see if the prisoners came this way."

"Where are you from?" the soldier asked, relaxing a little.

"Section six," Cory answered.

"And you came all the way up here without a weapon? Someone should have stopped you long before this."

"Everyone's acting really strange," Cory explained. "We think they put something in the water. It seems like those of us up in section six recovered faster."

"You guys get a lot of other stuff to drink," the soldier said, making a motion like drinking from a bottle.

"That's what we thought," Cory said. "I gotta go. The Major will put me on report if I don't get back pretty soon."

"Well, go over there to that big building. It's the photo lab. Tell them you're from section six and they should let you check out a couple of weapons. Everyone seems to let you guys have anything you want. Of course, that's if anyone there is thinking clearly again."

"Thanks," Cory said quickly. "Have you seen anything strange or out of the ordinary?"

"Someone left this vehicle up here," the soldier said, motioning to the Humvee. "I was sent to investigate it. It's one of yours, isn't it?"

"It is," Cory said evenly. "I ought to take it back to the compound. We think they were planning to use this as a get-away vehicle. The Major wants to put a crimp in their operation."

"What are you doing in that compound?" the soldier asked as Cory started toward the vehicle. "You said something about prisoners."

"It's top secret," Cory answered, opening the driver's door. "I can't say anything more than that. Where are you supposed to go after you identify this vehicle?"

"Back to parts inventory," the soldier said, his voice betraying his disappointment.

"Well," Cory said softly, "stay sharp. We still have some prisoners at large nearby. Do not let them get their hands on a weapon. They're dangerous, even unarmed."

The young soldier looked grateful for the hint of more excitement to come, and said, "I won't. You be careful, too."

"I will," Cory said, throwing the correct switch and starting the Humvee. He was more grateful than ever military vehicles didn't need keys.

He pulled away from the soldier, who stood watching, his mouth hanging open. Cory drove directly to the shadow where he knew Lori and Toby were hiding. They rushed toward him. Lori jumped in the front seat. Toby climbed in the back directly behind Lori.

"What took you so long?" Lori asked nervously.

"I met a friend," Cory said softly. "We're halfway home, kiddies. All we have to do is drive directly north to the ridge, then follow the road east. Piece of cake."

"Piece of cake," Toby reflected.

"Right," Cory said softly. "Let's go for a ride."

"Absolutely," Lori whispered. "The sooner the better."

They drove toward the cross road at the bottom of the junk yard. Toby turned backward in his seat and stared out the back window. Cory didn't stop at the corner. He turned left and drove in what he hoped was directly north.

"Cory," Toby said softly. "I think we have a problem."

"What?" Cory asked.

"That guard watched you carefully when you stopped to pick us up," Toby said. "He was walking toward us when you began to drive away. He watched as you turned the wrong direction and he became very agitated. He started to run toward us. I think he knows we're the prisoners who escaped."

"Well," Cory said quietly, "I don't think he can do anything about — oh, golly!"

Cory slammed on the brakes. A soldier in a black jump suit stood directly in front of the Hummer. He had a rifle trained directly on the windshield, directly on Cory.

"We have a problem," Cory repeated Toby's warning.

"Get out of the vehicle very slowly," the soldier almost shouted.

Cory glanced at Lori, then back at Toby.

"What do we do?" Lori asked. Her voice broke.

"You stay here," Cory instructed. "I'll see if we can bluff our way through just one more time."

Lori looked at him, and said, "What?"

"He may still be a little muddled," Cory said. "It's worth a try. I don't want to go back, and I think running him down might not be a good thing to do."

Toby nodded, but his face was washed with fear.

Cory opened his door slowly, carefully. He raised his left hand out of the door to show he was unarmed.

"I'm coming out," he shouted, stepping carefully to the ground. He brought his right hand out of the vehicle as soon as his feet were firmly planted on the ground. He kept them both high as he leaned against the vehicle door.

"Out here where I can see you," the soldier said.

Cory was not anxious to leave the shelter of the door. He stepped hesitantly to the side, glanced once at Lori sitting in the front seat with her hands to her face, and stood free of the protection of the door.

"Who are you?" the man asked, still pointing the rifle at the boy.

"We're from section six," Cory returned, keeping his voice as authoritative as he could.

"*I'm* from section six," the soldier returned. "I know everyone there. Who are you?"

Cory's mind was racing. He could see their escape ending in a pitiful whimper. He saw a second soldier, dressed in black like the first, approaching from beyond the first soldier. He knew he might talk his way out with one, but with two soldiers together he felt hope slipping.

"The Major sent us to check out the photo lab," Cory explained. "He thought the prisoners might be hiding there."

"No one has seen the Major in almost an hour," the soldier said. "And, you're unarmed."

"I wasn't going to bring my rifle out here to get shot by you," Cory said evenly. "You know our training."

"I do," the soldier admitted, "and you're not acting anything like one of us. I wasn't guarding the prison. I had another assignment. But you look like you just might be the prisoners who tried to escape tonight. Tell whoever else is in the vehicle to come out now. We're going to go back to the compound."

Cory heard the doors of the Hummer open, and felt his heart drop. Lori climbed out and Toby slipped out behind her. The younger boy immediately walked around Lori and toward the front of the car. Cory realized the boy's intent was to join him on his side of the vehicle. He was just rounding the right front of the vehicle when the soldier's focus shifted. The soldier moved the weapon slightly and fired a single shot just over the younger boy's head.

"Stay right there," he snapped.

"Absolutely I'll stay right here," Toby almost cried, his whole body shaking.

"Stop it!" Cory yelled. "You got us. You don't have to shoot us. We'll go where ever you want us to go."

The soldier moving up from behind the first was moving carefully, silently. There was something different in the dark shape, but Cory couldn't put his finger on it.

"You," the soldier said, pointing at Cory. "Move slowly to your right. You're going to join these two and we're going to walk very slowly back to the compound. You two step slowly away from the vehicle."

Cory looked around. There was no cover anywhere. The junk yard was 20 yards to their left, and the Quonsets at least 75 yards to their right. In between it was all flat and open. Except for the Hummer there was nothing to hide behind. The soldier was moving them away from that small island of safety.

"Come on," the soldier said, waving his rifle. "Turn around. You know where it is."

Cory turned slowly, and felt Lori and Toby close enough to brush his shoulder as they turned. Lori reached out and squeezed Cory's hand. There was a soft rustle behind them, and the three teens began to walk.

"You should get back in the Humvee," a deep voice said.

Cory stopped. It was a moment before he had the courage to look back. What he saw startled him more than anything else he'd seen that night. One figure, in black, stood over the limp, unconscious form of the soldier. He was the one who had come up behind the soldier. He wasn't wearing a uniform. He was simply dressed all in black. He wore a ski mask, a black, long-sleeve shirt, and black jeans. The soldier lay on the ground at his feet. Cory stared at him.

"I am very disappointed in you," the man said, pointing at Cory. "I expected you to be smarter than this."

His voice was deep, calm and warm.

"Yes, sir" Cory said, more because he couldn't think of anything else to say.

"Do you want to get out of here or not?" The man asked.

"Yes. Yes. But who are you?" Cory asked.

"Apparently your rescuer," the man answered. "The second one you've needed tonight. Follow me, Cory. You two get back in the vehicle."

Cory looked at Lori, she squeezed his hand again. He noticed she was breathing shallow, quick breaths. Toby nodded. He pushed Lori into the front seat and closed her door. Then he stood by the back door. Cory followed the man around the front of the vehicle.

The man pointed at the windshield and said, "This is bullet proof glass, not the bullet resistant stuff you see in the banks. Nothing will penetrate it. Nothing. The side windows are the same stuff. This vehicle is heavily armored, and carries an engine that could drive it clear through your house. You'd have to fall off a cliff to roll it over, and it'll go 45 miles per hour over the roughest terrain you've ever seen. Now, get into that vehicle and drive. Don't stop again. If someone else gets in your way run over them."

The man then took him firmly by the shoulders and pushed him into the front seat behind the driver's wheel.

"I don't know if I could run over someone on purpose," Cory said softly.

"If you have a big enough reason you can do anything," the man assured him. "These two are reason enough for anybody for now. Salah is depending on you to do your share. So are your parents. So am I. I don't know about the rest of them, but I don't do well with disappointment."

"What about him?" Cory asked, motioning to the soldier still lying off the left side of the vehicle.

"He'll wake in about ten minutes with a headache and sore back," the man said, pulling his mask off over his head.

He was tall, but his hair was grown out more than a soldier would have allowed. His face was deep cut, thin and angular. He stood easily on the flat ground next to the vehicle. He set the soldier's rifle gently in the back seat of the Humvee. Toby seemed to contemplate the weapon with distaste.

"The safety is on," the man said to Toby. "It cannot harm you. He doesn't need it anymore, but you might."

"It's good to see you again, Boothe," Toby said quietly, still eyeing the weapon.

"You, too, Tobias," the man said, closing the back door. "You should get in, now."

"Who are you?" Cory asked the man.

"Tobias's father knows me, and so does the sheriff back in town," the man said. "That would be Thomas's father. You know Thomas, I think. He's shared this adventure with you. The sheriff doesn't know I'm here. I'm afraid he wouldn't approve. However, I know these men, and I know this area. I needed to be here to help. No thanks needed."

"Okay, but who are you?" Cory asked again.

"I'm Boothe," the man said simply.

"Toby told us that, and that doesn't help much," Cory returned.

"It's not supposed to, Cory," the man said. "I think you should drive to meet your fathers. There'll be plenty of time for answers later."

"What if he wakes up?"

"I think I can handle that. Don't you? You'd better go."

He smiled grimly.

Toby was staring down at the dark form in the dirt. His eyes were mostly white in the moonlight, his mouth an open dark hole. He hadn't moved to get into the vehicle yet. He looked from Cory to the soldier, then back again. Finally, he walked to the soldier, bent over and patted him on the shoulder.

"I'm truly sorry," he said softly. "I hope you recover quickly."

Cory thought he saw a flicker of a smile flash across Boothe's face as Toby climbed into the back seat.

"He'll recover quickly, Tobias," Boothe said. "You can't stay here. You have to go."

"What about my father and Anisha?" Toby asked.

"Tobias, trust your father," Boothe said. "He'll be fine."

"They don't have any transportation," Cory argued.

"Salah will work something out," Boothe said, smiling. He slipped his mask on again. "Now, get going before any more soldiers show up."

"We have to go," Cory agreed. "What about you?"

"I'll be okay," Boothe said, smiling again. "You should go straight toward the landmarks Salah gave you. This street ends up ahead at a ball diamond. Turn right. About a block later you'll turn left. Follow that road and you'll be going in the right direction. Tobias, I've known your father many years. He will not find this situation difficult at all. On the contrary, the military is probably finding him a bit difficult. He still has a few cards up his sleeve."

"Cards?" Toby asked.

Boothe smiled through the mask, and said, "An Earth reference. Forget it."

"Thank you for the help, Boothe," Cory said.

Boothe nodded and stepped back from the vehicle. Cory hit the switch and the vehicle roared to life. He looked over the controls quickly, found the lights and turned them on. He heard Lori gasp, and turned in the direction she was looking.

Down at the other end of the base activity around the large hangar had increased. Soldiers were approaching the large structure from the north side. Helicopters were flying low down the runway from the north as well. They seemed to be heading for the hangar.

"What's going on?" Lori asked.

"My father," Toby said quietly, worry in his voice.

Boothe slapped the driver window with the palm of his hand.

"Go. Now!" He shouted.

Cory jumped, then slammed the vehicle in gear and headed north, as Boothe had instructed. In moments the Quonsets had hidden the hangar from them. They were alone in the dark again. He turned back to see where Boothe was, and could not see any trace of the man. The soldier was gone as well.

"Cory," Lori sniffed. "Just drive."

Cory reached across the vehicle toward her, and said softly, "We're out of here."

"Father always said freedom was the most important thing," Toby said quietly. "I didn't know what he meant until now."

The road ended at an intersection, just as Boothe had said. Cory swerved without stopping and hit the stop sign, clipping it off at the ground. The road passed an open field on the left. Cory could see a fence, a backstop, a baseball diamond. They passed a complex of buildings, and the road curved left in front of them. Cory sped around the corners, throwing both the other teens against the body of vehicle. The stop sign rode on the hood for half a block before it finally slid off the side. Cory used an expletive he knew his father would not have approved of. He glanced at Toby and realized he didn't approve, either. Lori just looked worried.

"We're going to find our parents" he said decisively.

He revved the engine, and the Humvee sped up the dark street. He was fastening his seat belts with one hand, and steering with the other. He glanced over at Lori. She was looking tense. Toby was leaning over her shoulder.

For the moment, they were free. And freedom tasted good.

Lori, Tobias and Cory left them next to the ruined fence. Salah reached out and took Thomas by the shoulder and pointed the opposite direction.

"Please take Anisha," he said softly.

Thomas picked Anisha up in his arms and was surprised at how light the young girl was. She smiled at him gratefully, and leaned into his chest. He felt her trust, and was a little surprised.

They walked across the back side of the compound. Thomas was a little confused. The entire compound was fenced in, and Thomas was sure he had seen only one gate. When they reached the fence, Salah paused. He leaned close to the chain link and was busy for several moments. Almost magically the fence parted.

"What did you do?" Thomas asked.

Salah just smiled the same simple, confident smile he'd used in the prison below. He pulled the sides apart and signaled for Thomas to go through. He followed, and paused at the fence again. Thomas was sure the fence hadn't been cut, and hadn't been broken in any way. The edges were smooth, and simply the last link in the fence. Salah pulled the sides together. There didn't seem to be any tension on either end of the fence. He leaned close, and the fence was whole. Thomas stared, incredulous.

"Chain link," Salah said with a quiet shrug. "So insecure."

He stood and walked away from the compound, indicating with a simply motion of his hand he wanted Thomas to follow. Thomas lifted Anisha closer to him, and walked into the dark open spaces separating the compound from the hangars a quarter mile away. The hangars were more brightly lit than the prison compound. The lights were white and brilliant as opposed to the orange mercury vapor lights around the prison.

Five or six buildings were grouped past the hangar. The hangar itself was the single largest structure in the area. A smaller hangar, though still huge by comparison to anything Thomas had ever seen, was attached on the right.

The distance they had to cover wasn't great, and the young girl was so light Thomas carried her easily. Salah smiled at the boy. It was that same smile that carried a simple, quiet assurance that everything was all right.

They reached the back side of the lesser hangar, breaking through the light almost like breaking out of water into the air. Salah walked to the large aircraft doors, which were closed, and stood next to them. He stared around the corner. Thomas leaned out and could see Salah's concern.

Soldiers were beginning to come out of the larger hangar, through doors at the right and left. There were fewer than a dozen. They were all in air force work uniforms, khaki's and camouflage. They looked confused and seemed to be wandering aimlessly.

"Time has been very important to us," Salah said quietly.

He took out the cube and whispered into it. He waited, nodded without speaking, and motioned to Thomas.

"We need to go in here," he said, indicating the lesser hanger they stood next to.

He hummed, and shook his head. He walked around the corner into full view of the milling soldiers. Thomas followed.

The side of the hangar was slightly darker than where they had been, but not dark enough to hide their movements. They were in a partial shadow.

Salah looked over at the soldiers, then at Thomas, then back to the soldiers again.

"We can go the way Cory and the others went," Thomas suggested.

Salah looked over his shoulder, and shook his head.

"What we need is in here," he said quietly, indicating the lesser hangar.

Thomas turned and looked, and saw the tarmac by the huge hangar filling with soldiers. A Jeep arrived. Several of the soldiers were now carrying arms. He looked at the wall of the lesser hangar and saw the door a few feet ahead.

"Well, there's the door," Thomas said. "Maybe we ought to go in. Can you use that cube and fuzzy up their minds again? It worked once."

Salah shook his head and said, "No. I cannot. We don't know where Tobias and your friends are. If we 'fuzzy up' their minds, as you say, they will never get away. I cannot protect them if we don't know exactly where they are. Also, we cannot use the process twice in so short a time. The chance of permanent change is increased with repeated use. I will not risk that."

"That's one thing I wouldn't worry about," Thomas contended.

"I must," Salah responded gently. "Even if the other children were clear of the base, I would have to consider the well-being and safety of the soldiers."

"They wouldn't consider our well-being," Thomas said harshly.

"I understand," Salah responded.

"Well, we can't stay here," Thomas said.

"We go into the hangar," Salah returned. "We will find transportation there. They have one of my vehicles. The one Tobias used is in this building. We are going to use it to escape."

"Toby said your SUV was broken."

"I'm not familiar with the terms you use," Salah said softly. "Assuming you were referring to my vehicle, I may be able to repair the damage. However, it may be beyond repair. If it is, I will need to fix it so they cannot ever make it work. Then we'll have to find another way to escape."

"What if we can't find another way to escape?"

"I like to think there are always possibilities, Thomas."

He walked along the side wall. The whole wall was featureless except for several doors at intervals to admit individual workers. They arrived at the first one and tried it. It was locked.

Salah whispered gently into the black cube again. For several seconds nothing happened. The cube beeped softly several times. Salah shook his head.

"It's not a power lock," he said sadly. "It's mechanical and complex. It cannot be opened remotely."

Thomas had been watching the soldiers milling around the compound several hundred yards away. He saw a group of them organizing, pointing toward them and moving their way. He realized their time was running short.

"Let me try," he said suddenly.

He stepped to the door and knocked loudly. Salah stared at him. A shadow appeared on the frosted glass window and the door opened. A soldier barred their way.

"What do you want?" He asked.

He was unarmed. He seemed more than a little confused. He was young, closer to Thomas' age than to Salah's. He stared at the little girl in Thomas' arms.

"The captain needs a platoon to help with the hangar next door," Thomas said easily. "Do you have any men you can spare?"

The soldier smiled weakly, and said, "I'm the only one here. All the others left when their minds turned to mush. What's going on, anyway? And, who's the girl?"

"The water's been drugged," Thomas said simply, ignoring the question about Anisha. "They really need your help over there." He motioned toward the group of soldiers heading their way. "Can you go?"

"What about you?"

"We need to check out the vehicles here," Thomas said softly. "The captain wants to know if there's a connection between them and the water."

"He must think someone is trying to gain access to them," the soldier said. "Okay, I'll go help where I can."

He pushed past Thomas and left the door open, the way free. Thomas watched him head across the tarmac, then ushered Anisha and Salah into the building. He closed the door and threw the heavy dead bolt. Then he took Anisha and strode toward the center of the hangar.

"Whatever you did to these soldiers is potent," he commented. "That was a lot easier than it should have been. They seem to be susceptible to suggestion even now."

"But not in groups," Salah said. "I am worried that someone may hurt themselves through lack of attention or inability to make decisions before the effect wears off completely. If that were to happen, I would be very sorry."

"Why didn't it affect Remmick?"

"There were some protected rooms," Salah returned. "He may have been in one of them. Certain kinds of metals, specifically lead or stainless steel, can protect someone to a certain extent. There are some people who have a natural immunity. We masked my children and you and your friends to protect you. We chose a low level so as not to harm anyone. All these are variables. Given the right combination and Remmick remains unaffected."

"Superman," Thomas said.

"What?"

"Superman couldn't see through lead, and he was invulnerable," Thomas returned. "You couldn't hurt him. That's rotten comparing Remmick with Superman. I liked Superman. Let's find something to get us out of here."

They had been moving out into the hangar. The roof rolled away overhead, rising to over a hundred feet in the center. Beams were exposed in a lattice of support, with lights hung among them to provide daylight brightness on the hangar floor. There were eight vehicles on the floor of the hangar. Three were stealth fighters parked near the other side. Two of these had panels open and it was obvious they were being repaired. The third seemed to be whole.

Thomas had seen the stealth fighter before at an air show at Hill Air Force Base, but here were three side by side, and he could get as close as he wanted. He stared at them, taking in every detail.

One vehicle was an Apache helicopter. Again, Thomas had seen one before, but this was up close.

The last four vehicles were different. Two were disc shaped, each twenty-five to thirty feet across. They had the look of inverted saucers with a bubble section in the center, presumably for the pilot and passengers. The third was a sphere, maybe thirty feet across and flattened at the top and bottom. The fourth was much like the third, only it was larger, and the flattening at the top and bottom was far more pronounced.

Thomas let his mouth fall open, and said, "Real flying saucers! Wow!"

"This one is a clever ruse," Salah said as they passed one of the saucer shaped ones. "There's nothing inside to make if fly. Somebody on this planet put it together as a joke, and these fools are still trying to take it apart piece by piece to see what makes it go. It doesn't go because it never did and they can't figure that out. They're wasting their time. This one is a ruse, as well," indicating the second saucer-shaped vehicle. "Unless I miss my guess, it was built by the same group that built the other one. They are very similar in construction. This one," he walked to the sphere, "is mine. Look at the damage here."

He seemed a little less than happy about the condition of the sphere. As they walked around the side they found a large, jagged tear in the skin of the vehicle. Inside clear plastic lines were tangled and cut. Salah reached in and played with the lines. He shook his head and hummed quietly to himself.

"I can see why Toby couldn't get it working again. The motivator's been disconnected. The stabilizers are cut. All the stealth functions are damaged. I'm surprised he was able to land it safely. I'm not sure I would have been able to. I will have to let him know how proud I am he was able to do that in spite of the damage."

"He was lucky," Thomas breathed, not really understanding what he was looking at.

"Luck is often skill masked," Salah returned, smiling and stuffing the plastic lines back inside the craft. "Some of this damage is the result of inexpert hands trying to discover how the vehicle works. What kind of thing did this to my vehicle?"

"He said it was a rocket," Thomas explained. "So, he couldn't keep this thing flying?"

Salah nodded, and said, "I told you he wasn't fully trained. He might have been able to protect himself and the vehicle. There is too much damage to repair here, and we can't carry it with us."

He touched a panel, and a section dropped back in and slid aside. He entered and fumbled around. Thomas set Anisha down. She looked a little upset, so Thomas reached into his pocket and handed her the box of discs.

"I need you to take care of these," he said softly. "Give them to me when I get back, okay?"

Anisha looked happier, and nodded.

Thomas followed Salah into the vehicle. Steps led upward, and Thomas followed them by feel. The interior was totally dark. He reached a place where there was a flat floor, and he was aware of Salah's presence just ahead working through something.

"The emergency lighting system seems to be off line," he mumbled. "If I can just... ah, there it is."

Suddenly the room was bathed in soft pink light. Thomas stared around at the interior. Everything was gray with a slight pink tint. The walls reflected the outside curve of the sphere. There were no hard corners; everything was rounded, and smooth. At the front, facing a solid wall, were four surprisingly normal looking chairs with safety harness systems. The chairs were molded to the floor as if they were part of the floor. In front of them was a panel with pink circles and squares printed all across the face.

Salah was touching various painted squares and circles in rapid succession. He seemed to be a little frustrated.

"Nothing is working," he said softly. "Wait. There."

The wall in front of them suddenly became a clear window to the hangar.

"Wow," Thomas said. "Can you see through anything?"

"It's an illusion," Salah said. "You're not really seeing through the wall. It's like your television. The wall is a screen, and the image adjusted to correspond to what you'd see if the wall were transparent."

Thomas nodded.

"Can we make this thing go?" he asked.

"No. It will require more repairs than I am able to do now. I'm attempting to disable it so your military will not be able to use it. There. That should do it. Come on. Everything will shut down in a few seconds."

Before Thomas could turn away the screen began to go fuzzy, and fade. Almost immediately the lights inside began fading as well. They stumbled down the stairs as darkness descended, and stepped outside. The doorway slid across the opening and expanded outward into place.

"The final power structures in the vehicle will be disabled in a few minutes," Salah said sadly. "I do not like doing that, but I cannot leave it here even partially functional, and taking it with us is out of the question. I may come back for it later."

"I understand," Thomas returned. "The prime directive. Don't interfere with a planet's culture."

Salah looked at him a moment, slightly puzzled, and said, "Bring Anisha."

He walked toward the fourth vehicle. Thomas started to pick up the girl, but she shook her head and handed him the box of discs. He slipped them into his pocket.

"I think I can walk now," she said.

She struggled to her feet. She was a little wobbly, but she managed to take a few steps before Thomas had to help her. Together they approached Salah.

He'd already opened the door to the craft, and had stepped back. The design and operation of the door was very much like the one in the previous sphere. It had simply slipped in and slid to the side. There was a bad smell emanating from inside the craft. He waved his hand in front of his face, and looked at his daughter.

"You two stay here," he said. "Let me see if I can get the circulation working."

He took a deep breath and entered the disk. Thomas stepped forward, found the smell too much to take, and stepped back immediately. He saw the light come on inside. A few seconds later the smell seemed to suddenly suck into the sphere, and was gone. Salah appeared at the door.

"Come in here, Thomas. Anisha, you sit still and wait for us. We'll be right back."

Thomas handed the box of discs to the girl. She accepted them with a weak smile and sat down on the concrete next to the door. Thomas stepped into the door, stepped up three steps to get into the main room of the ship, and looked around. It was very similar to the other vehicle. The chairs were smaller, the control panel a pale green, and the controls seemed to be gems instead of simple marks on the panel. Of the five seats, two of them were occupied.

The two bodies were very familiar to Thomas. He'd seen pictures of them on UFO shows, in the gossip sheets at the newsstands, even on science fiction shows. They were short, probably only five feet tall, with large bald heads and coal black eyes. They wore a simple robe that covered them from neck to ankle. Their feet were bare.

"Are they..." Thomas asked.

"Yes. The investigators never got this craft open. They died here, afraid to go out and unable to escape."

"What killed them?"

"I suspect starvation."

"Why don't they look like you?"

"They come from a different world," Salah said, amused. "They are Briori. They have a unique culture. They don't believe anyone else should see their ceremonial robes. These are reserved for only their race. They must have put these on when they realized their death was imminent. Others see them wearing a one-piece skin suit. To many it would look like they wear no clothing. Their eyes are usually clear blue, like deep pools of water. You can see into them, even get lost watching them. They are not unfriendly people, and we have a working agreement with them. There are certain tensions between our peoples that have festered for far too many generations. We have tried to mend them, but the Briori are resistant. Well, we need to place them in the sleeping compartments in the back. They will be sealed, and we can return them to their families later."

"Where?"

Salah walked across the room, touched several jewels, and a compartment slipped out of the wall. It was a bed. Salah walked back, and together they lifted the small body up and gently lowered it into the compartment. Salah adjusted the robes gently, almost reverently. He closed his eyes and said a few words in a language Thomas could not understand. Then he closed the compartment, touched more jewels, and a second compartment opened. They repeated the process with the second body. Then Salah spent a few moments running his fingers over the jewels. He stepped back and stood, head bowed, for almost a minute. After a moment, he turned to Thomas.

"Does it smell fresher in here to you?" he asked.

"Father!" Anisha shouted from outside.

Thomas was first out the door. She was sitting beside the sphere, hugging the box of discs close to her chest, and pointing. A troop of soldiers was entering through the door they'd come in. They were carrying rifles, and appeared to be looking for something to shoot at.

"Quick, Thomas, inside," Salah said from the doorway.

Thomas grabbed Anisha and lifted her into his arms. He turned toward the doorway.

A soldier, seeing the movement, shouted, "Halt!"

Others, picking up on the first, began to run toward them.

Thomas didn't pause, but jumped into the sphere. Salah stepped back, and Thomas turned to see the men running toward them, rifles ready.

"We're done for," Thomas breathed.

Salah smiled, and pressed a single jewel. The door closed, and the noise from the soldiers was suddenly sealed out. He turned and went to the control panel.

"I think this is the one," he said.

The wall in front of them suddenly opened and they were watching the soldiers outside surround the sphere. Thomas watched for a moment. He sat Anisha in one of the chairs, one that had been empty.

"How long will it take them to get in?" he asked.

"They've had this vehicle for years," Salah said, smiling. "We are the first to enter since it came here. How long do you think it'll take them?"

Thomas looked puzzled, and said, "Then the... those men must have died years ago."

"Correct."

"But, they didn't rot away to bones," Thomas said.

"The air in here has been free of bacteria and germs all that time. They were simply preserved by the environment. The odor in here was not them. It was their natural atmosphere completely stagnated. I recycled it and refreshed it. Their systems are quite sophisticated, even by our standards. There probably isn't much in the reserves, but we won't need much anyway. We're not going outside the atmosphere in this."

Thomas nodded, and said, "Why didn't they just fly away?"

Salah studied the panel, and began to touch the gems. After a moment the view outside was replaced with a screen full of writing. It looked to Thomas a little like cuneiform mixed with Egyptian. He looked at Salah, who was busy reading. He glanced at Anisha, who was also reading.

"It seems they strayed too close to the sun," Salah said softly. "How tragic! They made a mistake in navigation and landed here instead of the planet you call Mars."

"That's a pretty big mistake," Thomas whistled.

"It was for them," Salah said. "They drained their reserve energy stores protecting themselves from the heat. If they'd gone to Mars they could have called for help. The elements in the atmosphere could have provided them with enough energy to stay alive until help came."

"Why didn't they radio from here?"

"Your atmosphere," Salah said simply. "Their signals are blocked by it."

"We radio to our astronauts outside the atmosphere," Thomas said.

"There are more efficient ways of communicating than radio waves, son," Salah said calmly, touching the buttons on the panel. "Their communication systems are far less dependable than ours, or even yours. It's a kind of blind spot they have. We've offered to help them, but our relationship is tenuous and they have repeatedly refused our help."

"What do we do now?" Thomas asked. "I mean, this thing is out of gasoline, and those soldiers will get tired of standing around in a while."

"Well, let me see what I can do," Salah said softly.

He pulled the cube out of his pocket, and held it close to his lips. He blew gently on it, turned it, and whispered into it. He touched a few more gems and the display on the wall changed. A small yellow sun swam in an empty blue ocean across the wall.

"Let's see if your mother can help us," Salah said softly, speaking directly to Anisha.

The girl smiled weakly, and watched.

The sun changed color slightly, and started to grow. As they watched it continued to grow until it filled half the screen. Then the edges of the screen began to show margins of color, and the color spread inward, toward the sun until there was only a blue line separating them. The line grew smaller until the colors merged.

"What's happening?" Thomas asked.

"I believe you would call this a 'jump start'," Salah returned.

Salah blew gently on the cube again, and carefully slipped it into his pocket.

"Always thank someone for helping," he said to Anisha. "Especially if that someone is your mother. Thomas, I think you'd better sit down now. We're ready to go."

"That's it?" Thomas asked. "You mean, that's all they needed to do, and they could've flown out of here?"

"Only if there had been someone close by," Salah said softly. "You see, Thomas, I came here prepared. Even prepared, it has been very difficult. They couldn't contact their friends because of your atmosphere, so they were alone."

"You can call outside the atmosphere," Thomas said.

"The cube is only good over a limited range," Salah returned. "I would prefer direct communications, but one must use what is available. You'd better sit down."

"No seat belts?" Thomas asked, sitting down.

"They won't be needed," Salah said, punching in the orders to revert to the vision screen again. "The Briori have some techniques for protecting their pilots we've only begun to duplicate. We will be fine. Let me concentrate now."

The hangar was full of soldiers, seeming to take up almost every square inch of the floor space. Salah frowned.

"That's not good," he said. "If we try to maneuver too quickly, they could be hurt. If we go too slowly we won't be able to force the doors open. Well, I guess it cannot be helped."

He sat down, and from his seat he began to touch gems across the board. Almost imperceptibly at first, then quicker, the floor of the hangar began to sink below them. The soldiers were looking up at them with amazement, some with fear. Several were pointing rifles their way.

"If they fire," Salah said, "they might hurt others around. The projectiles will bounce back into the crowd. What would you say is the weakest place in the hangar doors?"

"I don't know," Thomas breathed. "Salah, if you're worried about hurting anyone, try running at the doors once, but stop just before you get there. That will give the soldiers the idea, and will give the smart ones a chance to get clear."

"That's a good idea," Salah said. "What about the less intelligent ones?"

"Hopefully their injuries will be slight," Thomas said, realizing Salah's reticence to hurt anyone.

Salah nodded, and rested his fingers on the controls. The ship backed away from the doors until the breadth of the hangar stood between them. He changed his fingers slightly and the ship darted forward, picking up speed, then stopped just in front of the doors. He repeated the maneuver, backing across the hangar. The soldiers began to scatter, running away from the doors. The hangar floor was quickly evacuated, and stood empty.

Suddenly a soldier came running out to the middle of the floor waving his hands above his head. He was shouting something. He pointed toward the side of the hangar, and shouted something that way. Immediately the doors began to slide open.

Salah sat back, and said, "That is very good. Thomas, you know your people."

"You have to thank him," Thomas said.

"How do I do that?"

"Do you have a public address system?"

"You mean to speak outside? No. I do not believe so. Remember, I don't know a lot about Briori ships."

"Then," Thomas said, thinking, "then waggle your wings at them."

"Do what?" Salah asked, amused.

"Do this," Thomas said, demonstrating dipping each wing with his hand. "It's kind of a universal symbol of good will down here. Airplanes do it all the time."

Salah nodded, and touched the buttons. The saucer wobbled back and forth. Suddenly many of the soldiers began to jump up and down and cheer, waving and shouting. Others were trying to close the doors again to prevent their escape. It was obvious there were at least two distinct factions on the hangar floor. Thomas wondered which ones were still functioning under the treatment Salah had given them, and which ones were beginning to think clearly again. He decided he didn't want to think about it. In the meantime, Salah moved the ship forward through the doors and out into the desert night.

As he cleared the hangar he turned on outside lights. The area around and immediately under them became bright. Salah turned the ship in a full circle to see where the soldiers were. They were crowding out of the hangar, following their progress. He brought the ship up slightly, till they were fifty feet over the tarmac, and turned toward the opposite end of the runway.

"I think it's time we check on the others," he said, as the ship began to pick up speed.

Thomas nodded, a broad smile on his face.

"Amen to that," he said.

Anisha looked at him, then back to her father.

"He knows the word," she said, amazed.

"I know," Salah said. "Are you surprised, daughter?"

"What word?" Thomas asked, watching them accelerate toward the end of the runway.

"Your use of 'Amen' was appropriate," Salah said, guiding the ship over the end of the field, past the high fence. "It is a word we have treasured from our past, from before our city was removed from the earth. We have always kept the sacred words of our fathers for when we returned to become part of the earth again."

"What are you saying?" Thomas asked.

"We were part of the earth once," Salah said softly, concentrating on the flight of the saucer. "I need to pay attention here. I haven't flown a Briori ship in a long time. Let's see what's under us."

The screen immediately changed perspective, looking straight down. Salah adjusted the lights so a large area of the landscape was illuminated. He drifted first one way, then the other. Then he sat back and pointed.

"That was your prison," he said distastefully.

The three buildings, blacker than the ones to the north, surrounded by a high chain link fence, washed with orange light, seemed to look a little less ominous from above. Soldiers drifted around the buildings near the gates. A group had already put out the burning Jeep.

"Over here is where the vehicle was," Salah said, drifting over toward the mountains.

The mountains seemed lower and less threatening from above as well. A lone man in black stood in the light of the vehicle. He had a body over his shoulder. He glanced up, seemed to relax, and flicked a simple wave with his free hand.

"Boothe, my friend," Salah said, a sad smile flowing across his face. "You still have much to learn. I am, however, grateful for your help."

"So, what are you saying?" Thomas asked.

"They made it to the vehicle," the man explained, smiling. "They had a run in with the guard, but I would venture to guess they are all three all right. The man you see down there helped them. If they go the direction I told them, they will be up over the ridge in a few minutes."

"Let's go find them," Thomas said enthusiastically. "I know Cory would love a ride in this thing! Do you want to pick up your friend down there?"

Salah suddenly smiled broadly and said, "No. He'll meet us at the rendezvous. He can take care of himself."

Salah switched views again, and turned toward the base. The planes were being taxied out onto the runway, and the helicopters were already becoming airborne and coming their way.

"That is not a good thing," Salah said quietly. "Those hovercraft will likely be firing on us in seconds. Maybe it's time we headed for the rendezvous ourselves. I'm afraid we'll have to trust your friends can get there without any further assistance."

"Can't you use a shield or something?" Thomas asked.

"I told you before, we have no such weapons," Salah said firmly. "This ship is much stronger than anything you have, but it is not invulnerable, and it can be shot down with your weapons. Tobias will tell you that. We have to go. We'll meet your friends shortly, when the hovercraft lose sight of us."

He touched the controls, and the ship soared straight up toward the stars. At first it seemed to Thomas they were rising very quickly. The view screen turned toward the base again. He could see the helicopters coming toward them. Further away he could see the stealth fighters preparing for takeoff. He realized how very slow they were going, then.

"Can't we go any faster?" he asked quickly.

"Not yet," Salah responded. "This vehicle has not been run in a long time. The motivators are sluggish. They need time to fully activate. We'll have to build up speed slowly. Don't worry. We'll be okay."

Thomas looked toward the base, and couldn't help worrying.

# CHAPTER 27

ory slammed on the brakes. The Hummer slid ninety degrees into a sideways skid. Dirt and rocks exploded around them. The vehicle slid to a stop. The road stretched away ahead of them, curving gently to the right, but heading directly toward the low ridge, now only a mile ahead. The moon highlighted the desert on either side of the road. The flat, white lake bed stretched out on their right. He sat at the wheel shaking, and looked over at Lori.

"Good eyes," he said to Lori. "Good voice, too. Very good voice. And, loud, too. We definitely don't want to run over a coyote."

He shook his head to try to clear his ears after her scream.

"Right," Lori breathed. "I - I thought it was a man."

"I don't want to hurt anything alive, either, Cory," Toby said softly, rubbing his own ears.

Cory nodded. He got out and climbed on the hood of the Hummer and looked back toward the base. Toby climbed up beside him. Lori stood on the ground looking up at both of them.

"You two were born in a barn," she said.

"Lighten up, Lori," Cory returned gently. "It's their car, not mine. Besides, it's their fault we're here in the middle of nowhere. Wow! What was that?"

He heard the report, an explosion like thunder. It shook the vehicle they stood on, and penetrated their bodies. Cory looked back toward the base. A ball of light floated high above the base. A shimmering skirt around the sphere gave it the appearance of a saucer-shaped anomaly. Near the ball he saw two, then three helicopters. They were vying for position around it. He could barely hear the helicopter engines. The thunder was from three fighters exploding off the runway to their left to join the helicopters. They rose, and banked out over the lake bed. The helicopters dropped toward the ground to give them room to maneuver. The fighters, given the air space, began to scream past the ball at exceptionally high speed. It was hard to decide just what they were trying to do, but it seemed clear they were threatening the sphere. The object continued to rise straight up, toward the stars.

"What is that thing?" Cory asked.

"It's my father!" Toby said with conviction, a broad smile spreading across his face. "He's found my-his-vehicle! They made it out of the compound too."

"*That's* your vehicle?" Cory asked, incredulous. "I thought you were talking about a four-wheel drive. Now I find out it's a no-wheel drive."

"There's wheels," Toby objected. "They're in the motivators. You see, there's the power source, and it- "

"Never mind. You tried to tell me. I guess I just wasn't listening. Remmick told me, too, but I thought he was lying. He lied about everything else."

"Yes, but the wheels are in the power source, and it --"

"If you boys are finished talking, I think we ought to go," Lori suggested.

"Well," Cory said, climbing off the vehicle, "they made it out of the complex. Only *they* did it with style. I wonder why they didn't take us with them. That would have been more fun."

"We better go," Lori said, pointing.

"But you wanted to know about the power source," Toby said plaintively.

"I know," Cory said, looking back the way Lori was pointing. "That'll have to wait."

Back toward the base they could see four sets of headlights racing toward the area the Hummer had originally been parked. Cory jumped off the Hummer.

"The helicopters seem to be backing off," he said softly. "Well, I hope they can shake the fighters."

"Father can go clear out of the atmosphere," Toby said quietly. "Then his speed is unlimited. How about your ships?"

"They can't follow him that far," Cory said, helping Toby off the hood. "But they're fast down here. If they decide to shoot him down, he may be in trouble. Does he have ray guns or phasers or anything like that? Can he defend himself?"

"No," Toby answered. "There are no weapons on the ship. We don't use weapons. But he should be able to go faster than that. He is moving very slowly. Maybe the vehicle is damaged more than he thought."

"Well, we can't do anything from here," Cory said. "Your father would be the first to tell us to get to safety. Those four Hummers will be after us in a couple of minutes. Let's get to that ridge he told us about."

He climbed in, and the others followed. He turned on the engine, and then, with a nod at Lori, turned on the headlights. The desert burst into view. The road ahead of them looked even more ominous. Cory shifted into gear and pressed the accelerator. The Hummer jumped forward, growling into the darkness.

The road began to drift right as the ridge grew closer. Cory pushed harder on the accelerator and coaxed the vehicle into higher speed. The rough surface of the road rattled through them as speed increased. The Hummer didn't even slow down as they turned and began to head almost directly east around the end of the dry lake bed. He pushed down on the accelerator again, and they picked up more speed. He kept his eye on the road, but stole a quick glance at the action across the lake at the air base. He estimated they were, maybe, four miles from the base now, and they were passing the ridge on their left. They had another ten miles or so to go. The Hummer was used to rough roads. He was sure they could make it now.

Toby tapped him on the shoulder, and said, "They saw our lights."

Cory nodded, and asked, "How do you know?"

"They're following us," Toby said simply.

Lori looked back, and said, "They are."

Cory pushed the accelerator all the way to the floor.

He felt the vehicle lurch forward, and asked, "Are they gaining?"

"Some," Toby returned. "Can we make it before they catch up?"

"We have the same vehicle," Lori suggested.

"But not the same driver," Cory complained. "I wish Thomas was here. We either go back to those cells, or we get away. I'm not going back, so here goes! Lori, keep your eyes on the road ahead. Toby, you keep watching behind us. Let me know how quickly they're gaining."

"Yes, sir," Toby said, turning around again. "Cory, if they're following us, maybe there's a way to go faster."

"How?"

"The road. It jogs ahead. Don't follow it. Cut straight across. We can save some time. They think we're stupid, but I bet you can drive as good as they can."

"Not bad, Toby," Cory said, smiling, and yanking the wheel to miss a Joshua tree and heading directly across the desert. "If we're lucky a couple of them will spin out right where we almost did. That's great! Toby, what would your father say?"

"If they catch us it won't matter," Toby continued, his face reflecting his distaste. "They may follow the road. Perhaps they'll be more careful, and a little slower following us."

Cory nodded, turning the Hummer to the left, and pressing his foot into the accelerator. The desert foliage whipped by at an alarming rate. Toby kept watch out the back of the vehicle. Suddenly they bounded off the desert sand and back up onto the road.

"That's it," Toby said softly, almost sadly after a short time. "One, two of the vehicles followed the road. The others followed us across the desert."

"So much for short cuts," Cory intoned. "Are they still coming?"

"Yes," Toby returned. "The two that followed across the desert are closer. The two that followed the road are further back."

Cory turned back toward the left again. They were driving toward a larger ridge now. There was a lower area where the road was headed. That had to be the pass Salah had told them about. He kept his foot all the way on the floor. The desert was flying by on both sides now. Dust swirled behind them.

"This is a race we can't lose," Cory said. "Just hang on tight."

Five minutes passed, and they were all holding tight to anything close. The Hummer bounced over the road, which was becoming rougher as they drove. The rise was becoming more discernible as the mountains flowed around them. Occasional rocks on the road bounced the Hummer hard, and Cory had to correct quickly. The vehicle slid and skidded around even slight corners in the dirt road. He yanked the wheel and barely avoided a rock, and sent the Hummer into a momentary skid sideways. He straightened the vehicle out and they were hardly slowed by the incident.

"Go right," Lori shouted, pointing.

Cory had to twist the wheel, and avoided another rock.

"The pass," Lori said. "I think I see it now. What do we do when we get there? The soldiers picked us up on public land once before."

"Salah said our fathers were there," Cory said, turning hard left, then right again. "I don't think the soldiers will want to take us into custody with our parents standing there. Brady will have guns, and he'll use them if he has too."

Toby breathed deeply, and said, "They're a lot closer, Cory. Two vehicles are catching up. Not very fast, but if we have much farther to go, we'll be in big trouble."

"I guess maybe a few more miles," Cory said, gritting his teeth. "Tell me how close they are."

"Maybe two ablio," Toby said, more softly.

"Two what?" Cory asked.

"About three miles," Lori interjected. "I can see them."

"You watch the road," Cory shouted. "Toby, use whatever measure you want and feel comfortable with. Just keep it consistent."

"All four are chasing us," Toby said. "The two in front are close."

"How close?"

"Maybe two... miles," Toby said. "We might be able to stay ahead of them."

"That's great!" Cory snapped. "We have the same Hummers. If I could drive as fast as they can they wouldn't catch us. I wish I could get a little more speed out of it, though. I bet Thomas could."

"Stop that!" Lori snapped suddenly.

Cory looked across the vehicle at her and said, "What?"

"Thomas isn't here," she snapped. "I'm tired of you constantly comparing yourself to him. You're different. He's different. And you're the one getting us out to safety. So just shut up and drive!"

"I only meant- "

"I said, 'Just shut up and drive,'" Lori repeated. "And I meant it."

"Sure," Cory returned, and fell silent.

The desert flashed past like an endless tapestry. Each Joshua tree and sage looked like the last one they passed. Even the mountains that were starting to rise on both sides of them were almost identical. Cory growled, and turned the wheel hard again.

"What's wrong?" Lori asked.

"The road is becoming erratic," Cory answered. "I think the ground must be harder up here. I may have to slow down to see the turns."

"No," Toby said, hanging over the front seats. "Don't slow down. Look up there. That's the ridge. All you have to do is get us there. My father said we'd be safe there."

"But there may be rocks," Cory complained.

"Then there are rocks," Toby said, turning back around to look back.

"You're supposed to be strapped in, Toby," Lori said, horrified. "If we wreck, you'll be the first one killed."

Toby shrugged, and said, "I can't look behind us very well with the straps on."

"Put 'em on," Cory said evenly. "Do the best you can looking behind you, but put the safety harness on. It's not important how close they get now. We just need to stay ahead of them."

Lori looked at him.

Cory said quickly, "I'm shutting up and driving."

Toby was quiet for several minutes as he figured out how to put the straps together. The vehicle bouncing over the rough road offered a challenge to his task, too. He slid the last of the five straps into the buckle, and looked up at Lori and smiled. He turned and looked back, straining at the straps.

"The vehicles following us are getting closer," he said. "The lead two are no more than a...a...a mile or so. The others are...a mile further. We can make it to the ridge."

"I know we can now," Cory said heavily, hearing the grind of the engine fill his whole body. "Then what?"

The desert floor had been rising gradually for some time. Now it began to rise much more quickly. They were nearing the top of Salah's pass, and help was supposed to be on the other side. Cory didn't let up on the gas. He wanted to get there, even if it meant wrecking the vehicle.

The steeper the grade became, the faster they seemed to be going. They topped the ridge. The road swung in a hard left, then a hard right turn. Cory managed to negotiate the left, but missed the right. The Humvee hit the rocky hills at the left side of the road and left the ground, sailing twenty feet down the other side of the pass before they hit earth again. Cory slammed on the brakes, and the vehicle skidded sideways down the slope, spraying sand and desert foliage everywhere. It skidded slowly to a stop. He slapped the buckle and let himself out of the harness, threw open the door and jumped clear of the Hummer.

Dust and dirt filled the air around them. The cool night air reminded him how much he'd perspired the last half hour. The moon was high in the sky now. Though everything around was visible, black shadows still dominated the landscape. The desert was empty. They were the only ones there.

Lori stepped out, and Toby followed. It took him a little longer to figure out how to operate the release mechanism. They stood in the darkness, listening to the near silence. Over the ridge they could hear the distant grind of the pursuit closing in.

"There's no one here," Lori said softly.

"I know," Cory said, looking around. "Is this the wrong ridge?"

"Father said this way," Toby said. "He's never wrong."

Cory breathed deeply, and said, "Maybe this once, he was."

The air was shattered by the sound of vehicles, and two Hummers crested the ridge at the same time. Both soared, engines racing, one a hundred feet to the left, the other a hundred feet to the right. They hit the ground in unison, breaks locked, and skidded bringing their headlights to bear on the three friends. The doors to the vehicles popped open and soldiers sprang out, rifles aimed, and in less than fifteen seconds Cory, Toby and Lori were the center of attention in the middle of a vast wasteland.

No one moved. The soft sound of sand shifting seemed to fill the night air. Cory could hear his own heart beat in his ears. He slowly raised his hands. Toby mimicked his movement. Lori began to sob quietly.

"You should never have escaped," one of the soldiers said heavily.

"Well," Cory said softly. "It seemed like a good idea at the time. What do you do now, shoot us?"

"Just don't move," the soldier returned. "We will shoot to kill if you do."

# CHAPTER 28

The first indication of trouble was the helicopters. As the ship rose, the helicopters formed a ring around them and followed them up. They seemed to have no trouble matching their speed. Thomas wondered at that.

"I would be surprised if they continue much longer," Salah said softly, letting his fingers play over the controls. "Air machines require air. We will go higher where the air is too thin."

The image on the screen began to spin, almost as if the ship were spinning to give them a good view of their adversaries. One by one the helicopters came into view from the right, and disappeared around the circle to the left. The pilots were almost close enough to touch. Their visored faces stared back at them across a very narrow gulf.

"I can almost count his nose hairs," Thomas commented. "Can they see us?"

"Remember; this isn't a window. They see only a silver, flattened sphere," Salah returned.

The helicopters continued to follow them upward, keeping their guns trained on the ship. Thomas stared into the muzzles of the guns, and counted the rockets each airship carried. He wondered how long it would be till they fired.

"What if they fire?" he asked.

"They won't fire," Salah returned. "They would get caught in the explosion themselves. They'll back off first."

As if at a given signal, the helicopters suddenly broke off and dropped toward the base. They put a great deal of distance between themselves and the vehicle Salah piloted.

"I hope they did that because we're getting too high," Thomas said. "I don't even want to think that they may have orders to open fire."

"We're not that high yet," Salah said solemnly, turning the screen toward the base. "Let's hope they have another reason to back off."

The fighter coming at them seemed to be deliberately trying to ram them. Thomas stood up, and watched as the plane flew just to one side. His heart raced as the screen revolved to follow the flight of the intruder.

"I thought he was going to hit us," he breathed.

"Not yet," Salah said. "We're moving faster now, but-"

A second plane flashed past, moving too fast to catch any details, or even to follow. Salah moved his fingers on the controls and the ship seemed to jerk slightly.

"What was that?" Thomas asked.

"Just an adjustment," Salah said. "The elements are beginning to clear a little. What do you think they will do if we don't slow our ascent?"

"I don't know," Thomas said. "I didn't think fighters would deliberately get that close. Salah, they shot your son down."

"My thoughts, too," Salah said. "I've got an idea, but I wouldn't try it without your full approval. I would need your approval, too, Anisha."

"I just want to go home, Father," Anisha said quickly. "Please do what you have to."

Thomas stared over at her, then back to Salah. Another plane flashed by, very close and a little above them.

"They're getting a little close," Salah said. "They are trying to get us to turn back. That might be an option. Thomas, I want to put this ship into a steep dive. With gravity, and the buildup of our engines, we can accumulate enough speed to break the sound barrier. It might be enough to carry us clear out of the atmosphere. It should clear the elements, as well, and give us full maneuverability."

"You mean, into space?" Thomas asked.

"Yes," Salah replied, smiling. "Did you ever want to see your planet from out there?"

Another plane shot by, even closer than the last. Thomas breathed deeply, feeling a kind of numbness close in. It was becoming difficult to breath, but he was sure it was just the excitement.

"Let's do it," he said quickly, and smiled as Salah stared at him.

"Not yet," Salah said. "You have to understand the danger. The only clear path we have is directly back toward the airfield. We will dive to build up speed to breakaway, and pull out in a parabolic course. I estimate we might be as little as fifty feet above the tarmac. If I miscalculate, we could end up part of the tarmac."

"I have to trust you, Salah. You got us this far."

"Well, there's more. The field might have defensive weapons. If they choose to use them, they could shoot us down. We'll crash in a fiery ball. Do you think your father would approve of me taking such a risk with your life?"

Thomas thought a moment, and said, "I think my father would do the same thing if he were here. And I don't think he'd approve of me going back to that prison. Is there anything I can do-Wow! They're really getting close now! If he got any closer, I'd have to let him have my chair. Is there anything I can do to help?"

"No," Salah said softly. "Just sit down and try to remain as calm as possible. Anisha, you've done something similar to this before. Remember when we circled the moons of Fiulari? This is the same only the earth will be below us. Now be very quiet. I need to concentrate."

He changed his fingers, and immediately the screen changed. Thomas felt a tickling in his stomach exactly like when an elevator stops at the top floor. A plane was flying straight at them. As they watched the plane was just off course, then more, than over flying them by twenty feet. They were dropping almost directly toward the runway below.

"We're falling!" Thomas exclaimed.

"No," Salah responded. "This is a power dive. We are using our engines to propel us downward. The planes will not be able to keep up with us now!"

He sat back, and Thomas saw a slight smile play across his lips. He had released the controls, and was simply leaning back in the chair and enjoying the ride. Thomas swallowed hard.

"Aren't you going to pull us out?" he asked.

"I've programmed everything," Salah said, still smiling. "If I did it right, we'll pull out on our own. There's too much at stake to rely on human reflexes, especially mine."

"Human reflexes?"

"Of course," Salah said. "I told you we were cousins. Didn't you believe me? The internal gravity should take care of most of the forces, but you'll still feel some pull at the bottom. Try to stay seated. If you lose your seat, stay flat on the floor till I tell you. It could get a little wobbly in a moment."

Thomas nodded, and held on to both sides of his chair. He didn't know what it was that was supposed to keep him in the chair, but he began to wish for an old-fashioned safety belt like the one in his jeep.

Like the one that used to be in his jeep, he reminded himself.

The base was coming up quickly now, and he could see the movement below. In seconds he was beginning to pick out individual vehicles, then individual soldiers. He watched in amazement as the soldiers began to scatter at the approaching ship. He clenched his teeth.

Almost imperceptibly at first, the course of the ship began to change. Instead of straight down, it was almost straight down. Then toward the ground, then angled. The craft cut a singular arc, pulling out of the dive rapidly, and seemingly at the last minute. Suddenly, and Thomas knew he couldn't tell exactly when it happened, they were screaming across the tarmac so close to the ground he was sure they were going to take the soldiers' heads off as they passed. The soldiers must have felt the same way, judging from the numbers who were falling flat on the concrete. Inside the ship there was dead silence except for their breathing, and the heartbeat Thomas could hear in his ears. He wondered what their descent sounded like to the soldiers.

Before he could think of anything else they were climbing again, slowly, then more quickly. Then they were going up much faster than they had before. The craft climbed straight up. Something dark flashed past, and Thomas realized they had missed one of the fighters by only a few feet.

"How did that feel, mister," he said sardonically.

Salah leaned forward, touched a few more buttons, and sat back again, smiling.

"We won't slow down now," he said. "The engines have cleaned themselves, and we're near full power. Nothing I've seen can keep up with us. I think we're safe."

Thomas nodded, and watched as the stars became clearer. The sky turned from black paled by the moon to solid black, even around the moon. The flight was different. There was a deep vibration that was quickly ebbing, and their path took on a smoothness he hadn't expected.

Salah touched the control board, and suddenly they were in pitch black. He moved his fingers over the keyboard and the screen rotated. Off on one side they could see the narrow edge of the Earth just beginning to pick up the glow of the sun. The screen rotated more and they were looking down at the black side of the planet. They were so high even the place the base had been was lost. Thomas breathed deeply. He was feeling a little light-headed.

"Trouble," Salah said suddenly, touching the buttons.

Almost immediately they saw a missile flying straight up at them. It didn't seem too big, but after what Salah had said earlier, Thomas grew worried.

"They shot at us!" he said.

"They did, indeed," Salah said quickly. "Thomas, what do those missiles key in on?"

"Huh?"

"What do they use as a target?"

"Heat, sometimes, or radar," Thomas stammered. "I don't know."

"Radar, then," Salah responded. "We don't leave a heat trail. Hold on. This will be very close."

He touched the gems on the board again, playing his fingers over them rapidly. Thomas could see from the missile below they were moving in short, erratic jerks. The missile seemed to be trying to compensate and follow the movements of the ship. The screen continued to focus on the missile, and he couldn't tell how close it was, only that it was coming up rapidly.

Salah said suddenly, "Hold on! This might be shaky."

He hit the controls, and everything happened at once. The screen revolved rapidly, and the ship jumped and jerked several times. The screen focused on the missile, and the projectile suddenly exploded. The screen was filled with clouds of smoke and fire. The shock wave hit, and enveloped them, and the ship bucked several more times.

Thomas suddenly saw blackness filling his vision. His last conscious thought was that the missile must have punctured the ship. He knew he was going to die in space.

# CHAPTER 29

ory stood stiffly, waiting. He glanced at Lori, who was still crying softly, and shaking with each sob. Toby stood calmly, but his face showed worry. Cory took a step closer to the girl. There seemed to be no reaction from the soldiers. He took another step, and one of the soldiers waved his rifle in a slight arc.

"That's close enough," he said simply.

Cory nodded slowly, and said, "Can we put our hands down? You know we're not armed."

The soldier shook his head, and said, "Only if you want one blown off."

Cory looked at Lori, then said, "I'm going to go over and stand next to her. She's upset."

"She'll live," the soldier said.

"Can you at least point your guns somewhere else?" Cory exclaimed.

There was no movement from the soldiers. Cory counted eight of them.

"Okay," he said evenly. "What are we waiting for?"

The soldier in charge didn't answer. Instead he raised his rifle into the air and walked around behind his own vehicle. He stood out away from it.

Cory could hear the growl of the other two hummers growing near. Suddenly the air was filled with the sound of engines, and the other two Hummers ground over the ridge. They pulled up in a much more leisurely fashion and slowed to a stop. The doors of the vehicles opened and soldiers began to climb out. One wore a headset that looked too familiar. He approached the three with an evil grin on his face. At a single motion from his hand, the rifles were lifted and pointed at the sky.

Cory groaned, and said, "Remmick! How did you get out of the prison? Salah said he sealed the door."

"You can't throw a bolt into a hole that doesn't exist," Remmick said harshly. "I put a shell into the bolt hole. The bolt only wedged, and all I had to do was push it open. There's an emergency escape hatch in the ceiling. That's right. It's hidden. There are special codes to unlock it. I suppose your...friend...didn't know about it. Not many people do. I had it installed specifically for an emergency like this. Then, of course, I had to climb over the fences. Cut my hand on the barbed wire. See? I'll take that out of your skin."

"You're insane," Cory said angrily.

Remmick continued to smile, and walked slowly around the Hummer Cory had driven. He passed close to Toby, nodded at him, and returned to his previous position.

"Theft of government property," he gloated. "Destruction of government property, drugging government officers and guards, escape from a lawful detention center, attempted murder-"

"We didn't try to murder anyone," Cory snapped.

"There was that soldier back outside compound," Remmick returned. "He'll testify you tried to kill him. And, there was that stunt back down in the valley. You left the road deliberately to get one of us to crash and burn. Are you going to try to convince me you weren't trying to kill someone?"

"Self-defense," Cory said softly. "Besides, Boothe took out the soldier. We didn't. The short cut was just to try to stay ahead of you."

"Boothe?" Remmick returned thoughtfully. "He's involved in this?"

"No. He was just there. You know him?"

"Of course, I know him," Remmick said, more strongly. "That's another thing we need to find out about. You've been associating with known traitors."

"I don't even know him."

"He helped you escape," Remmick accused.

He turned and spoke into the microphone, then turned back.

"We didn't mean to hurt anybody," Toby interjected. "We only wanted to go home."

"This *is* your home now," Remmick said. "You'll be here a long time. All of you will be here a long time. By the way, Boothe will join you. I've sent a detachment to round him up. Tobias, did you know your father left you here? Yes. He took off and left you here. Do you think he'll be back for you? Don't bet on it. He won't ever come back. And you'll be here the day I retire. Every single day, for the rest of your life you'll hear my voice and you'll know I'm watching you. You'll give up all your secrets, and the next time you or your people come here we'll be ready for you."

"Don't listen to this jerk, Toby," Cory said. "You know your father would never leave you. He'll come back for you."

"I know," Toby said softly.

"What about us?" Cory said, going over to put his arm around Lori. "Our parents are still running around. They'll keep looking till they find us."

"Lots of people have disappeared and never been seen again," Remmick said confidently. "Golly gee, children, I hope you haven't damaged this vehicle too much. If anyone has to walk back to the base it'll be you three. You can bet you won't get there before noon, and tomorrow the temperature should rise to over 110 degrees in the shade."

He turned to the troops surrounding them, about 16 soldiers now, and said, "Let's get them into the vehicles. It's time to get back."

"I think you'd better let them go."

Remmick immediately spun around, staring at his soldiers.

"Who said that?" he snapped.

"I did," the voice floated in from the perimeter.

Remmick looked up. Three men were walking down from the ridge. They almost ambled, taking their time, picking their way through the sage and cactus. They seemed very aware that all eyes were on them. Even in the dark Cory could see the traditional military desert uniforms they wore. The camouflage patterns seemed to flow with dark as the three blended together and flowed apart again. All three were armed. Two carried large barrel shotguns, weapons not typically associated with the military. The third carried what looked like a traditional hunting rifle, again not generally thought of as military issue. At a signal from Remmick, the perimeter soldiers barred their path.

"Just who do you think you are?" Remmick snarled.

"I don't know," the spokesman said softly. "Just who do I have to be?"

Remmick seemed to recognize him. His face turned noticeably darker, even in the headlights of the Hummers. His mouth moved as he spoke into the headset.

"I don't think that radio of yours will work," the man said, still in the dark behind the lights. "We've effectively jammed your signals. We need to talk, Remmick. Tell your guards to let us through."

"This is the biggest mistake you've ever made," Remmick snapped. "You're on government property, and you are under arrest. Just turn your weapons over to my men, and you can come back to the base with us."

"I don't think you have a thorough grasp of the situation," the man said softly from the darkness. "We just want the kids. That's all. Then we'll leave."

Remmick thought for only a moment, and said, "I'm getting a little weary of your small town ethics getting in the way of national security."

Cory stepped forward to try to see who was beyond the headlights, but he couldn't. The voice seemed so familiar. He felt a glimmer of hope returning.

The man said, "This is not national security. This is kidnapping, plain and simple. And we are not on government property. This is freedom ridge, and public property. Your base ended about a quarter mile on the other side of those rocks. One more thing: Before you give your men permission to shoot, you'd better look around you. Carefully."

Remmick looked out into the dark. He couldn't see anything because of the headlights.

"Turn them off," the shadow suggested. Then louder, "Turn off the lights."

Remmick signaled, and the lights went off. The area was bathed in darkness. Their eyes began to adjust. Slowly, along the rim of the ridge they could see soldiers, many soldiers, all wearing the camouflage uniform the newcomers had on. They were completely surrounded. Remmick shrugged, then pointed to the vehicle behind him. The headlights went on, and the newcomers were framed in its headlights.

Cory's eyes cleared, and he recognized Sheriff Brady standing between two of Remmick's soldiers. He broke out laughing.

"Sheriff Brady!" He shouted.

"Don't move," Remmick warned Cory. "How did you get here, Sheriff? This is such an interesting time. Is it possible you had something to do with this prison escape attempt?"

"I think you can safely assume that," the sheriff said coolly. "We should talk, Remmick."

The Sheriff had his badge pinned to the front of the military fatigues, and it reflected in the headlights of the Hummers. Behind him stood Cory's father, Bishop Morris, and Jacob Bennett, Lori's father. The three of them seemed strangely out of place in spite of the uniforms they wore.

Lori caught her breath when she saw her father, and started forward, but Cory held her firm.

"Just a minute," he said softly into her ear. "Let the sheriff work this out first. We're going home, Lori. Just be patient."

Lori nodded, and said, "Okay. Okay."

Cory smiled, and lifted a hand in a weak wave. Brady nodded, but his father waved back with a warm, satisfied smile.

"So, you still want to find out who has the real power," Remmick said. "I remember you men from that flea-bitten speck you call a town. You know, aiding a prison break from a military prison is serious business. I have the authority to protect this base from any threat. That would include an invasion of local militants."

"You still don't understand," Brady returned. "We don't want a confrontation. All we want is our kids."

"Are you willing to fight to take them?" Remmick said evenly.

"If necessary," Brady said softly. "That shouldn't be necessary, however. I had hoped you would see reason."

"What? You expect me to just surrender to you? I don't surrender to anyone," Remmick said firmly.

"We don't want your surrender," Brady assured Remmick. "We only want our kids."

"No," Remmick said simply. "Your meager arms are not a threat to us, you know. Now what do you intend to do when we arrest all three of you?"

Brady nodded, and shouted, "Colonel! I guess the general was right. I will need your help."

A single shadow left the group on the ridge and began to pick his way down the slope. He moved slowly. He seemed to be used to having others wait for him.

Brady, in the meantime, looked toward Cory, smiled and said, "Tell your men to let us go, Remmick."

Remmick nodded. The soldiers barring their way stepped back and the three men moved to the kids.

"Are you all right?" Jacob asked as Lorelei fell into her fathers' arms.

"Oh, yes, Papa," Lori said, sobbing, letting the tears soak her father's uniform. "I'm really all right now. I'm so glad to see you."

"Me, too, Sweetie," Jacob returned, his voice choked with emotion.

Cory held on to his father for a long time.

"It's good to see you again, Sonshine," Jon Morris said to his son.

"I suppose you're going to want to ground us again," Cory said, half laughing.

"I think you can count on it," the Bishop said, laughing. "We'll talk about that when I get you home. You've been confined to your room for a week already. Maybe we'll count that as time served. That'll shorten your sentence a little."

Cory laughed weakly.

Brady put his hand on Toby's shoulder and said, "I've met your father. He's quite a man. We are going to take you to him. He knows where we are, and you'll be with him soon."

"Thank you, sir," Toby said, his eyes glistening in the harsh headlights of the hummer.

"We're happy to see all of you," Brady said to them.

"Boy are we glad to see you, too," Cory said a little too loudly.

His father ruffled his hair.

"You've had a busy night," Brady continued, pitching his voice low so only they could hear. "We've been watching from the ridge. That maneuver around the dry wash scared a couple of us, but you handled it incredibly well, Cory. We're proud of all of you. You, too, Toby. We'll be going home now. Think you can handle that, Lori?"

"Oh, yes, sir," Lori said gratefully.

"Sheriff," Cory said, a little subdued. "We think Thomas is up there."

Brady smiled, and said, "I know. I told you, we've been watching."

"They're trying to shoot them down," Cory added.

"We'll have to trust Toby's father, then," Brady said, squeezing Toby's shoulder slightly. "We'll just wait and see."

His smile faded a little.

At that moment the colonel arrived at the perimeter. The soldiers started to bar his way, but the colonel barked an order. At a signal from Remmick they quickly moved out of his way. He approached Remmick directly.

He was a large man, in his mid-fifties.

"Remmick," Brady said exuberantly, "you know Colonel Madsen."

"By reputation only," Remmick said shortly. "Colonel, this is a military operation. We are about to return prison escapees to their cells. During their escape they have broken enough laws to put them in prison for the rest of their natural lives."

"You will release these children to the sheriff's custody immediately," the Colonel said shortly.

"No, Sir, I will not do that," the Major said evenly. "My authority comes from the highest level and gives me complete autonomy in carrying out my assigned duties. You cannot override my directives."

Colonel Madsen smiled easily, and said, "Let's talk about that. Your command was organized by General White, and you were under the direct command of Colonel Thane. Is that correct?"

"It is," Remmick snapped. "That chain of command was also top secret."

"For the rest of this, Major, I think we'd better step over here," the colonel suggested.

He led Remmick and the three adults to the side where the remainder of the soldiers couldn't hear. The teens edged close enough to hear what was being said. Colonel Madsen nodded at them as if giving them permission to listen in.

"I was confused when I noted that General White had retired over two years ago," the colonel continued in a friendly manner. "About that same time Colonel Thane was reassigned to Okinawa. So, Major, I was puzzled why, after the good General retired, your unit should drop out of sight."

"We were always out of sight," Remmick returned. "We're a top-secret- "

"Yes, Major, I know," Colonel Madsen cut him off. "You're a top-secret group. Even a top-secret group must report to someone. I was surprised, as was General Bowden, that we could find no record of your unit or your mission anywhere. That didn't seem reasonable. Every unit has records somewhere.

"Then, I thought, surely the paymaster general would have some records of your unit. That would give me a place to start. You surely wouldn't be doing this work on a voluntary basis. You have to be paid. I found records there."

Remmick smiled wryly.

"I followed that lead to your unit records hidden deep in the top-secret files in Washington."

"Just as I told you," Remmick affirmed.

"But," the colonel noted, "There was no record, no paper trail as to how they got so deeply buried. We know it happened right after General White retired. We just don't know how it happened."

"I'm sure I have no idea," Remmick said smoothly.

"Oh, I'm pretty sure you do," the colonel continued. "When I find out how it happened, Major, there will be some accountability. You can count on that.

"Now, since you cannot continue without accountability- "

"I report directly to the President," Remmick cut in.

"General Bowden and I spoke with the President, Major, on just this issue. He doesn't know who you are. He is unaware of your unit."

"He is protecting our top-secret status," Remmick argued, his face paling.

"He doesn't know you," the colonel responded simply.

Remmick took a half step back, but recovered his composure quickly. He seemed almost like a child caught with his hand in the cookie jar.

After a moment of silence, the colonel said more quietly, "Since you cannot exist without accountability, I have had your records transferred to my command."

"You don't have that authority," Remmick snapped.

"General Bowden thinks I do," Colonel Madsen said softly. "For that matter, so does the President."

Brady glanced at the colonel, and felt a great ease wash through him. He suddenly realized he was grinning broadly. He dropped the grin and composed his face.

Remmick seemed shocked to silence.

"Your operation here is closed," the colonel continued softly. "You will report to me on the 24th of June at Hill Air Force Base, in Ogden, Utah." He stared at the major a moment, then continued, "You will be in regulation uniform at that time. We will discuss the further disposition of your unit then. Under the direction of my men you will dismantle your operation here and turn over all facilities, materials and equipment to the commanding officer of this base. I understand most of your inventory was procured from here. It's fitting we return what we...um...borrowed."

"Colonel," Remmick stammered.

"I'm finished, Major," the colonel said evenly. "You seem to have some questions."

They stood facing each other for a long moment.

Then Remmick said, "I have prisoners..."

"Not anymore," the colonel responded. "Do you have any more questions?"

Remmick seemed to shrink, almost to deflate.

"No, sir," he said softly, hanging his head slightly.

"Then, Major, you have your orders," Colonel Madsen snapped. "You are dismissed."

Major Remmick suddenly snapped to attention and saluted. The colonel returned the salute. Remmick turned sharply and signaled to his men. They turned almost as one and disappeared into the Humvees. Engines snarled. The four vehicles snaked their way up to the road above them, which had become crowded with military transport vehicles. There were four in all, with several smaller vehicles. The Humvees edged their way past, and darted along the road back toward the base. It wasn't until they disappeared over the top of the pass the colonel moved.

He turned and strode slowly directly to the three teens. They looked up at him with some trepidation.

"I was going to address you as children," he said, standing easily in front of them. "You are not children. You are young adults. More than that, you are unusual young adults. You have been where few civilians have been allowed to go. You may have seen things that are highly sensitive. I would trust you can keep them safe and secure."

"Colonel," Cory said.

"As to this regrettable incident," the colonel continued, stopping the teen with a slight hand motion, "you may shed as much light as you feel necessary. In fact, my aides have already released a statement to the media. I believe you will find it accurate and satisfying, if not entirely complete in all details. I hope you will agree with the details we've chosen to omit. Your parents have copies of the statement for you to read.

"I know you will join with me in keeping Tobias and his family safe and secure. There are certain truths we should not reveal just yet. Tobias, you are entitled to your privacy.

"You are free to disclose whatever you feel necessary, but I would ask you to use the media statements as a guide."

He smiled for the first time since he arrived.

"In a moment you will be free to go with your respective fathers. I have one more task to perform here."

He singled out Toby with his eyes.

"Tobias," he said with authority.

Toby nodded nervously and said, "Yes, sir."

"Young man, on behalf of the United States Government I offer my heartfelt apologies for the incredible indignities you have been forced to suffer for no better reason than suspicion. When I presented the facts to the President he wept. That is the sign of a great leader. To all of you: Our deepest apologies.

"Now, the Humvee is at your disposal. You've done a fair job driving across the desert landscape this evening," the colonel said directly to Cory. "I would be pleased to have you in my command. Not for a few years, however. I think we can trust you with the vehicle until you are home."

"Yes, sir," Cory said, smiling broadly. He wanted to salute, but didn't know if that was appropriate. The colonel eased his discomfort by extending his hand. Cory shook it.

"You did a fine job leading your team this evening," the colonel said. He turned to Brady and said, "Is that about what you had in mind?"

Brady smiled, and said, "Yes, sir. For the moment. What's going to happen to Remmick?"

"That will be handled by us," the colonel said. "There will be an investigation, and the general will determine what actions we should take. In the meantime, he will not be able to change socks without permission from me."

"That's not fair," Cory blurted. "He had to disobey almost every law there is - "

"Easy, Cory," Bishop Morris said, holding his son's shoulders.

The colonel turned slowly toward Cory, and said, "No, Cory. It isn't fair. Sometimes life isn't fair. On my word I will not rest until those responsible are held fully accountable for their actions."

He raised an arm, and the soldiers began to close in. Lieutenants barked orders, and a Captain appeared at the Colonel's side. The Colonel turned to look at Toby. He studied him for a moment, and cleared his throat.

"Are you really from another planet?" the Colonel asked quietly.

Toby thought a moment, and said, "Yes."

The Colonel nodded, and said, "Are you going to invade us and take over, like the Major insists?"

Toby shook his head, and said, "All I want to do is go home."

"Me, too, son," the Colonel returned. "Sheriff Brady, please allow us to escort you back to Ely where we'll have another escort waiting to take you home."

"I would appreciate that," Brady said.

"Sheriff Brady and Mr. Morris, you are welcome to ride up front with me," the Colonel said, his voice tinged with humor. "In fact, I would be honored if you would. These youngsters will want to invite Mr. Bennet to ride with his daughter."

Bishop Morris looked over at Brady.

Brady said, "Don't worry, Bishop. They'll be fine. Jacob will be with them, and we'll be right behind. Let's let 'em make it the rest of the way home."

"They've earned the right to complete their journey," Colonel Madsen said.

They turned toward the Hummer. Several vehicles were appearing from around the rocks. They could hear heavy transport trucks from somewhere up on the road. A soldier ran up to the Colonel.

"Sir, a dispatch from intelligence," the soldier said, saluting.

He handed the paper to the Colonel and left quickly.

The Colonel nodded, and opened the paper. He scanned it quickly and frowned. Then he crumpled it and stuck it in his shirt pocket.

"I guess it isn't supposed to be easy," he said softly. "Brady, I have some troubling news. My men watched the craft we believe your son was in. It performed some incredible maneuvers to escape the fighters Major Remmick dispatched. In fact, it did escape the fighters, and climbed to an altitude of something over thirty-five miles. As it slowed at that altitude, and hovered, Remmick's troops launched a single missile with a conventional warhead. The report I have is that the craft was destroyed."

Brady looked at Cory, and Toby began to shake his head.

"No," the boy said quietly. "No. I won't believe that. My father is a better pilot than that. He would never let them destroy his vehicle!"

Brady snapped, "We have to go to the base."

"There won't be anything there," the colonel said softly. "We've launched a search. We're doing everything we can. Please, come with us. I'll keep you informed."

"My father isn't dead," Tobias shouted as they herded him toward the Humvee. "He isn't dead!"

# CHAPTER 30

Thomas woke slowly. He felt the room spinning. He looked up and saw Anisha first. She was on her knees next to him. Her face was pale, but she smiled. On impulse, he reached up and touched her cheek.

"He's awake, father," she said, glancing back over her shoulder.

Salah was immediately there.

"I'm sorry, son, but urgent matters were pressing. I neglected to adjust the atmosphere within the sphere," he said softly. "Please forgive me. I should have seen it when your speech became slurred. I thought it was the excitement."

Thomas tried to get up, but felt weak. He lay back down.

"What happened?" he asked, feeling a little foolish.

"The air mixture was wrong for you," Salah said simply. "There were gases not right for you in the mixture. We've become adjusted to them, and pretty much ignore them. The Briori thrive on them. Don't worry. There was no permanent damage done. But I am sorry all the same."

"The missile," Thomas said, this time succeeding in sitting up. "Did it hit us?"

"No," Salah said calmly. "But they think it did. I masked the ship the instant the missile exploded. It was a delicate operation to be close enough to appear to be struck, and still far enough to keep from harm. I didn't know about your missiles, or their capacity for destruction. I had to do a lot based on assumptions. I knew the damage done to my sphere by one of your rockets, and that helped some. Since then we have been watching the progress down below. And Anisha had an opportunity to speak with her mother."

Thomas saw the young girl beam, and knew she was going to be all right. Some of the color was coming back into her cheeks.

"A talk with mother can always make me feel better," he said, smiling at her.

"We finally have full power now, Thomas," Salah continued. "Those airships, the fast ones, could never catch us now. I think we're ready to join your friends, and pick up my son."

"They got away all right?"

"With the help of your father, and a few of his friends," Salah said. "One of my friends helped, too. Come and see."

Thomas stood uncertainly, and sat down in the seat quickly. He looked at the screen.

At first the screen showed only black. Salah began adjusting the view, and things began to move closer and become recognizable. Thomas could see moving lights, and the large complex of the base. Then he recognized headlights. Hummers, four of them, were driving over rough terrain back toward the base.

"Are they in the hummers?" he asked, alarmed.

"No," Salah returned. "I believe those carry your adversary, Major Remmick and his group. Watch."

He made more adjustments, and the view swung in an arc, and they were looking down at troops, barely visible in the dark, climbing into troop carriers and assorted vehicles. More adjustments, and they could see a single, black Humvee, headlights glowing, rolling down a twisting unpaved road.

"Are we that close?" Thomas asked.

"No. We haven't moved much since the missile exploded," Salah returned. "I've adjusted the magnification so we could see them."

"From way up here? You *are* Star Trek."

"No, whatever 'Star Trek' is. We're just people like you. Look."

Other military vehicles were pulling onto the road in front of the black Humvee. Still more were falling into line behind it as it moved slowly down a desert track. It was clear the black vehicle was being escorted.

"But, they've been captured again," Thomas said, pointing. "If they're in the Humvee, they're in deep trouble."

"Your father is there with them, and I believe these are there to protect them. You would say they are the 'good guys'. Their vehicles are well marked, and your father seems to trust them. Your father contacted them and secured their help several days ago. He had a bit of trouble explaining me. He had more difficulty explaining what I wanted to do to help. They finally accepted our plan, but not until I demonstrated some of our technology. They appear to be heading back for the main road, and then back home again. You will all be home again very soon."

He returned the screen to its regular settings, and the edge of the earth re-appeared, touched slightly more by the sun. Thomas could see they were beginning to move toward the Earth, into the blackness below.

"Are we going down to meet them?"

"Yes," Salah said quietly. "But I cannot allow this ship to come into the hands of the military again. We'll find a spot off the road and set down. Then we'll approach the road on foot and let them come to us."

"Right. The prime directive," Thomas said.

"You mentioned that once before," Salah said, running his fingers over the control board. "Perhaps you could explain it."

"It means, as an advanced civilization, you are not allowed to interfere with the natural progression of a more primitive civilization," Thomas explained. "Star Trek stuff."

"Well, I don't know about 'Star Trek stuff'," Salah returned, "but we are hardly more advanced than you. You are a little violent, but you are not primitive."

"But you have this," Thomas protested.

"The Briori have this, and I'll grant you that we have ships equal in most respects to this, but they're just toys and tools," Salah said. "It's never been the tools, Thomas. It's always the people. We're the same people, you and I. Whatever you may learn from us is your birthright."

"Then, why don't you want this ship to get into the hands of the military?" Thomas asked.

"They wouldn't know how to use it," Salah said simply. "They would waste a great many men's talents and energies trying to figure it out, and they would be unsuccessful. I just want to save them the trouble. Besides, in a few years we'll be here, and you'll receive the technology from our people."

"You're coming here?"

"Of course," Salah said. "We're the children of Enoch. You are the children of Noah. We've always been told that we must one day return. So, we are coming back."

Thomas thought a long time, then said, "You knew Enoch?"

"No," Salah laughed. "He died a hundred generations before I was born. I've read his scriptures, though, and he was a remarkable man. He helped develop a lot of these instruments."

"For the Briori, too?"

"Of course," Salah answered.

"Oh, wow," Thomas said softly. "Then it's all true."

"What is that?"

"The Bible, and the Pearl of Great Price," Thomas stammered.

"These books tell about Enoch?"

"Yes," Thomas said. "They said the nations of the Earth were so afraid of him they moved to far off lands."

"These are your scriptures, then? Do they say how Enoch felt about that?"

"No."

"Ours do," Salah said. "They say he was very sad. He did not want them to fear him, or to hate him, only to join him, as brothers everywhere should. What else do your scriptures say?"

"Only that his city was taken up to heaven by God," Thomas returned.

"Ours say Father helped Enoch remove our city to the heavens to preserve it," Salah said. "It is an interesting distinction, isn't it?"

"Who are the Briori?" Thomas asked. "Where do they come from?"

"From Earth," Salah said sadly. "All life in this part of the universe originated here. We've not been allowed to meet any other peoples. Your scriptures only tell of one city taken up? We know of at least four. One, sadly, was destroyed. Three survived. There may be two others, but we are uncertain of their fate."

"But, the Briori are so different," Thomas protested.

"Their science developed in a different way," Salah said. "They tried to improve that which the Father gave them. They didn't understand it was already perfect. Now, genetic engineering has made them as you see them. But they are still not too different to see they are Adam's children."

"But you don't think they are better," Thomas said softly.

"They live only a few short decades," the older man returned. "You can expect to live much longer than they do. And they are frail beyond belief.

They are easily hurt, and mend slowly. The must use advanced healing devices to help them mend when they are injured. They have a highly developed medical technology, but it is a poor substitute for a happy life. Should I go on?"

"I get the picture."

"Look, there is the convoy."

"Magnified or up close?" Thomas asked.

"We're close now," Salah said. "I've turned on the vehicle's shadow capabilities. They cannot see us. Not even this close. We'll be safe."

"I won't feel safe until I'm back home in my own bed," Thomas said sardonically. "Then I might have to look under the bed to be sure."

Salah recognized the reference, and chuckled. Anisha looked perplexed. Salah leaned close to her, said something in his own language, and her face brightened and she laughed. She replied in the same language, and Salah nodded. He looked back at Thomas.

"She thinks you are pretty special," he said. "She said you are the equal of any of the boys back home."

Thomas felt the color rise in his cheeks, and stammered, "Thank you, Anisha. You are very pretty, yourself."

The girl was looking better by the minute. Thomas reflected at how good he felt being free. That alone was enough to mend many of the injuries caused by their imprisonment.

Salah watched the two of them for a moment, noted the exchange of looks, and returned to the control board.

"Over there," he said. "That would be a good place."

The sphere swooped down over the convoy, and sped ahead of them. Then Salah banked and brought the craft down gently behind a stand of rocks. Even in the growing light it would be hidden from the road. He turned away from the controls, and held out his hand to Anisha. She got up and walked, still a little unsteadily, to her father. She carried the box of discs with her. Salah motioned, and Thomas followed him to the door.

As they exited the craft, Salah touched the wall and the door closed and extended into place. He walked around the sphere examining the condition of the shell.

"Excellent," he said softly. "It is unharmed by our close encounter with the military rocket. I will be able to return this vehicle in perfect condition."

He took Anisha by the hand and led her toward the road.

They walked around the end of the small ridge, and followed a dry wash to the road. It was less than a quarter mile. Anisha walked slow, but she refused to be carried any more. They arrived at the road as the first of the convoy crawled up over the rise a mile to the west. They stood, waiting. Thomas felt like a hitchhiker, and he laughed at the thought.

"You are happy," Salah commented.

"It feels so good to be free," Thomas returned. "My prayers were answered, Salah."

Anisha touched his hand and smiled up at him. Salah nodded.

"Freedom is too precious to waste," he said softly. "It shouldn't surprise you your prayers were answered, Thomas. Our Father loves us and will help us when we ask."

The first trucks rolled past, not even slowing down. Then there were two Humvees. Thomas felt some anxiety as they passed, but noted with some comfort that they were camouflaged in desert colors, not the black he'd come to dread.

The convoy stopped, almost as a single unit. The black Humvee was still several vehicles away. The Humvee in front of them opened, and a large, older man stepped out. He walked immediately toward Salah.

He stood several feet in front of him for a moment, surveying him as one used to judging men quickly. Then he cleared his throat.

"I am pleased to meet you again, Salah," he said formally. "You truly are a man of many talents."

"Thank you, Colonel Madsen," Salah replied. "I thank you for your help. We could not have saved our children without your support."

"We could not have done it without you, as well," the colonel said. "We work well together."

"It is my hope we have formed the basis for an ongoing relationship."

"That is my hope, as well," the colonel said. "I believe we have your son, and you have young Master Thomas Brady here. I'm sure you are as anxious to be reunited with your son as Sheriff Brady is to be reunited with his. But I have one more task to perform. This is your daughter."

"This is Anisha," Salah said, smiling as the young girl tried to hide behind her father.

The big man immediately squatted down in front of the girl so he had to look up to see her face. He wiped his eye briefly, then smiled at her.

"I am Colonel Madsen," he said simply. "You are Toby's sister. Your brother is safe. He will be with you in a moment."

Anisha nodded shyly.

"Young lady," he said softly, "not all men on our world are like those you have met back there. It is my hope that at some time in the future we may be able to, somehow, make up for what we have done to you. I am truly sorry."

He reached out, and took her timid hand in his great paw, and gently kissed it.

"That is a symbol from a gentler age, when we knew how to treat young ladies. Accept it as a token of my sincerity."

He rose, and stood at attention in front of Salah.

"I have been authorized by our government, and by the President to offer our sincerest apologies for what we have put you through," he said. "There is no way we can make up for what has been done to your family. Be assured we will hold those responsible accountable."

"I have my daughter back," Salah said softly. "I believe my son is in the black vehicle behind you. That is all I need."

The colonel held out his hand, and Salah took it. They shook hands for several seconds before the colonel released it.

"Well," he said gruffly, "God speed you to your destination."

"And you, Colonel," Salah returned.

"Thomas Brady," the colonel said gruffly. "You have endured a great deal of punishment for which you were not due. I am sorry. Cory and your father will tell you what you can tell those around you. Basically, it is anything you wish so long as you keep the identities of Salah and his two children secret. Can you do that?"

Thomas nodded, and said, "Yes, sir."

"You did well this night, Thomas. I'm am certain your father is proud of the way you have handled yourself. It is a pleasure to meet you."

He reached out and shook Thomas's hand. He stared directly into Thomas's eyes as he did so. He nodded kurtly and turned on his heel and retreated to his Humvee. Two more figures stood there, beside the vehicle. Thomas recognized Bishop Morris and his father. They stood back, casually watching the proceedings. He was anxious to run to his father, but he was sure it wasn't the right time. He waited.

The doors of the black Hummer burst open and Toby jumped out, followed closely by Cory and Lorelei. They were running across the sand as Jacob Bennet climbed slowly out of the back seat, a smile filling his face. He stood beside the vehicle, glancing back at Sheriff Brady from time to time. It was clear he did not want to interfere with the reunion.

Lori threw her arms around Thomas and smothered him with affection. Tears were streaming down her face. Thomas looked a little embarrassed by the attention, but accepted it.

Toby hugged his sister, whispered in her ear, and kissed her cheek. Then he looked up at his father. Salah simply opened his arms, and Toby let himself be wrapped in them.

Cory stood back a few feet, and watched. When the opportunity presented itself, he stepped in and slapped Thomas on the shoulder.

"I guess we both made it," he said softly, smiling.

His voice cracked slightly, and he tried to hide it, but Thomas could see the tears in the corners of his eyes, too. Thomas was feeling the same emotion.

"They told us," Cory said, his voice breaking, "they said you'd been blown up by one of their missiles."

Thomas felt his own throat tighten. He wanted to break the tension with a joke or a smart comment, but he couldn't think of anything.

"We were playing possum," he finally said. "We had no choice. I'm sorry."

"Don't be," Cory returned. "I'm just glad you're here now."

He reached out and hugged him. Thomas, after a second to catch on, hugged him back. All five of the prisoners embraced each other, Anisha somewhat shyly.

Then Thomas looked up, and saw his father, Brady, drawing close. He controlled himself only a moment longer. His eyes spilled over and he took two steps into his father's arms. Brady held him gratefully.

The other two fathers walked quietly to join the group.

This all took place in a matter of moments, but to the friends time seemed to stand still. It was the culmination of a trial by terror and seemed to last forever. No one wanted to break that embrace.

Brady pushed the boy away, holding his shoulders, and said, "They said you'd been shot down."

"I know," Thomas said. "Cory told me. They tried, but Salah is a great pilot. He kept us safe."

Brady nodded, and walked over to Salah.

"I didn't think you could do this by yourself," he said softly.

"I didn't," Salah said warmly. "We did it together. I brought them to you, and you brought them here. You have powerful friends, Brady. I'm pleased."

"Thank you for my son," Brady said. "Thank you for our children."

"And thank you for mine," Salah returned warmly. "When did the troops finally arrive?"

"Ten minutes before the kids got to the ridge," Brady returned. "I've never seen such efficiency before. They deployed in the dark in about three minutes."

"It took them that long to get there," Salah mussed. "You will be interested in this."

He pulled a computer disk out of his pocket, and handed it to Brady. Brady turned it over in his hands, and looked up at the man.

"I've looked it over," Salah said softly. "It was their evacuation plan. If our soldier friends here had descended on the base in any fashion, they would have had the children on a helicopter to some other hidden location."

Brady nodded, and said, "Colonel Madsen said as much. We might never have found them. You were right."

"These are for you as well," Salah said, taking the box of discs from his daughter and handing them to Brady.

Brady looked over the box, glanced up at Salah. Salah held a finger to his lips and shook his head slightly. Brady nodded.

"I would rather have been wrong about all of this," Salah said. "You have serious problems to work out here. It's such a waste of talent and energy."

Colonel Madsen returned to the group. He glanced at the discs, ignored them deliberately, and said, "I am hoping, Brady, that this comes close to evening the score between us. I don't want to go through the rest of my life owing you."

Thomas looked up to his father, who simply shook his head, and said, "You never owed me anything."

Madsen looked from Salah to Brady, then looked down at Thomas and said, "Son, your father is the bravest man I ever knew. He saved my life twice. Once in Afghanistan, and once in Iraq. I promised him if he ever needed help, I would be there. Brady, that still stands. Salah, until we meet again."

"It has been a remarkable experience working with you to rescue our children," Salah said softly. "I am pleased the children of Noah have such leadership. I look forward to future meetings. For now, however, I must go. Perhaps we should exchange sons here. I am anxious to take mine home. We have a small discipline matter to discuss."

Toby looked uncomfortable, but smiled. Anisha nudged her big brother, and smiled up at her father.

"We will be having similar discussions," Brady said, reaching out and taking Salah's offered hand. "Will we see you again?"

"Probably," Salah said quietly, "only next time I will do the driving."

"Agreed," Brady returned. "Next time you come we'll have better accommodations than my sons room for you."

Salah nodded.

"He stayed in my room?" Thomas asked.

"Your mother cleaned it up some," Brady said. "But, yes, he stayed in your room."

Cory took the moment of silence as an opportunity to speak up.

"I know you," he said softly.

Salah smiled, and said, "I didn't think you would remember."

"I have a scar," Cory said, touching his temple, "here. I have a feeling you fixed that for me."

"You needed immediate help. I am happy I was there," Salah said softly. "Your father told me you will be able to give blessings, too, when you're older. There is power in the priesthood if you keep yourself worthy, young man."

"I know. Thank you, sir," Cory said, reaching out his hand. "Thank you."

Bishop Morris caught Salah's eye, raised his eyebrows. Salah acknowledged with a gentle smile.

Salah shook Cory's hand, and said, "Be careful climbing the ladder, young man. It's very old and can be treacherous."

"I will," Cory said. "Then, we can go back up to the canyon?"

"You earned that right when you dug under the sentinel," Salah affirmed. "It is a blessed place. Take care of it. Respect it. I will tell you more about it when we return."

He turned then, and scooped his children close to him. Anisha pulled free, and stepped shyly to Thomas. She smiled down at her feet.

"Thank you for helping," she said softly.

Thomas smiled, and said, "You're very welcome. I wish you didn't have to leave so quickly. But, I'll be very happy when you come back to visit."

Suddenly Anisha stood on tiptoes and kissed him on the cheek. Then she turned and ran back to her father. Still slightly unsteady, she was moving more normally now.

"I will be very happy, too, Thomas," she threw over her shoulder.

Her gesture had not been lost on Salah. He glanced at Thomas; his eyebrows raised slightly. Thomas waved.

They turned and went back to the Humvee. Cory pushed him toward the driver side.

"I've been driving enough," he said. "It's your turn. Besides, you haven't lived till you've driven with Lori as co-pilot."

Thomas looked up at his father. Brady smiled and nodded, then noted that Lori and Cory climbed into the back seat. He climbed into the front seat beside his son.

Thomas stood there for a moment, and saw the sky ahead of them beginning to pale and turn blue. To the right he saw the rocks the space ship was hidden behind. As he watched, the sphere rose above the rocks, lifted higher and hovered. A thin shimmering disk-like shape began to form around the flattened sphere, and the whole began to take on a silver, reflective appearance. Then the ship shot toward the east, grew distant, and disappeared into the lightening sky.

Thomas sat in the driver's seat, and fumbled with the safety harness. Then he took the wheel in his hands, and stared at the instrument display.

Brady looked over at him, and said, "Son, do you feel confident enough to drive this thing?"

"Of course, I do," Thomas said, offended. "Just, would someone tell me how to start it?"

# CHAPTER 31

Thomas looked up from the corner table at the Frosty Freeze. Wendy reached over to squeeze his hand.

"It's just the wind," she said.

Thomas nodded, and said, "On nights like this, when it's dark, I get a little jumpy. I wonder if I'll ever get over it."

"Maybe not," Wendy said. "I wish I knew how to make you better."

"I know you do," Thomas said softly, wrapping his hands around hers.

Wendy suddenly brightened, and said, "Hey, look! Here comes Cory and Lori. You know, I don't think I'll ever get used to that. 'Cory and Lori, Lori and Cory'. I wonder if one of them would consider a name change."

"They're an item, all right," Thomas laughed softly, watching the two enter.

Wendy always seemed to know how to cheer him up. He liked that.

Cory ushered Lori in, and without hesitating they walked through the teens already crowding the place and slid into the booth next to Thomas and Wendy. Neither of them spoke. They just grinned, and sat back.

"Where have you two been?" Thomas asked, letting his voice carry an air of mystery.

"We went down to the reservoir," Cory said. "The moon is great tonight."

"First quarter," Lori agreed. "Just like a month ago when it all started."

There was a catch in her voice.

"Sometimes the whole thing seems like a bad dream," she said finally.

"Or a nightmare," Cory said softly, looking at Thomas.

Thomas nodded.

"I was just wondering if I would ever stop jumping when I hear a helicopter engine," he said.

"Me, too," Cory agreed. "The good news is: There aren't that many helicopters around here. Well, one good thing came out of all that."

He squeezed Lori's hand. She squeezed back, and dropped her eyes. A flush was crawling up her cheeks.

"You know, I think there's more going on here than meets the eye," Thomas said. "What do you think we ought to do about that, Wendy?"

"Not one thing," Cory said defensively. "And you'd better not try anything cute, either. By the way, tomorrow's your night for the Humvee. You got anything planned?"

Thomas shook his head, and said, "No, why?"

"No reason," Cory said. "It's just that Lori's father is giving a talk down in Richfield at a youth conference, and she wanted to know if we could go."

"You could ride with her father," Wendy suggested, smiling demurely.

Cory looked pained, and said, "Give me a break! Besides, we were hoping you two would like to go."

Thomas brightened up, and said, "I want to. How about you, Wendy? Want to go?"

Wendy thought a moment, and said, "Sure, it sounds like fun."

There was a moment of silence, and Cory said, "Oh, I almost forgot. Your father wants to see us in his office right away."

"Great!" Thomas exclaimed. "Did he say it was an emergency or anything?"

"No, he just said he wanted to see us," Cory returned. "That includes Lori and I."

"Did he say what he wanted?" Thomas asked, sliding out of the booth, and helping Wendy out.

"He said he had something he wanted to show us."

They pushed through the crowd, and headed toward the door. The teen night spot had become very popular since the incident the month before. VerDean had become a cult heroin since the storming of the Frosty Freeze. She'd lied to storm troopers for them. And Max, the cook, was signing autographs. Meantime Thomas, Cory and Lori had tried to keep a low profile, answer as few questions as possible. They tried to make it as clear as they could they wanted to be left alone. For them the incident was closed.

The black Humvee was parked prominently outside the establishment. That was one side benefit of their imprisonment that made sense. The men in black had blown Thomas's jeep to pieces, ostensibly to send a message to Sheriff Brady. Thomas had driven the Hummer home from Nevada. They had a military escort of two troop carriers and four other Hummers. Colonel Madsen hadn't trusted Remmick to leave them alone. The Colonel had refused to take possession of the vehicle at the time, saying he didn't have the personnel to drive it away, and that he'd send for it. Both boys thought that was strange considering he had four other Humvees and two troop carriers full of soldiers. A week later the title and a bill of sale had come in the mail, in Thomas's name, with new license plates and registration to match. The vehicle was Thomas's. He installed an ignition switch with two sets of keys, one for him and one for Cory. The vehicle needed nothing else.

"The government can't do that," Brady had said softly.

But they had. The Department of Motor Vehicles in Salt Lake had confirmed it was all legal and binding.

Brady, Jacob and Bishop Morris were still consulting lawyers over the issue of kidnapping and imprisonment. They found several interested enough in the case to take it on, two of them gratis. They said they expected a large settlement.

As for the government, there had not been a single word from them by way of apology or even inquiry about what had happened, other than Colonel Madsen's apology at their rescue, and a brief note with the Humvee title. That had simply indicated the vehicle now belonged to Thomas. There was nothing more in the note. Brady explained he believed it was a personal gesture from Colonel Madsen.

Cory slipped behind the wheel, with Lori to his right. Thomas and Wendy took the back seat. Cory slipped the key in the ignition and started it.

"Your driver wishes to know where you would like to be delivered," he said, trying to mimic a British accent.

"Carry on, my good man," Thomas responded. "To the constabulary, please."

Neither one knew which had the worst mock accent, nor did they argue about it. They laughed, and drove up the street two blocks to the sheriff's office. As they entered, they caught Brady sitting back on his desk watching a TV screen. The screen was turned away from them, so they couldn't see it, but they all saw the concerned look on his face as he watched.

He looked up and said, "Someone's coming in for a visit in a few minutes. I didn't plan it, but Captain Ferris up at the base called me a couple of minutes ago. He told me he'd just arrived, borrowed a jeep and was on his way."

"Who?" Thomas asked, concerned because his father was.

"Our old friend Major Remmick," Brady said.

"How soon?" the boy asked.

"A couple of minutes," Brady said. "That's not why I sent for you. You know the slide that occurred about the same time you escaped from Remmick and his army."

"Yes," Thomas returned, relaxing a little. "You said it was probably a second rocket from that helicopter that blew up my jeep. You said not to worry about it."

"That's what I said," Brady returned. "I was up there with Karl two days ago, and we started poking around. You see, we thought we could find fragments of the rocket and prove the military had been up there firing them. That would give us more evidence on our side. We didn't find any rocket fragments, but we did find something else."

"What?"

"We looked inside with our flashlights, down behind the rocks, under rocks, everywhere we could to find fragments. On one side we found a narrow passage just big enough for a human being. It was solid, deliberately built for access to the interior. Inside we found a gray, metal sphere."

Thomas looked at Cory, and mouthed the words, "The flying saucer!" and grinned broadly.

"Don't get too excited," Brady said, handing a small envelope to Thomas. "You will find this very interesting. It's addressed to you two. Sorry, Lori, but it seems Salah got to know the three of you very well. He was only worried about these two. Go ahead and read it, Thomas."

Thomas glanced at the front, saw his name clearly printed with Cory's, then slid his thumb inside the flap and lifted it. He unfolded the paper inside and looked over the short letter.

"Read it out loud," Cory said, irritated. "It's addressed to me, too."

"Okay," Thomas agreed.

"Dear Thomas and Cory,

I had to leave the Briori sphere here. I couldn't fly both spheres home, and I don't want Tobias to fly again for a while. I covered it with rocks to keep it hidden and safe till the Briori could come for it. That should be in a few months, when their position is optimum again. You won't see them. You will simply come up the canyon one day and the sphere will be gone. They won't want to interact with anyone on earth. They would find that both physically and emotionally painful. In the meantime, be assured that I have disabled the controls. You cannot fly it even if you could uncover it. Work hard in school; learn what you need to know. We will visit you again, perhaps often. And, don't forget: We're coming home to stay in a few short years. I promise you will see that day.

Tobias sends his best, and Anisha sends her love.

I am always your friend.

Salah."

Thomas passed the note back to Cory, and looked at his father, who was grinning.

"You wrote that, didn't you?" Thomas accused.

"I did not," Brady responded. "Why does it surprise you that he knows you as well as I do? I found it fixed to the wall of the craft. The ship is up there, just like I said. You may go up and look at it tomorrow, but if you move so much as one rock I will extend your grounding so far into the future you'll be a grandfather before you can leave the house again. And, I talked to your fathers, too, Cory and Lori, and they will back me every step of the way."

Thomas nodded, and said, "Okay. Why did you wait two days to give this to me?"

"I wanted to have the paper tested. Notice the corner of the envelope has been snipped off."

"What is it?"

"Just paper," Brady said. "A little more cotton, or cotton-like substance than we normally put into our paper. And there are some trace elements that we couldn't identify. It seems to be waterproof, fire proof and acid free. It seems to be created to last virtually forever. Other than that, it's just paper."

"I'll keep it," Thomas said, taking it out of Cory's hands.

At that moment the door burst open, and Remmick marched in, his face red and his teeth clenched. As soon as he saw the kids his mouth twisted in an evil smile.

"All we need for the whole gang is the alien cub and his father," Remmick said, pitching his voice in a particularly surly manner. "I have been put under a microscope since you aided and abetted an escape from a military prison, sheriff. I'm reporting to Colonel Madsen up north again in a few days. We were hounded and watched every second while we dismantled the facility in Nevada. There is no longer a secret facility, other than what has always been there. Did you see the article on that news program the other night? It has gotten so bad that I can't even use the bathroom without filing five forms requesting countersigned permissions. It looks like my unit will be disbanded. You seem to have powerful friends."

Brady stood slowly, and moved around his desk.

"Their orders come from the highest level, Major," he said carefully. "It's good to see you in a regulation uniform."

Remmick scowled, but didn't speak.

"It's ironic you should mention being under a microscope in front of my son and his friends," he said softly. "I don't want you under investigation, Remmick. I want you in prison. When that day of reckoning comes, I'd like to be the one who turns the key. You can be sure of that."

"You stole important government evidence," Remmick accused.

"You are referring to the DVD discs," Brady said softly.

"They aren't DVD's, sheriff. You can't possibly be able to view them. They're useless to you and your small-town locals. Where are they?"

"I have them," Brady returned softly. "It took me just one week to have a DVD player modified by one of our 'small town locals' to play back your surveillance recordings of my son and his friends. I've only reviewed part of one of those discs, and I don't think I will review the rest. They disgust me. I will destroy them."

"Those discs are important!" Remmick snapped. "They involve a top-secret recording method that shouldn't be out in the public."

"Neither should you," Brady said quietly. "Any recordings that follow children around twenty-four hours a day, including when they are dressing or showering, among other things," he said with extreme distaste, "are nothing more than child pornography in this 'small town'. And we have the Supreme Court to back us up on that. You want to take it to that level?"

"My authority was from-"

"The highest level," Thomas sneered. "We don't care. Colonel Madsen put that claim to bed out on the Nevada desert. Remember? He's your boss now, isn't he?"

Brady said softly, "Get out of my town, Remmick. The day you set foot in this town again, I will have you arrested for kidnapping, trespassing, and the promotion of child pornography. I will put you so far behind bars you'll think your prison back in Nevada is a country club."

"There's not a court in this land that would convict me," Remmick snarled.

"Go ahead and push your luck," Brady replied, turning away and walking toward his desk. "Colonel Madsen indicated the military would not oppose any action we chose to take. You overstepped your authority. You may yet be hung out to dry. And, I can't feel one bit sorry for you. For now, get out of my sight before I throw you in jail for just plain looking ugly. I'm sick of your presence."

"I would be happy to, Sheriff," Remmick said, his voice tense. "However, it seems I have a little problem."

"What could that possibly be?" Cory taunted. "Did someone try to kidnap you and hide you in a secret prison?"

Remmick glanced at Cory, then back to the sheriff and said, "I've been given an assignment."

"What kind of assignment?" Brady asked.

"Not to put too fine a point on it, you are my assignment," the major replied, his voice betraying his distaste for the assignment.

"What is that supposed to mean?" Brady snapped, stepping toward Remmick.

"I am not sure," Remmick said. "I'm going to be briefed when I report to Colonel Madsen. However, I've been told under no circumstances am I to let anything happen to you, your brats here, or to this town. I've been told to tell you I will be back and will be reporting directly to you."

Brady sat down on the edge of his desk.

"Reporting to me?" He asked, confused.

"Yes," Remmick scowled. "I think that means that, short of jumping off one of those cliffs up canyon, I am supposed to do what you tell me."

"Why?" Brady asked directly.

"I don't know," Remmick said, shaking his head. "I have to go now. We're still breaking down the facility. Colonel Madsen, as you said, will be meeting with me in a few days. Maybe he'll shed more light on this... this...assignment."

At that moment the door to the office opened. Remmick paused, his fist clenched. Brady stepped back away from the major. Remmick glanced over his shoulder.

Boothe nodded to the kids from the doorway.

"You said to stop in any time," he said to Brady. "Is this inconvenient?"

"Boothe!" Remmick snarled. "What are you doing here?"

"I forgot you knew each other," Brady said, a touch of irony in his voice. "I'd like that talk, Boothe. Could you wait a few moments? Remmick is about to leave. Remmick. Let me show you your discs."

Boothe stepped into the office and stood five feet behind Remmick. Remmick looked over his shoulder once again.

"You know I don't like you standing behind me," he said evenly.

"There are a lot of things you don't like," Boothe replied, his voice cold. "You're going to have to get used to some of them."

Brady cleared his throat, drawing Remmick's attention. He held up a stack of discs. He took the top one off the stack.

"I don't like these discs," he said, and bent the disc double.

There was a crack, and the disc snapped. Tiny bits of filmy foil scattered around the sheriff's hands. Brady threw the remainder of the plastic disc in the trashcan.

Remmick stepped forward, and said, "You're insane!"

"That's been said of me," Brady said casually, picking up another disc and snapping it cleanly.

The bits of foil sprayed from the break just as with the first disc.

"I don't intend these ever be played again," he said, holding up the third. "Kids, there were only five discs, one for each of you. There wasn't anything secret about the way they were made; except they were extreme time lapse." He snapped the third disc. "One disc for each of you. Each disc had a whole week worth of recording on each of you. I said 'had'. It's all gone now, Remmick."

Remmick was so angry he was trembling. His hand was drifting toward his side arm.

"I was better than you five years ago," Boothe said evenly. "Think about what I accomplished in prison with nothing to do but train seven days a week. You wouldn't have a chance with me alone, but you have the sheriff there, too. He's been where you are three times, Remmick. He's not as good as me, but he's certainly better than you. I'd think twice if I were you."

Remmick glared at the sheriff for almost half a minute. The sheriff sat on the edge of his desk smiling casually back at the major. He waited patiently.

The kids watched the showdown intently. They all breathed shallowly, and waited as still as they could.

Brady destroyed the fourth disc with a distinct flair. Tiny bits of ultra-thin foil drifted down through the light from the desk lamp and sparkled as they gently fell toward the floor. The air conditioner on the roof labored quietly, sending puffs of air into the office to disturb the descent of the sparkling foil. Outside on the street a car passed slowly, obeying the 25-mile per hour speed limit. And was gone. Almost an age passed in silence.

Then Remmick breathed deeply. He raised his hand away from his holster and smiled. It was a cold smile, an evil smile. He stepped back and looked at the kids.

"I am not going to enjoy my next assignment," he said, the touch of threat still edging his voice. "My one comfort is that you will know I'm around."

He pointed at each of the teens individually.

"If you are to report to me," Brady said, standing. "I think my first order will be to stay away from these kids. Period."

Remmick nodded, and said, "Another day, Sheriff."

He turned smartly and faced Boothe. Boothe merely stood still.

"We should have executed you," Remmick snarled.

"You should have tried," Boothe admitted, confidence in his voice.

Remmick stared eye-to-eye with him a moment longer, then stepped around him and headed toward the door.

"You'll be sorry you befriended this one, Sheriff," he threw over his shoulder. "He's far more trouble than you can ever imagine."

"Interesting," Brady threw after him. "He seems to have proven himself to be of great worth to us."

Remmick slammed the door, but whether he was reacting to Brady's last comment or just totally frustrated was unclear. A moment later they heard the jeep outside start, and pull out and down the road. Remmick was gone.

"Boothe," Cory almost whispered. "Sheriff, he took out the soldier- "

Boothe held up a hand, and shook his head quickly. Cory immediately shut up. Boothe smiled at him.

"You pick strange times to call on me," Brady said quietly.

"I saw the jeep," Boothe responded. "I just wanted to see if you needed some help. I see you had things well in hand."

"Nevertheless, I was happy to see you," Brady said softly. "Thank you. By the way, Salah sends his regards. He said to thank you for your help."

"He's a good man," Boothe said. "I only sent him to you. I knew you would help. You're a good man, too, Sheriff."

The four kids were staring at the two men in silent astonishment.

"I was in Iraq, too," Brady said, still breathing heavy. "I did back to back tours in Afghanistan and Iraq. You remember when I was gone, Thomas. The difference was that I learned to avoid a fight if possible. I have some scars that may never heal. Boothe knows that, too. You don't have to want to fight to be a good soldier."

"You could have knocked him clear across the office," Thomas said incredulous.

"Yes, well, I've wanted to do that for a while. But it never feels nearly as good as you imagine. Maybe Salah has the right idea. He doesn't like confrontation, you know. Come here. I want to show you something. You, too, Boothe."

"Boothe," Thomas said. "What was that thing with Remmick all about?"

"We have a history," Boothe said casually. "We don't particularly get along,"

"You can say that again," Cory said. "Sheriff, he took out a soldier- "

"Sometimes we don't need to hear everything," Brady cut in. "It's not necessary to embarrass individuals. Besides, Boothe couldn't have been there. He's restricted to the town unless he has my explicit permission to leave. He didn't ask for that, so I know he was here. Right, Boothe?"

Boothe smiled and nodded.

"Of course," Brady said, "if he'd have asked, and knowing what I know now of his character, I think I would've said 'yes'."

Boothe smiled. The kids all looked confused. Brady walked behind the desk. The disk in the machine was still playing. Brady turned the monitor so they could all see.

The screen was divided into three distinct sections. In the center was a clear view of the cell. The recording showed Thomas sitting on the edge of his cell bed eating one of the meals.

"That's lunch," Thomas said quietly.

"Yes," Lori said softly. "There's something that looks like carrots, and a piece of bread. We only got bread at lunch."

Thomas continued to eat slowly, deliberately. His shoulders were hunched, his spirit seemed all but broken.

The three in the room watched and remembered. Lori held her hand to her mouth, and Cory and Thomas sniffed, and blinked a little more rapidly. Even Wendy was moved almost to tears.

The upper right corner, smaller than the video, was an infrared image of the same scene. Except for color and a distinct lack of detail, the scenes were matched in every way. In the bottom right corner was a third screen. This one was green, and showed a hot spot in the center that pulsed about once a second. A yellow band circled it. It seemed to float in and out as Thomas chewed, swallowed or breathed. They watched, transfixed.

"It's his heart beat," Cory said after a few moments. "It's the third lens. Somehow it records heart beats."

"What's the yellow ring?" Thomas asked.

"I don't know, but this is weird," Cory said quietly.

Brady nodded, and touched the buttons on the player. The disc ejected. He closed the machine and turned it off.

"They got the technology for the third lens, as you call it, from Roswell years ago," Brady said softly. "They can watch you and see your heart beat. They haven't figured out the yellow ring yet. Salah said they would understand some of it eventually. But they would never understand its full meaning. So, he fixed it. It won't work anymore."

"You saw Salah? When?" Thomas exclaimed.

"Over a week ago," Brady said softly. "I wasn't kidding when I told Boothe he said 'Hi'. Don't get excited. You were down in St. George for the physical with Cory and his parents. He said he'd drop in from time to time. You'll get to see him again. He said he'd bring Tobias and Anisha along if you'd like. He'll even bring Amium by. You two boys met him, too, didn't you? Salah said Amium hasn't stopped talking about you. He was impressed. You know, Thomas, Anisha's a strikingly beautiful young lady now that she's healed up."

"Dad, she's a baby," Thomas protested, glancing at Wendy.

"You remember your mother is five years younger than me," Brady said. "That age difference won't mean a thing in a few years."

"Come on, Dad," Thomas pled, his face coloring.

Brady smiled, and said, "It was the third lens recording that Remmick wanted more than the pictures of you. I wasn't about to give him that because I didn't want him to have the pictures of you. He really believed they could recreate the technology if they had the discs. Salah said that wasn't possible, so that part of it didn't matter. So, I kept the discs. And, as you see, I destroyed them."

He smiled again, and snapped the last disc in half. He threw the pieces into the trashcan. He pointed to the trashcan.

"They're all there. You were recorded every second of every day for as long as you were there. I only watched Thomas's disc, and only enough to get an idea what they put you through. It was clear to me no one should ever see those discs again. Not even Salah's technology could put them back together again."

The kids stood very still for a few moments. Then Thomas smiled, and laughed.

"It's really over," he said, happy to hear his own voice.

"Of course it is," Brady assured him. "Lori. Cory. You're all really and truly home now. No one will bother you again. Not as long as I'm sheriff of this town."

Cory smiled and squeezed Lori's hand.

"This was a little more exciting than I expected," he said. "How about you, Lori?"

She nodded, and he realized she'd been crying again. He put his arm around her.

"Want to go sit in your living room with your dad?" he asked. "We haven't visited in several days."

"We want to come, too," Wendy said quickly, nodding at Thomas.

"Be home early," Brady said as they left. "You have church tomorrow."

He turned to Boothe and said, "Now, let's have that talk we've both been putting off."

Boothe sat slowly, easily in one of the chairs across from the sheriff's desk. Brady didn't go behind the desk. Instead he turned the other chair to face Boothe and sat down, both on the same side of the desk.

"What do you want to know?" Boothe asked calmly.

"Whatever you'd like to tell me," Brady returned.

"I think I'd like to tell you all of it," Boothe said.

"Go ahead, then," Brady answered. "I have as much time as you need."

# CHAPTER 32

For the first time in his life Thomas sat behind the sacrament table. He glanced at Cory as he took his place at the sacrament table next to him, and breathed deeply. He'd reached a decision over the last few weeks; beginning with the moment he'd seen Cory fall backwards off the ladder in the canyon. He saw, for one horrible moment, his best friend's life ending, and realized he could have been left entirely alone. He didn't like the feeling.

There was a flash of instinct, and, for the first time in his life he'd prayed. It wasn't the prayer of a primary child reading from a book. It wasn't the prayer of an adult repeating over and over the words taught in a catechism. He'd reached out and spoken directly with God, had made an instantaneous promise. What he'd promised was his bond now. Something had changed inside him.

He was aware when he'd gone to see the Bishop, the night Cory sat at home nursing a sore head, that the promise he made was one easily broken. It was a promise that was hastily made on the spur of the moment, in the face of more horror than he'd ever imagined he could live through. In their discussion he and the Bishop had explored whether the promise was one he was obligated to keep.

"Many people would not keep it," the Bishop had said gently. "They would let the things that happened up there fade and become dim in the past, and hedge their covenant. That's the word, Thomas. Covenant. Was your promise a bond on your word, or was it simply an unvoiced- "

"I said it out loud," Thomas sniffed. "I almost shouted it!"

"Okay," the Bishop affirmed. "Was it simply a quick and reflex response to what you saw happening? Or, did you mean it?"

"I don't know," Thomas had said softly. "I think I really meant it. I think about that moment and I get stomachaches. Bishop, Cory is more than a brother to me. We think alike. We feel alike. We share each other's ideas. I can say things to him I would never be able to say to anyone else. If he went away, I would be lost."

"I understand," the Bishop said quietly. "Thomas, I hope you're not placing your faith in the gospel in Cory. If you place your activity in the church, or your faith, in one person you could be in danger. You know that, don't you?"

"I know," Thomas said after a moment. "Cory's my guide, my example. I've always felt that. What exactly is faith, Bishop? How can I have the same faith Cory has? I mean, look at him. There are things he just accepts as true that I question and hesitate about."

"Don't make it any harder than it is," the Bishop answered. "Faith is a choice. You determine who, and what, you will believe in. Period. Then you act on that belief. That's faith. It is not a gift from God. It is a gift we give to God in response to all the gifts he's given to us."

Thomas sniffed, and felt tears running down his cheeks.

"What did you promise up there in the canyon, Thomas?"

Thomas listened to the Bishop's soft, sure voice, and wanted to tell him everything. He wanted to tell him all he'd promised, all he'd hoped, all he'd prayed.

"I promised God if he'd protect Cory," Thomas answered, "I'd do anything in the church He wanted me to do. I'd listen in Sacrament Meeting, I'd listen in Sunday school and priesthood meeting, and I'd work to go to the Temple. I promised Him I'd be the most faithful member of the church He ever had if He'd let me keep my friend here so we could grow up together. I promised Him I'd teach my wife to be friends with Cory's wife, and my kids to be friends with Cory's kids just like Cory and I were. I promised Him I would never again be afraid to pray to Him, and that I'd pray to Him every day. I...I guess I promised Him a lot."

The Bishop was silent a long time, then said, "You did, indeed. Did you mean everything you promised?"

Thomas nodded vehemently, and said, "Absolutely."

"Do you intend to keep your promise?"

Thomas nodded again, tears streaming down his face now, and said, "Yes. But, Bishop, I don't know how."

"Are you going to say your prayers?" The Bishop asked.

"Yes," Thomas said vehemently.

"That's the first step," the Bishop said, reaching out toward him.

The Bishop took his hand and folded it within his own. He remembered the warmth and the gentle strength there. He could feel the confidence flowing through that grip, from the bishop to him. He felt for the first time the strength in the church he'd always heard about but never really knew. Suddenly, in that moment, everything was all right. He could see how easy, how simple it all was, and he breathed deeply and let a soft sob escape his lips.

After a long moment the Bishop handed him a tissue, and he wiped his eyes and blew his nose.

"Now," the Bishop said softly. "Let's talk about your ordination as a priest."

Thomas breathed deeply again.

It happened the way the Bishop had outlined. Not a week had passed since they got back from the middle of Nevada, and the prison there. The Bishop had talked to his father several times, both in his office at the church and at home. On a sunny and bright Sunday early in the morning the Bishop had invited them into his office. Brady used his priesthood as an Elder in the church for the first time for his son. With the Bishop's help he ordained Thomas a priest.

He remembered his mother crying, and remembered the tears in his father's eyes. There were handshakes and expressions of support all around.

Now Thomas sat at the sacrament table. The sacrament song began, the congregation singing, and Thomas stood beside Cory as they broke the bread. For the first time in his life he knew what the covenant was all about. He broke the bread carefully, reverently. Then they sat down.

The song ended and Cory slid off the bench to his knees. Holding the card he said the prayer over the bread, and Thomas let the words roll through him. The bread was passed to the congregation. When the deacons brought the trays back, they folded the cloth, covering the bread and revealing the trays of water cups. Thomas knelt and took the card in his hand.

He had read the prayer over and over at home, but nothing prepared him for the wave of emotion that washed through him as he repeated the words at the table. He felt the tears streak down his cheeks, and his chest filled to where he thought it would burst. He finished with the "Amen", and, as he'd seen Cory do countless times, glanced over at the Bishop. The Bishop smiled and nodded almost imperceptibly. Thomas got up and helped hand the water trays to the deacons.

When the deacons returned, they placed the returned water trays on the sacrament table, and sat down. At this signal the deacons also sat down. The Bishop got up and approached the podium. He said a few words of gratitude for those who had participated in the sacrament, and for the reverence of the congregation. Then, with a smile toward Thomas and Cory, he excused them to go sit with their families.

Cory got up, and gently nudged Thomas to his feet. Thomas searched the chapel, and saw who he was looking for. They walked down the aisle together. Cory peeled off and slid into the pew next to his mother and siblings. Thomas stepped one row further back and slid into the pew. His father put an arm around him, and, for that moment, he realized he'd never been happier.

"I'm proud of you, Son," Brady said softly in his son's ear as the Bishop announced the speakers.

His mother leaned across and patted his knee.

"You did very well," Macey said softly.

Thomas could help noticing tears in his mother's eyes. He sat back, shoulder-to-shoulder with his father, and listened for the first speaker. He knew he was about to hear something very good. He knew he wanted to hear every word of that talk. He knew their family would be better from now on.

Thomas stood on the rocks on the edge of the lake. Near him were his parents. Cory and his father were on his left. His mother was not able to make the climb. Next to them was Lori and Jacob Bennett. Salah stood on his right with Toby and Anisha, his sister. He felt a tug on his shirt and glanced down to see the younger boy, Amium, standing very close to him. He glanced at Salah, who seemed interested in the sky, and the lake.

The sun was nearly gone. They stood in shadow now, with the shadow stretching across the dark, clear water. He cleared his throat and felt his father nudge him. He waited patiently.

Salah said quietly, "Which way does this canyon run?"

It seemed like such a strange question. Cory stared at Thomas, and Thomas shrugged.

"Well, the falls are back there," Cory said, "and the stream runs in at the other end. So, I guess that way, toward the falls, is west. Toward the stream is east."

Salah nodded imperceptibly.

"Where is the sun?" He asked.

The other two fathers smiled, and waited.

Cory looked up, and Thomas looked around. They both realized what Salah was saying at the same time.

"That way," Thomas said. "Then, that means the lake runs north and south, not east and west. The crevice the falls drop into twists more than we thought."

"But the slick rock between here and the mountains is riddled with folds," Cory exclaimed. "We thought it was all this canyon. If it's not, then there must be- "

"At least one more canyon!" Thomas shouted.

They looked at each other, and sheer joy spread across their faces.

Cory stared across the lake. The sun was lighting the cliff across from them. In the center a single finger of rock pointed up and seemed to be pointing to a particular fold in the cliff. Cory glanced at Thomas.

Thomas was taking it all in as well. He looked at Salah, who smiled warmly. His face reflected his surprise. He held out his hand and began tracing his palm with his finger.

"We are here," he said softly. "If we went this way, and the canyon goes this way, then..."

Salah nodded.

"Cory!" Thomas suddenly shouted. "That means..."

Cory laughed, but Salah interrupted them.

"It's time for you to go now," he said warmly. "It will be past bedtime by the time we get home. My children's mother will be worried."

Thomas felt a sudden hug from a small boy. He looked down to see Amium wrapped around his middle. His dark eyes stared up at him.

"Thank you," the boy said. "Thank you for saving my brother and sister."

Thomas leaned over, hugged him back and said, "My pleasure, Amium."

"You remembered my name!" Amium exclaimed. "Father! He remembered my name!"

"Of course, he did," Cory affirmed. "We're friends, aren't we?"

The boy beamed in the growing dusk. He wrapped his arms around Cory, who hugged him as well.

Tobias reached out a hand and said, "I'm glad I met you. I owe you my life."

"We owe you a lot, too," Thomas said. "You are more than a brother, Toby. I...I love you, and Anisha and Amium."

Cory's eyebrows went up in surprise. Lori nudged him and smiled. Brady hugged Macey.

He said quietly, "Maybe we shouldn't have stopped with one child, Macey."

She smiled back, and said, "It isn't too late, you know."

Salah turned to the two boys and said, "You have shown courage beyond measure. I have given you this gift. You know what I am caretaker of now. I expect you to be wise in the care of this knowledge. None of us can know what will happen in the future, but I believe our friendship will endure for many long years ahead. Your fathers and mothers are proud of you. I am proud of you, as I am of my son and daughter who were called to bear these trials with you. Stand tall and know you are loved by many around you."

He hugged each of the boys then Lori. Then he shook each of the parents' hands.

"Thank you for your help," he said to Sheriff Brady.

He repeated this with Jacob Bennett and Bishop Morris.

"Now," he said softly, "it's time to take my children home. We'll return often. We have family here now."

His eyes twinkled in the growing dark. He opened his arms as if rounding up the three children there, and they turned and walked around the rocks.

Both Cory and Thomas knew they'd be gone as mysteriously as they had arrived.

As a group they turned and began the long walk down to the bottom of the canyon. The parents were content. The boys, on the other hand, were excited. They knew where Sister Smith's lost city was.